THE INVISIBLE WOMEN

OF

WASHINGTON

a novel by

Diana G. Collier

CLARITY PRESS

Atlanta / Ottawa

LCCCN: 86-072862

Cataloging in Publication Data:

Main entry under title:
 The Invisible women of Washington
ISBN 0-932863-02-7

I. Title.

PS8555.046169 1987 C813'.54 C87–090044–7
PR9199.3.C64169 1987

Laser set by Keylink Systems, Ottawa

Clarity Press

Suite 469, 3277 Roswell Rd. N.E.
Atlanta, Ga. 30305, USA

and

P.O. Box 4428, Station E
Ottawa, Ontario K1S 5B4
Canada

PRINTED AND BOUND IN CANADA

This book is dedicated to

the women I have known

in downtown rooms

Acknowledgement

Grateful acknowledgement is made for permission to reprint the first four sections of this book, which originally appeared in *The Long Story* under the title "The Secret."

"How many sleepers we got tonight"?

The two black men behind the counter glanced idly into the bus station waiting room. Several people were sprawling or sat hunched into themselves on the long pewlike benches. On the farthest bench, an old black woman had stretched right out, her head propped up on a shopping bag, one arm flung out over a suitcase to guard it if she slept. She was staring at the ceiling, flat-eyed.

"Aw it's on'y eleven yet. The old lady. Probably that little blondie over in the corner there. When I come on shift she jus' 'bout run me out of dimes for the phone. Gone at it with the newspaper, y'know, goin' through them classifieds."

The two men exchanged a pointed glance. Each, in his time, had had short and long wars of attrition with the classifieds.

"Hey, there's Lennie again. Ain't he off by now?"

A sinewy man with hair slicked straight back was surveying the room, rocking a moment back and forth on his high-booted heels before easing on over to a bench near the lockers where the yellow-haired girl sat, eyes closed. He slid onto the bench beside her, waited a moment looking at her, then touched her shoulder on the far side, his face moving close to her neck. She started violently. He drew back, both hands raised as if she had drawn a gun, then grinning, he closed in again, talking to her, his elbows on his knees, his cigarette ash flicking down between his legs onto the floor. Red-faced, the girl stared away, one stubby-fingered hand lightly touching the cord that tied the powderblue suitcase pressed tight against her knees.

"Hey honey," one of the men behind the counter called out, "He telling you you can stay over night with him an' his Ma?"

The girl glanced up sharply. One hand pushed her hair back behind her ears, revealing a plump freckled cheek.

"Will you shut up, Hank," the cabdriver grunted in exasperation.

"Hey, his old lady lives in Pasadena. She ain't seen Washington in twenty year," Hank kept up, his voice jocular but his eyes hard. "Ain't nobody lives in that rattrap he got but him. An' they ain't no two beds, neither."

"Shit, Hank," the other man nudged. "You gonna queer it for him."

"Hell, I get tired of these guys cruisin' by here pickin' up on the country chicks like a horde of dogs in for the kill. Makes me think of my sister Jinny when she first left Wyattville an' went on up to New York."

"It ain't the same. You know Lennie's just lookin' for fun."

Their eyes shifted again to Lennie, whose arm had hooked over the bench behind the girl's back, locking her in to a little niche of intimacy. She contracted into her turquoise raincoat like prey beneath a lion.

"Anyway," the second man shifted awkwardly. "Who says this broad is country?"

1

"You ever see a country girl get on a bus without packin' enough sandwiches an' stuff to last a year? The bus ain't even out of the station, they got to start eatin', and they keep it up the whole way through. Sandwiches, bananas, stuff wrapped up in wax paper, sesame seeds..."

For a moment they considered the shopping bag next to the girl's suitcase. Each drifted off into his own thoughts.

"Hey Lennie," Hank started up again suddenly. "Ain't that Doris sittin' out there in your cab?"

Lennie's head snaked around, then he yawned, slapped his knees, and stood up.

"Okay, I'm goin'," he sighed. "How about a smile anyway?"

Relief blazed through the girl's face. She glanced at him for the first time.

"Hey, that's nice. Hey look — ain't she got a pretty smile?"

The men behind the counter nodded amiably. The girl wasn't pretty, but she was young and healthy-looking. In the neon dusk of the bus station, her fresh face seemed to glow.

"You that glad to see me gone?" Lennie leaned over the girl again, and her smile faded. "Aw hell," he grimaced. "What you think you are — an electric light goin' off an' on?"

A bus came in, distracting the two men at the counter as sluggish passengers stumbled through the waiting room towards the washrooms, some lining up to pump change into the coffee machine, others briskly making for the door with their suitcases and off into the night. Warm wet air came through the moving doors in gusts. As the bus pulled out again, a residue of people remained standing listlessly by the doors or pacing the waiting room floor, reading notices on the walls, the bus schedules, anything in print. After a time, they thinned out and the flickering neon lights reasserted their drone. But the long benches held more people than before.

"How many now, you figure, Calvin?" Hank prodded.

The second man shrugged. "All a' these." He frowned in annoyance at a Spanish woman who was murmuring a constant "chu-chu-chu" to the crying baby squirming against her breast. An older child sat separate, deep-eyed and silent, taking in the whole of the waiting room in a single remorseless glance.

"Jeezus H. Christ." Hank shook his head.

The two men glanced in unison at the clock.

"Well I guess..." Calvin said listlessly, rapping his knuckles against the counter, not in any hurry to leave though his shift was done. He wasn't married and lived in a basement room over on U Street.

"Don't it ever make you wonder?" Hank burst.

"Nah," Calvin said.

They glanced again at the clock the way they always did to fill in the empty spaces.

"I ever tell you about Jimmy from back home?" Hank started up. There was a long night ahead of him and he wanted to hold Calvin as long as possible.

"Jimmy, Blaine, Norwood, hell I can't keep 'em all straight," Calvin frowned. "You'd figure after two years nonstop, you'd a told me about 'em all."

"Naw, this Jimmy, this just happen last week sometime. This Jimmy come off'n a chicken farm just below Monck's Corners."

Calvin snorted at the name. He was from Baltimore.

"Sure we got names like that. Monck's Corners, Cracker Neck, Whippy Swamp, Nine Times. You think the whole damn countryside down there is empty?"

"At the rate they all pilin' in here..." Calvin muttered defensively.

"This here Jimmy — "Hank began, then he shrugged, lapsing into silence.

"Aw come on," Calvin gave in. He had nowhere to go.

"This here Jimmy," Hank began again, satisfied. "He come from the old Jones fambly, some twenty kid or more. He were one of the middle ones, useta fish with Blaine an' me. Then one day last month, outta the blue, he say he's off to New York City lookin' for a job. The Big Apple. He's thirty years old an' they never give him no job yet where he was. But hell, all his life, he ain't never been more than thirty miles from where he got born. Maybe you can't figure it, sittin' here where everybody's kinda cut loose and flyin' off. But lotsa them folks down there, they go off thirty mile down the road an' they feel like they done quit the country. So figure this," Hank started to cackle, his fingers slapping on the counter. "It takes one hell of a time to get from Moncks Corners to New York. Can't you jes' see him a-settin' there with his nose pressed up against the window, tryin' to keep all them towns in a line in his mind case somethin' happens an' he got to pick his own way back? An' all them towns keep on passin'. Darlington, Florence, Charlotte, an' passin', Raleigh, St. Petersburg, Richmond, an' still no New York. An' still his eyes bugged to the window, nighttime too, 'less they double back an' run him over the same track again. Cause how can them drivers keep on drivin' all them miles and never once get los'?"

Hank's head shook, one large hand raising to wipe the tears of laughter from his eyes. Calvin laughed too, sharp-eyed.

"A day an' two nights an' there he is, sittin' in the Port Authority, bag of groceries an' all. An' what you figure then?" Hank sighed. "Two whole days an' he jes' sits there in the station, watchin 'em come an' watchin 'em go, eatin' his way down the grocery bag an' out the bottom. More folks in two days than he ever seen in his life, black, brown, white, yellow, all them weird New York types. An' in the morning, the salesmen pourin' in from Jersey in a chain so solid you can't tell where one busload gives off an' another starts up. An' it

3

keeps up, all day an' all night. Two whole days he sit there, watchin' an' eatin' an' thinkin'. Aw hell, can't you see it?"

Calvin waited as Hank rubbed his eyes once more. He was waiting for the punch line.

"You know, two whole days he sit in that monster station without ever makin' his way to outside. Two whole days an' he never seen the light of day. On the third day, he jes' grab the bus an' come on back home. When the folks ax 'im how he like New York, he come on like a man of the world, real calm and quiet-like." Hank bent over, wheezing with laughter. "An' he jes shrug an' say — he didn't like it none."

Calvin grinned. "Scared."

"Didn't even make it out of the station, an' he come all that way."

"Scared shitless."

"He ain't no fool."

"You make it a week in the big cities, you can stay forever. " Calvin thrust his chest out. The story made him feel good.

"Y'know, I think about that sometimes," Hank said wistfully. "You look at these mean streets, you remember that country air, an' you think, holy Lord why all us crazy fools fightin' just to stay jammed up in here?"

"Me, I got stakes in Washington."

"Oh yeah? Jes' what you got here?"

"Job." Calvin frowned irritably. "Place to stay."

"Yuh." The word came out in a release of breath.

"An' if there's somethin' to go for out there, how come they all a-pilin' in here?"

They looked at the clock again.

"Hey, that little blondie, she go off with that jerk?"

They glanced over at the bench by the lockers where three milky-faced young army men sat, heads nodding miserably.

"Over there."

Their glances turned to the bench where the old black lady lay sleeping, her arm still flung over her suitcase. Stretched out in the opposite direction, head propped into the corner, the girl lay with her turquoise raincoat draped over her legs and partially covering her face. An arm protruding from beneath the raincoat flicked restlessly over the suitcase rope. Between them, they had secured the whole bench.

"See that?" Hank grinned. "It don't take her long."

"Long enough. This the second night she been holed up in here."

❂

As Alex Vandernikke approached the office door, a girl crouching beneath the steps bolted towards him, dragging a suitcase by a

4

rope. He shook his umbrella, pointed it toward the rental hours of the women's residence posted on the door. She drew back beneath the steps without a word.

Looking at her now through the small office window as he washed his hands, he fought off a tug of sympathy. If he gave a damn, sooner or later she would try to use him in some way — to get by on some rent, to move from room to room to room searching for a better one, to get something fixed that was unfixable — the taps or the bugs. The stream of complaints, the duplicity, the effluence of a sea of troubles dropped its silt on him when there was nothing he could do, not about any of it, but his job — weed out the crazies and drunks, prevent funny-business, and get rent for every second from the others that stayed.

He was not unsympathetic — he wiped his hands very carefully with the towel — he was not cold. His every instinct had to be braked and held constantly in check. For they would push him to the limit. And what good was his understanding if it put him on the street as well? That was the rock base of it: there was nothing he could do — not about the high rents, the stink from the toilets, the old women who trailed ash in the halls, the noise, the forbidden cooking that drew in roaches, the windows that stuck, the air that didn't move. As there was no squeezing repair money from the holding company down in Florida — God knew who the owner was, or even if he or they were Americans — so there was no controlling the ceaseless innovation and destruction of the women's efforts to survive, to force their needs or their condolences into the claustrophobia of their rooms. Like an irrelevant principle of order in an immense clash of forces, he kept clean and aloof, absolutely without condemnation, despising no one, doing his job.

When he opened the door at ten, the girl beneath the steps burst into the room, sending rainwater flying as she shook out her coat right there on the floor. She stood there glaring at him and shaking the coat, the noise of its flapping setting up a commotion in the outer room. He folded his hands on the counter and waited.

"It was rainin' out there to beat the band," she gasped. "You coulda let me in at least. I coulda stood just inside the door there, not botherin' nobody." Her face pulsed with anger, then abruptly she swallowed it. "You still got a room?"

"We got one."

She dropped the raincoat over her suitcase and propped one elbow on the counter.

"It rain like that all the time in Washington? Lord!"

"You want a room?" His voice was brisk and clipped, the way he had learned to speak to officers in the army to avoid interruption.

"I just come up from Carolina. Lord, I was on the bus seemed like forever. I never been out of Beaufort much. You know Beaufort?"

"I got one fifty-four a week." If he talked with them about other things, even the weather, it seemed to create a relationship of some kind, and next thing he knew they were trading on it. That was the first insight he had had into how it worked. Later he decided they knew it worked that way, which was why they bothered to chat him up in the first place, and that eased his conscience as he cut them short. But it hurt to know they thought him, not scrupulously impersonal — just a mean old man. It was a point of pride that he proved them wrong by always working to the letter, never veering off toward revenge.

"Last night you said thirty-nine."

"I never said we had any rooms at thirty-nine *now*, I just told you the rates like you asked. I said we got rooms from thirty-nine to sixty, and that's a fact."

"I come all this way by taxi." She pointed helplessly at her suitcase. "Everywhere I been, I had to lug this thing 'cause it don't fit in the bus station lockers. I thought it was gonna slice my hand right through. By the time I get it on the right bus to get out to some place, the room's taken. Then I got to pay the busfare back — over a dollar it comes to, an' for nothing. An' I got nowhere to go back to anyways but the pay phone where I was at. An' I make five more calls, an' half the places are gone already an' the others, I can't figure how to get to 'em 'cause I don't know the city an' they don't know which bus to take that connects up with the bus that reaches them. An' some of the people sound weird. Mean, or suspicious, y'know?" She stared at him earnestly. "An' some of 'em kept askin' if I was black an' where I worked, an' if I got a letter of reference from the place I lived before. But I got nothin' cause I lived at home. An' then they want all this rent — first month, last month, deposit — Who's got money like that? They want to take the whole thing that I come with," she burst out incredulously. "Finally I told myself, Abby-Jean, you gotta get out of this bus station 'fore you pour all your money down the phone. So I got a taxi this morning. I was here at *five* — She broke off, her face stark.

"You make up your mind, you let me know," he said abruptly, and escaped to the desk in the inner office. He was perspiring. Carrying a suitcase the size of that thing, he thought in a fury, no fault of mine. Either they knew all the tricks or they knew nothing, nothing. Either way, it aroused in him a sensation of mayhem, like the splintering of wooden beams, the creaking of foundations, and he wished he was back in the army again. He went to the sink to wash his hands once more, lingering as long as he could with his hands beneath the cold water before the telephone called him back. Each time the telephone rang, he could see her wince in the outer room, her eyes searching him anxiously to see if the room had gone.

In the silence between calls, he stood at the window looking out at the construction work across the street. Two black workers were stretched out on the steps of a magnificent brownstone having a smoke. If it were afternoon and George Waddell had drifted in for his shift on desk, without fail he would be hearing some laconic remark like "On their butts again, over there," as Waddell remarked every afternoon at about break time, sitting paunch up by the window, one foot on the desk, one hand on the blinds. "I've been watching them go at it all spring and not a change in that building do I see," Waddell would say emphatically, his face taking on a shrewd vindictive gleam. It was useless to point out that the workmen were only gutting the building, preserving the outer frame of turrets, cornices and bay windows intact, the way the smart young professional couples who were moving back to the inner city liked them.

In patches all down the block, the mysterious transformation was under way, turning bruised houses with long grass licking up the brick walls, porches creaking with families on afternoons soporific with the solitary clink of beer bottles, into polished homes with windows that reflected sunlight with a deep resonant sheen, dazzling the eye with glimpses of stained glass, arcane lamps, mahogany, a wealth of plants under sunlights. Wherever the renewed houses were, a silence was created that impinged on the surrounding clamour. Alex Vandernikke watched the invasion as if it were the encroachment of a disease, a moribund white arm stretching out to wither with a touch — his job. Even the residence, evacuated, gutted, sandblasted clean again, might become big condo money some day.

Again he answered the phone, mechanically listing off the weekly rates for the rooms. Though only one room was free and already several women had pleaded with him to hold it, they were dashing right down, to each one in turn he replied, If you get down here and it's free, it's yours. Perhaps five would come and four would leave in frustration and anger at the futile trip. But that was no business of his. The room was free until it wasn't, until the money reached his hands. In the meantime, he saw a justice in letting them race. Each one had a chance though all but one must lose. He took credit for the former. The latter was no business of his.

"Hey Mister!"

He stood perfectly still without turning.

"I thought about it, an' can I see the room?"

"You working?" He turned abruptly towards her, then caught himself angrily at the foolishness of the question, remembering she had just come up from the South.

Her eyes raised to his fearfully. "Uh-huh."

He nodded curtly, and the old irrational anger surged through him at the lie, coming always like a slap in the face no matter that he knew it wasn't personal. He felt a constriction in his stomach, then numbness as his understanding worked it through and had done with it again. Watching her quietly, he took in the white blouse with the pocket over one breast that looked crushed and worn.

"Least I'm goin' t'be," the girl stammered, driven by natural honesty to clarify despite her need and exhaustion.

"You're not working now," he said dispassionately, eliminating any accusation of the lie from his face.

"I got some money," she cried out. "What's it matter to you, long as I pay?"

"Just got to know that you can. Don't want to have to jerk you out later."

"Well I can. Word of Honor — "

The girl's gaze dropped to the floor, her face bright with surprise. That was no good with him now, stripped from her before she'd had a chance to think.

"You want to see all the money I got here?" She raised her purse, daring him to look inside it.

A heat went over his face, shooting out to his hands.

"You going to show me the room now?"

He heard the triumph in her voice without resentment, and nodded.

○

Three burnt-out cigarettes stood butt-end up on the stair railing beneath the pay phone, like remnants of a vigil. In a surrounding radius the length of the cord, the linoleum was pocked with tobacco burns. A section of the wall around the phone had been repainted to blot out an ancient swarm of names and numbers, and a fresh history atop the new paint had already begun. A newspaper, crushed open at the classifieds and heavily scored in black, had been trampled by other passings before their own.

"You got the use of the phone." As Vandernikke passed, he moved the newspaper to one side with a scrape of his foot, then continued his climb to the third floor without glancing behind him. Abby-Jean clambered after, panting noisily as, with her left hand, she hoisted her enormous suitcase from stair to stair, all the while trying to keep the shopping bag and manual typewriter in her right hand from catching in the slats in the railing. Either her arms were too long or she was simply too short; with every upward step, the bottom of her suitcase hit the rim of the next stair, needing a further jolt to land it squarely on the step above. Puffing and banging, onward she came, her eyes fixed on his back, looking down only when he reached the third floor landing and glanced back briefly to survey her struggle without moving to help, watching her climb the way a man might wait for an elevator to come.

He hated her right off, she thought confusedly. Why else to answer her small talk about the rain as if she had asked him straight out about the rent. First he made her wait; then he was in some unholy rush. Now she couldn't speak to him at all, her natural impulse to banter about nothing, to like and be liked, somehow clouded by a suspicion she didn't understand. It made her feel ashamed. Maybe the only way to restore her credibility would be to shut up and, certainly, ask nothing of him, nothing ever?

Turning brusquely, he walked down the corridor, stepping mechanically to one side as an old woman darted out from behind one of the doors, a towel twisted around her head. Startled by the unexpected presence of a man, she pulled her scanty kimono tighter over an exposed breast, then slipped past them, mortified. He poked the bathroom door open with a forefinger and gestured inside.

"You have the use of this bathroom. There's another at the end of the hall."

Abby-Jean's head dipped hesitantly into the bathroom. Her nose wrinkled. It smelled of sweat and cigarette smoke. Involuntarily she glanced behind her at the row of doors, unable to tell behind which the old woman had disappeared. There were no sounds now, no evidence whatever of life though the building presumably was full. Taking a deep breath, she towed the suitcase forward once more, unable to stop its scuffing and scraping as it shimmied over the rug's edge onto the floorboards and back again.

Vandernikke had stopped in front of a door at the end of the hall and was waiting quietly, staring at his shoes.

"You ought to have left your things downstairs until you'd seen the room."

"I'm gonna take it," she burst.

Head tilting to one side in a refusal of opinion, he unlocked the door, allowing her to pass by him into the room.

She glanced back at him in surprise. The room was painted bright yellow with blazing orange framing the two windows in the corner, making her think of sunshine and orange juice in a way not entirely agreeable. Both blinds were drawn, but still the colors raged. At the top of the window frames, the orange paint petered out, as if a previous tenant had tried and failed to reach the upper sill. The jagged edges made the room seem to implode.

"Anyway — anyway — I oughta get a cross breeze with these windows here — " she started up hopefully, picking quickly on the good point. Then she tried the taps on the sink, opened and closed the door to the small closet. At a loss for more to do, she turned around once in the center of the room, struggling inchoately to peer into the days and months of it ahead.

"No hot plates, no cooking in the room, no visitors after 11."

"I'll take it."

"Fifty-four dollars." He was looking at his watch.

She counted it out for him, then stared at him anxiously as he pocketed it after counting it again. "I don't sign nothing? I don't get no receipt?"

"Come to the desk by noon."

Her gaze faltered, then returned again anxiously to his face. As if he could read her thoughts, he frowned sharply.

"Okay, that's all right," she said, unable to show her distrust longer, ashamed and embarrassed by it, forgetting that the thought to distrust had been sown by him. It made her feel as if she were guilty of something herself, if not now then before. Why else would it cross somebody's mind to suspect somebody else?

He nodded, stepped out the door and shut her in.

Eyes watering suddenly, she lay down on the bed, her feet carefully hanging over the edge to avoid marking the bedspread.

"Geez, right downtown," she cheered herself. "I was lucky to get one right downtown. An' when the cheaper one comes up, I can just shift on over."

Then she sank into sleep like a stone.

When she awoke in the late afternoon, Abby-Jean noticed an odor near the windows by the desk. The smell was sweet yet fetid, materializing through a covering layer of incense like a corpse rising from a marsh, taking on a presence in the room. Raising both blinds, she stared out the windows at walls on either side, the diagonal wall so close that she shrank back, glimpsing suddenly a bare male foot propped up on the window sill a few yards away. Between the walls, though, there was a narrow alley, a channel for air. She heaved at one window then the other. Neither moved. A twinge of fear, like a premonition of claustrophobia, of suffocation, sent a little burst of heat over her body.

If a man tried it, she thought hopefully. Her face hardened. She remembered Vandernikke. Grasping the more promising window, with a suck of breath she heaved. Shrieking, it opened. But as her hand let go, it rattled inexorably down. Twice she tried to balance it open, each time lower and lower, but at no place would it hold. Taking out a bottle of Halo shampoo from her suitcase, she lowered the window upon it, sticking one hand out the scant seven inch opening, waving it futilely to generate a breeze. The smell remained, cloying yet unlocatable, making her think timorous unformulated thoughts of the woman before her. What had she done in this spot, the woman who had painted her room this yellow, this orange? She gazed back at the walls by the bed where a small dent in the wall had sent out shooting cracks in the paint. The dent was the same height as the door handle. How hard did you have to let it fly to make a hole like that? The thought sent a quiver through her like an eddy from a violent shock.

She squatted over her open suitcase on the rough shag rug, squeezed out a white cotton nightie with pink flowers on it, and draped it over the chair. She put her soap and toothpaste out on the bureau by the sink, then placed the manual typewriter on the desk with the instruction book beside it. The sight of her things in the room reassured her. As a last touch, she put the pictures — Mums and the girls strung out like clothes on a line in front of the house in Beaufort, her younger brother Bud grinning, his foot propped up on the dash of the truck, three shots of her sister Lucy's first child Benjamin, Lucy and Harry together before Harry vanished out west, her two nieces in Orangeburg, and Great Auntie Tifford from Davenport, now dead — all there on the desk facing the bed so she could see everybody when she lay down and not feel so strange and alone.

She stared at the pictures mournfully. To see them in a place like this — But there had to be jobs in a city this size. When she got one and could send money home, what need for them ever to know it had started out like this? Why tell them when they would worry, when something simply had to be done and there was no going back anyway, not with the girls already moved up in the beds. It made her feel older and wiser already, this beginning of a secret. She gazed at them with a sudden, inexplicable pity.

Bounding away from the bed, she began combing her hair, watching her face eddy in the ribbles of the mirror above the sink. It was corn yellow, yellow enough to look dyed if it wasn't for the pink in her face and her pale lashes. Robust-chested, with arms that thickened toward broad shoulders, short-legged and sturdy, she exuded a hefty energy that seemed dauntless, unhurtable. Yet there along her lower arms, the flaxen hair stood out in agitation, the entire surface coarsened by a rash of goose flesh to which the swift pulse of her feelings gave rise.

Struck by a thought, she turned abruptly to the plastic shopping bag, dumping its contents — some cutlery, two cups, two plates and a pot — onto the bed. Seizing the dinner knife, she thrust the window wide open and jammed the knife into the crevice between window and wall. It held. A thin breeze reached her outstretched fingers.

"Hah! You potlicker!"

She turned again to her toiletries, her face shrewd. Uncapping the bottle of Kentucky Blue Grass cologne, she pelted out a volley of droplets over the rug, the chair and the bureau. The room was engulfed in a sweet soapy smell. Face blooming with triumph, she opened the door and peered down the hall.

Down all the length of corridors, there wasn't a soul.

Disappointed, she turned back into her room. The bare foot had disappeared from the window across from hers; she could see a plastic plate with a knife askew, the yellow remains of egg in swirls beneath it, sitting on the radiator. The outside light cut into the room, exposing a small space, leaving the rest in shadows. She too, then, was invisible in the day and could leave the blinds open wide. As she pressed against the corner of the window so that her face was aligned with the narrow channel between the walls, she caught a glimpse of one of the magnificent beech trees that lined the street, its foliage so thick and resplendent that it blocked sight of the buildings behind it. As a slight breeze passed through its leaves, scattered undulations of silver followed the deeper swells of green. The sight thrilled her. She had a room with a view, the only window on the entire length of wall that didn't stare a few feet across to another wall or worse, another window. A room right downtown, then, with a view. Hah!

Neck stiff from craning to see the tree, she returned to sit on the bed, gazing at the yellow walls, the orange window frames, trying to imagine them white or robin's egg blue. With pictures on the wall of shrimp boats in the canals near Beaufort. With fish netting strung all along one wall, there, with shells caught in the net and plants winding through, the way Lucy and Harry had had. Her face clouded, then brightened again. With curtains on the windows instead of blinds, a frill along the top, so that when the breeze came through, the cotton would lift gently and rise; all of it white, so white and fresh that you would think you were in a lighthouse on some pinnacle along a rocky coast with the wind dashing in off the bright blue sea, gulls dipping in the sunlight overhead. Something like that Old Spice commercial —

She rose quickly from the bed, taking three steps across to the window again, but looking back this time at the sink, the bureau, the door. Planning. If the sink were not there — But it was. The bureau, though, could be shifted to another wall, to the corner where the bed was now. There only, if it wasn't to block a window, a closet or a door. And in turn the bed could only go where the bureau was, unless she put it there beneath the window with the desk to the wall instead. She would be able to sit on the bed and see, way down the narrow channel between the walls, the beech tree. But then whoever stood at the window across the way could see her as she lay on her bed. A man perhaps. If he stood at the window, it would be almost as if he could stand over her and glance at random into the heart of her life.

No, she shifted towards the sink, there was only one place for the bureau, where the bed was, and for the bed the same. But the desk didn't have to be there at the window forcing you to lean across it to look outside. The chair could be there, right in the path of two meagre currents of air, while the desk — was there anything that said you couldn't put a desk right dead center in a room? It would remind her to practice her typing. She wouldn't be able to take two straight steps without banging into it.

Energetically she pushed the desk towards the center of the room, its feet catching and having to be lifted onto the gritty shag carpet. Which way to point the desk — towards the window, the door, the wall where the bed was, or the chair? She tried them all, starting to sweat, looking at each one from several vantage points to get a real feel. But no matter how she placed the desk, the result was the same: it looked like it was waiting to be taken out of the room. And the armchair, now placed in the corner with a window on either side, was too low to place her directly in the path of the faint pants of breeze.

12

And in order to glimpse the tree at the end of the alley, she would have to raise herself, not just to the edge of the chair, but a good two inches higher. Disconsolate, she moved desk and chair back to where they had been, which had been the best, indeed the only, way that they could be all along. Hot and grimey, she sat on the bed. Nothing more could be done with what was here.

She leaned back on the bed, about to put her hands out on the bedspread to brace herself, then she started upright once more. She turned her palms upward. The pad of each finger was a sooty grey. She had almost put them on the yellow bedspread, the only thing that was crisp and almost spotless in the room. She thrust a tentative finger at the wall at the head of the bed where the blazing yellow surface took on a dun sheen. Someone's head against that wall, day after day... As her finger touched the wall, it left a soft grayish smudge that made her suddenly acutely aware of the surface of the wall. There were actually shades to it, much like the ripple of skin on an arm, carrying slight shadows, changes in texture. While whatever had been beneath was invisible, it nonetheless left ridges and indentations in the painted surface which, though hidden by the blazing yellow, seemed to throng with a welter of small scuff marks, random flecks of now-dried droplets, blurred dun areas where flesh had left a deposit of oil visible only in its accumulation and overlay with dust. The mark her finger left was neither more nor less distinguishable than the rest.

Face burning with a new determination, she went to the sink and washed her hands. There was nothing to clean with in the room, not even a rag. Pulling a kleenex from her purse, she wet it and began with the bureau. Within seconds the kleenex had turned deep grey, small pieces of it breaking away and sticking to the top of the bureau. She flung it with a heavy thud into the metal waste basket beneath the sink, then pulled out a pair of pink panties from her suitcase. They could be washed after. She had to clean it now, had to be free to touch things and not wonder *what, who* —

She began with the wall by the bed. The panties, thickly lathered with hand soap, merely left a swatch on the wall slightly lighter but no cleaner, drawing attention to the failure of her effort, adding her mark to the others engrained there. The irrelevance, indeed the worsening effect of her effort left her blankly pondering the wall. Who knew what scars the yellow paint was hiding? Cleaning out the chicken coops back in Beauufort was a stinking job, but the filth never made her feel like this — queer. Something intimate, stagnant, the private filth of who knew how many other people.

She leaned back against the wall angrily, letting the back of both her arms press against its surface.

"There. Don't hurt you none."

She moved a bare arm in an arc over it, then inspected her white flesh closely, thinking how if no filth came off when she scrubbed the wall, then maybe none came off when she only touched it? She

13

turned her head slightly, letting her cheek rest against the wall. Good. She wasn't afraid of it any more.

"It's only 'cause I don't know who it was," she said out loud. Yet for minutes after raising her cheek from the wall, she could feel its pocked surface there on her skin.

She wiped the desk clean. While wet, it looked good. It even gleamed. But when it dried off, she couldn't help thinking, not how clean it looked, but how chipped and scarred. The more she tried to change the room, the more she saw the things that were wrong. But the desk was clean now. She studied it, satisfied. Dropping to her knees by the carpet's edge, she drew the panties in a wide swath, following the line of the baseboard until the grating sensation beneath her fingers forced her to stop. The cloth was black, laden with small particles and hair. She sluiced the panties under the tap, but they stayed dark grey. Ruined. Vengefully she scoured the remainder of the floor, keeping her knees always on the bare board, leery of the rug whose thick pile was no joy if you thought of what could be hiding inside it.

Finished. She stepped once more into the empty hall, lured down the corridor by the noise of a television, halting in front of a door which was slatted like a shutter. Though she couldn't see anything through the door at eye level, when she glanced down, she could see two slippers, gold with black pom-poms, thrown askew on a rug like her own, and behind, the bluish light from the television casting a fractious glare against the darkness. She stepped back abruptly. The slats had enticed her to peer into somebody's room. How could you relax in a room like that with God knew whose nosey nose passing by outside?

Turning, she saw a sign posted in the corner of the landing across from the slatted door. DON'T COOK IN THE ROOMS. IT BRINGS IN ROACHES, the sign warned frankly. Directly beneath, two garbage bags sat propped against the wall, an empty egg carton protruding from one. Involuntarily she glanced back at the slatted door. It seemed like the kind of insolent thing someone would do who watched TV in the dark in the middle of the day.

Beside the garbage bags, there were some movie magazines and paperbacks tossed against the wall. Her glance flickered over the titles as she delayed, listening hopefully for someone coming, someone to talk to, but the TV game show host shouting "Harriet Egan, it's your lucky day! COME ON DOWN!" and the shrieks and applause blotted everything out. For a few moments she lingered in the hall, her head tilted to one side like a bird listening, before retreating to her room in shame at the thought of being caught hanging about in the hall, so hungry for a friend.

Opening the door slowly, she tried to see her room as if for the first time while still remembering that first time in order to see if she'd made it any better. The door shut quietly behind her. Nothing. There was no change in the appearance of the room, none at all, except she wasn't shocked at it any more. Maybe the room wasn't so bad after all? Or maybe she couldn't see it as clearly as at first. Maybe she was already beginning to fit the room. As the closing door muted the sound of TV down the hall, she relaxed a little. However small, here inside, this space was hers. It offered relief from the outside.

She sat on the bed, her shoes carefully placed nearby so that she wouldn't have to walk on that rug with bare feet. She could feel more than hear the reverberation of disco music from the bar beneath the residence. It sounded mean, threatening, when she heard it from outside, when she wasnt swallowed up in it. The sound reached her only as a throbbing, as if it were part of the teeming that had threatened to overwhelm her from the moment she arrived in Washington. Even here in the refuge of her room, her body was still tense with it. So many people. She lay back on the bed, trembling. People everywhere. All kinds. She was feverish from it, the thought that she would have to go out once again to eat, and soon before darkness fell, filling her with fear. Suddenly the prohibition against cooking in the room took on full meaning. For any and every meal she would have to go out, day after day after day. Where would the money come from for that? She shrugged the thought off. It was impossible to worry that far ahead.

Pulling on a maroon jacket sweater, she tiptoed into the hall again, quickening her pace at the sound of a woman's voice, rushing towards it hopefully. As she neared the second foor landing, a large black woman using the phone glanced at her once with soft shy eyes, then turned her body in toward the wall in a futile attempt to keep her conversation private. For several steps approaching and passing, Abby-Jean could hear the undulating reproach murmured over and over, "Why you can't do that? Uh-huh. Uh-huh. But all s'I'm a aksing is why? You know what I mean, why. Why you can't do that, huh, why?" The large soft volumes of the woman's body pressed closer against the walls as Abby-Jean passed, moving briskly ahead to show she wasn't listening. The slow Southern accents of the woman's voice gave her a pang. She glanced back once at her orange and blue striped pants and yellow top, all cotton and fresh as sunshine. She would be from the country too, she would be frightened too. Perhaps she wanted to go home, perhaps the question she was asking over and over with that gentle urgency was, why can't you come and get me, why can't you take me out of here, why can't you bring me home?

She faltered. She wanted to go home. She wanted to go home too. The thought she had smothered rose from her like a bird crashing against some inside window. She wanted to go home. Was there a soul in all these blasted rooms that didn't grieve for the chance to get on back home?

She heaved the front door open, and was out on the street again.

There was nowhere to eat, nowhere regular. The wide streets lined by massive rich-looking buildings were silent, as if some state occasion were over and only a few hilarious diehards were left in the wake of vanished crowds. Along the route towards K Street, scattered restaurants had unfurled their tables out onto the sidewalk, terrace-style, with occasional canopies or large garden umbrellas spread out to protect the smart-looking men and women who drank in lazy clusters beneath. But for the fact that no one took any notice of her, Abby-Jean would have rushed on by, mortified even to be on the street itself, there in the presence of lower-echelon civil servants whom she mistook for presidents of banks and their glamorous wives. As it was, her eyes could run quickly over the menus under glass tablets posted like warnings outside, while passing waiters only glanced at her and moved on without offering to usher her inside.

The menus were confusing. Some prices were reasonable while others were — Someone like herself could eat there if she ordered something called Vichyssoise at $2.50, and kept away from veal milanese at $12.00. As a waiter glanced up at her, vaguely questioning, she stumbled quickly away, thinking *Lord, what a fuss. Worse than a swarm of gnats.* You had to be a certain kind of person to put up with all that, and she wasn't. She was like — she shrugged — like everybody. It was those others, the ones with the sleek suits, that stuck out. And yet it seemed that every restaurant she passed was one for them. It took her aback seeing so many of them all at once, looking at her if they saw her at all, as if she had to be dying to be in there with them, as if she had to nearly fall over backwards with admiration and envy. She felt a tidal crest of self-affirmation and stalked on by the menus, not looking.

The next street seemed more hopeful since it seemed more obscure. As she paused in front of an empty patio, feeling free to look over the white iron chairs, a waitress' head poked from the interior shadows and smiled at her, saying smoothly "How are we doing this evening?"

"Lookin' for somethin't'eat."

She grimaced. Now there was nothing for it but to go in. A waitress, though, that was a good sign; in order to have a man waiting on you, you probably had to pay more. She took two steps behind the knee-high white iron pickets that created a sense of enclosure, and sat as soon as possible at an outer table. What a terrible choice. Stuck out there by herself amid all those vacant white iron tables, so nearly in the street that anybody passing might look over her shoulder at what she ate. Everyone in the world watching her, surely. Stifling the urge to bolt, she rose slowly from her chair, pushing it back under the table with a dreadful sceetch, then snuck in towards the protecting wall. Better. She had control of it now with her back to the wall.

The street was almost vacant, disturbed only by a slow-moving car and a man walking briskly, his suit jacket flaring in the wind he created. And yet still she sensed tumult, a throbbing in the air just beyond the empty street and silent buildings, a humming in the trees that billowed over embassy avenues, that shimmered around gutted inhabited houses with windows shot out and boarded over, that ebbed and swayed next to street lights and in the traffic circles where lone men sat out late at night long after kids spraying water at the fountains had gone home.

She was beginning to settle in the chair, feeling almost calm, wondering why the waitress was taking so long since the place was empty, when her gaze fixed on a girl coming toward her along the street. She stared intently at the girl's flat shoes, her way of carrying her bulky purse crammed with a thousand things, arm flat against her side and wrist turned out, almost as if she were dragging it. She was walking quickly as if she saw nothing, was looking for nothing, yet from time to time her glance shot out around her as if to get her bearings again. Watching the girl's swift self-conscious progress, Abby-Jean felt a shock of recognition. Was that how she herself looked, as noticeable as that? But for sitting behind the phalanx of white tables, she would never have known it. As the girl passed their glances met, the girl's dropping abashedly to her feet then raising again in doubt, shy with recognition before she rushed quickly on.

How could she know? Yet Abby-Jean remembered herself in the past two days blundering through crowds, that instinctive feel for people like herself and those others not, remembered those frightened forays, her very body alive with noticing, as if she were a fish passing through strange waters, each fin delicately probing, questing, not touching solidity but recoiling from the external impressions, the tricks of movement carried through the water. Too many impressions, not too few, causing her to stumble along like a fool. Unconsciously her eyes sought out her own — skinny whips of boys that shot the plush cars up from underground garages, threatening always to hurtle across the sidewalk to the street, grinning bravado at her fear and insolence at the older black men seated tilted in chairs, the guardians of the keys. Or women in stores, women behind counters, women in crowded buses, burdens in their arms. The vendors of ice cream, crazy hats, fruit, jewelry, umbrellas. Service station men and bus drivers. Looking always for people like herself, finding them everywhere, even here where it seemed so rich and dead, even here in streets frozen with banks and insurance companies and law offices, sprouting through the seams with all the force of nature breaking rocks. But after working hours, she could see it plainly, downtown was not for them. There was nowhere to eat, nowhere regular. And here she was sitting like a fool, full of dreadful apprehension of the menu bearing down upon her in a waiter's hands.

There were six pages of it! It was two feet tall, on parchment paper with rough edges, enclosed between padded leather covers with Biblical lettering in gold! The thing had a long golden tassle hanging down. She turned the pages dizzily, not knowing where or how to begin, looking at the prices, panic-stricken. Had the waiter given her a breather and retreated a moment inside, she would surely have bolted. As it was, he stood over her waiting an aeon of time.

"This." She stabbed at a price on the center page.

"Hamburger steak," the waiter read out. "And with it?"

She stared at him. Wasn't there, at $10, a meal?

"What vegetables," the watier said. "Vegetables are ordered separately."

"Carrots," she blurted.

As he still hung over her, she burst out in desperation, "That's all," as if, but for dire threat, he would remain standing over her, murmuring "And with it?" to eternity.

"Shall I take this away?"

She nodded.

The food came at last, looking sculptured and minute on the large plate. She began on it laboriously, chewing and swallowing with effort. The smell of it made her feel weak. She could taste nothing, only feel it pass in lumps down her throat, watching it diminish on the plate. Thick waves of heat were beating through her. Ten dollars. With the carrots, more. It was a calamity!

She glanced up, saw a middle-aged couple at an adjacent table staring at her blankly. She stared back, preoccupied, fork halted halfway to her mouth, and their eyes dropped at once. Yet when she continued eating, she saw they were staring again. She stopped eating altogether then, her face ablaze. There were tears stark and hot on her face! She'd been crying over her food!

Putting her fork down, she tried to wipe her tears inobtrusively with the back of her hand, feeling them threaten again as she pictured herself snuffling over her plate. The urge to bolt pumped through her like volleys of a cannonade. Resisting, she picked up her fork with determination. The meal was going to cost her as much as dinner for a week; she was going to eat it all.

There was no bread. Was that extra too? Maybe the waiter just hadn't bothered, deciding he could do just half a job for someone like her who wouldn't know the difference. Maybe he had insulted her many times already, subtle deviations or omissions in the usual thing, noticeable to others, undetectable by her. With difficulty she swallowed the last carrot, then glanced about her. She'd finished it all. The middle-aged couple no longer watched her, picking at something in shells with their forks. Where was the waiter? Wasn't he supposed to come, now she'd done? For several moments she sat waiting, feeling her face grow hotter. There was something in his delay in bringing the bill, surely, that showed the color of his attitude toward her? She stood up abruptly, unable to bear waiting further. As she gathered up her purse, he materialized at the table in front of her. Did he think, then, she was about to sneak out without paying? Her chest heaved with the exhaustion of it.

She snatched the bill from the little plate on which he had extended it, face down. So she was to leave the money on the plate, as if a straight settling of accounts hand to hand would be an indignity to them both. $15.85. She counted it out exactly to the last nickel, the stack of ten ones causing the bill on top to tremble. As he came over to retrieve it, she pulled out an extra dollar from her wallet. A peculiar expression came over his face as she extended it to him.

"That's for you," she quavered, stumbling through the grand gesture. Deftly he took it between a second and third finger, snapping it to his palm, then crushing it into a pocket without a word of thanks.

She picked her way out through the white iron tables to the street. Once beyond the knee-high iron picket fence, she glanced back in amazement. The middle-aged couple were leaning back slightly in their chairs so the waiter could place yet another set of plates on their table. All around them in clusters, the white iron tables were empty, looking ready to be stacked and taken in. In the dim twilight, the small terrace area seemed dismal and make-shift. The sight of it angered her. Her stomach hurt. She had been robbed.

She hurried back to her room, stopping once in mid-stride, stricken with the memory of her outstretched hand offering yet one dollar more. She would brood over it for weeks, the way all the women in her family did, brooding over a misspent dollar with the same sharp passion and regret in weeks and months that followed, until a backward glance at their whole life's course seemed one long lament for money that had gotten away.

There was no handle on the inner door to the women's residence, just a lock fitted into the heavy slab of wood. As she struggled with the poorly fitting key, two men passed through the small entranceway that served as antechambre to both residence and bar, a slender grey-haired man in an expensive suit, very frail and drunk, with his arm slung about the shoulder of a younger man who wore no shirt beneath his leather vest, his bronze arms and chest exposed, his hair strangely orange-bronze. She pressed against the door, but they were oblivious to her, the young man maneuvering the older clumsily through the outer door and down the steps to the street, cajoling him and shaking his body from time to time with a brutal humour that the older man, head reeling, drunkenly wistful, seemed to endure as his due.

Quickly Abby-Jean forced the key into the lock, heaved, then released the door, letting it swing shut with a thud behind her. From the darkness at the foot of the stairs, she could hear a woman's voice at the landing above where the phone was.

"Oh yeah? Well he's been after me all the time. Two weeks now. Sure he has. Says he's gonna sneak right up here into the room, he says. You can tell it to them others, I says, but not to me. You get to know things after a while, you don't stay as green as you was. Oh Lord, but he keep on after me 'til I don't know what I'm gonna do."

Despite the vigorous complaint, it was a boast which seemed to be having difficulty in getting across to the other party on the line. Mounting the stairs, Abby-Jean saw a short corpulent woman in pants, her face daubed a vehement red at cheeks and mouth. As her head was small and neat compared to her ballooning body, it made her look like a clown.

"Sure, he told me that too. Yeah, and that. He told me that too. Yeah, I said to him, y'know what I said? Haw. Listen here. Lemme tell you what I said. Will you hang on a sec? Lemme tell you —"

As Abby-Jean passed, the woman's voice lowered momentarily then redoubled as if the lapse had given ground that had to be rewon. Her voice shrilled up the stairs to the third landing and down the corridor, punctuated by brief silences as if she were speaking into the earphone of someone deaf. Despite all her effort, it was as if she hadn't been heard, for she laboriously repeated the same phrases again and again, her voice frank with the urge to communicate, innocent in its boasting. Like an announcement to the whole three floors of silent rooms, it gave notice that she had friends, had a life of her own out there in full swing. Abby-Jean listened to its rise and fall with envy.

Passing slowly along the third floor in the hope of running across anybody else, she glanced at the garbage bags under the roach sign with new sympathy. Behind the slatted door, it was quiet and dark. Reaching her room, she switched on the light and stood blinking in the glare of the two bare bulbs above, buffeted by waves of Blue Grass Cologne. She was starkly visibile to anyone glancing from a chain of windows across the way. Anyone could take in the whole of her life at a glance. She rushed across the room to jerk the blinds down.

She sat on the bed then lay flat out, stared at the ceiling, sighed, then jumped up to the mirror to comb her hair with an iridescent green comb. Pulling a makeup bag from her purse, she squinted at her eyelids. What better time to find out if she could turn her fat lids into almond eyes with a well-placed line of brown pencil like the cosmetic ads suggested? Now when there was no one to laugh, to shove her arm, to call her away to help with the — Now when there was no one and nothing to do.

For over an hour she struggled, making the line thicker first in the corner, then at the apex of the lid, then darkening the whole of the lid, extending two lines straight out to her hairline: all of the possibilities. Failure. She would never have almond eyes. But somebody would love her just the same. Her face became stricken, passionate. The magazines tried to frighten her that it happened for almond eyes alone, but that couldn't be true. There was something special about her, round eyes or no, something — she couldn't name it, but it lapped and surged within her. If the magazines were to be believed, then all the sweet flow of love in the world would stop, afraid to believe in itself due to no almond eyes. How to think that when it churned here within her, beat hopeful in the breasts of her sisters at home, even within the woman on the phone at the foot of the stairs. Love calling for love, loving itself, believing it could draw to itself, believing it could never, not forever, be denied.

Too agitated to return to the bed, she opened her door and went a few paces down the hall, listening. No one. Still no one. Would there never be another soul down all the dim yellowish halls? If they were in, what were they doing in their rooms? She heard no sound of television or radio, no conversation or laughter, not so much as a footfall or a cough intermingled with the dull thud of music from the bar below. She returned to her door then turned back sharply as if to catch anyone who might appear just because she was giving up. There was no one. Her door closed behind her with a muffled click, a click that might have hid the sound of another door opening. She swung her door wide open again and peered into the hall. Truly, no one. She returned to sit on the bed, then lay flat out, then stared at the ceiling, then sighed.

How about a shower! She rose again, grabbed her nightie from the armchair where she had draped it carefully, then suddenly released it. As the white cotton dropped onto the plastic, a roach slid dizzily down the white folds, careening from frill to frill, gaining a momentary scrambling foothold then dropping off at last, a slick brown pellet, to the floor. Its shiny back bobbed and glinted as it beat an erratic retreat over, under, through the rough shag pile of the rug to squeeze through a crack in the floorboard. Silent and bemused, she watched its tortured course, then glanced quickly at her suitcase to be sure the zipper was done up tight. Picking up her nightie, she gave it two brief flecks with the back of her fingers, then hung it on a peg so that it didn't touch the wall.

Laden with soap, toothbrush and towel, she halted in surprise at the closed bathroom door. Her face lit. Someone! Someone who had come down the hall so silently that, despite her constant instinctive keening for some outer sound, she hadn't heard. She stood outside the door smiling and shifting from one foot to the other, hearing the rush of water into the tub. Someone!

Humming under her breath, she turned into the second parallel corridor of doors, on down to the second washroom. There the shower was nothing but a tiny metal triangle wedged into the corner of a room where only a toilet and sink should have been. She stepped in without removing her thongs, let the stiff jet of spray beat against her neck and back, maneuvering carefully so that her naked body didn't touch the soap-streaked tin a few inches to either side. The heat of the water felt sharp and good. Soon she was singing aloud, the bar of soap clutched between her legs as she sluiced the water over her breasts, rinsing the foaming white lather down.

A momentary relaxation loosened her grip, and the soap bar skittered down over her ankles to rest in the drain. She bent towards it slightly, then straightened abruptly with a short, hesitant laugh. When she bent, her body had slammed against the clammy metal wall. She took a mincing step forward, bent slightly again, and again her buttocks collided against walls grey with corrugations of ancient lather. No matter how she fretted about trying to keep her flesh from touching the filthy metal, the triangle was too small to permit bending without the slamming of naked flesh against its walls.

It was so ludicrous, her soap melting away in the drain as she thrashed about, that she gave in to the urge to be silly, giving a little shriek amid giggles at each recoiling bump of her body against the walls. She moved the soap with her toe, tried to press it against her ankle then slide it along one leg with her other foot. At two inches above her ankle, the knee of her propelling leg slithered against the wall, and down the soap dropped again. Suddenly she was claustrophobic and breathless. Leaning forward, left cheek and buttocks plastered against two walls of the triangle, she grasped the soap, then scrubbed the contaminated skin with vigor.

Her thongs scattered water on the rippling linoleum as she burst out. Who in their right mind thought a person could shower in a hole like that?

Pausing a moment by the other bathroom, she eyed the open door wistfully, glimpsing long dark hairs in the tub. Whoever it was had gotten away without being seen. Looking both ways down the empty hall, her eyes fell upon the garbage bags and tottering stack of books beside them. Tiptoeing over, she took the top book and fled with it to her room. Glancing once at her nightie, she inspected the bed, then got in in the raw and pulled the thin sheet up to her neck. Her heart was beating wildly.

What if I went crazy in here, she thought.

Suddenly the room seemed foreign, a little distorted. She raised her hand and stared at it. Her own freckled hand. It looked strange, as if it had a life of its own. On the opposite wall a large roach crawling laboriously toward the ceiling lost its footing and fell with a sharp ping into the metallic wastebasket by the sink.

Crushing an inside page in her haste, she propped the book up against her chest and read:

When Maurice picked me up at Adorno's driving the mazzeratti, I wasn't impressed, not after a summer in Europe with the Spicer- Joneses, whom I met through Countess Titania, a friend of my aunt's. Not, of course, that our New England family had much more to offer than blue blood, Yankee style. But if you're five foot seven with jade eyes and flaming red hair, and a body that Nastasia wouldn't recommend for Vogue but would give her eye teeth to have — or is it to get her hands on? Well you can get around, need I say more?

The trouble was, naive idiot that I was, I'd done all my getting around with one Baron de Mourne, with whom I'd fallen hopelessly in love. What a dizzy whirl — the Hunt Club, the yachts, the galleries, the Mediterranean at night with a man who knew everything, who made women's eyes turn as he passed. A man, might I say, who seemed to only have eyes for me. Who gave me silk blouses from Diacardia and a teaset of belique, who lent me his limo on Wednesdays and Fridays, complete with Fritz, who had a special eye for the most marvelous boutiques. It was Seventh Heaven, my summer in Europe. How could it all have come crashing down around my ears?

Maybe Maurice would say something clever over scampi and I would forget it all, even the incredibly handsome Baron de Mourne. Dear Maurice, who was so entertaining and, happier still, so very rich. Things could be worse, I thought as I stepped into his mazzerati. Much worse. I'd talk to him about a controlling interest in the Tricciana, and *then* we'd see —

Abby-Jean lowered the book, unable to keep her mind on it. Were there such people? Or was that something else you just found in magazines? Maybe they were rich and beautiful, maybe they had everything, but they seemed so nasty somehow. And so many of the things they talked about, she didn't understand.

As she turned her cheek against the pillow, *Call Me Princess* slid from her hand. She lay without moving, trying to think of something beautiful to fall asleep on, a trick her mother had taught her. From the bar below, she could hear words now, overriding the dull disco beat, repeating the same phrase over and over like an incantation:

Gotta *BE* somebody
Gotta *BE* somebody
Gotta *BE* somebody

23

For over an hour she clung to the memory of the beech tree glimmering and swelling in the streetlights beyond, and fell asleep at last with the light still on.

○

There it hung on the second floor landing like the hub of the universe: the phone. Each time it rang in the first days, even before she left the number with a string of personnel offices, Abby-Jean galloped down from the third floor landing to answer it, anxious to talk a second, if only to call someone to the phone or relay a message, hoping always it would lead to something, at least to the sight of faces in her flight through the halls.

"Don't give up if it seems a long time. 411's at the end of the third floor hall and I got to go up one flight of stairs, but I'll come back an' tell you if she's not there, I wouldn't just leave you hangin' on the line," she would say before carefully stretching the receiver down until the cord hung straight, leaving it skimming gently near the baseboard rather than letting it knock pell mell against the wall. Then off she would hike to 411, then back again quickly if no one answered her knocks and timorous "Hey you got a call", to pant the bad news. If the caller asked to leave a message, she would repeat it over and over on her way back up to her room to write it out, then return to wedge the message in the crack of the absent woman's door. It meant a lot of running up and down. Sometimes the small white squares of paper stayed wedged in a door for days before disappearing.

But sometimes women answered when she knocked. Whether they thanked her or just brushed past toward the phone, intent already on the call, they all had the same way of opening the door — just a little at first, with their head peeping round, then their whole body squeezing out without the door being opened any wider, so that it was impossible to see behind them into their rooms. Which she couldn't help trying to do — not because she meant to be nosy, but to compare their rooms with her own, to get a better idea, so to speak.

And she never knew what to expect behind one of those doors when she knocked — a huge black woman in a sleeveless white blouse with her hair tied in knobs all over her head, a shy black girl, slim-bodied and graceful, wearing Indian or African prints, an oriental woman with short-cropped hair, a white woman of indiscriminate age with pallid eyes, dressed in a security guard's uniform like a man. Older women with voices that seemed to crack with the moving of their bones. Voices raw from cigarettes, accents, drawls. And from each room, in the little gust of air from the opening and closing door, came its smell — sweat, powder, cigarettes, perfume, food, lysol, pine-scent, incense, beer, and lingering and permeating it all, the special smell of each woman.

Each time as they hurried off to the phone, leaving her wistfully trailing along behind, going always as far as the landing to check that the caller hadn't hung up, she felt a pang at the way they forgot about her as they ran off to make their connection with the city outside, a connection that in itself seemed something marvelous to her. But sometimes the calls were terrible — loud angry voices, tears. Sometimes she wasn't sure if the call had been answered at all, women pressed into the corner niche, low-voiced murmurings with their faces right up against the wall, struggling for privacy. Then afterwards, the sound of feet in the hall, a closing door, then silence, silence, as if never had a soul passed at all.

Often as she sat at her desk practicing the typing, her open door failing to attract company, she could hear someone going through a session on the phones. There would be the rattle of change in the pay slot, dialing, a few trailing sentences, silence, then the sound of change and dialing once again. For half an hour perhaps, the phone gobbled up change as somebody looked for a job or another place to live. Sometimes snippets of conversation reached her from a floor and a half away. "From Georgia. *Georgia.*" Then a pause. "Well I don't give a damn if I sound black to you —" The receiver came down with a crash. Or "Well I know it's Wednesday but I got a day off, that's why I'm not at work...At the CV on Wyoming, I got their number here, you can call if you don't believe me... Well look, I gave you the number and now you don't want to call. If you still don't believe I work, what can I do?... It is *too* your problem, it is, it —" Then silence.

Sometimes it was as if the phone got its appetite up, like a slot machine with an unlucky player. She would hear them begin, and after a few calls would know it was going to go on that way, call after call with no headway, and maybe though there was nothing to do then but keep on, it was awesome how they did so.

From time to time the phone rang late at night, after three. The first time it happened, she heard it through her dreams, the dream changing to accommodate the sound, a dream of her brother running to meet her up the long white beach on St. Helena, running and waving, and each time his mouth opened, the ringing came out of it, even the gulls swooped ringing, until at last she was awake and recognized the sound for what it was, lying motionless still, waiting for the ringing to stop or be answered. Surely if she was awake at the far end of the third floor, others were lying awake too, listening to it ring, and they were closer. Why couldn't someone on the same floor answer the damn thing for a change? She lay a moment longer on the bed, obdurate, bleary and vague with sleep until the dream vision of her brother running towards her electrified her. A call this late, an emergency surely, if not for herself then for somebody else? What was wrong with them all that nobody answered, everybody lazing in the warmth of their beds.

She leapt up, not bothering to shuffle about on the shag rug in the darkness for her slippers, wheeling out the door and down the hall, running on tiptoe. Hang on, she thought breathlessly after each ring that seemed the last, just hang on, I'm coming, I'm nearly there, I'm right — She grasped the receiver and leaned back against the wall, hearing no dial tone.

"Hi you-all, I made it," she burst into the phone, face round with chuckles at her success, one foot scraping quickly down her other leg to rid the sole of the particles of dirt and small things accumulated in her barefoot flight through the halls.

There was silence on the line, still no dial tone.

"Hey," she whispered. "Hey, is somebody there?" She gazed up and down the halls changed from daytime grey to dim yellow under the bare overhead lights. Raising her other foot, scraping it down along her leg, she glanced over her shoulder at the blackened sole, thinking how she would have to wash her feet in the tub now. The sink in her room was too high to get a foot in.

An exhalation of breath came from the other end of the line, caught up quickly, like a swallowed sigh. She nearly dropped the phone.

In all the building, there wasn't a sound, not even from the bar below. Whispering hello once more, she heard the urgent angry word as it hissed through all the halls, heard it as if she were behind the many dozen closed doors where eyes, now open, stared unblinking, thoughtless, into darkness. That very hello carried over a labyrinth of wires out into the dark unsleeping tumult beyond where someone sick, crazy, febrile with loneliness, hung on it, savoured it, picturing her perhaps in this very cotton nightie, standing anxious and exposed, one-footed, at the phone. It was as if the building walls had collapsed and a fevered hand reached in to clutch her thighs.

Mortified, she hung up quickly then snuck on back to her room. All the others knew what it meant, then, a call like that in the night. Knew tonight it had been answered once more by somebody new who would never answer a call in the night again.

Toward the end of her second week at the residence, Abby-Jean's term of duty at the phone came to an end. A young Vietnamese girl moved into a room by the phone, and when it rang she answered it before Abby-Jean could reach the third floor stairwell. Craning over the bannister to glimpse the girl's thonged feet at the phone below, Abby-Jean would stand there listening for her voice, then her footsteps as she went to relay messages. The call was never for her; those who received calls rarely bothered to answer the phone. So she knew about the Vietnamese girl. Another like herself only newer yet. It made her think of the Vietnamese girl warmly, tolerantly, like someone with rich years of experience. But Lord, how she missed not being the one to answer the phone! Still when it rang, she rushed to the landing and waited glumly for the thonged feet to beat her to it.

Then another newcomer. Several times when the phone rang, she saw a middle-aged woman in a duster open her door on the landing below, and stand outside it thoughtfully. Their eyes would meet as they waited, listening. A floor apart, they would smile gravely at each other, each inclining her head to show how important it was to know whether the call was for her. Something in the woman's quiet face went out to her. But they were a landing apart, too far apart to speak. They could only smile foolishly and shrug, and go back to their rooms after a moment or two because it wasn't possible to delay any longer, straining eagerly towards each other, a landing apart. Nonetheless, it gave her something to take back to her room, a communication of sorts.

When it happened a few more times, it was agreed that they knew one another.

❂

"Of course, it's not New York. Washington's not New York," Louise Crisp advised Abby-Jean, who sat in Louise's only free chair, smoking the cigarette she had chosen from one of the different brands spread in modest profusion there on the bed. Louise Crisp didn't smoke. The cigarettes had been bought for whoever came to visit her, offered as soon as someone entered her room, then offered again immediately at the butting of each one. The conversation continued unabated through a gathering haze, for Abby-Jean smoked them to be friendly until she was ready to choke.

"Half the people you'll meet here will be from New York, and they'll tell you that right away. That Washington lacks the spice of New York. Then they'll try to pretend that they're better than you because they're from New York. Even if they've lived here twenty years, you'll still catch them saying, 'Of course, back in New York...', as if that was where they really lived and not in Washington at all. I get angry, of course. I'm no fool. I know it's not the same because I'm from New York myself. But Washington is Washington and there you are. You can't expect it to be New York. You must take it for what it is, with its own marvelous ways."

Abby-Jean nodded, trembling, feeling exhilerated by the idea of not expecting Washington to be New York but taking it for what it was. She felt both small and enlarged at once to be hearing the two great cities spoken of so commandingly, and stared eagerly at Louise, at the deep red lipstick that made her full lips stand out against a face still starkly pale in mid-April, at the wealth of short metallic graying hair held back by a tortoise-shell barette on one side. When she spoke, her voice granulated and throaty, tinged with a luxuriant unplaceable drawl, Louise Crisp had a way of tossing her head back from time to time that forced her to refasten the barette. It was a dramatic self-assertive gesture that gave her words intelligence and passion.

"Here you have the diplomatic community, people from every nation in the world. You may not get to meet them — they keep to themselves, you know, they run in a closed circuit — but think: they are here, so are you. You see a magnificent limousine with shaded windows glide by and you think — Kuwait, Zaire, Indonesia. Somebody exotic from the far side of the globe, and you, Abby-Jean Brown, have seen him pass, and you know."

Abby-Jean nodded uncertainly, unsure as to what she would then know, her gaze shifting away from the woman in her late forties who sat in a duster and slippers on the edge of her bed. In order to make a place for herself there, Louise Crisp had heaved a pile of clothes on hangers to the far side of the bed and crammed several paper bags, crushed and rolled closed, beneath it. Along the walls and in the corners of the room, there were bags of various sizes similarly rolled or open — paper bags, plastic bags, bags with crests of department stores or supermarkets on their sides reading Shop-Easy, Kresge, Gimbels, IGA. From the open tops protruded knitting needles, crumpled clothing, pamphlets, utensils.

Louise's room was a little smaller than her own but it overlooked the street. Though one could see trees without straining from the two windows, the fact that they were placed side by side prevented a cross breeze. The walls were off-white, preferable to the glaring yellow of her own. But the closet, from which boxes seemed to bulge, was surely much smaller than hers. The sinks were the same. Louise's carpet had a finer ply. They discussed the differences noisily before sitting down, agreed how assets balanced liabilities on both $54 rooms, and speculated as to the failings of the room at $39. Though Louise Crisp had sojourned in several of the other rooms at one time or another in the past decade, she hadn't run across the cheaper one yet.

"The government is here, and the military, and the civil service. Think. You have senators, congressmen, generals; you have heads of departments, judges, bankers. You have the White House, the Pentagon, the FBI." Louise paused as if waiting for her to catch up. "I'm not saying you can expect to meet them — you have your set and they have theirs — but the buildings where they work are there for the naked eye to see. Marvelous buildings made of brownstone, limestone, marble. And down every major road in the city, you can see the Capitol dome. All the avenues come from there, like arteries from the heart."

Her voice seemed to throb. The way she spoke about the city as if it were in the palm of her hand took Abby-Jean's breath away.

"You have the Georgetown people, the university and all, they're another lot. They stay where they are, though you might see a few around here, some crazy looking people at the art galleries up the street. And then," Louise's arm cut a broad swath about her that covered miles of the north, east and south, "There's the blacks. I've got nothing against them," she said.

Soon Abby-Jean's lap was heaped with pamphlets describing scenic tours, theatre and movie listings, restaurant guides and art galleries. Louise gave her a listing of lectures being given at some institute or other, of poetry readings at the university, of military bands in the public parks. She fingered them, daunted, stopping to pore over pages torn from several newspapers listing what could be done in Washington for free.

"Go ahead, take them, they're free. There'll be new ones next week. I know where to get a load more of these if I need any, so don't worry about me."

Abby-Jean glanced at her shyly. No matter how dazzling the portrait of Washington, she wanted to say something in praise of Beaufort. A conversation wasn't a conversation unless one got in one's own little piece.

"I like Beaufort n'all," she began. "My whole family's there. I'm the only one that's moved on but I don't think nobody wanted me to go."

"You were different from them, that's why you left. They don't have the courage to go themselves, so they try to hold you back."

Abby-Jean thought a moment. There was something startlingly sweet in the idea of being different, but something tiresome too, and besides, she couldn't really see that it was true. How many souls in all of Beaufort thought there was somewhere better in all of God's earth? How many who didn't sniff the salt air, watch the Regatta parade, work a garden in the declining sun, and praise God that they were themselves and nobody else in that very spot on earth that contained the whole of their efforts, their memories, their dreams? It wasn't that they were content with what they had, she couldn't say that, though it wasn't always how much they had that measured their peace of mind. But their hopes were in that place. They weren't longing for Washington or New York.

"We're travelers. Adventurers," Louise Crisp said. "We live in a wider world."

For a second time, Abby-Jean felt aflame at her words, then was quickly abashed as if she had misrepresented herself.

"I just had it in mind to get a job and stay here. In a hotel cleaning, or something in a restaurant somewhere."

She hadn't really thought it out, resting her confidence in the hundreds of things that she knew how to do — how to cook and to clean, how to make beds, how to look after kids and keep them in line. She knew how to weed thoroughly, how to pick berries fast, how to paint walls without streaks and wash windows. She could even drive a truck, though she didn't have a license for that. It wasn't believable that someone with all that and hoping to learn more couldn't find some kind of work, even in hard times like these.

Louise Crisp nodded slowly.

"But that's just until I get my typing speeded up," Abby-Jean burst, a sense of fairness to herself in turn making her disclose the dream. "I figure to be a secretary an' get a job in a air-conditioned office somewheres."

Louise Crisp drew in her breath in volume. "That's marvelous!" she exhuded. "You could be a temp like me."

Abby-Jean felt a burst of energy like when she gathered her muscles tight before a leap into the sea, feeling the old boat rock and give way beneath her. It would be something to be like Louise... What was a temp?

The way Louise described it made it seem more demanding, more rewarding than she could have dreamt. Not everyone could be a temporary secretary, you had to be good at what you did. Because every time they sent you out, it was as if somebody had hired you above everybody else for a brand new job. Everybody was depending on you — the agency you represented, the employer faced with an emergency perhaps, the woman whose work you were taking over, for if you did something wrong it might take weeks to discover and a month to undo. You had to be able to remember instructions the first time you were told because asking again made them lose confidence in you, ready as they were to think you were dumb. You had to be sharp from the first, for they forgot how long it had taken to break somebody in to the job that you did. But not too sharp, on the other hand, so as to make the other girls look bad or set a record that they might have to keep, day after day and year after year, slowed down by the boredom of doing the same old thing. It took a delicate touch to be the best the boss had seen, yet not set him questioning the women he had. If a temp was good, people appreciated it beyond measure, praising her more in a week than they did people they'd had for years. That she herself had been offered permanent jobs by the score was a proof of how good she was.

Louise Crisp's eyes narrowed and her voice became stronger yet.

"But if I had taken one of them, what would I know? Nothing but that. As it is, I've worked in publishing, advertising and insurance, in hospitals and factories. I've worked for doctors, dentists, lawyers, architects and engineers. I can look out over a city and know what life's like of a day for thousands of lives. You can't imagine the people I've met and the things I've learned. And I've traveled. I lived in New York of course, but that's not all. I lived in Boston too, in Providence, in Atlantic

City. And I lived in Roanoke, Reading, Baltimore and Atlanta for a while. Sometimes I go south for the winter, to Miami."

The terror of the first two nights in the bus station was forgotten as Abby-Jean savoured the panoramic listing of the cities' names.

"You have to expect that it makes people envious, people who live all their lives in one spot. I have a sister who stayed in North Carolina with her husband all her life, while I have been up and down the entire length of the eastern seaboard many times. I try to explain to her how my life's very broad, but she's just too narrow to see. People don't know what they don't know. They get so rooted where they are that they see nothing at all. You see, they can't place anything because they have nothing to compare it to. But when I come in to Scranton, say, and they're hard on me at work or when I try to find some place to stay, well I put them in line with others like them in all the towns that I've known. I can see beyond them, I can place them where they are. I can say, well, so you are the local this, the local that, and all the importance of them and their set fades away. But think if I'd lived there forever, how they'd crush me down with their ways."

Louise's head tossed back again with such a vehemence that Abby-Jean could imagine a younger Louise for whom that gesture habitually cleared from her face a luxuriant flow of hair, a passionate girl who had a way of sitting with her face straining upwards as if she were at once trying to keep above a flood and to pitch into the pulsating blue.

"When you're a temp, you don't have to take any of that. You get restless or angry today, and within a week, you're on down the road."

On down the road, Abby-Jean thought with a shudder.

"You see what it means," Louise Crisp said.

Abby-Jean's heart was beating rapidly.

"Freedom," Louise Crisp breathed.

They stared at each other intensely without noticing it, each coursing down the channel of her own thoughts.

"Have another cigarette."

"Lord, I couldn't."

"What about one of these?" Louise pulled out a slim pack from a bag beneath the bed. "Black Russians."

Abby-Jean stared at the black-papered cigarettes with gold tips.

"Maybe I'll just take one for later, if it's okay with you."

"Take the pack. I know where to get more of these."

They haggled about it for a little.

"What about coffee then?"

Abby-Jean agreed.

Louise took two steps back toward the wall, so that Abby-Jean could pass through the channel between the bed and a second chair heaped with clothes to get out of the way. Then she reached for the percolator down behind the TV set, pole lamp and chair, near the wall switch down beneath the bed. When she had it, they squeezed past each other to their former seats again. Louise raised the lid and frowned.

"I'll just drop the dregs in the toilet down the hall. Never put *anything* down the sink in your room. Here —" She gathered up TV listings cut out from a couple of newspapers, pressed them into Abby-Jean's hands. "Feel free to change the channel, I don't mind, and —" She glanced about the room. "Have a cigarette of course, and —" Her glance searched the room again without finding anything else to offer. "I'll be just a minute," she said apologetically, backing out of the room.

Abby-Jean glanced at the TV set appreciatively. What an asset to her new life, to come and visit Louise and get a chance to watch TV!

A grinding sound came from the keyhole.

Abby-Jean leaned forward in her chair, her face intense. Louise Crisp had locked the door behind her. She had locked the door! Her glance traveled quickly over the room, taking in the yellow dress that seemed freshly ironed hanging slightly askew from a coat hanger crooked over the top of the closet door, the meagre row of religious and prophetic books on the window ledge, the towel draped to dry over the other chair so laden with clothing that Louise hadn't even tried to clear it. Was there something so valuable here? Did Louise Crisp expect that she would loot the room while she was away? That she wouldn't protect her things from anyone else, wouldn't guard them as if they were her own? Good Lord, she had only gone down the hall. Breathing lightly, she leaned forward, listening for returning footsteps from the hall.

When Lousie Crisp re-entered the room, she was staring intently at the TV, visibly too engrossed to even be aware of her return.

"There." Louise deposited the percolator in shining droplet-covered pieces in the sink. As she glanced over her shoulder, she caught Abby-Jean's eyes as they raised in apprehension then quickly returned to the TV. For a second she stared at her blankly.

"Why, you thought I locked you in!"

Abby-Jean reddened. What if Louise guessed some of the fantastic suspicions she had been having? That she was on to some of it was obvious from her brief frown, a second of tiredness, before a wry tolerant smile found her face again.

"When I left the room, I didn't even notice that I was locking the door. It's taken years to get the habit to come no matter what. Someone can be in and out of your room in a second, don't think that she can't. Only a fool would go out and leave her room unlocked, no matter how near she is."

Abby-Jean blanched. She couldn't remember if she had even shut her door, so eager had she been to rush down at Louise's signal when the phone had lured them again to the landings of the second and third floor. What a good job she had nothing worth stealing!

"People will take anything. You may think it's nothing but to them... Locking the door had nothing to do with you. If I didn't think you were a good kid, I never would have let you in."

They sat silently a moment.

"I'm sorry, Louise."

"Well, you didn't know."

Abby-Jean's eyes lowered. Because she was much younger than Louise, she had taken it as only natural that Louise might try to please her for the reward of her company. But if she was a blockhead —

"You sure know a lot," she said softly.

"If you want to know anything, just ask."

"What're you doin' about the bugs?" Abby-Jean blurted, seeing an opening for the question at last. " I can't put nothin' in the bureau drawers because of 'em. I got my underwear an' all still locked up tight in the suitcase to keep it safe. Lord, I see 'em crawlin' the walls. An' sometimes they drop off, like they made some kind of a mistake, didn't remember to hang on, an' down they go, z-i-i-t-t-t, like a pea into a pail. POING! It makes me feel weird to think that they made a mistake, 'cause that makes them individual, like people."

She paused for breath. Now that she was on the subject, it was as if a festering grievance had begun to ooze forth.

"I was washin' the other day. I got my towel hung on a rack on the back of the closet door, an' I had the door open so it was near to the sink where I was washin' so I could reach across for the towel to dry. Then I felt somethin' soft on the back of my arm. I looked down, an' there was a roach. Now my arm wasn't touching nothing an' I know it didn't crawl from up my legs, there's no way I wouldn't know about that. But my towel, see, it was about five inches from my arm. So the way that I see it, here's this roach swingin' on the end of my towel, the very furthermost tip, with no place to go. An' then five inches away, he spots my arm. For all I know, it looks big as an airfield to him. An' then —" Her face teetered on the brink of laughter, then of distress. "—He made a JUMP for it. I swear to God, that's the only way he could've got up there on me. He made a JUMP for it. So I struck him off an' he hit the floor on the run. I grabbed my shoe an' I started hittin' after him, BAM, an' I missed 'cause he dived down in the pile of the carpet, an' BAM, he flips out an' still running, an' BAM — you know how crooked they run — but I got him, BAM, BAM, an' he's off again, crookeder 'cause a part of him's there on my shoe. But he don't die. There I am crawlin' after him on my hands an' knees, hittin' him direct time after time an' he don't die. He keeps wobblin' on an' on, his shiny back tiltin' from side to side, an' every time I hit him, he stops a minute like he's hunkering up his strength again before he makes another bolt for it. I hit him twenty times, an' still he don't die. *He just don't die,*" Abby-Jean exclaimed. "Lord, it turned my stomach, I just couldn't

33

stand hittin' him no more. So I threw my shoe into the corner an' watched him stagger away."

Louise Crisp's pallor intensified.

"There are no bugs in here. Not a one."

Abby-Jean glanced at her dubiously. The women's residence was joined on either side to buildings like itself, and on it went, on down the block. If the roach population were driven from one building, it would course like a wave to the final building wall at the end of the block, then seep irreversibly back. How could a single room stay free? Obviously they were all in it together and yet, looking at Louise who was staring fixedly out the window, she felt she had done something terrible by talking about it, that she had insulted and wounded Louise. No matter that the building had bugs and that was the truth, she sensed from Louise it should be something beneath her dignity to admit to it, to dwell on it even worse, as if dwelling on it would push grimey seams into all the things inside one that were beautiful, that struggled to exert themselves in the world outside.

"I guess I oughta do something,." she stammered. Having roaches from time to time in Carolina had never bothered her. There the roaches came in from *outside*.

"Here." Louise reached down under the bed, pulled out a red and gold tin from a paper bag that seemed to contain more of the same. "Roach powder. The best kind."

She explained where to put it: all along the baseboard at upper and lower seams, in any cracks between the door or window frames and the wall, in any cracks in the floor, around the sink where the pipes went through the walls, around the drain. In short, at any and all the tiniest crevices that might connect to outside. Abby-Jean glanced at the paper bags pushed against the walls of Louise's room, suddenly aware of traces of the white powder extending along all the walls like a witches' ring.

"There are no roaches, not in here." Louise said lightly and tossed her head back.

Abby-Jean fingered the red and gold tin gingerly, placing it atop the stack of pamphlets and clippings, under the pack of Black Russian cigarettes.

"You have to realize that some people are strange when it comes to roaches," Lousie said with a level glance.

Some people seemed to feel, she explained, that if they didn't move right in shoulder to shoulder with the roaches, they weren't a good sport. That was because they didn't want to create a fuss as if they'd never seen a roach before, didn't want to be too prissy and make everyone else ashamed. Roaches are only roaches, they would say jauntily, what harm do they do? But she had noticed that people like that probably hadn't had roaches much, didn't have the prospect of roaches stretching out in front of them for the rest of their lives.

"Even if we can't get rid of them," Louise's head tossed back, "Even if we have to live with them, why should we start saying it's okay?"

Abby-Jean frowned. After two weeks, the roaches revulsed her more than in the beginning, as if a membrane layer of insensitivity had been worn through. Now whenever she lifted something, she waited for the bug to drop out. She had pushed her bed away from the walls to keep them from crawling directly from the wall onto the yellow bedspread, and from there up onto her face. While drifting into sleep, she was careful never to drop an arm over the side of the bed for fear of what might crawl up it from the floor. Who could be crazy enough to pretend that roaches were okay?

"Time for the coffee." Louise's smile was sudden, brilliant. She didn't want to talk about it anymore. Ferreting two cups and spoons out of one of the crushed paper bags, she washed them painstakingly in the sink though it was apparent that they were already perfectly clean.

Passing by the windows with the coffee, she stopped a moment, staring down.

"What you lookin' at?"

"Just the cat down there crossing the street."

"Oh," Abby-Jean said, disappointed.

"Look! See how its body lowers when it runs, how its ears flatten out to the side and its tail seems to float along loose behind? He keeps it low and inconspicuous like that when he's scared and trying to sneak by."

Abby-Jean's eyes followed the fleeing cat.

"Did you see how, when he reached the bushes by the side of the building there, his tail gave a twitch? It didn't go upright, the way a cat's tail goes upright if it's hungry and coming for a dish of milk. Just a little twitch, like a kink of nerves, of relief because he's safely across the street and hidden in the bushes again."

"Yeah."

"It's so interesting! It's so marvelous!"

"I guess."

"Most people see nothing."

Abby-Jean's head hung. No doubt she was one of those. But then, she had a special way of seeing particular to her, she too noticed things that others wouldn't, had her own little savvy. She could see into the heart of things. That's what it was.

They settled back and enjoyed the coffee.

"I gotta go now," Abby-Jean said abruptly, remembering her open door.

"Anytime you want to come and watch TV — Anytime. I mean that."

"You come an' see me too. I'd be glad for you to."

They stood nodding and smiling at each other awkwardly, their faces straining to communicate: *come, sometime soon, come,* as if each could see over the shoulder of the other long hours of solitude while the city swarmed relentlessly about them.

"One more thing," Louise Crisp said, reaching her purse off the bed, pulling out two cashier stubs on the back of which addresses were written, one in pencil, one in pen. "I saw signs for rooms in these places. I always jot them down just in case. It's always a good idea to know —"

"Maybe you'd rather keep it for yourself?" Abby-Jean glanced at the stack of dresses on coat hangers laid out on the bed. Surely if anyone were thinking of moving, it was Louise. The idea that she herself might be looking for another place already took her aback. She had just moved in.

"Oh I'm leaving Washington," Louise said lightly.

"You're goin' now?" Abby-Jean cried. It was too much, to lose a friend and a TV all in one day.

"Soon." Louise glanced idly about her, gesturing toward the bundles stacked against the wall. "Doesn't it look like that to you?"

"I thought you was moving in, maybe. That's what I hoped it was."

"Well I was." As Louise's glance trailed over her things once more, she seemed to become entangled amid the clutter. "Just it's three months now and I can't seem to get anything unpacked and put away. I just sit here in the middle of it all and wonder."

Abby-Jean gazed at her earnestly.

Abruptly Louise tossed her head back and clipped the barette, breaking out of it with a sharp little laugh.

"You get to know yourself after a while. It must mean that I'm moving on."

○

Was it possible to feel conspicuous and anonymous at the same time? From the moment the heavy unmarked door of the residence swung shut behind her, Abby-Jean could feel the men hanging about on the street watching her. They were everywhere — always one or two on the high steps of the apartment building across from the residence, one or two on the porches of the houses on the way to the convenience store, often five or six on the street leading to the rotary, grouped by a bus stop, ignoring the buses that constantly stopped, shed people then lurched on. Yet as she passed the art galleries, she had to step off the sidewalk to get around a stout older lady in a mohair pancho and a young man whose immaculate white T shirt had a blue painted circle which made a bullseye of his left nipple. Totally oblivious to her, they were talking volubly, taking occasional quaffs from bell-shaped wineglasses right out on the street without a thought for the endlessly passing patrol cars which never even batted an eye.

In the center of the traffic rotary, there was a small park with trees, a water fountain, benches, and men again: solitary older men, boys in groups of twos and threes, black men, white men, orientals, some hunched over a game that she didn't dare glance at. If any women were sitting out on the benches, she felt free to stop awhile, perched on the corner of their bench, relaxing in the anonymity, free then to look around without that queer feeling of vulnerability that lingered even when she kept her eyes busy by looking in store windows. When the women left with their purses, their paper bags, their books, she could stay on for a time, hoping the memory of their presence lingered among all who remained. But soon some man would come up and sit beside her, or another two benches away would begin to glance at her, and she would wonder if he was wondering who she was sitting out there all alone and whether it meant something — And that would drive her on, filled with a loneliness so intense that surely it showed, surely anyone could see from her face that there was no one in all that sprawling city she could turn to. No one who, if she were suddenly to vanish, would even notice she was gone. And once they knew *that* — what then?

The thought maintained a thrill of fear throughout her body. Even in Beaufort, television let her know that there were crazy, violent, mean people in the cities who would stop at nothing, cared nothing for your life, had no limit to the things they'd do. But in Beaufort, it looked exciting because of how quiet Beaufort was, and she hadn't really believed TV anyway, not until she got to Washington. Then the TV people were on her mind all the time because she didn't know, and didn't know what she didn't know. It made the buildings look hard and bright, and people's faces hard and bright and, when she closed her eyes, seamed with shadows. She began to feel strange, as if she were losing touch, drifting, so she talked longer than was necessary to cashiers, to waitresses, to sales clerks in stores, to women in line for buses, until she felt sure they wondered what kind of crazy lost soul she was. The sense of behaving oddly was itself unbalancing. It was as if she were drunk and, meaning to walk a straight line, found herself slipping, laughing helplessly, slipping to the side. But how to behave normally when nothing was normal, when she had no job, no friends, nothing but a room, and was scared to death besides? Who wouldn't be strange without an anchor in all this seeking, straining, drifting, hungering city?

Time was an enemy. When she awoke in the morning, she stayed in bed to use up two hours of it, then was forced out at last by the mounting heat in her room and the knowledge that if she didn't get out and exhaust herself during the day, night would find her pacing her room like a small fierce animal in a cage. The weekends, when she couldn't look for a job, were worse. Then she just walked. She walked by the White House a few times and discovered to her surprise that it looked just like the postcards and the pictures in her schoolbooks, no more, no less. It was hard to believe that the President and his wife were perhaps no more than 500 yards away, very nearly breathing the same air. She checked herself to see how she felt at such a moment, but she felt nothing. It made her wonder if she wasn't a good person after all. There were people pacing about outside the iron picket fence carrying placards which read PEACE IS DISARMING and JOBS, NOT WAR. People against the government. It was weird, a little scarey. The words on the signs passed her by in a blur. She didn't dare take any of the flyers they were handing out. Who knew what kind of people they were? She tried to think who they looked like on TV. They were drug addicts, maybe?

So she walked on some more through department stores, pharmacies, shoe boutiques, dress stores... But it was exhausting, her daily parade through aisles of merchandise — dresses, blouses, wigs, coats, coffee percolators, dishwashers, sofas, microwave ovens, TV sets. And on it went — vacuum cleaners, blenders, barbeques. Barbie dolls with wigs, inexhaustible wardrobes, houses, horses, trailers and teasets all their own. After a while she stopped turning the price tag on toasters, desk lamps, housecoats, towels, for the small things were as far out of reach as the large ones. Everywhere there was merchandise — merchandise on shelves, merchandise on racks, merchandise in bins. Because she couldn't afford to buy anything, all the merchandise seemed to blur a little, losing its individual identity, becoming a glass thing she couldn't have, a little brown wicker thing she couldn't have, an electric thing she couldn't have, a furniture thing she couldn't have — all the things in their hundreds and thousands, in their acres of shelf space, blurring her eyes as she reeled on past. And all the while there were convex mirrors at the end of aisles and four directional cameras at intersections set to catch her if she tried to snatch one single thing from all the piles and hide it — where? The strength of her desire left a wake of revulsion. The things crowded her, impinged on her until she didn't want them any more, not when she was back in her room, not until she had to go out past the stores with their bright displays once again.

Never had she been such a bother to herself. She couldn't walk forever. Sooner or later she had to sit down, and to do that she had to pay. If she were so foolish or unlucky as to take a coke in a restaurant where there were waitresses instead of in a self-serve franchise, then they would be after her to buy something else before ten minutes was up, and she would have to pay more or get up and start walking again. Time was money, all right. It cost her just to get through it.

Then came the incident on K Street. The aisles of the discount drugstore were piled high with merchandise that couldn't be crammed on the shelves. There were no customers in the store.

Stopping at a display of lipsticks set out like a row of shining candles — Nude Beige, Paramount Pink, Can't Wait Vermillion — Abby-Jean picked out a tube of Strawberry Frosted. Immediately a replacement rattled into the plastic slot. When she opened the tube, she saw the color wasn't as advertised below the slot, and when she nicked it the slightest bit on her wrist, the color changed again. If she could get it just right, maybe she'd — maybe — She had to be careful choosing if she didn't want to throw her money away —

There were two little nicks on her left thumb when the salesgirl butted in, saying "Can I help you?" with frightened eyes. She had on some of everything ever sold in cosmetics, a young girl like herself with enough makeup on to obliterate a face of forty.

"I gotta do it myself or I'll drive you crazy," Abby-Jean smiled politely, careful not to put it the other way around. The salesgirl shot her a troubled glance, then moved away.

Within seconds she was back. Abby-Jean glanced up in annoyance. Despite the fact that another customer, a well-dressed elderly woman, was wandering around unattended, here the salesgirl was, dogging her again.

"Here. What about Cherry Ripe?"

Abby-Jean gaped at her. The salesgirl had taken Cravin' Pink right out of her hands, stuck it back in the little slot marked Golden Honey. She shook her head obstinately. Cherry Ripe was nearly purple. One after another, the salesgirl sorted lipsticks out of the plastic slots, insisting on holding them all in her own hands as she showed Abby-Jean the colors, holding the open caps as well, dropping one, putting two others, miscapped, back in the plastic slots with a crash.

"Really, y'know, thanks but —" Abby-Jean kept saying, and the salesgirl kept on, glancing with terrified eyes over her shoulder, a pink flush rising to her face that was visible even beneath her already pinkened cheeks, until both of them were in a tizzy. She kept dropping things, trying to keep them all in her own hands. It was impossible to show a person lipstick, Abby-Jean thought, if you never let her touch it. And the salesgirl knew it was impossible, it showed in her apologetic eyes. Yet still she kept on in a high-pitched voice, saying whatabout-this and whatabout-that, until Abby-Jean was ready to flee. But she couldn't move. Something about the frenetic performance made her feel trapped, spellbound, as it poured over her. And she really wanted to buy a lipstick — she had almost decided —

"You. Get yourselv' to the front of the store."

The salesgirl broke and ran, dropping the lipsticks on the counter. Spotting Cravin' Pink amid the jumble, Abby-Jean reached out tentatively just as a small peroxide-haired woman swept in to scoop them away from her. Back the lipsticks shot into the plastic holes: flack—flack—flack — put away with such vehemence that Abby-Jean had the sensation of boxes closing upon boxes, lids sealed inside lids, the whole kit and kaboodle swallowed up inside some recessed plastic vault and covered over with a cloth like the dead.

"I think I'd like to —"

"You. You're t'ru in my place. You get out."

"Beg pardon?"

The elderly customer was staring at her an aisle away, looking up over her glasses from the Get Well card section.

"You heart me. I've had it wit' you."

Abby-Jean glanced at the elderly customer who had been in the store looking at the cards just as long. Why her? Whatever had she done?

"But I was only —"

"*OUT!*" The woman took a step towards her.

She fled to the door. Reaching it, she turned back, glimpsing the woman enthroned behind the front cash once again.

"Y'old witch," she cried out.

"I'm callink the cops right now." The woman's hands reached out for the phone there ready on the countertop, her voice a low spitting whisper.

Abby-Jean burst out onto the sidewalk, her face ablaze. She strode quickly along, not looking in the store windows. She was afraid of them now, afraid to go in anywhere. Still her body trembled at the unexpected assault. They must have thought she was going to steal. Whatever had she done to make them think that?

She began to envy the men. If they had nowhere to go, they could just stop, lean against a wall and watch people pass. They could at least stand still; it would take a cop to move them along. If she had a house, she could have sat out on the porch or the front steps. Even with an apartment building that gave onto the street, she could have sat out front. But as it was, the steps that led to the residence were the very same steps that led to the disco bar below, in through a private door. None of the women from the residence ever sat there. Why was that?

She was going to sit out on the steps. She had an excuse to be there. She had a right to be there! Relieved, she turned back toward the residence, her pace quickening. Just to sit outside and watch people pass. Maybe somebody nice would come along, and they'd talk for a while to break the ice, and then —

She reached the residence, mounted the steps, slipping past a bikini-clad man in a long blonde wig and a shirtless boy all in leather, to dart with relief behind the windowless door.

Returning to her room, she sat on the bed dolefully. So that was why none of the women from the residence sat on the steps outside. No matter that the rooms got stuffy, that it was frightening to walk out alone after dark, that they had to pay to sit elsewhere, they kept away from there.

40

Trapped! The yellow and orange of her room stung her eyes. She went to stand pressed against the window held open by the dinner knife. She could barely feel the air coming in. Straining, she glimpsed the beech tree at the end of the narrow channel between the buildings. As a slight wind passed over its leaves, it blew silver. Her body clung to the window, hungry for the breeze that all her desire couldn't entice inside. There would be hours yet before she could sleep, hours of sitting on the bed, lying on the bed, getting up to comb her hair, cleaning her teeth, lying on the bed, looking out the window, listening for sounds in the hall, reading at the new book *All I Desire*, trying to open the other window further, lying on the bed, lying on the bed, lying on the bed. Until her head throbbed and her eyes saw black spots from the bright undiluted bulbs overhead and her heart cried out, oh who will love me, who will find me here?

Pulling back the chair at her desk, she shoved the manual typewriter over to one side and began to write letters by hand, one to her mother, her brother, one to each of the girls, all on slips of paper from a small yellow pad.

Dear Mums,

I bet you can't guess what I done today. I went over and saw the White House. See, I told you I lived smack in the center of town. I seen a guy standing on the steps but I don't think he was nobody. I been looking for jobs and working on the typing at least 3 hrs a day so don't worry. I think of you and everybody all the time, you know that? Sometimes I remember back to times when I was rotten and I'm real sorry now. It's cause I was a kid then. You know? Now I'm getting to be mature. Not that it's not great here. I know lots of terrific people but there ain't no one like you all. Does Dibsy still cry cause I'm gone or has she forgot me alredy? Just cause I'm here ain't like I'm disappeared or dead or something. Anyway nothing bad's gonna happen so don't worry. Life is sure strange, it's not what you think. I mean, here, its even more not. You know? Well anyway I know you'll never forget me Mums and that's one thing.

XOXOXOXO

Abby-Jean

When she read the letter again, it made her wonder why she had never known she loved Mums so much. She closed her eyes and in the splintered darkness saw all the family's faces, thought how frail and alone they each seemed. Sometimes it was as if they were five dogs tied to a stake, all pulling in a different direction to get away, and that stake was old Mums. Oh, it made her cry. Oh, in this terrible darkness there was nothing but people, their faces like shining lights, nothing but the hands and kisses and holding tight of people, who found and lost each other in their struggles and their injuries. Oh, she thought of them all and of herself and how when she came to die, there'd be nothing but that, the memory of the people she'd known and loved, and everything else would fall away. And it was so clear, she felt fearful and luminous, and wondered if she was dying now.

Lying back wet-eyed on the bed, she listened to the sound of thunder and sirens and the disco below until only the fear remained. Where were they, what were the women doing in all those rooms beyond, that the outside should pour in on them in such a wash of sound?

She rose from her bed again to open the door, and peered down the yellow corridor. Walking down it, she couldn't hear a thing, not even her feet on the runner. Ahead, a crack open, a door moved as if at the suck of non-existant wind, closing the space to her eyes. The door to the next room was ajar. The yellow light of the hall fell across the naked legs of a woman stretched out on a bed pushed right next to the open door as if to catch a breath of air from the hall. Unlike her own room where the blinds glowed through the night from the alley light below, this room was darkness, darkness and a rush of thick air. She had found it at last, the $39 room.

She paused at the top of the stairs, listening like a bird, her head turned, breathing lightly, her heart noisy in her chest. She heard singing. The voice, very low, seemed to stop after each line as if the impulse which impelled the song was drained at the end of each line, then irresistably renewed. Impossible to tell from behind which of the closed doors it came, four in a box there, all in darkness by the cracks beneath. The voice wasn't beautiful. It was raspy as if from too much smoking, the voice of a middle-aged woman. And yet the sound, beating against the silence, resisting the silence, throwing the silence back, sent a shudder through her that was almost a thrill.

Shall we gather at the river....
The beautiful... the beautiful ... river
Shall we gather at the river...
That flows by the throne of God.

Abby-Jean paused, one hand on the stairwell railing, her face closed and deep, waiting for the singing to go on. Several moments she waited, almost somnolent, then the voice began again with a surge.

YES we'll gather at the river...
The beautiful... the beautiful...

And that was it.

42

Slowly she padded down the stairs to the second floor, paused outside the door at the foot of the stairs, then knocked once. The sound seemed startling, disproportionately urgent. She had begun to edge on down the hall when the door opened. She ran back.

"You're still here! I been down here knockin' day after day an' you never answered. I thought you was gone!"

"Apparently not," Louise said wryly, then she smiled.

Abby-Jean glanced over Louise's shoulder into her room. A multitude of plastic and paper bags still lined the walls.

"I hope I'm not disturbin' you."

"I was only writing a letter to my sister."

"Oh Louise, I feel so bad — "

"For the love of God, come on in. Take a Black Russian from the pack on the bed!"

○

"This look okay?"

Abby-Jean was wearing her best dress — the other one. Though she stood teetering on her chair, the mirror above the sink was too small for her to tell if the wrinkles caused by packing were visible when the dress was worn. She still kept it locked up in her suitcase to save it from her room.

"Turn around."

She turned around slowly, trusting Louise's inspection since it was Louise who had suggested she might want to dress up a little in case they passed places for rent while they went for the evening walk. At first she had resisted, denying that she wanted to move just yet because facing up to superintendents was so tiring. It was unbelievable, of course. Having succeeded in getting in, most women at the residence spent their days trying to find a way out again. Louise was adamant. All the time, every day, she had an eye out for some way to try to make her life better. It was a habit with her. But if that was so, Abby-Jean wondered, then how was it Louise was still living in a dump like this?

"You look great. Besides, you're young. You don't need to worry at all."

"I wasn't worryin'. And anyway maybe we won't see nothin'. I never do."

She glanced at Louise sharply, waiting to see if another list of collected addresses would emerge from her purse.

"Maybe I look too dressed up, now?"

"No." Louise eyed the rows of cotton frills that crossed her breasts. "No."

Abby-Jean stared at her feet in misery.

As the residence door clicked locked behind them, Louise stood on the steps outside gazing upward.

"Look at this sky! Just look at it."

Abby-Jean's head tilted toward the rose-grey heavens. Any sky would have done, just to be out of that room.

"Hot in there," she muttered.

"You think this is hot. Just wait."

They walked slowly for it was a spring evening, mid-June, and night was a long way off. It was good to dawdle along the streets secure in each other's company, to linger chatting in front of store windows, to wander a lazy half-circle across the rotary park glancing mildly over the backs of the dice-throwing men. A strong sweet euphoria made Abby-Jean want to lie down on the grass right there, no matter how patchy it was. For a moment they stopped, watching a stray dog rub his shoulder into a little bank of grass, his tongue lolling out in a big smile. He skidded his body onto his back, grinding and squirming his shoulders into the grass and dry dirt, snuffling and groaning with pleasure.

"Look at him! We useta have a dog —"

Abby-Jean reached out to pat him, then felt Louise's hand jerk her back. The dog scrambled to his feet hastily, watching her as he bounded sideways twice then darted away, street wise.

"He was havin' such a good time. Makes you want to roll around down in the dust there with him."

Louise scraped the ground with her foot doubtfully, implying that this, this wasn't clean dirt.

"Blitz, that's what we called our dog."

"I used to have a cat named Sophie before the superintendent found out."

They were silent a moment in memory of Sophie.

"Look! Look over there! The blue hydrangeas by the wall! Have you ever seen a larger head?"

Abby-Jean scrutinized the blooms. They were large, though not perhaps the largest —

"Oh look at them. How marvelous they are! And there's nothing else growing there either. Maybe the seed was blown from a bush somewhere else, and this one has hung on!"

Abby-Jean stared again, something in her quickened by Louise's voice. Yes. Yes! The more she looked at it, *yes!*

As they strolled through the sidestreets down which traffic never ceased to flow — always a car squeezing out of a parking space, pressing at them at an intersection just before they reached the curb, shooting across from some unexpected direction at a rotary — Louise pointed at things, the gable on a house, a mauve panda on a window ledge, a car with New Hampshire license plates reading *Live Free or Die* and exclaimed or laughed out loud. Then they would pause a second, nodding over it. It made a block's walk so interesting, Abby-Jean thought, if you noticed things like that and pointed them out to a friend who then noticed them, and maybe said something too. It seemed to change the objects, to make them glow. Now she even pointed to things first, for Louise's way of noticing things was infectious, and she didn't have to be the one pointing to be interested. "Marvelous!" and "Wonderful!" rang in her ears.

"See there, Louise? That kind of a step? You could sit out there at night an' watch folks pass."

"Once I lived in a place where there was a bench outside. You could cook your food in the cooking room, then sit out after where it was cool. We used to sit out until late at night. The women who didn't get a place on the bench talked to us through the windows. We got to know each other because of the cooking room and the bench. You can't imagine what it was like to have the common room, not just because you could cook and didn't have to pay to eat outside, but because there was always somebody to talk to in there. We all made our own meals, cutting our own vegetables on our own newspaper spread out over the table in case of germs, you know. Sometimes there would be five or six of us at a time peeling carrots or potatoes, slicing zucchini, shredding cabbage, everybody checking out everybody else's meal. Everyone had her own pots and pans, her own cooking ingredients and spices, her own cutlery, even her own special plates kept in a locker all her own. Some women only had odd cups and dishes of course, but others had a place setting where all the dishes went together: cup, saucer, bowl and dinner plate all the same pattern. You could see how they showed each woman's idea of herself, set out there on her place mat in a neat little setting while she cooked her food. I remember somebody had thick beige plates with a wide brown ring that reminded you of farmhouses, men and wood-burning stoves. Somebody else had a white set with drawings of hunters and horses jumping bridges. Or big flowers in mustard, cherry and green. Even the odd settings took on a kind of character when you knew whose they were. Good God, they looked like their cups, I swear."

Louise chuckled, remembering.

"Think, if we had a cooking room and a bench outside."

They walked on down the street silently, thinking of that.

"See that place up there? The open window on the third floor? I lived there once."

There was a small electric fan on the ledge, its propeller whirring crankily.

"It looks nice."

"Same as ours. No point you trying there."

They poised hesitantly at the curb, scanning down the two side blocks to check them out before venturing along them, diverted from their course and off down another street at the sound of loud voices, at the sight of young boys hanging around an old car, diverted again from a narrow street where several families sat out in chairs on bare earth kids had run the grass off, veering back altogether at an area where there were whole streets of ramshackle houses with no windows, some with the gaping holes boarded up, and everyone was black. East and north they zagged, talking excitedly about the things they noticed, skirting the blocks where something touched off a fear within them that didn't need to be spoken to be communicated. It was impossible to tell when a street that looked good might cross or even become a street of dusty reeking poverty. Impossible again to anticipate a renovated street with new olde English lamp posts and sandblasted buildings, at once reassuring and unnerving in its vacancy. While there would be no people there likely to attack them, there were none to defend them either. Down such a street, they "noticed" less, taking in everything silently.

"You have this sort of thing in Baltimore and Boston and New York," Louise said.

"Imagine living in a place like this. Just look at the doors." The heavy oak, the huge brass knockers, shone.

Louise shrugged. "If it was me, I'd put in different lamp posts than these."

Abby-Jean stopped to consider. It hadn't occurred to her to criticize.

"But it's all very beautiful, of course," Louise said quickly. "Who could say that it's not?"

"Someday I'm gonna get a place like this. I wouldn't have to take the whole thing. I'd just live on the second floor."

Abruptly Louise began to walk on.

"It would be after I got a good job, natch. An' maybe my sister would come in too to share the rent. We could have a bedroom each. Bud could even come."

Louise walked on.

Maybe it was too late for Louise to think of having something like this, Abby-Jean thought, and shut up. Clutching Louise's arm, she paused a moment in front of one of the renovated houses, gazing in and down through the black bars protecting the window. Oblivious to their exposure to the street, a young couple were enjoying cognac in snifters, seated casually at opposite sides of a fireplace across from a burnished antique table. Abby-Jean gazed silently. So many things. Green, orange, purple, yellow upholstery, with show lights, plants, lamps, books, wall hangings enough to dazzle the eye. In a vaulted room like this, the yellow and orange — how different from in her own room. Was this what the woman there before her had struggled to capture when painting the room? And the elegant couple in their reclining clothes, the woman's hair sleeked back in a knot behind, little wisps at the ears — how strange to be looking in on them with their beautiful things all exposed to the street yet part of another world.

She glanced at Louise, abashed. Places like this were for people like those. Those were the kind of people you found in the *basements* of places like that.

"Come on," Louise said. "You don't like to hang around too long on streets like these."

A cross street got them away from it, back into clutter.

"What about that building?" Louise pointed to a large building with long rows of small windows cramped together. "I used to live there once, but maybe it's changed.

Abby-Jean gazed at the building hesitantly, taking in the fretwork on the exterior walls. It looked okay. They often looked okay. Then you got inside.

"I'll wait outside," Louise murmured. "I'm not dressed for it. Things will go better for you without me."

"They'll ask me to fill out some forms, I know it," Abby-Jean protested. "Then I got to say I got nothin' they need."

"Go and see."

From the spacious lobby, Abby-Jean glanced back once through the glass doors at Louise with her blunt-cut greying hair, white jacket sweater and low heels. Louise, how strange, she thought, seeing her hovering outside the door beyond sight of the central desk, paler in the outside light, her face diffident yet raised up into the last of the sun. Louise, looking frail and vulnerable out there, a little shabby and childlike in the jacket sweater and loose skirt. Then a middle-aged black couple wearing what she knew were holiday clothes passed in through the doors, and when she looked out again, Louise was gone.

In ten minutes, Abby-Jean was on the street again, embracing Louise exhuberantly.

"Oh geez, Louise, what a find! A little fridge an' a complete stove. Clean 'n all, with a shine to the floor. They got a TV in there too. An' even so, it don't cost quite as much as where I'm at. An' it's *clean!*" she repeated.

She was pulling Louise off down the street.

"What are you doing?" Louise said sharply.

"I gotta go get my stuff. I got to hurry. The guy said he'd hold it for me. I got to cart all my stuff over before it gets dark."

Louise was watching her levelly. "You didn't give him any money?"

"Couldn't. I got it stuffed in my brazziere in case somebody grabs my purse. I couldn't get at it, right in front of him, there." She pulled Louise's arm.

"It's that good? Are you sure?

"Sure I'm sure. I *saw* it."

"You're sure of the price?"

"I asked for the weekly rates an' he handed me a card. I saw it written down. Thirty-five dollars, it said."

Louise pushed back through the glass doors and straight up to the desk, with Abby-Jean straggling behind her.

"I want to rent a room," she said in a loud voice.

The young man at the desk glanced at her hesitantly, then at Abby-Jean standing behind her.

"I want to rent the room at $35 a week. I'll take it now." She opened her purse, held her wallet out in her hand. "You can take me right on up."

Abby-Jean gaped. Louise was going to take her room, right in front of her very eyes, the chance at a good room making her change her plans to leave Washington just like that. Now, without the slightest shame, and herself too astounded to stop her — She stared, stricken, at the young man whose glance wavered between them.

"I don't know if we have —" he stammered.

"Don't give me that garbage. I'm going to take the room, and if I'm going to take it, you can show it to me now. Do I see it or not?"

Flat shoes or no, Louise seemed powerful now. The young man's face was sheepish as he handed her the card. Louise glanced at it, brushing her hair back from her eyes with a quick hand. She glared at him a moment and he shrugged.

"These are weekly rates?" she asked caustically.

Then he got angry back. "Daily rates. Daily. We don't rent by the week any more. This place is a hotel now. It's a whole different story when it's a hotel."

"But weekly rates was what I asked," Abby-Jean blurted, edging nearer, trying to catch sight of the card again.

"You really think you could get a room in a hotel at $35 a week?"

He gave her a long cold glance that was somehow meeting her eye, somehow not.

"But you heard me say —"

"Oh never mind," Louise said, propelling her out to the street again.

They stood at the sidewalk's edge watching the traffic pass.

"What if I'd dragged everything over! They'd have put me out the next day. Oh Lord, an' the money gone! I couldn't 've stayed another day."

"I knew something was wrong. I knew it."

"There I'd be on the street an' my old room gone. By 10 o'clock tomorrow somebody'd have it for sure. An' then what? An' then what?" Her face was white. "No money an'out on the street. Oh Lord, that was close."

She stumbled along after Louise, still looking back at the hotel.

"The only way to get to the bottom of it was to try to take it myself. Then if something went wrong along the way —"

Abby-Jean stared at her, grieving.

"What?"

"Lucky I was with you, that's all."

They walked on facing the traffic.

"All these places are turning into condominiums or hotels. It's just a way of owners making more."

"I'm such a rotten person, Louise —"

"Look, there's another one. And it's nice, I know. I used to live there."

"Oh I don't think there's anything vacant —"

"Just go and see."

"Its getting dark soon —"

"I'll wait."

Abby-Jean trailed up the long sidewalk, glancing back stiffly before going inside. Within minutes, she had returned.

"Nothin," she announced cheerfully. "Let's go."

"But you're back already. How could you do it so quickly?"

"I just asked the old lady sitting there, an' she tole me no. Okay thanks, I said, an' that's all."

"No, no, no. You don't do it like that."

"Either they got rooms or they ain't. That's all there is."

"Maybe she has a room and you didn't convince her to give it to you. Even if she doesn't have one now, she'll have one sooner or later. Don't think she's going to give it to you just because you come up and ask. Here, let me show you how."

"I already been in there. What're they gonna think of me comin' back?"

"Just keep an eye on what I do."

Louise took off her jacket sweater, dropped it neatly over her arm, then they went in. In the lobby, two elderly women wearing lipstick and bright round earrings, their hair done carefully up, were nested in upholstered chairs on either side of a small table.

"Good evening," Louise said.

"Yah, she's the —" Abby-Jean whispered.

"There's something about a spring evening that makes you glad to get out of the car," Louise said, her voice more smooth and more Southern than usual. "If I only leave it around the corner for a few minutes, I won't get a ticket, I hope?"

The two old women shook their heads in unison and smiled. Abby-Jean watched their faces intently, unable to tell what they were thinking. But they would be smart; she was coming to expect that. They looked and smelled like two pieces of expensive candy.

"I think you were speaking with my niece just a second ago? Oh, excuse me, my name is Mrs. Crisp — Louise." She extended her hand to each of the women, presenting Abby-Jean and repeating their names.

Abby-Jean hung back, watching Louise gesture to the street, to the mysterious interior behind the women, mentioning Baltimore, Boston and New York, saying how she had once lived in this very building and hoped they still kept it as well, for she felt responsible for her niece even though she had a good job at the pharmacy and could take care of herself at age 21. The superintendent listened with her head tilted lightly on her forefinger, nodding, making remarks when they were called for, enough to be pleasant but not enough to propell it on. From time to time her glance seemed to bend, dropping from Louise's eyes to her loose skirt, her flat black shoes, then breaking away to cail out a few gay words to an elderly man in a pale yellow sportsjacket who was edging in short panting steps through the lobby.

When she did that, Abby-Jean took it as a signal they were dismissed. She could barely prevent herself from grabbing Louise's arm and pulling her away. Still Louise kept on, until surely there could be nothing more about the weather, the inside lobby, or Baltimore, Boston and New York to be said. She drew back, watching the white skin at the back of Louise's neck, her white stockingless legs in the flat shoes like a girl's legs beneath the loose rim of her skirt. How she hung in there, that Louise, dipping and faltering over their fathomless calm like a sea bird beating into the wind.

When Mrs. Jarelzowski mentioned the average rent as if in passing, Louise carried on fluidly as if such an amount were beneath consideration.

"Can you take my niece's name, Mrs. Jarelzowski?"

The superintendent shifted in her chair. There was a list.

"Can I bother you to put my niece on it, Mrs. Jarelzowski. If you don't mind?"

Sighing, the superintendent rose and limped across the lobby to a small mahogany desk from which she drew a blank piece of paper.

"Your name again, dear?"

"Abby-Jean."

Louise nudged her.

"Brown."

The piece of paper dropped back into the desk drawer.

Outside the doors, they walked slowly to the street, Louise chatting serenely to her all the while, making it seem like they weren't beating a retreat.

"Now. If you ever go back there, they'll remember you," Louise said. "Someday when you get a good-paying job."

"You get to not like them," Abby-Jean whispered. She would never go back.

"They weren't so bad."

"It's only a stinking room. I used to live in a house," she added, almost disbelievingly.

They bobbed against one another on up the street, Louise explaining what superintendents could be like — how they could hold back on a room until someone slipped them money, how they said there were no rooms or said the rent was higher than it was if they didn't like your face. How sometimes they made you fill out forms before they'd even take you near the room at all, or demanded bank account numbers or letters of character reference just to stall you off or frighten you away. And even if you filled out the forms, sometimes it was all a charade because they never meant to contact you again. There were plenty of people who worked hard all their lives who could never expect to get a decent place, no matter what.

"But I thought they wanted to rent what they got," Abby-Jean burst, her feeling against them hardening. It was as if there was a war going on between those who needed and those who had places to rent.

"As if they need to worry," Lousie scoffed. "There are too many people looking. That's why they get like that. Their job isn't to rent a place — anyone could do that. It's to weed people out. Their job is to *not* rent a place."

"What if a person can't get nothin' at all, though. What about the person?"

"They go back to where they came from, I guess."

"Geez." Her thoughts were flooded with images of the city emptying, of waves of exhausted poor people, white, black, yellow, red, dragging large powderblue suitcases back to the bus station and on home to Davenport, to Augusta, to St. Petersburg, to Beaufort. "What if they can't go home again, Louise? What if —"

"Then they sleep in doorways, on benches, anywhere. The police take them to flophouses or charity places if there's room. If they feel like it. But mostly they just tell them to go over somewhere else if they're in a nice area, or they leave them alone. Unless they're dead, of course." Louise shrugged abruptly. "I don't want to talk about it."

Abby-Jean felt a chill. After a few days like that, getting dirty and worn from the street, how could you ever get on your feet again? When you got to looking weather-beaten and scarey? She might have been on the street herself tomorrow but for Louise, it could happen as suddenly, as simply as that! At least she had the family in Beaufort to fall back on. Praise God for that. But what of all the sad ones, the orphaned and estranged, the lost and forgotten, who hadn't a soul to be their lifeline in all this precarious world?

"It's getting dark." Louise frowned.

Some of the cars coming toward them had their headlights on. The trees lining the avenue were dusky nodding shadows.

"Let's get back. I don't like to wander about after dark."

Thought of her room made the humid night air call out to Abby-Jean like a deep ocean swell that would bear her out and away, dropping upon her like a fine spume, herself rising clean-limbed, moonlit and ghostly through the waters. No matter how afraid she was of the city after dark, the night air beckoned her away from that room.

"It's not as if we're wanderin' around. We're lookin' for a place."

"Last year over on Florida Street, a young black boy pushed me down and took my purse." Louise shook her head. "It cost a lot."

"That's why I never carry money in my purse."

"It was the stitches in my knee that cost a lot."

They glanced about them. There was no one coming down the street, nothing but the constant passage of cars.

"It won't happen now, not with us two."

Abby-Jean shot a glance at Louise out of the corner of her eye to see if that was true. Under the streetlight, Louise's face looked blanched and worn.

"I'll protect you," she joked, putting an arm about Louise.

"You?"

They went on another block arm in arm, drawing closer together as a long-haired young man approached, then relaxing at the sight of the grocery bag in his arms, TV dinners and Fritos poking out the top.

"Okay now this is the last," Louise said, stopping in front of a large brick building.

Abby-Jean looked at the building mournfully. "Anybody gives me trouble," she muttered,"An" I'm gonna let them know. I'm not gonna sit there an' pretend it's not happening if somebody starts treating me bad."

She pushed the button labeled INQUIRIES several times, gazing at the row of mail boxes, half of which bore names. The lids of several were skewed ajar.

"What you-all want?" a man in an undershirt called harshly from inside.

Abby-Jean took a few steps forward, felt Louise press behind her rather than wait outside alone in the gathering darkness.

"It's about a room?"

The two of them edged toward him along the hall, bumping against each other.

"See my wife in there. It's got nothin' to do with me."

Abby-Jean eyed him timorously as she passed — a heavy young man with a paunch caught and held firm by the hitch of his pants. He was sweating profusely, shifting from one foot to the other, upset about something, a wheeze in his breathing like sawdust slowing down a machine.

"I wash my hands of it. It ain't no business of mine. The Lord bring this place down around my ears 'fore I say it is. And my wife's a good woman, that's for damn sure. I'm gonna smash anybody says she ain't."

Somehow the last words reassured them.

They followed his pointing finger through the kitchen to what seemed like a bedroom but for the plaque reading OFFICE on it, their route plagued with children's toys — a large red and green dumptruck, a garage assembly kit whose hundred pieces were scattered over the floor. Plastic marines lay fallen on their sides, still crouched. But there were no children in sight, and the low sound they heard coming from behind the door was surely a woman, crying.

They tilted back toward the husband, not moving their feet in the clutter, but he had gone off down the hall, leaving the door wide open. Behind them, a small wooden cuckoo clock ticked noisily against imitation walnut panelling. A row of trophies glimmered spotlessly atop the TV, crowded there amid cardboard-framed photos of kids. On the wall above hung a pastel seascape dated /65 of a girl holding an umbrella looking out over the water.

"Ma'am?"

Abby-Jean rapped gently against the door. There was no break in the gentle controlled sobbing. They glanced at each other, abashed. Somewhere on a floor above, the noise from a television got louder as the commercial came on.

"Ma'am?" Abby-Jean called again, louder.

There as a sudden silence as the commercial and the sobbing ceased at once. Footsteps moved across the ceiling above. It seemed as if they could hear the woman on the other side of the door listening, could feel the heat that dropped over her body as she realized she had been overheard. There was a low snuffle, the sound of a nose being furtively blown.

"What is it now," a female voice said huskily.

"It's just about a room but I could come later."

They heard a sigh. The succeeding silence was obliterated by blaring sirens and a barrage of shots from overhead, then people shouting at each other long after the shots had died away. Glancing toward the outer door, they saw the husband pass by again, one hand waving palm up to ward off any communication. Yet they sensed he was hovering nearby.

The door marked OFFICE opened, and a tall woman in slacks and a green orlon shirt blouse stepped out, flicking on the light switch in the room behind her as she opened the door. She had been crying in the dark.

"Don't mind me." She stuffed a kleenex up the narrow sleeve of her blouse, then smiled apologetically. "Feel a little silly."

Abby-Jean gestured helplessly.

"One of those days," Louise said swiftly.

The woman nodded. Her eyes began to shine with tears again, and to cover it, she began picking up pieces of the plastic garage scattered around their feet.

"Left these things around all day." As she picked up the pieces, some dropped out of her grasp. "Oh hell." She swept them away with her foot, sending them skidding across the linoleum to come to rest under the sofa. "Come into the office. We can't stand here."

They entered the bedroom, sat down on two hardbacked chairs near a large desk that seemed to dwarf the bed behind it. Passing behind them, the woman shut the closet door on a pair of blue flannel pyjammas. From the next room came the plaintive sounds of children fighting.

"Now," she said, putting on black-framed glasses and staring at them impersonally. "What is it."

"Oh — a room. You have any?"

"Probably."

"Can I see —"

"Not until Friday. I'll know by then."

"How much," Louise said.

The woman told them, her voice flat.

Abby-Jean sighed. "It's a lot." She didn't add, for a place like this.

"I don't set the rent." The woman's voice was suddenly sharp. A color rose to her face. For a moment it seemed she was going to cry again, then she took off her glasses and stood up. "Come back Friday or —" she paused as if remembering Abby-Jean's reaction, "Or don't. Whatever —"

They butted and bumped around the chairs getting out, Abby-Jean glancing once over her shoulder to see the light switch flick off again as the woman shut the OFFICE door behind them, remaining in the darkness, leaving them to pick their way out through the livingroom.

In the hallway, they ran into the husband again.

"All finished?" he demanded, running a hand through blond curly hair.

They nodded, passing by him. He tagged along after them.

"She's a good woman, my wife. She just had a bad day."

"Happens to everyone," Louise said.

"The order come down from the management company over on L Street, there, Millward, Hewitt. She don't raise the rent of her own accord. It's got nothin' to do with her. She don't even send out the letter."

The urgency in his voice stopped them. He went on in a whisper.

"The only way we even knew they sent the letter out was when the folks started comin' down. All morning they come down, right after the postman come, then another string of 'em come in after work around six. You wouldn't believe how it was. There was cryin', yellin'. Old Mrs. Morgensterner, she starts cryin', what's she gonna do? The old lady — thin as a rail, she don't eat nothin'. She can't move out, she tells me, then she can't stay. She gives her notice an' she takes it back. Three times she comes down with the notice written out on a piece of paper, an' three times she takes it on back up. How do I know what she's gonna do? I left. I got out of there.

"'This is your thing,' I said to the wife, 'Got nothin' to do with me.' She don't want me to go. She wants me to stick around and catch it too. She thinks 'cause there's a man in the room, it'd cool them out. Huh," he half chuckled, "I ain't no fool. 'Let's close up for the day,' I said. 'Let's take a walk. When we get back home, they'll have it under their belts by then.' No, she says, 'cause she wants to let 'em know it wasn't her what raised it. She wants to let 'em know she feels bad too.

'Cause normal days, she jaws with 'em in the halls, you know what I mean? We come up from Richmond. She don't know no one else. She gets lonely in there with the kids, so she jaws with 'em in the halls."

He paused for breath, shaking his head.

"But when they come troopin' down one after another, ain't one of 'em remembers *that*. They's strangers. We can hear 'em talking loud in the halls, up the second, third, fourth floor it goes, up like a fire. There's doors slammin' from the basement on up to the sixth. You'd think somebody'd kicked over a hive of bees. You don't know what bothers you worst, the yellin' or the whisperin'. An' the wife standin' beside me cryin' these was her *friends*.

"'We get friends on the outside from now on,' I say. 'Ain't I told you all along not to make no friends in here?' 'This is where I live,' she says. 'I *live* here.' She don't want people hating her, a whole buildingful of folks hating her in their sleep. 'They're gonna hate you no matter what,' I says. 'It comes with the territory.' But she wants to tell 'em it's not her that's doin' it, she wants to get 'em to see the whole mess from her point of view. 'You're crazy,' I tole her. I could hear her out in the hall tellin' 'em 'Remember how I kept the heat up last winter? There's others would've cut on the heat an' made a little on it, too.' But it won't wash, that about the heat, with summer comin' on an' folks startin' to steam in their drawers. How they gonna worry way ahead to winter when the problem with the rent is now? An old gent who seen what a box it were don't yell no more, he starts to cry. He had this fit of coughin' with his handkerchief out but I seen through all that 'cause there was water in both his eyes. 'Now hold up,' I told the wife. 'The next time you just leave 'em yell.' An' I walked out of the place right then an' there."

Alternately nodding and shaking their heads, they edged toward the door. He followed them right along.

"When I come back, she's mad as H—, an' it's at me. 'You left me to take it all alone,' she yells, forgetting how I tried to pull her away an' it were her all along that wanted to stay. 'See what my life is,' she cries, an' she's lookin' at that painting she done we got hangin' up on the wall. You wouldn't believe the names she tole me people called her, how nasty they was. You wouldn't believe folks could be so cruel. I was smart to leave all right. When you add the whole thing up, I was thinkin' smart that time."

They stared at him perplexed, unable to follow his reasoning.

"I couldn't have held back, I'd have popped 'em, don't you see? Then where'd we be?"

In the glimmering light from the street outside, his two large arms raised in a massive question.

"One of those days," Louise soothed. "That's all it is."

All the feeling in him seemed to subside. Both arms slapped down. "It's a bitch."

"You bet your life."

"I'd go back to Richmond if I could pick up something there."

"You'll feel better tomorrow. I always do."

He glanced at Louise sharply, then shrugged.

They made their goodbyes peaceably in the dark of the doorway. He stood there leaning against the mailboxes, half looking at the moon, half watching them go.

"Geez," Abby-Jean said, the word blowing out softly over the exhaust-laden air.

Louise nodded, moving quickly down the street for night had come and they were still a long way from home. Abby-Jean kept pace beside her, her face dark and pale as the long moonlit beaches off the Carolina coast.

"Come on, snap out of it," Louise elbowed her. "Sometimes it's a wonder all people do is yell."

"But how much you think they raised it, Louise?"

○

To the seven unprocessed women in the waitingroom, it looked like a love affair. Abby-Jean, third among them, didn't know whether to stare or go back to checking for green beneath the small ruby ring on her left third finger. Foolish as she felt to be watching, it was hard to pretend she hadn't noticed the interviewer as she lingered in the doorway, lavishly complimenting her find. The two women seemed to have developed a real feel for one another in that brief half hour in the back room. It was quite a little flurry, quite a little show, full of vivacious gestures of shared self-relish, full of dips and dives.

"Erica, this is simply terrific, you're so *exactly* right. When Mr. Almond phoned yesterday, I had to tell him it might take three days at least to find, you know, the sort of — And now I can send him — You!"

Surreptitiously seven pairs of eyes scrutinized the unblemished cherry handbag, the way it matched the cherry silk blouse beneath the white suit jacket, the way the woman stood, the lean smoothness of her, relaxed, even slightly aggressive. An expensive package all in all: young, white, middle class at the least. Six pairs of eyes glanced down, away, as the women yawned, sighed, shrugged or exhaled it off with another cigarette. In the practice room beyond, a large black woman was typing furiously, her head bent over the machine. All through the hallelujiah chorus, her typewriter throbbed like a kettle drum. If effort raised sweat, she'd be floating in a sea.

"If only there were more like you," the interviewer confided, her voice loud enough nonetheless to bring her grievance home to seven pairs of ears. Their distant gaze swept the circle of waiting women only a few feet away. Seven pairs of eyes stared hard at the abstract pictures on the walls or across at a row of shifting, tapping feet, or directly back with an antagonism they didn't notice. Through the doorway, the sound of typing seemed to speed up until it was really quite astoundingly fast.

"As long as I've made myself clear, Jannah," the lucky one said, sounding troubled nonetheless. "I'm only doing this kind of work until the management slot comes up."

"Of course you are, dear. But it's always best to apply from the inside. What you have to do is get in. After all, just getting *in* —"

"Well, true, but men don't have to go this route," the young woman was saying as they drifted together toward the door.

Returning, the interviewer sighed to the receptionist and they disappeared together behind the slatted wall without a glance at the waiting women. The women outside could hear them planning their vacations back there.

Abby-Jean returned to the job of filling out the form. On it there were spaces for descriptions of four previous jobs from recent history on back. Her only job at Wendy's in Beaufort seemed naked and insignificant, taking up no more than a single line. Nonetheless, it required some thought to decide whether Dr. Melrose Dudley, a dentist she'd seen a few years ago, would carry more weight under Recommendations than Libby Jakes, her homeroom teacher the year she finished high school. Would either of them remember her? Certainly Josephine Dawes who worked with her at Wendy's would, but Recommendations meant: list the most important people you know. Knowing Josephine Dawes, wherever she was now, surely wouldn't get anybody far.

On her left, a small woman with a permanent in the frizzy stage had been writing tirelessly for the past half hour. Now she was spelling out all she had done in the years 1960-62. But on her right, a plump girl her own age sat with the form still blank in her hands. Behind it protruded a sheet of white embossed paper.

"Ain't you gonna fill it out?"

"I got this instead."

The plump girl handed her the embossed sheet. Sarah-Mae Carruthers, it informed her, had been a Girl Guide, had played thè xylophone in a marching band. She liked music, liked to read; she had a penpal in Kenya overseas. Known at her high school for being courteous, prompt and a good speller, she had many friends in Alexandria and hoped to be able to visit Europe one day. Her ambition was — there was a smudge on this line and something whited out — to be a corporate secretary. By the end of it however, Abby-Jean had deciphered that Sarah-Jane Carruthers had worked only once before, part time filing in a lawyer's office. Still, the long embossed sheet made her seem like somebody worth reckoning with.

"You do this yourself?"

Sarah-Mae shook her head. "Paid to get it done. Twenty bucks." She thrust out her lower lip, blew up, and her bangs rose slightly. "Better work," she said, grinning more broadly as the nervous tremor in her voice showed through. " I got counselling along with it for just twenty more. Forty bucks."

Abby-Jean stared at the sheet in more distress than before. Nearly a week's rent to put on a show like that! It made her feel naked in comparison. If only Louise hadn't pressed her to apply for a secretarial job. She wasn't ready for it yet.

"Hah," the small frizzy-haired woman on her left piped up, staring pointedly at Sarah-Mae's resume, winking at Abby-Jean, then returning to her own voluminous efforts on the agency card. "Hah," she repeated, her small body jerking vehemently as if she had hiccoughed.

"You got one of those things too?" Abby-Jean asked the woman beside Sarah-Mae whose card remained blank.

"Oh I been running around after jobs all morning. I just had to come somewheres where I could sit down." Leti Mitchell's nose was a little red at the tip. She was twisting a lilac-bordered hanky in her hands. As she sighed, more years crept into her pert middle-aged face, until she looked young and old at once. "So I just been sitting here like a bump on a log. I can't face filling out another form."

Every time Leti lowered her eyes to the agency card, the day swam before her eyes. The ad for a saleslady at a Georgetown boutique listed no phone number; there was no way to save herself a trip by checking it out in advance. So she phoned the Office of Public Transport the night before to check the bus routes, and verified what they said on a disintegrating kitchen map. Twice she awoke in the night to check the time. By six o'clock she was up, showered and dressed, by seven undressed again to keep her clothes fresh. By seven-thirty, anxiety drove her back to the shower, making her miss the eight o'clock bus and its connection over to Georgetown at 8:23. But she had planned for something to go wrong, and would still arrive early on the 8:45. Fifteen minutes later, back at the bus stop, she was thinking of raglan sleeves and trying to recall brand names.

She beat her way off the second bus crushed and sweating, getting out too early by about five blocks. Arriving before the manager, she wasn't allowed to wait in the store, so she bought coffee a few doors down. Returning too soon, she hovered outside in the street, her nose at the window. At last she snuck back inside, wandered through the racks as if she were shopping. Some of the silk blouses — just passing them over her hand could cause them to catch and run. Such beautiful clothing — even if she was all wrong for it, the designers never taking into account the needs of short women broad through the thighs —

The manager came at last, a heavily made-up young woman who draped her netted shawl over a chair before heading for the mirrors. Leti edged over. Who knew how many covert applicants were cached in the store already frisking the racks? Tapping the young woman on the shoulder, she panted apologetically, "It's a very nice store you got here, I've come about the job?"

The young woman glanced over her shoulder, then away again. "Oh we want somebody young."

And that was it. There was nothing to do but walk out.

"When you think of the coffee, the bus tickets, how it all adds up, " Leti Mitchel murmured as if all along she had been talking aloud.

The waiting women glanced at her and nodded as if all along they had been listening. Somebody's stomach rumbled and they all looked down, keeping their eyes on the magazines on the waiting room table: *Career Woman, Glamour, Vogue.* It was awkward to hear the stomach and wonder if it meant —

"Soon as I got out of Jessica's Fancy, I phoned over to my Employment Office," Leti Mitchell went on aloud. "He said he might have something but I'd have to come in. 'Tell 'em for God's sakes, hang on, I'm coming', I said. 'Take it easy, okay?' he said." She glanced at them apologetically, tugged on the little pink scarf at her neck. "Guess I was rude."

"The hell, so you were rude."

"I don't like it when people treat me bad so I try —" There was a murmur from their left that seemed to agree with both. A stomach rumbled again.

"So I was off like a shot for the buses again, and I got back to his office before noon. 'No rush, no rush,' he says to me. 'You might as well go and get some lunch first,' he says as he hands me the address. The place was right back down here, where I just come from."

"Go and get some lunch," the woman across the way snorted. So it was her stomach rumbling, they knew.

"I thought maybe he was trying to tell me something. You know how they are."

There were sighs, snorts, shakings of heads.

"All of this *don't rush.* I would have gone right over but he got me worried by telling me that. Everybody knows if you want to get a job, you got to go quick, jobs don't hang around and wait. But sometimes they know something at the employment office, I thought, so I figured I better go get a cup of coffee at least. Maybe there was some reason behind it. So I had coffee and I thought and I thought, but I just couldn't make nothing out of it at all. After a while it didn't matter that I hadn't figured it out, I'd taken long enough not to rush. So out I raced, back on the buses again. But when I got down to Patterson, Quigley & Quince, the job was gone."

The women groaned in sympathy.

"If you hadn't had that coffee," Abby-Jean said.

"It was just before noon that they filled it."

Abby-Jean frowned. Leti hadn't had a chance all along.

"Well keeps you busy, don't it. Gives you something to do."

"Maybe he didn't know when he sent me. The poor man, with so many people after him —"

The woman with frizzy hair looked up from her card blue with ink front and back. "Hah," she said loudly, then wrote in some more around the edges.

"He probably just called you in to look busy himself."

"Oh I don't think he'd do that," Leti's face dropped. "It's not his fault there's no jobs. Poor man, I know he tries." She persisted in wanting to feel sorry for him.

"Sure he tries. You can't say he never sent you out for a job."

"Sometimes a job is already taken," Sarah-Mae said with authority. "But they advertise it anyway."

Abby-Jean's frown deepened. That made no sense, she couldn't believe that, but a murmur of concern rippled through the circle of waiting women that broke into a flurry of questions when the receptionist returned, settling with a flounce into her chair and putting on a zesty professional smile.

"Miss, excuse me? I've come about the ad that begins 'Love people?'?"

The receptionist glanced brightly at her watch. "Which one is that?"

"It goes, 'Love people? Expanding retail company looking for receptionist for complaints dept.' You know the one?"

"What about 'Lawyer seeks bright efficient clerk typist for interesting work filing'?" Sarah-Mae cut in. "You still got that?"

"I came about 'Love to travel? Diplomat seeks —'"

The last question was cut short by an emphatic "Hah!" amid the clamour.

"We'll talk about it after you've been processed, dear." The receptionist was addressing a woman three times her age.

"I bet they let that last ad run all month," Sarah-Mae whispered. "You never catch up with jobs like that. They're just bait."

Abby-Jean nodded silently, keeping her eyes on the receptionist's face. The woman who had asked about "Diplomat seeks" showed no sign of leaving. It didn't matter what was gone as long as there was something left.

"Okay two more," the receptionist said, not glancing up as the large black woman who had been typing furiously made her way from the interviewer's office to the outside door unescorted.

Abby-Jean followed the small frizzy-haired woman to the practice room, sitting by the door where the black woman had sat. In front of her, sheeted in plastic, was the letter she would have to copy as many times as possible in three minutes. Soon the frizzy-haired woman's typing pounded like a racehorse in the home stretch, so fast that the woman seated between them stopped typing and stared at the wall.

60

Tentatively Abby-Jean touched the Olivetti, starting back as it sprang into action. Maybe her hands were too big, too strong? Practising on her manual typewriter had made her heavy handed for an electric. It flew on, out of control, registering errors at the slightest accidental contact of her fingers, registering errors even when she paused to think, forcing her to stab at the letters one by one and hold her fingers away in the intervals. Harrassed and mortified by the piercing notes of her lone keys striking in counterpoint to the frizzy-haired woman's full orchestra of sound, she tried desperately to speed up but the keys only jammed. The back of her neck prickled as she sat prying them apart. The woman beside her still stared at the wall.

Beneath the copy letter she spied the black woman's practice sheet and searched over it avidly. It began flawlessly:

We have all known people who are different from ourselves and it is these differences that make life interesting. Sometimes, however, it is unfortunately true that certain differences cause some members of our society to receive unequal treatment at the hands of the society as a whole when it comes to jobs, for example, or housing. Consider this: Suppose one man wears a green tie, another a yellow tie, and a third wears a blue tie. Now wouldn't it be absurd if we were to say that a man who wears a green tie should be prevented from getting a certain job because his tie is green, or that a man wearing a blue tie shouldn't be allowed to live in your neighborhood because his tie is blue?

Whatever color tie a man wears we must recognize that he has a right to live in whatever neighborhood he wants if he can afford it

and so on and so on. But by the middle of the page, small mistakes had begun to creep in, becoming more frequent until, toward the end, recognizable words disappeared alto- gether in a jumble that went on for four unbroken lines. Slowly the exercise pattern a;sldkfjghfjdksla; began to emerge, but there were errors even there. Suddenly on the last line, it cleared up completely and the typing was flawless again. Her gaze swept back to the startling four lines of jumble. They had occurred while the interviewer and the young woman in white had danced their duet in the doorway! She had outpaced herself; then, rather than slow down when they might hear it, she had let the machine run on into chaos.

Peeping out of the testing room to remind the receptionist she was waiting for the test, Abby-Jean spotted Sarah-Mae filling out the agency card.

"What about your resume?" She eyed the embossed sheet that was now diminished by being folded into four.

"Won't touch it." Sarah-Mae's face was beet red. "They want it all on their own forms."

"Huh."

"Keeps their files looking neat, don't you know. So I have to transfer all this stuff. But most of it don't fit nowhere." She shrugged miserably.

Abby-Jean glanced over her shoulder at the agency card. Sarah-Mae had been reduced to a single line. One consolation for not having worked much — it lessened the amount of writing you had to go through in filling out the forms. Imagine if your work experience stretched back thirty years—

"Twenty bucks, pfft," Sarah-Mae said as Abby-Jean turned back to the practice room, a snap of her third finger sending the resume skidding to the floor.

After the typing test there were others: vocabulary, spelling, grammar, calculating problems where you had to use X. Then another sheet to fill out telling how she felt about herself, about others, how she saw her future stretching out before her. Were these tests too? She labored over them, searching herself for the truth. They asked questions she hadn't given much time to before, and on each she wanted to explain how it depended —

"For God's sake, kid." The woman who had asked about 'Diplomat seeks' bent over her. "Don't fret so much. Just put down what you think they want to hear. Look —" She took Abby-Jean's pencil, made large tick marks on the squares of her card dealing with the operation of office machines. "Most of these only take minutes to learn. Why should you miss out on a job just for that?"

"But what if they ask me to run it and I mess up?"

"Say it's a different model than the one you know. Happens all the time."

Abby-Jean tried to smile thanks. She could see the sense, even the justice in all that. But it was a lie! It made her see the woman a little differently despite her kindness in helping. Maybe that showed how hopeless she was?

The receptionist came in and swept the tests away. "Go in and see Jannah now. She'll evaluate your deportment."

Her what? It was too hot to be wearing a slip —

"Mrs. McLynn?" Abby-Jean said to announce her presence, reading the name from the little bronze plaque.

"Jannah, call me Jannah, we're all friends here," the coppery-haired woman said perfunctorily. "We value the relationship we have with our girls and we, uh — sit down over there."

No matter how hard she tried to listen, Abby-Jean found she was watching Jannah instead, inhaling her perfume. You had to work to be able to dress like that, she thought. Maybe you had to dress like that to be able to work? But it was Jannah's nails, nine coral talons, that held her spellbound. On the tenth, the index finger of her right hand, there was a gold cap like an Aztec mask atop the nail. As Jannah talked, flicked through her tests, touched that finger speculatively to her cheek, Abby-Jean's eyes, mesmerized, followed the nail.

"I said, would you have any trouble answering the phones."

"No'm," Abby-Jean said after considering a bit whether to bring up how it depended —

Noticing the tremor of irritation passing over Jannah's face at her slowness, she gathered herself to answer the next question without delay.

"And you can run all these machines — the xerox, the adding machine, dictaphone and so forth?"

"*Yes ma'am.*"

"Jannah. Please."

Abby-Jean sighed.   In Beaufort, saying ma'am would have counted for her, but here this woman wanted to make like they were friends.

"Well I think that does it," Jannah said, her chair rolling back over the carpet to let her stand up.

Flustered, Abby-Jean remained seated.   How could it be over already before anyone had even asked why in particular she was here?   And what was the result?   It looked like nobody was even going to tell her that.

"It was the 'Treat yourself.   Insurance company in super new building' ad I come for," she ventured.

"Yes, well we'll see."

"It's not gone, is it?"

"I'm afraid —"

"I just picked out that one 'cause I figured they'd have air conditioning and that's a must," she took the expression from one of the ads, "with me."

Jannah's eyebrows raised.

"I'd take anything."

Jannah's hips leaned lightly against the edge of her desk. "We'll let you know if anything comes up."

"You mean you got no jobs?   Or just nothing for me."

"It's light at the moment, but things are always coming in." Inexplicably, she gestured toward the window.

"You mean you got nothing at all?" She couldn't believe it.   What of the people in the waiting room.   Did they know this?"

"Now we have you on file," Jannah said positively.

Abby-Jean nodded, mute.   Because they had her on file, because there was still hope some time in the future, she didn't dare protest and scuttle her chances.   But to have waited, to have labored and hoped all for nothing even before she began —

"I need a job." She hung on in her chair even though Jannah had reached the doorway.   "I don't know what I'm gonna do." Tears came to her eyes.   Searching with Louise for a better room the week before seemed ludicrous now.   Who knew how she'd survive where she was? Perhaps if she stayed right here, if she refused to leave the office, if she just let her body go limp? Anything, to keep Jannah from just walking away so easily, calling 'Next' and drawing another hopeless one in.

"Everybody needs a job."

Abby-Jean quailed. It wasn't as if she meant to be selfish about it. The thought of all the other people, millions like herself on the loose from one end of the country to the other — Feeling submerged in the tide, she bowed her head but kept on sitting there nonetheless. Surely there was something more to be said.

"Next!"

A thin woman wearing glasses and flat walking shoes entered, smiling uncertainly, seeing Abby-Jean still sitting in the place where she had been motioned to sit. She took up a position at Abby-Jean's elbow, hovering by her chair like a bird by a cliffside nest, gazing at her with large apologetic eyes.

"Sorry," Abby-Jean murmured to the thin woman and got out of the way.

She surveyed the outer lobby, seeing two men now among the replenished group of waiting women. A faint resentment pulled at her at the sight of them. But then, women were running after construction jobs and heavy labor in the hope of better pay. Everybody was running every which-way, helter-skelter wherever the money pulled.

Two tired looking women were scanning her face to read how it had been in there.

"They got nothing," she said aloud to save their time, to let them go home.

The two women nodded and didn't move. Everybody heard her but nobody moved. Either they thought it would be different for them or, having come this far, it required more will to give up than go on. And then there was always the file, the thread of a hope of a possibility. Behind her the thin woman emerged from the office, eyes down, skirting by her swiftly as if hoping to pass through the waiting room unseen by ten pairs of eyes that raised at the slightest movement. Had Jannah asked her, too, whether she thought she was so important?

Abby-Jean followed her out. They got on the elevator together and watched the numbers go down.

They picked you off one by one, Abby-Jean was thinking. But who would have the face to say 'What makes you think you're so important?' to millions of people standing there all together? Who could do that? Lord, millions with families needing, young folks wanting to get married, wanting to have children, wanting to send money home? More millions of lives hanging on that. Her eyes were round. It was getting to be such a big number that it was hard to get her finger on all that it meant.

The elevator door opened and the thin woman got out without a word. Abby-Jean darted after her, wanting to talk then hanging back as she saw her look around frantically then head toward the information desk by the farthest eleavator where an elderly attendant sat consoling a thin little boy. The child's eyes were red but his face was dry. He had been crying some time back before the old man had soothed him.

"I tole you to stand *there*," the thin woman's voice raised piercingly as she pointed to an indistinguishable spot along the corridor wall. "Cain't you see what a fright you done gave me?"

The little boy burst into fresh tears as she swept him away.

Abby-Jean straggled out after them. It wasn't a good time to talk about the millions. It was too hard to get through a day without having to think about that. But it amazed her, walking along K Street, how for other people life seemed to be going on as before. She saw people working in banks, in offices, in drugstores, in restaurants. The people driving past in cars, surely they had been working too. Millions. It was hard to get a feel of that on K Street before the 5 o'clock rush under the bright spring sun.

○

The commotion broke loose at the very moment the door to the women's residence swung shut, its ponderous thud with the slightly delayed click giving rise as always to the sensation of something final happening — the closing of a vault, the discrete muffled chunk of a coffin lid descending. Standing motionless at the foot of the stairs in a pacified exhaustion that had been the purpose of her all-day walk, Abby-Jean gazed upward toward the second floor landing where a door had just slammed shut like a rifle report. Elsewhere, several voices and a regular blunted thumping carried on unabated.

All at once a long-haired woman appeared at the top of the stairs. She flung herself down in such a rush that it seemed as if her legs were crumbling beneath her until, catching herself midway, she halted, fumbling in her purse to light a cigarette. Across the front of her white uniform — a waitress, a drugstore clerk, a hospital attendant? — there was a grey smudge where fallen ash had been heavy-handedly wiped away.

"A mouse in my room," she burst out at Abby-Jean as she passed, voice cigarette-hoarse, disgusted. She dropped her match on the stair.

"A mouse —"

Abby-Jean half grinned, thinking: a mouse now, that wasn't much, not like a rat or a horde of roaches. To date she had only seen rats by the sewers outside but roaches — Lord, those she was getting even in her dreams. When she was awake, anything at all moving suddenly on the fringe of her vision registered in her consciousness as a slick speeding roach, making her mistake a moving hand for a roach, a falling pen for a roach, the waving string to an overhead bulb or a blind, or even their shadows, for one more slithering, scuttling roach. Always, the sudden motion producing a flash of abhorrence even though she no longer bothered to try to kill them.

The woman crashed on by, her face introverted. An anger flashed from her that seemed to strike out at the whole of the building and Abby-Jean herself as part of that constant injury. Several times Abby-Jean had seen her skirting the halls, face closed off, not wanting to talk, a kind of shock hidden in her eyes. Once she had been beautiful; now her face was torn by age. Like a wounded animal run to darkness, each new presence meant only exposure.

"I got to get out of here," the woman muttered under her breath, "I got to get out," speaking to herself as she clattered on down as if Abby-Jean weren't there.

Only a little mouse, Abby-Jean thought, stung. But the woman's last words reverberated through her like an echo to cries of her own.

Feet thrashing on the stairs, she sped upwards toward the sound of voices and the thudding, intermittent now. Part of the noise was from the TV, she discovered as she poked her head around the open doorway. But the noise coming from the four middle-aged women squeezed around a card table — Elizabeth sitting too high on the bed, Margaret too low on an orange plastic lounge chair, Etta on an upright chair hemmed in against the wall, and Maybelle Johnson, seated with her back to the hall door taking up the whole of the aisle — wasn't exactly negligible either.

"Hey girl, how much would you pay for one of these here?" Maybelle called out over her shoulder by way of invitation, and Abby-Jean came on in, grinning a little at the sight of Elizabeth, so tall and rangey, seeming to loom over the card table while Margaret, so much shorter, seemed to peep over the table top like a child. On the bed lay a grey knitted wool sweater with little birds in yellow and pink that flew down the front, and beside it, an angora sweater, dazzling white.

"I'd pay hundreds, if I — Where'd you get something like that?"

An appreciative glance flickered among the women.

"Margaret made 'em," Elizabeth butted in, seeming to boast as she pointed a long blunt-nailed finger straight across at Margaret, who sat with her cards in one hand, knitting needles and an unfinished sweater on her lap ready to be taken up while the cards were shuffled and the next hand of bid-whist was dealt.

Margaret's round face went pink to her curly gray hair as she showed Abby-Jean the work in progress: turquoise, a cardigan this time. A woman she'd met while working part time in Macy's downtown had ordered four of these. With any luck, word would spread and she could go into making sweaters full time.

"You never know," Margaret said. "It might take off, then heigh-ho, I'm out of here. And Libby too," she added.

Elizabeth's sage brown eyes were fixed on her cards in perplexity as if she hadn't heard a thing. A humour line seemed to suddenly shoot from the corner of her lip up past her nose, but her eyelids never raised.

"Geez, I wish I had somethin' good to sell," Abby-Jean said.

"You watch out when you say that," Maybelle snapped. "You don't want folks takin' you for one of them."

Her head tilted toward the TV atop the bureau where at least three of the seated women could see it. The gesture with her head kept Maybelle's cards, tucked securely in both surprisingly small black hands placed firmly on the table in front of her, from risking any exposure to either side. Abby-Jean stepped into the room squinting, making out a montage of signs reading ADULT BOOKS, of downtown streets where girls and older women loitered about under floodlit marquees, cigarettes dangling in their hands, makeup making their features ghoulish through the black and white TV snow. There were close-ups of their lips as they smoked, of their eyes. The four of them stared at the TV screen phlegmatically, while Etta didn't bother to try to see. She had chosen her seat to get away from it.

"There's plenty of ways to get rich," Margaret shrugged, turning away from the Special on Prostitution.

There was a snort all around, even Elizabeth glancing up sharply and grinning.

"Shor they is, I jes' never felt like it, is all."

When Maybelle laughed, her vast bulk shook a little all over, but the cards in her hands never moved.

"Well there are," Margaret persisted. "You could open a dress shop. You could go into the travel business. You could invent something that everybody needs. Computers or something, you could get into them."

The women glanced at her, at each other, and said nothing. Etta played a card. It hit the table with a sharp snapping sound.

"You could open a little restaurant," Margaret went on unperturbed. "Or a laundromat. What about a White Hen grocery store? Or even just a store selling ice cream —"

There was a brief discussion over an ice cream wagon which terminated abruptly after Elizabeth demanded laconically, did they know how much money somebody had to have even to think of setting up any of that?

"If you could think up some service to do for people that have money," Abby-Jean offered. "Something you could run around an' do yourself, that wouldn't cost a thing to get started. The way I see it, you got to keep people with money in mind 'cause they're the ones that got it to spend. All you got to do is think of somethin' they want that they haven't got yet, somethin' they haven't even thought of, maybe."

"You hear of people walking their dogs," Elizabeth said, then she glanced up at the ceiling where the paint had gone ribbly as if searching her memory. "And watering their plants when they're away. I heard on the radio of a guy phoning up insults for people or tellin' their girlfriends goodbye — things they want done but got no taste for, themselves. He was making a living, he said." She shook her head, grinning.

"It's no life. There's no life in that," Etta said sternly. "We ain't all kids." Her florid face, made starchy by her white, white hair, gave her the crisp, efficient air of someone who worked in a hospital. She worked in the cafeteria.

"Anyway, whose phone you think you'd use for all of this?"

They glanced up to see a small ravaged-looking woman standing in the doorway, leaning against the frame.

"Well I got tired of thumpin' on the wall to shut you all up." She glanced over her shoulder in turn at a large long-haired woman with a tanned leathery face who had come up quietly behind her.

"Hi," the tanned woman murmured, then stood there silently as if she had been part of the group all along.

"There's folks makin' money on them game shows," the small woman turned back to the group. "If you could get on one of them —" Despite the gauntness of her chest, the way the sinews seemed to show through like cords in her arms, her stomach was distended like a volleyball. As she stood there, thin shoulders back, leaning on the doorframe, it seemed to thrust at them painfully.

Etta shook her head in disgust. "You ever see people act like such damn jackasses? Shriekin' an' hollerin' an' jumpin' up an' down the second some fancy-haired shyster waves a bill beneath their nose? Hah, I'd rather starve in my room."

"They don't let 'em play, they don't shriek like that," Maybelle Johnson said. "That's what I hear."

"What about contests? You could enter them."

"Do you know what the odds are on that?"

"Well I got my number, I don't care," the small woman in the doorway said.

"You could sell flowers," Abby-Jean said, then added before anyone could ask her where she would get the flowers from, "Or baking. I seen them out there on the street sellin' cookies at fifty cents a piece."

"Where you gonna bake, Abby-Jean? On your window ledge in the mornin' sun?"

They had a good laugh over that.

"Well, if you wasn't here, I meant." Which was the problem that had prodded the discussion on in the first place.

"Hoh, look at that one!" Margaret cut in, her eyes on the TV. Head cradled in masses of dark curly hair, semi-profile in the picture frame, a very young woman gave a long cool glance into the camera that deepened in insinuation as her lips slowly parted and her upper lip furled — the look of a woman who had just been hit. Who was aroused by it. "She makes a lot at it, you can bet. Did you see that wham-o look she just give?"

They stared at the screen attentively. A long sleek car, shafts of light glistering off its chrome, glided towards them out of billowing clouds of mist.

"You up in them clouds?" Elizabeth demanded. "That's the commercial, you nit!"

Margaret stared at the TV, blinking. "Oh. I thought she was one of them." Her face reddened. "It's the way she was lookin', after all."

"*That's* them."

There was a shot of a police waiting room where women sat in a line. As the camera panned down it, one of the girls pulled up a large black purse to shield her face.

"It's a terrible thing." Margaret shook her head.

"Well I guess," Elizabeth exclaimed. "I guess she's ashamed."

"Poor little —"

"You don't have to do that. Me and my sister, we was poor all our lives but we never done that," Etta said. "Just 'cause you're poor don't mean it's right. You got your respect. You want a daughter of yours to grow up like that?"

After shots of a speeding ambulance, a hospital ward, the announcer's face filled the screen once again. She was a chic-looking woman in an expensive tailored suit jacket that showed she meant business, her professional voice alternating fluidly between gravity and anger as she described how thousands of young girls drifted yearly toward the inner cities to find themselves caught in the coils of prostitution, often syphilis or drug addiction, and an early death.

"A terrible thing," Margaret said again.

"Them big shot liberals, they feel a whole lot sorrier for the whores than they ever felt for me," Elizabeth cut in. "Every time they want to talk about poor folks, they got to talk about some whore. You'd think all poor folks was nothin' but whores, pimps, addicts an' thugs."

"They get off on it, that's what," Maybelle said. "They just bustin' their noses to get in there an' see. It makes a good story for them."

"They don't got nothing against whorin' itself."

"Not their daughters," the ravaged-looking woman said bitterly.

"I got mine started on the Church early, that's what I did," Etta said. "I got her goin' to Church to protect her from all that. I watched her like a hawk."

"That's what you gotta do," Maybelle nodded. "You gotta sit permanently on their case."

"She's out in Costa Rica now," Etta said. "Savin' souls."

"Sometimes I think kids, they take it bad," Margaret said. "They can't see very far along — to the time when they won't be young. They just don't know."

They pondered Youth, all but Abby-Jean, with distant, knowing eyes.

"If they're gonna go some way, they're gonna go," the small ravaged-looking woman said. She took a step away from the door frame to stand upright, her thin shoulders thrown back, her stomach carried forward on lean shanks. "It's them makes the choices, after all. We got freedom of choice, I believe that. It's that, what brings us up above the animals. It's that, what gives folks any right to dignity — that they could've just let go but they didn't. They hung on when nobody gave a damn. They took what come on their backs and didn't throw it off someplace else. They never said 'I can do this here, who would blame me?'" When the tendons in her neck pulled tight, the skin pulsed with feeling. Her straining face, with its two small pouches of skin, dewlaps, on either side of her lips, seemed to be directed at some point in the wall above Etta's head.

The women listened quietly, nodding. They believed in their responsibility for their lives over the long, long run. It didn't have anything to do with feeling responsible for being poor, for the material conditions of their lives. It was a moral thing.

"Still," Margaret murmured, her face raised toward the screen where now there was televised golf. "You just don't know."

"It's better not to judge when you got no idea what went on," Elizabeth pitched in.

"That's true! That's true!" the small ravaged woman cried excitedly. "Only God knows what folks have been through that made 'em do what they did. Only God can look into hearts an' see. God'll know what you could've did when the time comes."

"In the meantime, who's to judge?"

"Nobody! Nobody's got the right to judge!"

There wasn't one among them prepared to say a word against that. A contemplative silence came over the seven women now crowded into the narrow carpetless room and out into the hall until Abby-Jean, thinking how God would know what she could have done and wishing she knew what God knew herself, started it up again.

"If you could learn to do something better than anybody else," she began again. "If you could sing, maybe, or dance, or play an instrument —"

The women gazed at her silently, all of them over thirty, thinking how it was a little late for singing or dancing or playing an instrument now. A sheen had come over their faces from the increased heat from so many bodies in such a small room. Margaret was fanning her face with her hand of cards, exposing them on the backstroke.

"I wanted to be an artist once," the tanned woman with long hair said.

Everybody turned toward her for she was speaking for the first time, taking in her rawhide bolero over a plaid shirt, her earrings and necklace of tiny strung beads. Though her cheeks were a deep leathey brown, her forehead was alabaster, protected from an apparently constant exposure by the yellow sun cap she was holding in one hand. The hand was large, chapped red, reamed, as if it had been scouring dishes for thirty years.

"But I thought you was an artist," Abby-Jean said. Surely she had seen that very tanned capped face behind one of the little tables set out by street vendors on K Street. Atop her table, laid out like a deck of cards on a piece of Indian calico, were dozens of tiny ink sketches in stiff mauve cardboard frames. They all showed couples walking along Pennsylvania Avenue with the White House behind. They looked good, too, except for the couples being somehow a little longer and thinner than they ought to be.

"I was a sculptor. I was a sculptor for years and years."

A murmur of admiration went through the small gathering.

"Oh not any more," the tanned woman said quickly, as if it were a question on which she wished there to be no mistake.

"Got tired of it, huh?"

"One morning I woke up and realized that I wasn't thinking of anything any more but how to survive. That's all I've thought of ever since."

When her other hand raised to grip her long brown hair at the back, holding it up to let air get through to her neck, they saw it was as red, as nicked and scarred as the other, and felt sorry that she had done such a terrible thing to her hands, and for no money, too.

"I've been thinking of writing a book," a voice said forcefully.

Abby-Jean turned. It was Louise, leaning calmly against the corridor's far wall.

"What about, Louise?" she asked, bewildered, thinking of *Call Me Princess,* belique teasets and all that.

"A temporary secretary. What her life's like."

"But what would happen?"

"Well you know, you could have the temp come in, in the morning."

Abby-Jean nodded, looking at Louise hopefully. "Then show if the boss was nice to her or not." Carefully Louise smoothed her hair back.

"An' then what?"

"Sometimes they are. But then again, sometimes they aren't. Sometimes they get worked up over some problem and take it all out on her. She has to handle it so they keep in line."

"Uh-huh," Abby-Jean said slowly. It didn't seem like the kind of thing you usually found — books about war, about millionaires, criminals, mistresses and spies. Surely surrounded by all that, people in charge of publishing wouldn't have much time for books on secretaries' lives.

It wasn't even a romance. She glanced down quickly for fear of disappointing Louise then her eyes raised again as she was heartened by a thought: if it were a love story, now, and they got together in the end? A girl coming to the big city, Washington, from Beaufort perhaps?

"What about a book about a janitor?" the small ravaged woman wanted to know. "She works at night in a Washington office building with another woman who doesn't do a good job. This other woman is always leaving butts in the ashtrays or missing spots when she mops, an' the first one always has to come round cleanin' up, behind."

"Or one about a woman who works as a night guard in a bank building," Elizabeth cut in. "And she has a friend who works part time in a department stores and knits beautiful sweaters on the side," she added before Margaret could jump in.

"I always thought you could write a beautiful story about a mother and her daughter," Etta said. "The whole thing would be made up of letters, 'cause the daughter's in Costa Rica savin' souls. She's got to do the Lord's work, even though she wants to come home an' take care of her Mum, who ain't gonna be able to work in the hospital kitchen many more years. She writes her Mum once — twice — a month, sayin' how glad she is with this life, how she understands now how wise her Mum was for pushin' her that way, an' how thankful she is. An' the mother writes back an' says she understands how it is with the Lord, an' how she's stood on her own two feet all her life an' doesn't mean to start takin' folks from the Lord just to look after her. She'll be hanged if she will, she'd rather starve in her room. It ain't until the end of the book that you find out that only one of the daughter's letters got through. The rest is held up in —" she grasped for a place "— Miami. You find this out after the mother is dead."

Etta looked sternly down at her clean white nails, clipped short, as a murmur, half of praise, half sympathetic, circled the room.

"Then one day this woman janitor, this janitoress, her number comes in," the small ravaged woman pushed her plot line along. "And everything's different from then on."

"The book the temp writes," Louise said, "Becomes a best seller."

"Oh Louise, d'you think it could?" Abby-Jean asked. Maybe they'd want a picture of the girl from Beaufort on the cover?

The room divided into optimists and pessimists, the optimists saying how interesting a book like that would be, the pessimists saying if it didn't have money or sex, it wouldn't be interesting to Them, and They were the ones who decided.

"I have a better idea yet," Margaret broke in excitedly. "You could do a serial for TV. About a temp, a security guard or whatever."

Abby-Jean glanced at Louise. A TV serial seemed to make the idea of a book pale in comparison. But if the serial were about a temp — Louise's face had gone stoney. She didn't seem to want to talk about the book any more.

72

"I can just see this TV serial about the night guard in the bank building," Elizabeth grinned. "You get this long still shot of a corridor with big windows at the end, the curtains drawn across. Then for the whole thirty minutes, not a blinkin' thing moves." She cracked up.

"Course you'd have to go to Hollywood, I expect," Margaret speculated vaguely, her cards fanning slowly in front of her face which was glistening now. "You'd have to get in touch with movie stars or TV directors. That would be Step Number One."

Deflated, the women let the idea drop. They saw what a leap Step Number One was. For several moments nobody said a word.

"What it comes down to is a job."

"What it comes down to is two jobs," Margaret cracked.

"People with two jobs are just greedy," the small ravaged-looking woman intervened sharply. "They want everything. Folks who already got one decent job, I mean," she added hastily. "Folks who got enough to survive. Greedy, I say."

"That's true, that's true," Margaret murmured. Her concentrated stare seemed directed beyond the line of pictures of Maybelle's sister's children atop the cigarette-pocked bureau, right on through the dun-coloured wall. "We want everything now. Look at us. Two cars, one for the kids. Eating out, going on trips. More appliances than we'll ever use. Blenders, micro-wave ovens, air-conditioners. Perfumed toilet paper. Electric toothbrushes — who needs one of those? All you ever hear about is things, things, THINGS, until you got THINGS coming out your ears. You start to think to yourself, can't we ever get enough?"

"It's greed, that's what it is," Elizabeth nodded. "Folks have gotten greedy."

"Nobody can think about a damn thing but chasing the Almighty Dollar."

"It's a terrible thing, greed."

"That's what it is, though. That's what's wrong with the country today. It's nothing but greed," the small ravaged-looking woman said. "The Lord'll curse us for it."

The murmur of assent from the seated women gathered volume among those crowded in the doorway, until it became one massive vibration of indignation that throbbed down the hall.

"You don't have to have so very much, after all," Margaret said.

The murmur of assent washed back over them again. In its wake, a silence fell.

"Lord," Elizabeth murmured, fanning her wet face with the score pad. "I wish to God there was a bigger window in here."

○

Saturday night. Abby-Jean lay sprawled atop the dun-colored sheet, heels on her pillow, head toward the door, the yellow bedspread folded into squares and placed atop the typewriter on her desk. On the typing manual lying open beside it, the words NOW IS THE TIME FOR were captured inside the stain ring left by a can of cherry soda, the can itself chucked slot downward on a newspaper crammed into her waste basket. A residue of cherry chemical trickled a wet red smudge down the advertisement leader, DIAMONDS: LOVE HER TONIGHT. As the last minutes of twilight shed a growing darkness into the room, the booming music from the gay bar below the women's residence seemed to mellow, slackening off earlier than usual after a hard-driving day begun at noon. The melodic strains of "Sophisticated Lady" reached Abby-Jean through two floors of single rooms, making her ache for all the things in her life that had never happened yet.

It was still early. She twisted restlessly on the bed, one knee raised up, the other leg balancing upon it at the calf, her toes lilting softly to the music, the hairs on her leg turned into a brown-gold sheen under the bare ceiling bulb. That was what somebody would see if they were to bend over and peer out through the stairwell window of the building across the way — this bare leg waving above her head cut off by the window sill — just as she, if she raised her head, would see their legs turning at the landing before going on up. She no longer cared if they saw her. She couldn't bear to pull the cracked blinds down and be entombed once again in her room.

In the interim between songs, she listened vacant-eyed to a rustling in the wastebasket that was either roaches, chicken bones sliding on down, or both together, and saw again in her mind the white Caddy going on up the road. Going into the sunset in her memory, up a rosey strip of Carolina road, rising and falling gently over the small hillocks, never seeming to get further away, just hovering in the sun-streaked air, looking pink like a flamingo. Josephine Dawes' sudsy fingers grabbing her wrist as she pretended to wipe the counter, both of them staring out through the big Wendy's front window after the Caddy with the DC plates.

"That's classy. That's us, huh? America! Them Japanese can put out a cheap car, but they got nothin' grand. It's America knows how to make you *dream*."

Josephine Dawes stared longingly after the receding Cadillac and the unseen driver as if she would love him forever. As Josephine's silver-nailed fingers raked down her raven hair and set the plastic bracelets on her arm aclatter, Abby-Jean eyed her own reflection in the window beside her: shorter, short-necked, pink-faced with corn yellow hair.

"This place is dead." Petulantly Josephine snatched Abby-Jean's dishrag from the countertop, tossed it into the sink, then added bitterly, "But I ain't."

Abby-Jean nodded absently, her eyes on the rosey trail where the Caddy had been. There would be a man in a suit driving it, she thought, a three piece suit. He would look down at her from his world very far away, not interested in her in the least. If for some reason she found herself in the car beside him, she would feel conspicuous and uncomfortable. They would be going to places where she would understand nothing.

"I got friends all over. D'I ever tell you that?"

"Yah, I think you mentioned it last week a hundred times."

Josephine was always hounding strangers about the big cities, struggling to grasp what the place was like at the same time as she implied that she'd lived in someplace else just as big. Sometimes they left her an address, a telephone number to call them up if she ever found herself up there. Painstakingly she copied the names into her address book, listing them not by name but by city: Buffalo, Charleston, New York, Washington.

At closing time, the two of them would walk out into the moonlight, but only Abby-Jean would be drinking in the ocean-sweet air. Josephine would be hankering down the roadside, fixing on the car lights, fuming how in the darkness the guys could barely see her. She hiked along fretting and complaining, wishing and dreaming as Abby-Jean paced the roadside listening to the choirs of insects, thinking: dizzy Josephine. It was like a sickness she had.

Seeing Fripp Island with its luxurious new multi-level beach homes, its tennis courts amid the palms, its guard in a little glass cubicle with a striped road barrier suddenly ending the public road, brought it on strong. Hitching in to Beaufort, Josephine had gotten a ride in a peacock green El Dorado, and every time the elderly lawyer asked when she wanted out she said "Not yet." So he drove on past Beaufort, over the bridge, through Lady Island, through St. Helena's, straight through to Fripp with her, right on past the barricade, and cruised around the whole of the island with "Not yet" ringing in his ears until the immense circle returned them to the sentry post once again, giving away Josephine's claim to live there.

Josephine got Fripp fever then. Afternoons off found her out by the roadside made up like a Hollywood star, trying to hitch onto the island again. It was so hard the first time seems like an accident. A carload of local boys stopped to gape at her and blocked sight of her just as a porsche, like a sleek silver pellet, shot past. She stomped off along the gravel embankment in a huff. Horn blaring, the old Plymouth spun gravel at her as it screamed away. Then there was nothing but Josephine and the highway, the marshes and the frogs, her with silver sequins pasted in a spray above her eyes. Not a Buick, not a Mercedes, not an Oldsmobile that wafted in silent grandeur along the inter-island highway, Fripp-bound, so much as slowed down for a second glance. In fact it seemed that they even speeded up as they coasted away, that they crossed the center median in passing to give her a wider berth, their passing beating billows into the humid sea air.

"It's the stuff on your eyes," Abby-Jean advised. "Maybe they thought you was a witch." She cracked up.

"Look, they wear that in *Vogue*. I seen how rich people look."

Abby-Jean glanced up at her from the sliced tomatoes. What was vog? Now that Josephine had seen the houses out on Fripp, why go again? Everybody on the mainland joked about the people out on Fripp. Here they had such lovely houses and they couldn't seem to handle them, sending out constantly for plumbers, electricians, painters, gardeners. The Geechies living in their trailers out in the bush on St. Helena's came in with tales about the rich men's homes that they'd helped to build — how they wanted the fresh new wood painted to look like it was twenty years old with the paint already worn away —

"If I take the stuff off, who's gonna notice me?"

"You don't wanna get noticed. Why you think they got the guard up there? They don't want nobody from here around there."

"It goes like this," Josephine said feverishly. "I get in, I just walk around the tennis courts a little. Or maybe up the beach with my bathing suit on. He sees me —"

"Who? Who sees you?"

"It doesn't matter, they're all rich out there. But he's the son. Tall, blond. He sees me. Who's that, he says. I've got to have her, he says. She's got to be my wife."

Abby-Jean blinked.

"Yes," Josephine insisted, her face haggard. "The second he sees me, he wants to marry me. He knows it's the only way."

Abby-Jean thought of the Caddy with the DC plates again, and savored for a moment her own dream: the door to the Caddy opening, a boy in cowboy boots who looked much like Ronnie Patterson getting out: blond, freckled, wild but serious. It didn't have to be the door to a Caddy opening, it could be a Chevy, a Ford van... It didn't have to be Ronnie, either...

"You want to come along with me? Maybe there's somebody up there who'd go for you. Y'never know."

Abby-Jean's knife demolished an onion in swift sure slices. "Won't catch me running after them."

"We do it like this. We take your brother's boat —"

Abby-Jean glanced up sharply, her face shrewd.

"And early in the morning, we drift out of the canals an' over to Fripp. An' then —" Her imagination gathered for the leap. "We capsize. Yeah. We crawl up on the beach. Our clothes get lost —" She frowned. "Don't want my hair to get wet."

There was no one in the Wendy's, nothing but the bright lights, large swaths of glass reflecting them back from the darkness outside, clean counters, clean floors.

76

"Josephine, ain't you got no pride?"

Josephine wiped the mirror behind the counter and stared at herself.

"Y'all don't have to come. Probly it would work out better if I jes' went out alone at night so the guard couldn't see me, took a little short cut through the marsh, then waited 'til the sun come up."

"But Josie —"

"That seems to me like the logical clear-headed thing to do. That seems to me like the smartest way."

There were two faces in the mirror now, Josephine's and her own. Long black hair, long corn-yellow blonde. The bracelets were clicking like mad as Josephine brushed her hair, tightlipped.

"I ought to get more, don't you see? 'Cause I'm pretty. I am. What about them baseball players, them big hitters? They expect to get more. They don't see why they should settle. If you got something good people need or they want, then make people pay. That's how it works. If I wasn't pretty —" She glanced straight at Abby-Jean's reflection, "—then I could see sittin' around takin' what come. But I ain't like the rest of you. I look like them in the magazines, an' I only want to get what oughta be mine."

Abby-Jean sighed, put her arm around Josephine's thin shoulder. "Look here, Josie, don't cry."

"How can I help it, thinkin' what I ought to have?" Her teeth were chattering. Smudges of her eyeshadow cast haggard pouches beneath her eyes. "I read them magazines an' it drives me wild."

Abby-Jean stared at her own plump freckled face in the mirror. It was a pleasant-enough kind of face, her own. Healthy-looking. She couldn't call it pretty. For the first time, she saw the Mercy of that.

A week later, she was out at the Dawes house delivering lozanges and magazines to Josephine, who hadn't been in to work a day since then. She knocked at the door then called out loud when no one answered, the sound of her voice carrying down the road to a distant neighboring house where it set the dog to barking. There weren't any trees to muffle the sound; the house was on a bare unfenced knoll some four feet away from the dirt arch of a driveway that lost the main thrust of its contour in the beaten-down stamping ground in front of the house, then regained it just before rejoining the narrow two-lane pavement. Raised from the ground by cornerstones, the squat square house was made entirely of new brick. Though the front steps weren't on yet, already a series of cracks ran up the wood of the new door, revealing a paste-like texture beneath. When she pushed the door it opened. She had to heave herself up to get in.

"Hey, somebody?"

"In the back. C'mon through."

She turned the corner, eyes smarting from whitewash still fresh on the walls.

"Where you at?"

"Here. *Here.* You bring me anything?"

Josephine lay propped up by at least three pillows, her single bed in the back room jutting out between two frameless windows. The floor was still rough plywood tacking, but there was a small fuschia rug by the bed for Josephine to put her feet down on. Abby-Jean dropped *Women's Day, Junior Miss* and *Glamour* onto the checkered quilt, the bounty of her tips for the week. Josephine raised herself on one elbow to look through them, and the sudden motion in the bedclothes caused a tiny ballet dancer atop a music box to pirouette once to "One Enchanted Evening" before toppling over onto the quilt.

"You don't look so bad. What you got?"

"I got exposed."

"You got what?"

"I was out in the elements too long an' I nearly caught my death. We ain't animals, y'know. We can't just stand out under the trees."

Abby-Jean nodded.

"Specially if we get wet. Specially if it rains."

"Yah. Who'd do a dumb thing like that."

"I nearly thought of callin' it off right there. My hair looked like H."

"You went out to Fripp!" Abby-Jean pictured Josephine pale under the moon, shivering and cursing amid the roar of bugs. Drenched. Afraid to go near the houses for who knew what kind of pervasive alarm system they had out there. Waiting amid the palmettoes and Spanish oak with their grisly moss hanging down, waiting for dawn to come.

Josephine eyed her sullenly. "So what if I did."

Her silver nails picked at a bluebird embroidered on the pink satin overjacket to her pink cotton nightie. For several minutes she stared abstractedly at an ad in *Glamour* showing two women in nothing but panties and bra, followed down a winding staircase by two men in tuxedos. THE MAIDENFORM WOMAN: YOU NEVER KNOW WHERE SHE'LL TURN UP, the caption read.

"Well aintcha gonna tell me?" Abby-Jean asked softly.

"Tell you what?"

"How it was."

"Aw, y'all know Fripp. Y'all know what it's like."

"I never been out there. How would I ever get to be out there?"

"Housecleanin', maybe?" Josephine grinned mordantly.

"Nope. I never."

Pages of lipstick, blush-on, eyeshadow, lashliner and perfume ads spun by beneath Josephine's fingers.

"Josephine, I'm dying to know."

Josephine shrugged.

"I'd never tell anybody. I'd never tell a soul."

Josephine's expansive breath ended as an accusation. "You wouldn't believe what it was like."

"I'd believe whatever you say, just you tell me the truth. 'Course," she got up off the bed, "If you're feelin' too sick —"

"It was like this." Josephine sat up in the bed, then harsh brakish coughing stopped her for a moment or two. "I biked out there around four, huh, before the sun come up. There was nobody on the road for miles an' miles. It was only 'cause of the moonlight that I could see at all. Nothing down that road for miles an' miles, with the marshes comin' up suddenly on either side, full of crickets an' frogs an' what-not, an' the hush-hush-hush beyond the rushes of the tides. I was peddlin' like a fury down this moonlight-grey strip with the whole of the nightlife in the bush boomin' an' crackin' an' raspin' an' roarin' all around me. I had to get off into that clump of trees the other side of the guardhouse, huh, before the sun come up.

"That was the worst part. 'Cept for the lizards crossin' the road, you ain't got no trouble there. But to plunge off into the bush in the dark to keep out of that gatehouse light — First thing I done as I took the bike off the road, I slid down an' put my foot straight into a bog. Lord, it made this suckin' sound, I thought I'd die."

The two girls burst into peels of laughter.

"*Suck*, it goes," Josephine gasped. "I thought I'd pee."

They doubled over again.

"The guard never even looked around. I hear this music, *Honey while you're sleepin' I'm jes' thinkin'*, coming from the booth there, this little glass two by four. Then I seen he was sleepin', his face drug up alongside the glass, out there all by hisself in the pitch dark night. An' here I got mud all up my white flare slacks when probly I coulda just walked straight on by. I snuck over into the trees. Then the rain come down. I could see the red line of dawn over top the canals, an' I never been so mad. Here the rain was pourin' down on me, an' over there the sun was comin' up bright an' clear. Even through the branches of the Spanish oak, it got to peltin' me sharp as gravel spun out from passin' cars. I hear the rain go zingin' down into the long grass like bullets gettin' buried in the earth. A sharp wind come up from nowhere off the marshes an' sent that rain borin' right into me until my hair was drippin' down my face like seaweed. I started to cry. But I hung on."

Abby-Jean was shaking her head.

"I don't care what you think." Josephine reached for her brush, sending it in swift long strokes through her hair.

"I never said a thing."

"Everybody tries to hold you back, like crabs in a bucket." There was hysteria in her voice and her eyes were wild.

"Look, how 'bout I brush your hair."

Josephine handed her the brush without a word. Eyes closed, she preened like a cat beneath the long carressing strokes, then her thin frame shook with coughing. Abby-Jean's hand rested quietly on her shining hair.

"When it dried, my hair turned wispy. All hoary like a clump of Spanish moss."

"You got beautiful hair." The brush came down the raven tresses in one satiny stroke, fine hairs full of electricity lifting towards her hand as the brush passed over it upwards to begin a stroke again.

"I brought my makeup bag along an' my brush too. So I could fix my hair okay."

"Well that's one thing."

"I took off my slacks an' left 'em under the tree."

"You what?"

"I had my two-piece on. What d'you take me for anyhow?"

"Geez I wondered for a minute how far you —"

"Thanks a lot, hey."

Quietly Abby-Jean began brushing again. It was several minutes before Josephine resumed, her voice light and breathless.

"I started out walking down a long clear beach lined with houses, all glass an' sundecks — you wouldn't believe all the shapes they come in, like they was put together like them woodblock Chinese puzzles you get in the store. Here we go, I thought, this is it! It was a windy day an' my hair was flyin' like a flag. If He'd 'a seen me then, I swear —" Her voice caught. "But there weren't nobody around the whole damn place, 'least not out there where the wind come up swift off the sea. I kept on goin', with the gulls hurlin' about an' the sand slick as mirrors to walk on, an' the sky that fresh blown morning blue. The tides was low an' gentle, runnin' up to me, then poppin' loose in little crinklin' frills up to my toes. I kept an eye out along the row of houses — Oh you should've seen them, Abby-Jay. They had sundecks lookin' out over the water in all directions. They had windows the size of this room here. An' drapes an' stain glass an' fireplaces an' — I don't know. Them houses had a way of lookin' so thought-out somehow. They wasn't all gigantic but there was something about each one — It was like lookin' through a magazine. There wasn't no toys or junk litterin' the lawns. Everything was all special an' in its place an' perfect. An' down the whole row of them houses, beachside, there weren't a living soul. There it was, *Paradise!* and there weren't no one there but me. An' I walked for miles."

Josephine sighed and Abby-Jean, despite herself, sighed with her.

"You saw nobody, huh."

"Not out on the beach. But I saw a few later on gettin' in an' outta their cars. It was the only place to see 'em. I walked along those rows of big Caddies an' Buicks an' T-Birds for maybe two hours, watchin' 'em at it. It looked like that was all they did, gather round them cars. Get in, get out. Yak, yak."

"Well how about it? You see one you liked?"

"They was all old," Josephine said. "And white."

"Yah... Well, sure. So?"

80

"I mean, they was white all over. The men got white slacks an' the ladies white skirts or jackets. They mostly all got white hair. They's white down to their stockins' an' shoes. An' as they go walkin' along, they's all white an' trembly. An' there's no place to go dancin', just a big place to eat. Lord, they looked borin' as hell."

Abby-Jean nodded phlegmatically. That was the end of it, then.

"When I went back to find my clothes, they was gone. I nearly froze to death bikin' back home. April ain't that warm."

"No, it ain't."

"Fact, I nearly died." Josephine hunched down again in the bed, her forehead and sallow cheeks glistening.

"Well, see? It weren't so much."

"Don't be dumb!" Josephine cried. "There ain't no comparison between this house an' theirs. Just 'cause I don't like them don't mean I don't want what they got. It drives me crazy thinkin' how dead they are an' how they got it all. I don't see how it can be. It don't make no sense at all. Why them an' not me?"

Abby-Jean put a hand on her forehead. "I think you got a fever again."

"I can't see how there can't be some way for me." Josephine writhed on the bed. "I ain't made for this life here. I don't want to be a nobody."

"You sayin' I'm a nobody?" Abby-Jean confronted Josephine on the bed, her face hot and incredulous.

Startled, Josephine said vaguely, "Oh, you. Well I wasn't thinkin' about you so much as —"

Abby-Jean stood up. She was going to walk right out.

"Oh, look here," Josephine said plaintively. "I never meant nothing bad against you-all. It was just a thing you say."

"I never say things like that. I don't know nobody who does. I don't know where you get it from."

Josephine gathered the satin outer jacket around her.

"When you think of it, most people are nobodies. If that was so bad, then nearly the whole world'd want to die. I don't see where you get off talking about nobodies as if most of the world's people wasn't worth nothing. Everybody I love is a nobody, according to you."

Josephine's eyes seemed to crinkle.

Abby-Jean sighed. "How you feelin'?"

"Bad."

"Here. Pull the covers up."

"I'm gonna go lie out on the road. When the first fast car comes, that'll be the end of me."

"Come on, Josephine."

"Why shouldn't I have what they got when they're no better than me? Good looks got to be worth something."

Perplexed, Abby-Jean eyed Josephine as she shrank back in the bed amid a black halo of hair, wasting away with wanting to get next to those people she couldn't stand.

"You ain't all that good-lookin' though," Abby-Jean said at last to bring some perspective in.

Josephine raised herself up on one quivering arm. "You go away. I never asked you over here to keep attackin' me."

So she left, hopping down from the stepless front door straight into a pile of mud just as Priscilla Dawes Williams came carreening into the driveway all squeezed up in the Dodge beside her brand new husband, Twitch.

Josephine never came back to the Wendy's again.

Two weeks later the postcard came, picturing the Capitol dome turning pink beneath a twilight sky, reminding Abby-Jean again of the white Caddy going on up the road, hovering in the twilight like an exotic pink bird. On the back, the message began without wasting any space on a greeting.

> I'm up here in Washington visiting a very good friend, Mr. Lawrence Mallory. He's a chemical engineer (does that sound right?) or something. He's been real good and a help. He got me this motel room all my own and says he's gonna help me set up somewheres else. If you ever come on up, Larry'll know where I am. 376-1891. I'd sure like to see you if you ain't mad. I ain't going back to Beaufort, never. I'm having a terrific time better than

The last sentence had to be squeezed in at the bottom in tiny writing so all the words could get in, using up the last bit of space where a name might have been signed. But it was Josephine nonetheless. There was a lipstick smudge on the card.

The postcard was right there in her breast pocket when Edward J. Davis walked into the Wendy's and announced he had taken over. Within a week, a swarm of Davises had descended on the Wendy's from the surrounding fifty miles — sons, daughters, cousins, nieces, second cousins removed — enough Davises lined up to serve part time from morning to night seven days a week. Edward J. explained regretfully that with all those Davises needing work, there just wasn't room for a Brown.

Unemployment set in.

Around November, the battle between Abby-Jean and her mother began, carrying on through December and January like a war of attrition: brief explosions with long silences in between. No matter the long and painstaking reasoning that assaulted her, Adelia Brown's response was always the same. She would turn to Abby-Jean, pointing her finger with such vehemence that the flesh along her upper arm would shake.

"You ain't goin' to Washington. You're stayin' *here* where it's *safe*."

Then she would go on peeling carrots, hanging out laundry, feeding the chickens, ironing her blouse for wearing to work at the Post Office in the afternoon. She never raised her voice, but sometimes her eyes got squinty before she said it, as if she were struggling with the possibilities, thinking them through. Then her face would tighten and the answer came out the same.

Finally Abby-Jean played the postcard from Josephine.

"It's not like I wouldn't know a soul. I'd just go on up an' stay with her."

"Who's this Josephine?"

"She useta work at Wendy's, you gotta remember that."

Adelia Brown went on sweeping, pummelling the broom, letting the grit go sailing right out the front door where the wind blew it away when usually she bent over and caught the last little bit in the dustpan.

"I don't remember no Josephine. What kind of a girl is she, anyway? How'd she get on up there, her own self?"

Abby-Jean showed her the postcard which now read: "I'm up here in Washington visiting a very good cousin, Mr. Laurence Mallory —"

"You're *stayin*."

"I don't know why I'm even askin' you. I'm free an' white an' — Look at Meryl Culley that went over to Columbia. An' then Dallas Wilson, she got a job up in Pittsburgh. An' Janice Baker didn't go nowhere an' look what happened. She got a load in the oven an' Freddie had to leave the farm lookin' for a job if he ain't run off. 'Cause there ain't nothin' here an' you know it an' there ain't never gonna be."

"There's no place nicer than Beaufort. You'll go a long way to find nicer folks than here." The aging blonde woman rubbed her large hands down her dress. They always had a floury look, no matter the hours she spent weeding in the garden out back.

"That ain't what I was sayin'. What I was sayin' was —"

"You go runnin' off to the city an' then —" Adelia threw up her hands. "God only knows. What kinda churches they got up in Washington, you ever think of that? They don't care nothin' for nothin', I heard, up there. An' here're you, wantin' to rush headlong to perdition. They'd drive over you like you was gravel on the road."

"How d'you know? How d'you know? You never been nowhere but here. You don't know nothin' but this."

Adelia Brown's glance climbed slowly up the broom handle until it reached the top and jumped off straight over to her face.

"I know what I know. Praise the Lord."

In April the government took the food stamps away.

Fear of what she was determined to do seemed to swell up in Abby-Jean like a balloon then jerk loose, sending her darting senselessly about the room, so rattled she could hardly pack, sneaking her things out of closets, out of drawers at four in the morning, tiptoeing around the twins' bunk, dragging the suitcase out past Bud asleep on the couch in the front room. Managing all of that only to be defeated at the last moment by something that all her planning never foresaw: that the sole powderblue family suitcase wouldn't stay closed.

No matter how she jammed the catch, it just wouldn't stay closed. It was a sign, a hex, that left her shaken, thinking how disaster had sprung up already before she'd even left the house, here where she was still safe on home territory. Who knew what could hit her up north. White slavers? Drug addicts? Terrorists — would they be after her too? Anything seemed possible in the dead of night. She sat on a kitchen chair, staring dolefully at the suitcase with its hump on the side over her boots, only one of the clamps holding it closed, and wondered if there was anything wrong with reconsidering. Then she thought of the skipping rope out on the porch, and suddenly it was too late for changing plans. Getting the rope, she pulled off the bright red wooden handles and stuck them in her suitcase so that Dibsy would have no fragments to mourn over, then looped the rope around the suitcase, pulling it fast and tying one knot on top of another. It held the suitcase solidly shut. And that was a sign, she thought.

The moonlight came in through the kitchen window as she wrote out the note, the paper crackling atop the crumbs on the kitchen table, the small house sluggishly cosy with its night sleeping sounds as she wrote:

> I phoned Josephine and she said come on up. So I did cause it's for the best. I still love everybody, you know that. Nothing ever happens less you make it.

> Abby-Jean

It didn't seem right to leave the note there on the table where she'd written it, though they'd never miss it there. Trembling, she taped it to the kitchen door window as if it were pointing out the direction that she had gone. Suddenly she had to sit down again, feeling immensely sad for herself. So this was it, the way she finally left home, sneaking out like a thief in the night. A real thief too, when she thought of her Wendy's savings, never once fully considered as her own, out of the dresser drawer and in her purse now.

She put her hands on the table to still them, trying once again to go over the reasons why her leaving was more than inevitable: why it was necessary. But nothing came. All she could see was the white Caddy winging up the road, turning pink in the sunset. Like a bird of hope. No matter that suddenly she couldn't see it, couldn't see it at all — herself with a secretarial job with the government, some kind of downtown apartment like Mary Tyler Moore, with money sent home for the girls, enough for college for somebody, maybe? — No matter that suddenly she couldn't see it, there was the bird of hope winging toward darkness, and Josephine's exultant words, "It's America knows how to make you *dream*" ringing in her ears. Dream beyond reason, hope beyond hope, why not her as much as anybody? Why not her, just a little?

Quietly she picked up the powderblue suitcase, the shopping bag full of food for the trip, the old manual typewriter, and slipped out the door.

On the bus, Washington-bound, she kept her face turned toward the window, watching stores, buildings, tennis courts, the big K-Mart Shopping Center pass through her reflection in the glass as if all the homesites, the known and familiar world, were passing one last time through her mind. What had begun had surely begun, it was well on its way now, she was gripping her life as it hurtled toward the future like a rider on a runaway horse. Getting dizzy with fear as the miles mounted up, as even the vegetation that covered the earth outside became different from that she had known at home. Thinking of Josephine, not thinking of her, thinking how, no matter, it was all beyond Josephine now. Herself hurtling to Washington, why not, it was as good as any place to hurtle to. Thinking how at least her long distance telephone call from the bus station early that morning would never be known by anyone.

"Hello," a man's voice had answered, then just a second later, she heard a woman's voice say "Hello?"

"Is this Mr. Laurence Mallory I got?"

There was a momentary silence on the line, then the woman's voice said "Larry?"

"Who's this?" the man said sharply. He sounded mad.

"Oh I'm callin' long distance. You don't know me."

"Well what is it? — I'll take this, Janice, you can — Yes?"

"I'm callin' about Josephine Dawes?"

"Larry?" the woman's voice said.

"— I don't know any fuckin' — Who?"

"She said I could always get in touch with her through you," Abby-Jean whispered. Out on the platform, they had just loaded a powderblue suitcase tied by a rope onto a Washington-bound bus.

"Josephine Dawes. Doesn't ring a bell, honey. Check with the operator, okay?"

"But she —"

"Look, that's it, okay? I'm warning you —"

The dial tone clicked on the line again.

Whatever had happened to Josephine, Abby-Jean wondered once again lying stretched out, top to bottom, on her bed in the women's residence. Though she had kept an eye out for Josephine among the women whom poverty and circumstance had driven to these three floors of squalid rooms, she couldn't imagine glimpsing

Josephine's raven hair, her row of white plastic bangles, in a place like this. Josephine wouldn't tolerate it; she would get out, would do — whatever was necessary. Anything —

That she herself wasn't prepared to do *anything*, hadn't even the remotest idea of how to go about such a devious and reckless — whatever — made Abby-Jean feel weak, suddenly less capable, younger than Josephine. All she knew, all she wanted, was to work hard, and now after two months it was beginning to look like she wasn't going to get anywhere with that. Now, out of Beaufort, maybe Josephine was the knowingest one.

Beaufort. Lord, it made her sigh. That and Saturday night seemed to swell up inside her in a longing too potent to drift with the notes of *Misty* that floated up from the gay bar below. Outside she heard high heels on cement, then a car door slammed. She could even hear the sandy grit of its tires as it pulled from the curb. Yet closer to her down the vacant corridors, there wasn't a sound. She glanced at her raised leg resting heavily upon her crooked knee, at her foot that tapped the cloyed air in no relation now to the music's beat below, gazing at the golden brown sheen of hair atop the smooth flesh, the strong thick swell of her calf. She had nice-ish legs, she thought. Someday there might be somebody who — She lay back benumbed, eyes turned to the ceiling where a crack in the paint sent out fissures like a dried-up riverbed, then turned on her side and cried.

So lonely. She was afraid to go out into Washington's bright darkness alone. Afraid of her desires too, and of the boys and men who wanted sex from her and nothing or something more, but never love. Wanting them in the heat of her imagination, then shrinking before the hot and cold eyes of strangers. Hearing them when she refused, even if they only thought it — "What's so special about you, bitch?" — torched by desires of their own. Relating to her any old whichway because there was nothing, no one to say they couldn't, her own torn aching self not enough all alone. Erupting from then receding into the anonymity of the city, often after little more than a squirmish, a plea couched in a threat, then refusal, then gone. And who knew, who could ever trace, their lies in between? Only her own situation, where she was herself — that was nakedly clear.

How to picture marriage here? Here where there were no rules, where even the question of it seemed vestigial as a tattered scrap of lace from a grandmother's dress, here where time measured itself in minutes, hours and days, and trying to gaze beyond the rim of two weeks seemed like dropping off the edge of the known world into fathomless mystery. No matter that she herself stayed shut up in the room, no matter that in terrified moments and hours it seemed that never in her life would she escape this wretched haven that had been so very hard to find, the world outside seemed torn up, rootless, whistling around her like the wreckage of some enormous wind. And still despite the terror that came creaking from all the inner corners of her mind, all that cried for *Life!* within her fretted and bludgeoned itself against the suffocation of these walls. To touch, to give, to work hard, to belong somewhere. *Lord, to get out of here —*

She heard a burst of laughter in the hall. With a swift roll she was on her feet and at the door. On the floor below, several women were talking at once. She listened for signs of anger that would force her back, afraid, behind her door again. There were none. And they were carrying on their conversation out in the hall where it was anyone's game. She trotted down to use the phone.

Elizabeth and a whiplike jean-clad girl were talking to someone through an open door.

"Aw, ya bend me double. Christ, I never heard nothin' so ab-surd in all my fuckin' life," the small girl was saying as she slapped her thigh. She did a complete twist around in the hallway, one sneakered foot skewing out on the backturn in a rhythmic jerk that was both grotesque and svelt. Though she was small and gaunt-chested, it seemed to magnify her presence by three. In the second that her back was turned, Abby-Jean could glimpse how her red hair was shorn close at the back in several levels like a series of fringes, from the last of which, right at the nape, a long blonde tuft curled inexplicably down. Maybe someone had cut her hair using three different bowls?

"Well maybe you don't understand, Lynn," Elizabeth objected, though her own lips were twitching, her warm heavy-browed eyes flickering between humor and disapproval as they peered some distance down into Lynn's. Her cotton shift, patterned with blue peaches and yellow leaves, was lopped off high above her elbows and extended barely to her knees, making her tall rangey body seem all knees and elbows and long, long neck. With her strong bruised legs thrust square into shaggy blue bedroom slippers, she looked as if she had stepped into a couple of mops.

"It would be a shock if a person wasn't thinking. Isn't that so, Margaret." Elizabeth peered into the doorway, her face thoughtful now.

Abby-Jean nodded at them, then edged in. She couldn't hear what Margaret said.

"How much you think you'd go for, Margaret?" Lynn was grinning, her face sly.

"Are you gonna stop?" Elizabeth towered over her.

There was a murmur from inside the room.

"I don't care if she's just young," Elizabeth muttered. "I never heard of nobody forgivin' me nothin' 'cause I was fifty."

"Aw Margaret knows I was teasin'." Lynn stared at a split in the seams of the floor runner, pried it apart a little further with her toe, making it worse.

"What's goin' on?" Abby-Jean put in.

"Some things are only funny from the outside. Think how it must've been, bein' Margaret," Elizabeth moralized, then despite herself, her upper lip twitched again.

"Listen Margaret, you want a pocket calculator?" Lynn offered, stepping inside the doorway. "Here." She handed a pink fluorescent comb with small gold flecks in it to Elizabeth as she stepped out again. "Sorry, I just run out," she said to Abby-Jean.

"What's goin' on?" Abby-Jean said again, watching as Elizabeth's finger ran down the teeth of the new comb, then her eyes raised to stare at Lynn speculatively.

"Well I gotta get outta here, it's Saturday night, hell," Lynn said. "No use pissin' around here in the hall, right? Leave that fuckin' shit to the men, right? Joke, joke."

They watched her hoo-hoo-hoo on down the hall, walking like a man with her elbows stuck out.

"You wonder what they're comin' to," Elizabeth said. "Them young people today."

"Yah," Abby-Jean said.

For several moments they stared speculatively down the rows of doors.

"Well, Margaret..." Elizabeth's broad palm stroked down the door frame as she looked around her in all directions again, finding nothing further whatsoever to comment upon. She shifted her weight and sighed, then wiped her brow with a crushed-up kleenex. It was hot.

"Hi Margaret," Abby-Jean peeped in. "How y'doin'?"

Margaret was sitting in a stuffed chair at the far end of her room, the length of a bed and a bureau turned sideways away. Seated with her feet resting up on her bed, she could have touched finger and toe to opposite walls of her room. The chair's placing enabled her to look outside down the channel between the buildings to the front street through what was half of a bay window, the landlord having divided what was once a fair-sized room into two very small rooms by means of a partition wall. Elizabeth shared the bay window with her on the other side of the wall.

"Nothing wrong with me," Margaret said. Her glasses glimmered beneath the light of her stand-up lamp, preventing Abby-Jean from seeing her eyes.

"It's Saturday night, huh." Abby-Jean sighed, leaning against the doorway, as if the phrase were a trans-generational lament.

"Huh," Margaret said, and turned on the little radio beside her.

"...*go ahead with the MX missile to show the Russians that we're determined to do what it takes to prevent war. He said —* " She flicked it off.

"Well Margaret," Elizabeth said and sighed again.

"Go on, do your washin'. You don't see me kickin' up a fuss," Margaret said. "I'm just waitin' for The Mystery Hour, that's all."

"Don't see how you can stand that horror stuff."

"It ain't real."

All three heads tilted to one side as a torrent of voices from the gay bar below sang out *Strangers in the Night* in a spray of pitches, obliterating the piano refrain.

"Gotta get movin'," Elizabeth muttered. "Work at eleven tonight."

With a step, she vanished into her room, leaving Abby-Jean lingering in the doorway.

"Those your kids?" she asked Margaret, pointing to the baby snapshots propped up on the bureau.

"Oh those are Fanny's boys," Margaret said. "Lane, Laurence, Lester and Jeffry." She took off her glasses. Abby-Jean could see the smile bloom all over her face.

"Here, I'll bring 'em," Abby Jean said, seeing Margaret's grey curls bob as she heaved one pom-pommed slipper off the bed. Hand-knit, the slipper was pink on the sides, the sole grey from the floors beneath.

"You can bring the whole stack," Margaret said, then hesitated. "'Course it might not be interesting to you —"

"Sure it will." Abby-Jean felt lonely enough to pour over pictures of strangers that had obviously been hungered over before, some bending and curling a little at the ends.

As they went over the snapshots, the boys grew up before her eyes. She had just about decided to get Margaret to introduce her to Lane when Margaret turned another picture of him dressed in khaki face down like a card. She turned the snapshot of Laurence as a soldier face down too. So handsome! Abby-Jean grieved. Still there was Lester and —

" — has three kids of his own now. He lives out in Pritchetteville, I think, to be near the cement works." Margaret beamed. "He's an awful good boy." She showed Abby-Jean pictures of the grandkids. "That's Fanny there. Look at her. Y'ever see somebody so proud?"

Abby-Jean swallowed her disappointment.

"What about Jeffry?" she asked hopefully. The last snapshot of Jeffry standing with his arm slung over a younger Margaret's shoulder, grinning aggressively into the camera, was the most fingered of all. Margaret's hair was reddish then, the same color as his.

"Lester sends her money regular as clockwork every month."

Margaret had taken Jeffry's picture and shoved it back midway into the deck of snaps as if forcing it back in time. Abby-Jean didn't ask any more about Jeff.

"I think he's dead." Margaret sighed and tossed the deck of pictures on the bed.

All gone, Abby-Jean thought with a pang.

"He sent money to me. I wouldn't take it and now he's dead."

Margaret's head nodded over to one side as if she were going to cry. Abby-Jean put her hand lightly on the foot still resting up on the bed. Margaret's support hose felt thick and rough beneath her

fingers. She must have been too tired to take it off despite the heat of
the room.

"You done a lot of walkin' today?"

"What?" Margaret's head jerked toward her and she reached for
her glasses.

"You want me to go?"

"Oh I was just bogged down in my thoughts. I was doddering
again."

"Aw come off it Margaret, hey? Listen, tell me what everybody
was laughin' at a little while back."

"Oh that." Margaret's mouth set stubbornly.

"Less you don't want to —"

"Oh it wasn't nothing at all, really. You talk of doddering." Margaret
shook her head.

A silence fell between them. Abby-Jean stared out through the
half bay window. It was so dark now she couldn't even see across to
the brick wall. In the inhalation before her sigh, she could taste the old
person smell that two tightly-wrapped lavender sachets on the
bureau were useless against, here where the hot dank air set a glister-
like sweat over all that didn't live or breath. Her thonged feet tapped
abruptly twice in the fetid air. Her spirit beat against the walls.

"...because it was Saturday night after all, and what did I have to
rush off home for?" Margaret was saying. "I thought to myself, well I'll
just take a little look around for a change. It was payday, y'see, and
my check was there safe in the bank. I was looking for — I don't know.
I walked for blocks, you know how you can, store to store.

"I was just wandering around, picking things up, putting them down,
thinking —" Margaret glanced up. "I don't know that I was thinking at
all," she muttered. "I walked around a while from store to store, and I
got to feeling pretty good 'cause I hadn't seen a blessed thing I
wanted. So I thought I'd have a nice piece of strawberry
cheesecake as a reward."

Abby-Jean chuckled and gave her a soft punch in the calf just
below where the pink quilted kimono came down.

"I wasn't going to go out of my way to get it, mind. Just if the
chance came up somewhere I was passing by, then I'd go on in."
Margaret's lips pursed; she tried to look severe. "I walked for blocks
and blocks and never found a single place. You'd think they didn't
make cheesecake any more."

"'Least you never went out of your way," Abby-Jean poked.

"Well I did. In fact I got lost," Margaret added crossly.

"Huh..."

"I wasn't paying attention. Usually when I walk, I keep an eye on
the streets. Now I'm coming up 10th Street, I say, then turning at F, then
another block — I keep saying it to myself as I go, like winding up a
string I can pull myself back on 'cause I don't remember so good any
more. Today — it was like I was dreamin', then all of a sudden I came

to. Well I looked around, and in God's name I didn't know where I was. Jesus Lord, it gave me such a fright. I looked around and for a minute I couldn't even remember what city I was in. Not even what city. I couldn't have told you the year."

Margaret's fingers began to pick at the quilting in her kimono, at one of several spaces where the thread had come loose and the pattern disappeared altogether. She had plump, vigorous fingers, round and smooth like her arms, her legs, her dimpled face. With the kimono cinched up tight despite the heat, her body looked bulky, a series of spheres.

"I looked up at the street sign. 9th and H. I couldn't have been more than a few blocks from the White House. Good God, I was only a few blocks over from Woodward's where I've worked for years. All the blocks are numbered and lettered so you can't miss, and yet it clutched my heart the very same. All around me the stores were closing up. I couldn't even see to get a cab out of there. I don't know where everybody went, how they got out of there so quick. The streets were still as death, all shabby, dirty and dark like in a movie about the end of the world. And there I was, waking up out of a dream and still lost somehow, no matter I could see what street I was on. 'Cause no matter what the street sign said, none of it looked familiar to me. I just stood stock still for a minute or more, arms flapping and gasping for breath. Things look so different with night coming in."

Abby-Jean listened silently, nodding.

"I started down H, then north. I think I almost started to run, I was so scared. An old woman — yes I am, I'm sixty-five — out alone on these streets at night. Good God. Even a flea could've knocked me down. Yes, I ran along thinking *Jesus! Jesus!* and then what did I look up and see? A bunch of women over on the next corner, waiting around in a line. Lord, I was so glad to see them, a dozen at least, I went puffing on over like a bird to its nest, right over smack in the middle of 'em, and put my knitting bag with the sweater for Fanny down. It doesn't matter which bus they're waiting for, I thought. Any bus would plug me in to my own line home.

"You don't know how relieved I felt at being with them women. A long string of them, tired-looking like me, waiting for the bus now that the stores was closed up, the last shift, maybe, anxious to get on home and get their shoes off. I was standing quietly, keeping to myself and still I was clinging to them all the same. With a dozen women there, who could hurt me? It was even kind of pleasant out there in the warm night. We was all just standing around, there weren't any line, no one shoving to keep her place. We was all just kind of scattered around dog-tired and waiting, and it seemed friendlier to me that we didn't keep the line strict. A body could wander in and out among us like a passing breeze. It were mostly colored ladies there, it come to me, but there was whites too, and nobody minded nobody anyhow. We was all alone, it seemed. And I remember thinking how nice it was to be out there with the beech trees shimmering in the streetlights and the big international hotel all lit up over there, and not in this hell-hole back here."

Abby-Jean's gaze dropped. Somehow she had never thought of the residence being as bad for the older women as for herself, had easily interpreted Margaret's endurance as a lack of need. And yet for all that, Margaret sweated in the heat, choked in the suffocation, grew desperate in the solitude as did she.

"We stood there waiting just a while, and every now and then a car come by slow. I kept expecting one of the ladies to give a big wave to her husband and climb on in. It was taking the bus so awfully long to come, no wonder they got their husbands down to pick them up. But I guessed there was some mixed up signals 'cause nobody stopped and nobody got in. And the women were getting restless like me. I could see them starting to shift their feet and pace around. And then I noticed something queer." Margaret glanced at her shyly. "Nobody was carryin' a thing. No groceries, no shopping bags, no newspapers, no flowers, no supper-hour knitting, no nothing."

"So?"

"Well think. Half of 'em didn't even have purses. And then I craned my neck around and what I was afraid of turned out to be true. There weren't no bus stop, neither."

"Huh," Abby-Jean said blankly.

"They was whores," Margaret said.

"No kiddin'!"

"I wasn't thinkin', I guess."

"Well it ain't somethin' you necessarily know."

"Well that's it. They looked just like ordinary girls and women to me — tall, thin, short, stocky — all kinds. They wasn't all dressed up in any particular kind of way. Not even sexy or nothing. Womanflesh, that's all they had to be. There was fifteen at least, and across on the other corner, the same. Each one of them stuck out there single all by her own, and yet they seemed herded together some way. Everybody standin' silent an' alone, like tombstones in a graveyard, dark an' ghostlike under the streetlights, waitin'. And the cars kept on slowin' down, then passin' by. What kind of a man, you got to ask, would have the face to stop by a crowd like that and yank out one? What kind of man? Nobody seemed to care much anyhow 'cause they was all lookin' at the ground half the time, nobody sayin' nothin'. Not waitin' there to be appreciated, just waitin' to be took.

"I grabbed up Fanny's sweater and hiked off across the street. Then I stopped and looked back at them one more time. It was so quiet, so sad, so lonely and dull. I never seen so many in a group like that, and there they were, only a few blocks from where I work every day! There they were, swirlin' down the main streets in torrents, like jetsam coming in with the tides. I saw a big car drive up and I thought

Hoh! They got one at last. But a fancier-lookin' woman in it, that's all it was, with a red light inside the car makin' her glow.

"Somebody's makin' it, I thought, a pink Caddy like that. Most of 'em looked dirt poor, but the pink Caddy lady, she'd have money, you can bet. She'd not be makin' no minimum wage and workin' herself blue."

Abby-Jean had glanced up sharply at the mention of the car.

"You look at these whores down here only blocks from the White House and you wonder how it can be. And then you think of all the rest that goes on. All the payoffs and graft, the wheeling and dealing, the people who got fortunes who never did a thing, the people it costs you, just they breathe." Her plump hand waved circles in the air as she struggled to come to grips with the idea, unsure how the fleecing was working, sure only that it was. Giving up, she broke off, stared out the window where darkness blotted out the channel to the front street. She seemed tormented suddenly, her mind on something else. "And I can't help but wonder, was I wrong."

"About the pink Caddy?" Abby-Jean asked. She ached to hear more about that.

"He sent me money, I wouldn't take it and now he's dead."

Margaret's elbow was propped up on the chair arm, her hand cupping her chin, fingers over her mouth. Her round body seemed to swell with a sigh that was followed by two little shudders. She was near crying over Jeffrey again.

"I said to him, 'I don't want to see money of yours, Buster, if you can't tell me straight where you got it. I'm not touchin' money of yours you got crooked some way.'There he was with the money held out in his hand, his face gettin' red. 'Aw c'mon, Aunt Peg,' he said to me, all embarrassed. Then he wanted to just leave it on the kitchen table but no, I kept on at him until he had to stuff it back in his pocket again. It was five twenties that I shamed him for." Margaret whispered. She turned to Abby-Jean, her voice urgent. "There's people throw away five times that in a day without turning a hair, and how they got it, justice couldn't bear seein'. Then here I was, all fluffed up 'cause he'd laid his hands on a hundred dollars some way, my poor sweet boy, an' he was even givin' it to me." Her face was stricken.

"Well you could take it now," Abby-Jean offered practically.

"After that, I never heard from him again."

"That don't say he's dead."

"I made him ashamed, don't you see? I made it so he could never come to me without answerin' for what he was doin'. And he never got to doin' things he could be proud of, so there was nothing for it but to steer clear of me. Then these past five years, I could feel it, he was departed. I couldn't feel him out there in the world no more."

Abby-Jean said nothing then, believing it. But Jeffrey couldn't have even reached forty. What reason could there be for someone to die so young? Not a car accident surely or a disease. Who knew what might have happened in the direction his life had gone. It made her flinch, thinking on it, suddenly picturing the redheaded body skewed out bloody on a cheap hotel floor, in a police morgue, disintegrating in the sea. It was as if Jeffry had walked into a fog, parts of his body disappearing as they penetrated the silver sheen, swallowed up in the savage mystery beyond. If he was dead, someone had killed him. There was a sudden rushing in her eardrums. She glanced across at Margaret turning the pocket calculator left on the ledge over and over with a steady thwack-thwacking sound. Tears were streaming down her cheeks beneath her glasses. She didn't raise a hand to wipe them away.

"I was too proud."

Abby-Jean tugged on the pink handknit slipper. "I bet Jeffrey, he knew you were thinking of him."

"Pride can be a terrible thing. Sometimes its got no sense to it at all."

They sat a while together listening to the passing cars outside, each lost in her thoughts until a terrific thud against the wall behind Margaret, as if a bed had rammed against it in full force, jerked their minds back to the small room where they were once more. Their gazes locked and froze. The ramming sound against the wall came again, then after a few minutes, again. There was no talking above it. Their embarrassed glances searched the four corners of the room for an innocuous place to land.

"I usually listen to *The Mystery Hour* at ten." Margaret wiped her face quickly with the back of one plump hand, flicking the radio on loud with the other.

"Anyway, I gotta go." Abby-Jean got up hastily. "You okay, Margaret?" she asked, her hand on the door.

Margaret's five splayed fingers urged her away.

Stepping into the hall, Abby-Jean saw Elizabeth heading toward the outside door on her way to work. In the gloom of the lower hallway her large body and the night guard's uniform made her look like a man. She stood a moment peering inside a crumpled brown paper bag before heaving the door open and stepping out at last into the palpitant night.

Returning to her room, Abby-Jean flung herself on the bed, her head hanging over the side with her hair streaming down. She closed her eyes and saw Josephine, Margaret, Jeffrey, saw the pink Caddy winging its way through a stream of neon lights to disappear in the dark night beyond. A scream rising from below announced *The Mystery Hour* was about to begin.

❂

An announcer in a white suit was sitting behind a display of white electronic consols in a white room — or so it seemed on the portable black and white TV that Abby-Jean watched half-heartedly as she waited for Louise. Seated on a cracked plastic chair pushed as far back as possible so that Louise could edge by her to make the bed, she glanced idly over the paper, plastic and mesh shopping bags crammed with Louise's things that were still heaped against the walls. There was no bureau to put them in, so she couldn't tell by the bags whether Louise had at last decided to stay put or move on. But along the baseboards of the narrow room, visible in the spaces between the bags, the defence line of roach powder had been renewed.

"By the year 2000, there will be computers in the family home. Whatever a person wants, he will be able to simply push buttons and the product will arrive... Already, however, scientists are questioning the hazards of sterility and isolation in the human environment. Could this be us, very soon? Dominated by machines which provide us with everything we want but happiness? What does it mean?" The camera panned through rooms of ascetic modern furniture and abstract paintings, through glass walls overlooking neat white plots of grass, then zoomed to the faces of well-dressed men and women staring past one another.

Abby-Jean sighed impatiently, unable to focus on the program that appeared to be science fiction or educational, she wasn't sure which. She watched the pictures change. The sound drifted past her as if it were a part of the noise from the traffic outside. Then she glanced at Louise sharply, wondering whether to tell her what day today was or not. Louise's face was gleaming with sweat.

"I'd never let them near my sheets," she was saying, shaking her freshly laundered sheets out of the Glad-bag onto her bed. The sudden sweetness exuding from the thin cotton made Abby-Jean's nostrils tingle. For a moment, the room seemed fresh. The scent came from two crumpled anti-cling tissues that Louise took from the dryer to stick inside her pillowcases before putting the pillow in — another trick to hide the musky stench of the room. Her stock of Javel water, Mr. Clean and lysol stood in a little corral beneath the sink. She had at least twenty dollars worth of cleansers down there, with two withered jayclothes spread out over them to dry.

"A few months ago, I was all set to move into a cooking room on Florida Street until I found out they weren't going to let me do my own sheets. For God's sake, why not? What was it to them?"

"Maybe they just wanted the excuse to keep getting into folks' rooms." Abby-Jean shrugged. She was glad that the management was doing the sheets here; it saved her trekking through the traffic to the laundromat like Santa Claus with a garbage bag of laundry on her back. It was hard to tell from one week to the next whether the maid had come to change the sheets, though. The fabric was too worn to ever look fresh. The only way to keep track was to keep her eye on some hole, and the one she had her eye on these days had been around for quite a little while. But minus the sheets, she could do the rest of her laundry in her sink, pinning it to dry on a string that stretched from her door handle to her chair.

"You never know who's touching them or where they've been. You never know whose sheets you're getting back, or how clean they are now. Maybe someone with a disease. You just don't know. And there's no reason to think they'd do a good job. That's why I do mine."

Abby-Jean scowled. Sleeping in the sheets of someone with a disease —

"You're givin' me the crawlies, Louise," she complained, taking a green iridescent comb from her purse to run through her corn-yellow hair. "You gonna be long?"

"I just want to wash up."

Abby-Jean groaned. "I got time to go pay the rent, that means." Anything, to get out of the heat of the room.

The residence office was crowded for late afternoon. Three women with suitcases and one with a packsack sat dolefully on the chairs. Two older women, both gaunt and ill-looking, stood at the desk holding on to each other's arms for support.

"Look, you know if you don't live here, I can't receive mail for you here," Alexander Vandernikke was saying. "It's against —"

"But can't you let me use the address, just? Even if you don't got a room, let me use the address, just? I don't ask to live here — just let me say I do. I got to have a address or I can't get nothin' from nobody. What's it to you?"

Alexander Vandernikke turned away. He was going to wash his hands, Abby-Jean knew. Whenever he was cornered by some rule, that was all he could think of to do. He never ever considered breaking it.

"Any mail for me?" she cut in before he could get away.

He glanced at the boxes behind him. "Name?"

Every day for months, she had asked him for mail. Disgusting!

"I'm going to the moon," the woman who had wanted an address said in a strange voice beside her. "I'm not going to stick around here."

"Nothing for Brown," Vandernikke said.

"You sure? Abby-Jean Brown?" Tears started to her eyes. Nothing from her mother, Bud, Dibsy or the girls when if she'd been at home, there would have been a cake. No one had remembered. "Can't you check again? Maybe something got into one of the other boxes by mistake."

His fingers ticked through the envelopes in the other boxes. There weren't many so it didn't take long.

"Maybe somebody took it. Oh I didn't mean you," she added hurriedly. "Just there might have been a few dollars inside. You sure you seen nothing? I really didn't mean you. But I can't see how it could be I got nothing."

"FORGET IT."

Abby-Jean jumped. But the woman who had wanted an address hadn't even been speaking to Vandernikke. Her friend let her arm drop.

"Well anyway," Abby-Jean said as if she didn't care about the mail, "I just come to pay the rent."

She took out her checkbook. It thrilled her, that checkbook. After all, Bud was afraid to even go into a bank. But then, he'd never had a wad of savings to be able to start an account up.

"Sorry, no checks," Vandernikke said flatly.

"But George Waddell, he took one last time."

"He shouldn't have."

"Well he did." Abby-Jean gripped the counter. The rent was due today and it was too late now to go to the bank. "But you know me. I been here three months now an' I paid each week regular every time."

Vandernikke's head turned to one side, as if he were listening to his hair turning grey.

"Look, I'll be in here first thing in the morning with cash, okay? If I was tryin' not to pay, would I have come in here at all?"

Both Vandernikke's hands raised lightly from the counter palm up as if to say "Well don't ask me" before he turned away. Now he was really going to wash his hands, Abby-Jean thought. Maybe her mistake had been in talking about money coming in the mail, making him think the rent depended on that. She should have been more careful. And now the word was out, ten to one, she'd never get it. But it wouldn't be Alex Vandernikke who'd take it. It would be George Waddell.

Beside her, the two older women stood looking at each other. It was as if their partnership had become unbalanced and they couldn't walk away. They were thinking what to do next, and because they didn't know, they just stood there looking as if their minds were drifting.

"Tomorrow morning. Honest!" Abby-Jean called to Vandernikke who stood in the interior office by the sink, then she brushed past the standing women, the sitting disconsolate women, glancing down as she passed them because she had a room.

Louise was out waiting on the street. She had on her good yellow dress, the one that seemed to be always hanging freshly pressed on the back of her closet door, free from the crush inside.

"I feel like something different. Want to eat in Georgetown tonight? It's on me."

"Oh Louise!" Abby-Jean's eyes glistened. So something special was going to happen today after all, just when she felt so forgotten and alone. She nearly blurted her secret out to Louise, then decided against it. The silence she kept made her feel strong, and it was good to feel strong again. Since coming to Washington, it was hard to tell whether she was getting stronger or weaker day by day. One thing was sure: she knew more.

"White wine, what do you say?" Louise said, getting into the spirit of it. "I always used to have white wine on Friday paydays in New York."

"Today's Thursday," Abby-Jean said, then added, "June 28th."

"So we're early."

They were off!

They pointed out and exclaimed over everything — foreign sportscars, stained glass, Boston ferns in bay windows — on the route to Georgetown, then sobered when they reached the major promenade of small fashionable boutiques and restaurants. Then, weaving behind Louise through the crowds, Abby-Jean was too busy watching to speak. The icy ash blonde in her flared white pantsuit, the curly-headed young man in jeans who wore an earring in one ear, the girl in the low-cut peasant blouse who wore no shoes — all seemed the same in some way. Even the people that weren't dressed up were dressed down in such a way as to hint they were special. To Abby-Jean, it seemed as if they all knew each other, and she and Louise were the only strangers there.

"What about Le Bonheur?"

Abby-Jean glanced through tinted glass at a lime-green dais crowded with white wrought-iron tables, then shrank back. How to sink down somewhere safe in there without a dither? There were two women wearing enormous hats —

"It's gonna be expensive, don't you think?"

"Not too bad." Louise was reading the menu pasted up on the glass.

"Well," Abby-Jean braced herself, "I suppose you could get white wine in a place like that, all right." She glimpsed the menu and bristled. She wasn't going to stand for Louise paying like that.

"I don't want to go somewhere you don't like," Louise said.

They searched up and down the main two blocks, dragged away from the more expensive restaurants by Abby-Jean, pulled back from the unlicensed cheaper cafes by Louise, compromising just when it seemed hopeless with a licensed pizzeria where tiffany lamps hung above rough wooden booths.

Settling in while Louise ordered at the counter, Abby-Jean read the pizza prices from a plaque on the wall, noticing at once it was as expensive here as at Le Bonheur. She eyed the booth across the way where a piece of crust had dropped forgotten beneath the table, then glanced up to see Louise approaching with two glasses of red wine. She grimaced, then thought how after all Louise needed somebody to go with if she wanted to go out and have a good time. Besides, she noted regretfully, seated further on up were two good-looking boys her own age who might have come on over if it weren't for Louise being old enough to be a mother to them all.

"You don't know how good this makes me feel, Louise. I was itchin' to go someplace special today."

"I said to myself, when this three week stint is done, I'm going to have a fling, I don't give a damn what it means." Louise was wiping the rim of her wineglass with her paper napkin. "Wait," she said, and wiped Abby-Jean's glass too, rubbing the outside rim then holding it up to the light.

Abby-Jean took a sip of wine and settled back against the booth. Elegant as Le Bonheur or not, it was a relief to be out of her room, exciting to see people passing on the street outside as she dallied over wine. She leaned forward again, her face ablaze.

"No kidding, Louise. It was so lucky that you come up with this idea to go someplace special. I coulda felt real bad the whole day."

"It makes you feel in the world," Louise said.

"You know what?"

Louise shook her head. She was wiping the forks the waitress had dropped on the table in front of them. Abby-Jean snuck a glance at the waitress to see if she had noticed this being done and gotten mad. Surely you didn't have to do that in a place like this? Probably it was another habit of Louise's that she didn't like to lose, but it made Abby-Jean feel peculiar nonetheless. She didn't like to behave as if she thought she was too good for everybody else.

"It's my birthday," she blurted.

The announcement seemed to lose its force as it left her lips.

"Well," Louise glanced up at her, smiling hesitantly and raising her glass. "To you."

"Yah," Abby-Jean said shyly, then added in a rush, "To the both of us, hey?" She stared around the room greedily. "This here's better than MacDonald's or Treacher's."

"How old are you anyway."

"Twenty."

"Lord, you've got your whole life still out there," Louise sighed. "My God, I think of when I was twenty —"

She stopped with her wine glass held to her lips, and Abby-Jean watched her remembering. Then she tossed her iron-grey hair away from her eyes, her head remaining tilted slightly to one side and up. There was a crimson smudge left on the glass from her lipstick that she didn't wipe away.

"I only brought it up 'cause I wanted you to know how lucky the timin' was," Abby-Jean said. "I was feelin' so strange. Nobody remembered me at all."

"I remember the first time that happened to me," Louise said.

"You sit in your room an' you think: there's nobody in the entire world that knows what day this is. There's nobody out there thinkin' of me. It's the only time somethin' good's supposed to happen 'sides Christmas, and now look. Lord, I was ready to cry."

Abby-Jean's eyes reddened as the lost feeling came over her again. After all, who was Louise? Nearly a stranger, somebody she had met in a residence for women, somebody who was always threatening at any moment to pack her bags, let go her room and move on to Baltimore, Boston or New York. And what then? Would they ever think of each other again after that?

"I'm glad I asked you, then. People have to stick together. I know how it feels."

"When's your birthday, Louise?"

Somebody turned the music tape up and Louise's birth date was obliterated in the blare of

Do you LIKE it
Uh-huh, uh-huh
Do you LIKE it
Uh-huh, uh-huh

"I remember once in New York," Louise said through the noise. "It was my birthday and nobody knew."

Abby-Jean bent forward over the table, straining to hear. Louise bent toward her, raising her voice until she was almost shouting.

"— working for Angela Ricardo in one of the big brokerage houses. I'd been working there for three months, just typing in the outer office, you know. Whenever Angela needed someone extra, she always asked for me. I used to get sent to impressive places like that quite often."

Louise paused, then tossed her hair back, her head on an upward tilt.

"But the morning of my birthday, I could see something special was going to happen. Caterers came in and set up a table right across from me. They brought in salami, pickles, cheese-dip, potato chips." Louise paused to recall all of the food. "Little sandwiches, crackers, olives, rye-crisps, more cold cuts —"

Abby-Jean was nodding avidly.

"Celery and carrot sticks, potato salad, a fruit basket piled high with grapes —"

Her sigh gusted across the table.

"Sure, and there was liquor too even though it wasn't even lunchtime yet. There were bottles of champagne tied in red ribbons and wine glasses laid out in rows. In the center of all that, there was a birthday cake. My God, you should have seen it. Everybody on the whole floor came around."

"Oh Louise! They did all that for you?"

"It was Angela's birthday," Louise said, tossing her hair back. "Her birthday was the same day as mine."

Abby-Jean nodded enthusiastically. "So when they found out it was your birthday too —"

Their pizza came. Louise wiped the knife clean, then cut them each out a slice.

"So when they found out," Abby-Jean repeated with her mouth full. The pizza had everything on it — mushrooms, green peppers, pepperoni — everything! Louise hadn't held back on a thing.

"Oh I didn't tell."

"But when there was all that food, a big splash like that? You could have just mentioned it, quick. It wasn't like they was gonna run short on account of you."

"It was her celebration," Louise said.

"Your birthdays the same day — you could've had a good laugh over that."

"It would have spoiled it for her."

Abby-Jean frowned, picturing a gathering of people in front of the heaping table, a well-dressed lady holding the hand of a younger Louise as the semi-circle sang Happy Birthday to them both and clapped.

"I didn't want to cut in," Louise said. "I didn't want to push myself forward."

"You could have just mentioned it, like, and then dropped back after they sang —"

"You don't understand," Louise murmured. "I was the temp, after all."

The taped music extinguished her voice again as the singer worked herself into a frenzy:

Do you like it like that
Do you like it like that
Do you like it like THAT???

Abby-Jean stopped chewing and listened incredulously. Did the singer really mean — *that*? Lord, it sounded as if she was — The groan of release rocketed over the booths, scraped against the tiffany lamps, mingled with the odor of pizza and scudded along the gritty floor. The blatant sexuality was somehow frightening. Abby-Jean's eyes met those of an older man in a crushed summer pinstripe suit. He was staring at her hard. She ducked her head away so he couldn't see any more of her thoughts.

"Besides," Louise was saying as Abby-Jean's attention recovered, "I had a good time, didn't I? I had a birthday celebration even if nobody knew. I could sit there eating her cake and know it was my birthday too."

Abby-Jean's face became stubborn. Somehow she would have let it be known.

"But what a celebration! I never forgot it," Louise breathed out, holding her wine glass in such a way that Abby-Jean knew she was reliving it.

"You got no family to send you a card?" she asked. "A family ought to send a card, I think, when they can't bake you a cake."

"I have a sister in North Carolina," Louise said. "But we never write. I move around too much for her to keep track."

"All you got to do is send change of address —"

"I got tired of her asking me why."

"You got to move, these days. Everybody knows that."

"Elsie's lived in North Carolina all of her married life, ever since she turned seventeen. Jimmy had a job with a textile company down there, so they settled down and started paying on a house. 'You ought to get married, Louise,' she was always saying to me. Well I had my life. There were good things in my life too."

Abby-Jean waited for the speech on the temporary secretary life, on Baltimore, Boston and New York. It didn't come.

"People always say, why don't you get married, as if it was something you could just walk out tomorrow and do. They never think that maybe you wanted to but things never came up that way. They make it as if you were trying to be unhappy somehow. They never think when they ask that, that it hurts you. And I could have said things right back to Elsie, like in the last years when they discovered Jimmy had that disease in his lungs from the plant, Brown Lung, and finally couldn't go to work any more. I could have said, well now there you are with an invalid for the rest of your life — no more job, no more house after a bit, just caring for him. You thought you were getting ahead and now see. But I never did. I know what's cruel."

Louise straightened up in the booth, lit one of the cigarettes that she usually carried to hand out to others, then shook one out for Abby-Jean. She tossed her hair back.

"I know what's cruel," she said again harshly.

Abby-Jean nodded silently, leaning forward again because when Louise went on, her voice was low. She could feel the wine heating her ears. A small pink spot had come out on Louise's chin.

"She told me Jimmy was sick, but it wasn't until I phoned one Christmas that she told me he'd got too bad to work. I never knew he was sick like that. She never said a word. I almost think she was ashamed to say that things were going bad after how she had bragged before. But then she started crying on the phone about his lungs, about how careful they had to be, for if he caught the least little thing he'd be done, and maybe he would anyway, no matter what. He needed a sterile environment, that's what the doctor said. She was going crazy making sure of that. They kept him downstairs in the front parlor where Elsie kept plastic on the furniture. She was always scared something would mark her good things that she could never buy twice in a lifetime. She had a mohair rug in there she used to go over with a hair comb just so the pile would rise up smooth. I swear, you couldn't find a cleaner place in all the world to put Jimmy than in there."

Louise stopped, smiling as she remembered the mohair rug.

"'I'll come down,' I said, 'Don't you worry. I've got an important job here but I don't care.' 'Oh but if it's an important job —' she said. 'Blood's thicker than water', I said, 'I don't care.' I got on the bus for North Carolina that night. I was in Baltimore then, only ten or so hours away."

"She was glad, I bet," Abby-Jean said. "She was glad that you come."

"When I got there, she started crying before she got the screen door open. I wanted to give her a kiss, but before I could she whispered 'Don't move' and went back inside. Well there I was, barely inside the porch door, out there where they keep the washing machine. But I did what she said. I put my suitcase down and waited. She came back with a blanket. 'Take off your clothes,' she said. 'My God, out here on the porch?' I cried. I didn't believe her at first. But then I could see it was that or else. She turned off the light. 'Nobody'll see you,' she hissed at me. 'Do it quick and you won't get cold.' I took off my dress — it was this one, my yellow dress, spanking new back then. 'Take everything off,' she said and held out a plastic garbage bag for me to put my clothes in. 'This is crazy,' I told her. But I couldn't keep on after the way she cried out — Louise! —

"She wrapped me in a blanket and we went running through the hall in the dark to upstairs. She ran a hot bath for me, then came in with some clothes of hers for me to wear. She had already taken all of mine off to the dry cleaners, everything in the suitcase too. Okay, I thought, and kept scrubbing. I was just ready to get out of the tub when she passed me over some shampoo."

Louise shot Abby-Jean a brief glance, then began wiping together the crumbs on the table with her napkin.

"She told me to wash my hair, too."

"Oh Louise, you didn't —"

"I did. What could I do?"

"You want a cigarette? Have one of mine."

Louise shook her head.

"'Who knows what kind of places you've been? Who knows what conditions you live under?'" Louise's eyes flashed. "That's what she said to me."

They sat quiet a moment, thinking of the residence.

"He must have been real sick," Abby-Jean said.

"He used to be a big robust man. It wrung my heart to see him lying on the couch, thin, like a dish towel spread out to dry. He was coughing his lungs away."

"You want another glass of wine?" Abby-Jean's face was intense, concentrated. "I could buy it."

Their small argument over it took the silence beneath the music away. The second glass of wine made them feel relaxed and warm, both leaning back against the wooden benches carelessly.

"She was just scared. Your sister Elsie was scared," Abby-Jean started up again.

"Look, I understand it all. But I'll never go back to North Carolina.

Abby-Jean stared at her sadly.

"Whose birthday is it anyway?" Louise's voice was suddenly chipper.

"Oh, mine," Abby-Jean said.

"Too bad you're here with me," Louise winked, "Instead of some good-looking boy."

"It's just as good with you."

"Oh nonsense. I understand."

But Abby-Jean could see that pleased her nonetheless.

"I'd have given you something. A card. You should have said earlier."

"Geez, Louise, this here is plenty." Abby-Jean's gesture took in the tiffany lamp, the wine glasses, the music against which their voices struggled. All in all, their celebration must have chalked up quite a bill, and here Louise hadn't even gone to Le Bonheur. Feeling suddenly guilty, Abby-Jean reached into her purse for her wallet.

"No, no, I said I'd get it," Louise protested.

Abby-Jean flushed. "I just wanted to show you something," she stammered, searching through a mass of employment agency cards, finding her social security card at last. But it showed no date, and she had no driver's license. But there on an old school card, her birthday was incorporated in the last digits of her student number.

"See that?" She showed Louise the card with her thumb underlining the digits 062862. "That proves it's my birthday today."

Louise sat back abruptly, stared at the PEPSI sign on the far wall.

"I never should've told you about my birthday in the first place," Abby-Jean cried. "I couldn't help it, that's all. An' I only showed you the card 'cause ever since I got here, people been acting like they thought I lied."

"It's hard in this kind of life," Louise murmured. "You come out of nowhere and that's where you go."

"Not me. I come out of Beaufort, South Carolina, an' someday I'll go back."

There were tears in her eyes.

Louise raised her wine glass. "To Beaufort," she said, then she smiled.

Abby-Jean grinned back appreciatively and raised her glass. "To —?" Despite Baltimore, Boston and New York, she didn't think that Louise started out from there.

"Roanoke."

"To Roanoke, Louise."

They settled back in the booth, content to stop fighting against the music, its solid hammering wedging in between them, excusing their silence. From time to time their fingers would tap on the table in response to the rhythm, but that happened almost inadvertently. There wasn't much in the repeated words 'Shake your MOney MAker' to think about, Abby-Jean thought, not like country music where there was a story and a guy telling you how he felt.

She glanced about her. The pizzeria was nearly empty now, despite the music making it seem there was a big party going on. It was a surprise to be in a place where there was that much noise and find there was nothing going on at all. The hollowness at the heart of it made her ache. Here where the music said it was happening, there was nothing, no one. No one but a pale, enduring Louise, relayering her crimson lipstick again.

Abby-Jean sighed. Louise glanced at her and smiled.

"Is there somebody special back in Beaufort?"

"Oh —" Abby-Jean waved her hand. No names came to mind to answer the longing that she felt.

"You have a boyfriend here?"

"Nobody wants to get to know you," Abby-Jean said. "Nobody wants to take the time. They just want you to sleep with them. If not, goodbye, there's others that will. They say, what's wrong, you don't like sex? I don't want 'em to think that I'm weird. An' I always feel good about it until the time comes an' then —" She shrugged. "I want them to like me, I guess."

"I know," Louise murmured. "And there's nobody to care if he treats you bad, nobody to say 'You never should have done that to Louise.'"

Abby-Jean glanced at her.

"We should get going, don't you think?" Louise said, looking away.

She put her cigarettes back in her purse, went and paid.

They wandered back toward the residence slowly despite the storm-black sky, enjoying the last moments of twilight, feeling the air's liquid eddies about them, the heat going out like breaths from the scorched pavement and sidewalks, billowing out in scent from the Georgetown lawns and trees. A red sportscar shot past and they caught sight of blonde hair whipping, heard a laugh peel into the evening sky. Abby-Jean stared after it with longing.

"I know what it is to be lonely," Louise said. "To be lonely that way."

Their eyes met then dropped. So it didn't go away, Abby-Jean thought. If you were alone, it went on and on.

"You feel like a cat sometimes," Louise said.

Abby-Jean nodded. It was true.

"Sometimes I lie there at night in the residence and I think that I can't go on," Louise said. "Sometimes I feel like I'll burst my skin."

They passed over the ravine out of Georgetown toward the hush of the storm.

"Sometimes I hear somebody's got someone, up there in the rooms," Abby-Jean said, her voice raised against the swish of passing cars.

"So I get dressed," Louise said over her shoulder. "I get dressed and go out for a walk. Just a walk. That's all. I got out for a walk. Within an hour or so, I'm back in the room again."

They walked faster, glancing anxiously at the sky overhead.

"Sometimes I can hear them," Abby-Jean panted. "Right through the walls, even though they're rooms away."

"There's men who know how it is, who keep an eye out for older women like me. Because I'm living like this, they think they can take advantage of me, as easy as that. I have to be careful, with all the cruel things they're ready to think."

Abby-Jean had to walk swiftly for Louise was pulling out ahead. From behind, she glimpsed the soft thickness of Louise's iron grey hair, the slender form of her body in the prim yellow dress, her pale arms with their slight thickening of flesh, an older woman's arms, graceful still.

"I have to fight to keep my life clean," Louise's voice rang.

They broke into a run for shelter, back to the stew of the residence in the rising grit-ridden wind.

○

Long after the storm had cooled the evening air, the residence remained locked in a heat so thick that walls and floors and the living bodies in between were slimed with sweat and a residue of grit. Already sweating from her race back to the residence, Abby-Jean flung herself naked on the bed and waited for the heat to pass. Instead it lifted only to bear down on her again, reinforcing the heavy atmosphere that made a presence out of nothing, an omnipresence soaking her there as she lay, not moving a muscle, hoping to lie still enough for the burden of it to pass away. Hoping that by barely breathing her body would quieten to neutrality, that by ceasing to resist the heat, a quiescence would overcome her, allowing it to pass through her unobtruded like light through a film of gauze. Eyelids closed, flickering, for twenty minutes she bore it.

It didn't stop. She was smothering!

Panicking, she thrashed to her feet, stumbling through the turgid air toward the windows where the blinds were drawn, maybe stopping some fresh current from outside. She thrust her hand behind the blind, waved it back and forth outside through the narrow slit that the window would open. Cool light air — she felt it tingling against her fingertips. One desperate heave sent her desk scudding across the carpet. Shunting, pushing, pulling, she struggled with her bed, slamming it at last into the corner where the desk had been. Now, elevated by the pillow and folded bedspread beneath, she could lie with her face just a foot from the current that passed, gentle and forceless as a sigh, between the two windows overhead.

But if she raised the blinds to let it come in, anyone looking from the row of windows in the buildings across the way could see her lying there naked on the bed. Closing the blinds or putting on her nightie would eliminate in a stroke the small advantage of the air filtering in. To preserve it, she would have to turn the light out and lie naked in darkness, left defenceless with her thoughts, unable even to read a magazine. She hesitated a moment, one hand on the blind, transfixed by the vision of an endless stretch of nights spent torn between light and heat as the summer bore down.

Reaching for her thongs, she crossed the rough shag rug and turned off the light. Hoping to increase the air current, she opened the hall door. But the air in the hallway was even hotter, more stagnant than that in her room, and if there was any current created by the open door and windows, it was that of the fetid air of the hallway swamping her room. She waited a minute for the first invasion of it to pass, thinking once the hot dead air had moved out, the channel of circulation would be clear. But it was as if exhausted air from some forty odd rooms pumped into the stagnant corridor in endless supply. No matter how much of the suffocating mass from the hall invaded her room, the tiny fissure at her windows could never suck the whole building clear.

She closed the door against it, cutting off too the dim rectangle of light from the hall that laid a yellow stripe across her bed that would have exposed her nakedness, even if lying with her light out, to God knew who that might pass along the hall outside. Stumbling back in darkness, she flung herself on the bed again and felt the heat of the room bear down. To touch anything was an abrasion. Heat seemed to emanate even from her pillow. She swept it to the floor, turning stomach down, spread-eagled on the soiled sheet, her cheek grinding into its damp.

A low trill of laughter escaped her.

"This ain't real," her voice said.

Her eyes pierced the darkness, catching the outline of her desk left haphazard in the center of the room. Somewhere along the row of windows outside her own, a light went on, sending a small flash of light across her body before it went out again. A dim reflection of the light in the alley between the buildings below lit a square on her opposite wall.

"Gotta get this cut off," she muttered, scratching together with one hand the long wet coils of her hair from her neck, pulling them above her head, away from her skin. Moving gingerly a few inches to the left to spread out over a new stretch of sheet, she tried lying still again with a sigh.

It was no use. She rolled onto her back, lying full in the damp, then heaved an inch or two more to the right.

"Well, that done it." Now the whole surface of her bed was wet. As she sat upright, carefully placing her feet on the thongs, a trickle of perspiration ran down her back. She took in a slow deep breath. Like a pressure on her chest, the air frightened her.

"It's not like it was carbon dioxide poison or something. There's still oxygen in it, only it's hot," she reassured herself aloud, finding a comfort in talking to herself, as if she were someone else in the room with whom she was sharing her fears. For she had begun to worry about the air — whether air that thick and dead could be breathed, or whether like a miner in a pit, she might fall asleep and never wake up again.

There was no need to worry about falling asleep. The fear of not waking up early to get the rent to Vandernikke was enough to keep her awake. She wanted to be able to give it to him the moment he got in, to make sure nothing would go wrong. Surely there was no reason for anything to go wrong. No matter how she hated this place, what if she lost it? My God!

From down the hall came the sound of rushing water, obliterating the whorling sound of a siren passing outside. Someone was taking a shower to get cool. Straining to hear, she caught the sound of the triangular shower cubicle at the end of the hall as well. She rose, crossed the room to the sink and let the water run, holding her hands, her wrists and as much of her forearms as possible under the lukewarm trickle. Then, soaking her facecloth in the water that never became cooler, she returned to the bed, lay down with the cloth on her forehead dripping onto the sheet beneath. As the water dried, it gave a faint sensation of coolness there on her forehead. The facecloth became warm. She turned it over, felt the momentary cool once again. Then she spread it over the whole of her face and lay still, feeling the water dry. But she had to take it off her face after a while, when it too became smothering heat bearing down.

Returning to the sink, she doused the cloth in water again, then swathed it over the whole of her body. Down her back, down her arms, over her breasts, her stomach, her thighs, the water ran in trickling droplets to the floor, and as it evaporated on her skin, the relieving coolness came again. But by the time she reached the bed, her skin was feeling tight, slightly prickly where the water had dried, hot and sensitive to abrasion. For what seemed like half an hour she held off, then returned to the sink and did it all again. It would be the last time. Her facecloth smelt leathery, and now when she applied it to her skin, a foreign smell lifted off her, as if she had lathered herself from a cake of dried animal sweat.

She raised her watch to the window light and groaned. It wasn't even midnight yet — hours to go before dawn. She tried to think about the beech tree, raising her head to the window to refresh her memory of it, but she couldn't see it there beyond the garish circle cast by the alley light's gleam. She tossed again. The tightness of her skin had been relieved by her own perspiration. It was difficult to think of anything with concentration. Her body tossed ceaselessly, trying to find a bearable spot on the soaking sheet. If it weren't for the disco below, she might have ventured outside to sit on the stairs, but by the noise it was reaching a peak hour down there. The stairs would be overrun by more of the startling people she'd seen before, some of them dressed as if they were going to a masquerade. In Beaufort, in a heat like this, she could always have gone outside to sit on the porch or taken a walk under the moon. But there was no escape here, no safety in the streets outside. She couldn't even sit on her window pane, for neither window could be forced open wide enough to permit a body to pass through. She was trapped.

Slowly her thoughts became random, dissociated, the way images pass in a dream — her mother's face, Louise's, giving way to enchanted faces of people from the disco below, Jeffry's death mask, then her mother's face again, passing before her wraithlike, meaningless, so distant and unknowable that it seemed there was no one, no one whose recollection could beat back the miasma that overwhelmed her in the toxic darkness of that stifling room. She gave in to the disintegration, let it go on, drifting deeper and deeper into that whorling strangeness that had terror on its outer rings, terror in the centripetal pit, an impersonal diffused terror that numbed rather than aroused, the ringing of an ocean in her ears ...

Suddenly she was absolutely lucid. Raising her watch again to the light, she saw an hour had passed. Had she slept? Surely not, and yet it seemed as if one part of her consciousness, snapping to clarity, had caught another deeper consciousness in the act of probing a problem in a lucid way all the while that she herself, so to speak, had lain sunk in oblivion. As if She were still there when she wasn't, going on intensely about something without her waking self knowing. Oh, oh it was strange.

The heat hadn't let up a bit. She twisted onto her stomach, carefully stretching her arms onto the sheet above her head rather than letting them hang over the side of the bed where, if they touched the floor, roaches might run up her fingers from below. But it wasn't just the roaches. She had the feeling — *ridiculous!* — that there was something lurking under the bed, something that would grab her arm and pull her under if she let her hand down. She hadn't been afraid of something like that since she was twelve. She raised herself on the bed, thrashed about in a fury in the darkness. If this heat were a thing, she'd tear it in two. She'd throw it against the wall. She'd knock its head against the sink until it was broken and smashed. Until it gave out and left her alone — She sank back down, her body racked with sudden harsh sobs.

Lord if only she were home. All this and no job. What would happen when her money ran out? And how to go home? How to say the job with the government she had bragged about so no one would worry had suddenly just faded away? They would believe that surely, with so many people getting laid off that it was almost surprising to think of anybody getting hired any more. Was it a crime to go home? Tears stung her eyes again. How to go home and see the disappointment in their eyes, hear the complaints as everybody moved back down in the beds. They thought of her as gone by now. It was better for everybody that she was. There was more all around with her gone. Maybe she could even help out if she got a job. What if George Sanderson ever managed to sell the house and they all had to move out? What if Mums lost the part time work at the Post Office? What if somebody got sick? She had never seen so clearly how they were hanging by a thread back there.

Christ! Christ! Now that she'd been in the room for hours, the air was worse than before, heated by her body, poisoned by her breath. Her bones were starting to ache. All up and down the bed, creaks and folds seamed the sheet like crevices in a dried river bed except that the sheet was wet. Everywhere she touched, it was wet. She rose to her knees, pressed her nose to the window's narrow opening, breathed in the thin stream of air that was imperceptible two feet away from it. For several minutes her face strained against the crevice ensured by her dinner knife jammed in the window frame above, then slowly her body melted back down onto the bed, her arms falling over the side. Let grab her what might, she didn't care. The sense of miasma overcame her again.

And so it went in cycles, hour after hour of fitful tossing dreams broken by moments in which she was lucid enough to observe angrily that she still hadn't slept, until around four in the morning a jet of air from the window swept over her, sweet and balming as a sigh, and a deep sleep released her at last. Outside the sky whitened in the east to the chitter of birds, and the light in the alley below blinked off.

Two hours later the sky was an irradiated blue and the heat was on the rise again. Bleerily Abby-Jean awoke, threw back the sheet she had pulled up, then sank into sleep again, unable to pull herself out of it now that it had finally come. An hour later when the sun cast a bold white stripe across her face, she reversed herself on the bed, lying face down where her feet had been. There would be no more sleep. The bank! Just as well! She was trembling. When she moved her head, the entire room reeled. Sitting upright, she ran her comb through her hair, its teeth catching in tangles that dried sweat and the water from her facecloth had stiffened overnight. Not taking the time to wash, she dressed and staggered outside.

As the residence door chunked shut behind her, she took a long deep breath. The violent throbbing in her head seemed to pulse through her body. Going down the stairs, she gripped the railing to steady herself, taking more deep breaths as she went along, as if the fresher air in her lungs could eliminate the melting uncertainty in her knees. Already the traffic was heavy in the streets. She stood a moment on the last stair, watching an old man shuffle down the street in front of her. With each step, his feet moved a scant three inches. He too, she felt certain, had come from a place like hers, driven to seek the morning freshness outside. Others like herself — fleeing their rooms — she saw them everywhere.

Moving down the street toward the rotary, she passed out of the shade of the building and into the fluid eye-shattering sunlight. She struggled forward, her eyes riveted to an empty bench in the rotary island. If she were going to faint, it would be better to do it over there. Her head like a bird wheeling down the air by a cliffside. A police car passed as she tottered along, and she straightened up shakily. Lord knew what they'd think she'd been up to the night before, with the case of the shakes that she had now. Was her dress zipped up all right in back? She'd hardly given it a thought in her rush to get out.

She made it to the bench and sat down. A lucky thing. It was the last bench free in all the wide circle of benches in the rotary island, some occupied by still sleeping men, others by single people sitting alone or in twos or threes, gazing distantly toward the sky through the shade-bearing trees. Out on the dusty grass in the circle's center, two black men lay asleep in a sprawl so contorted they might have been men who had fallen when shot. In all the bleery ring there wasn't the sound of a voice, just the early morning traffic swirling round on all sides, air-conditioned cars passing by with their windows rolled up. The relief they breathed in was as private as grief.

There was a rustle in the grass as one of the sleeping men hunched himself up on one arm and shook his head. She could almost hear his ears ringing from where she sat, restlessly chipping at the wood of the bench. His nose was running and his face beaded with sweat. It took away a little from the envy she'd had of the men's freedom to sleep out where the air got cool. She watched him closely. He was as oblivious to his exposure as if he were totally alone — leaning back, groaning, watching the traffic pass, hearing the sound of it, the sound of air-conditioning from a spray of sources mixing to a faint continuous numbing hum that made the air alive as a swarm of locusts, beating down on the only silence within it, that silence deep and resounding inside him. He shook his head again.

Time to get on. She picked herself up, propelled herself down the street, pausing to buy a banana from one of the street vendors that dotted Connecticut, their tables assembled in the early twilight hours to catch the morning rush. Nearing K Street, she saw a solitary man who had been standing against a white marble wall step out purposefully in the path of a passerby. The two steps he took forward reminded her of the kid's game, Mother-May-I? "Yes, you may take two GIANT steps forward —" and the player took one swooshing step, balanced a second, then took another, drawing herself up smartly after the distance Mother allowed had been covered. Ahead of her, the encounter took no more than a second, was followed by the man regaining his place at the wall by two giant steps back. There was a military precision about it, as if it were planned and executed rather than done haphazardly, as if the man cleared himself off the street afterwards rather than hang adrift.

When he stepped out again to approach a man carrying a briefcase, she saw he was begging, and her hand started scratching around in her purse. She heard his soft Southern voice say, "Suh, 'm hongry," that was all, his case simply and objectively stated and no more. The man with the briefcase slapped his pockets impatiently and shrugged, wheeling on by. The words sent a little electric flash through her. Lord, if he was hungry, surely she had something left, a quarter — But the beggar, on the backswing of his routine, had returned to his place at the wall. She glanced at him hesitantly. He didn't seem to see her. A short solidly built man, he reminded her of one of Billie Lyman's sons, one of the tomato growers from the Islands. It made her feel bad to just pass on by when she'd found that quarter now, but how to hang around waiting when he was staring persistently in the other direction? She couldn't just go over and give it to him.

She slipped into the bank around the corner, sighing as the air-conditioned cool enveloped her, then glancing down as she met a teller's eyes. Lord, it seemed that anybody with a job could make her feel bad these days. And here she was, after all, the holder of a bank account. How many of the people she had known had ever held one, instead of cashing their checks in the check-cashing store? The bad side was: every time she wanted money, they checked her account to see if enough was there. Every time they got to read the steadily declining amount. Before every withdrawal, there was the little argument over whether she was herself when her ID proved insufficient. This time, as the teller handed her a little piece of paper with her balance printed on it so only she and the teller would know how bad it was, the shock made tears start to her eyes. She pulled out a kleenex, sneezed into it, covering her face.

"You sure this is right? I figured I had more than that. I just know I had more."

The teller put the slip in the machine again, and the figure repeated itself.

"How much more?"

"Five dollars at least!"

There was a substantial pause before the teller said impassively, "Maybe you added it up wrong."

"Yah I guess. I guess it had to be me." Abby-Jean's eyes flashed. Maybe it was her, it probably was, but then maybe it wasn't, what about that? She wanted to fight somebody, she felt mean, she didn't care if she was right. Five dollars less! Whenever she looked around for someone to blame for all her misery, it seemed there was only her standing there. A machine, who could argue with that? Like the air in her room last night.

She stuffed the little bundle of cash that was the rent into the billfold section of her wallet, put $20 for the week into the changepurse, then fled the bank. She wouldn't be able to pay the rent for much longer. What would happen then? Would they come and jerk her out as Alex Vandernikke had forewarned? What about the welfare she had applied for? THe hateful thought of getting it was turning into abject fear that she wouldn't, that they'd be able to turn up some reason out of all their rules.

Turning off K Street, she spied the beggar still at his post, shoulders erect, hands at his sides. A Southerner all right, she could tell from the way he begged: politely, keeping his dignity. You couldn't tell a Northerner begging from somebody holding you up, according to Louise. Feeling a small swell of pride both at the South and at the shrewdness of her observation, she walked past him slowly this time so that he would have a chance to see her, holding the quarter ready in her hand so she could give it and run. God would see her giving it and spare her from coming to this. One of Billie Lyman's boys in a tight spot like this, somebody from Beaufort, oh Lord —

She walked past as slowly as she could, he saw her, and yet he didn't budge from his post by the white marble wall. Maybe he didn't feel like begging any more, she thought, maybe he'd had enough. But just as she passed, she glanced back to see him take the two steps forward again, intercepting a man in a three-piece suit coming out of the bank behind her. The man dodged out past him without so much as a glance, holding his flaring suit jacket in towards his body with one hand momentarily in case it got touched. The three words "Suh, 'm hongry" seemed to evaporate in the traffic. He took his two steps back to the wall.

He only begged from men! She could hang around on the corner for an hour and he'd never ask her for a dime. No matter what kind of trouble he was in, he wasn't going to start approaching women. This other way — she could see how he had it worked out — it was more like a business encounter between men: take it or leave it. There was no pleading in his abrupt return to the wall.

Yet they barely saw him. All the care and planning and dignity of it was lost on them. They brushed on by and the three words meant nothing to them. Probably they thought he was lying or a drunk. They wanted to think that, they had to think that — how else to pass right on by? And never think of him afterwards, go on home to lunch or dinner, to pack it away, never giving him a thought after that brief second of irritation when he burst in on their consciousness, never asking what they would do themselves if it ever came to that. To see somebody begging, somebody wretched, miserable, needing, was normal to them. Nobody batted an eye.

She felt a thrill of fear. She would remember him, that was for sure. She would never forget him, never! He should beg like a Northerner! Maybe it wouldn't take long for him to learn.

Reaching the residence office, she glanced at her watch. Surely it wouldn't matter if she dodged back to her room to wash up before taking in the rent? She wanted to get her face washed before handing Alex Vandernikke the money. If it were unwashed, he would know. As she heaved open the residence door, the dead heat came at her like bad breath. She chugged on through it, up the stairs to her room.

There was a piece of paper wedged in her door. There were two! She pulled out the card, reading on the outside "If you lived to be 100..." then inside "You couldn't be sweeter than you are today. Happy Birthday!" It was signed "Elizabeth and Margaret" in the handwriting of one of them. No doubt Louise had told them last night, and one or both of them got out early in the morning for the card. She grinned broadly. Imagine that, them getting her a card when they barely knew her. Avidly she reached for the second paper, her glance focusing on it sharply when it didn't come away with her first casual jerk. Its stiff paper was cut so that it could be securely hung around a door knob. Bending over, she read the message printed on it incredulously, an announcement to the world: LOCK CHANGED DUE TO NON-PAYMENT OF RENT.

Whoosh, the prickly heat came up from her toes, up under her armpits, under her ears at the back. Look at the thing they'd done! Like calling her a criminal in front of everybody! Who would ever know she'd gone to the office the night before and tried to pay? That she'd tried to pay and they hadn't let her and now they'd done this, changed the lock on her room the very next morning without giving her so much as the chance to get to the bank and back. Whoever might have seen the thing in passing would remember it again whenever they saw her coming out her door. Her heart beat rapidly.

114

How was it that here she'd done nothing wrong and still they'd made her feel so ashamed.

As she burst into the residence office, George Waddell glanced up at her, grinning widely, wiping one hand on the khaki shirt spread smooth as the skin on a boil over his belly, leaving faintly discernible fingermarks crisscrossing fingermarks that had been left there before. She leapt forward to the desk and began pouring her grievance out.

"I never even hadda chance. The other hand-washin' guy knew I was goin' to pay, I told him Word of Honor —" Her eyes narrowed; maybe that was it. "You change the lock on a person's door quicker 'n a fox snatchin' eggs. Here I was out gettin' the money too, the very moment you're up there changin' the lock, think of that! I even come in here with a check last night like you took before but no — he won't take it, an' if you will an' he won't, then there's no good reason 'cept he hates me."

George Waddell was watching her, a smile on his face.

"It ain't fair, it just ain't fair. You do somethin' like that an' I'm gonna — I don't know what — but it ain't fair," she dropped off weakly. She should never have started out mad and demanding. If he held that against her, what could she do? What could she do about whatever he decided?

"Did you try to get into your room?"

"Why should I try to do somethin' like that when the Notice is right there hung around the doorknob tellin' me my key won't fit the lock?" She thought how she should have brought tne Notice with her. That would have made it plain enough. "Look, I got the money right here in my purse. Will you please let me have the room back?"

"You like that room, huh?" He chuckled.

"Who's sayin' that? All I'm sayin' is I want it back."

He grinned at her, resting his elbows on the desk, the knuckles of his clasped hands knocking against it lightly.

"You gotta give me my stuff back at least. I got clothes in there. You can't just lock up a person's clothes. It's the same as stealin'. I gotta get in." She was on the verge of tears, thinking how maybe she was going to lose her clothes as well.

"We never changed the lock."

"What?"

"Nah. We just stuck on the Notice."

She stared at him.

"You could've got in if you'd tried."

"Then what've you been doin' lettin' me run off at the mouth? Why didn't you tell me right off?"

He looked back at her through half-closed eyes, still grinning.

"Oh, like to get a reaction. It always tickles me. You'd be surprised how some of 'em react. You never know what some of 'em are ready to do."

The last sentence trailed in the air as he watched her, one hand pressed against the khaki bulge of his stomach, leaving more sweat marks there. The small portable electric fan seated atop the mailbox pigeon holes turned slowly from left to right, the current of air skimming directly across his head causing the hair combed from deep right to left over his baldness to lift in frail waving tendrils. He was grinning at her as if it were all a big joke and yet something had changed. She was aware of his power now.

Silently she took out her wallet and paid, her ears ringing, the sound of the commercial coming from the small radio on the desk in the inner room filtering in meaninglessly: *It's the Ree-ull Thing...* Her lips muttered the words *Coke* is under her breath without her thinking as she counted off the five tens, the four ones, her mind a preoccupied blank through which the commercial flowed as if it were a shirt slipping down a laundry chute, dropping indiscernably atop a discarded pile of *You deserve a break today, Makes you feel squeaky clean, and Dodge trucks are RAM tough.*

Opening the office door, she emerged into the hot sunlight again and stood staring at the door to the residence. She didn't want to go back up there. Let the Notice stay on her door. Whoever didn't know all that was about would likely find out soon enough, Notices on their own doors, each Notice serving as a threat to everyone who read it as she passed on by. Her stomach convulsed. What had others been ready to do? What had they maybe gone ahead and done?

She strode off down the street in a tumult, her head bent low, long oily strands of yellow hair straggling over her cheek, reminding her by their abrasion of how she hadn't washed. She was going to cry right there on the street. First the fear of fainting, then of begging, and now this, crying on the street as the concrete hissed and glared under the torrid sun, the street grit blew in little stinging jets against her bare legs, and people came at her from every direction and butted on by. Toyotas passed, Fords, Oldsmobiles, a long low white El Dorado with its spare tire like an elegant brooch on the back, a black man with an elegant white hat, worn aslant, at the wheel. The lustrous spreading beech trees, the oaks, the magnolias bursting around and over bricks and pavement, sweating scent and reaping a glaze of dust. The blare of passing traffic, of delivery trucks being loaded, unloaded, the hum and drone of air conditioners, voices, radio, TV, a barrage of words, of signs: Lady Clairol, Players Mild.

She was scudding along, her hair an oily mass flung over her back, head held up high to catch the welling tears in the pockets of her eyes and keep them there. So hot. She was stinking, surely. Yet she kept on. She was going somewhere, she was going to get there, where she didn't know, bedevilled, purposeful, pushing on past half-open windows throttled with air conditioners, hot condensation drops splatting on the sidewalk and evaporating in seconds, full open windows with stained curtains sucked in over cluttered ledges, weeds and high bushes spiking up the contoured brick, on past monuments, past wire litter cans brimming with styrofoam cups, waxpaper, a torrent of flies zinging in, humming, darting pearled wings coming to rest an instant, a feverish crawling, then off in a zinging cycling furor again.

Across the street she spied it. She cut across toward it without hesitation as if it had been her conscious destination all along, pausing only briefly to glance at a little notice board out front where white removable letters on a black background under glass proclaimed : AND HIS NAME IS LOVE. Underneath, the hours for morning and evening prayers were posted. All that was visible of the church was the side of a wall of large brown bricks; the rest of the contours of the building were obliterated by other buildings crowding in on all sides.

She walked in along a dark corridor with a wooden floorboard, grit in the seams of the planks. It smelled of human sweat and dust, as if people had been exercising or playing some sport or holding a meeting. There were no windows along the corridor; it was dark, mostly cool. Tiptoeing, she banged into a metal-legged plywood table, her fingers running along the chipped surface to guide her forward. In the far corner of the room she peered into, there was an arch-shaped window through which light pierced, and at the end of a row of old-style pews, a dais with a lectern for the preacher. She walked a few steps into the room, decided God wouldn't mind she was a Baptist, and sat down.

Her hand reached into the wooden shelf nailed to the pew in front of her, hesitated between the Song Book and the New Testament, and pulled out the latter, glancing at it, her eyes coursing rapidly over the passage "Now Herod the tetrarch heard of all that was done by him and he was perplexed, because it was said of some that John was risen from the dead..." She stared at it for a few moments, flipped over a few pages, tried to read, then put the book down.

"Listen —"

The word echoed. She shrank into herself.

"Listen, I'm an okay person, huh? I am."

Throughout the bare dusty room, there wasn't a sound.

"I'm not tryin' to say I ain't a sinner or that I'm perfect or nothin'. But surely I ain't all that bad? I just can't believe that I am."

A fly hit the solitary arched window at the front of the room then spun away, the sharp ping reinforcing the silence.

"Since I come up to Washington, this feelin' started to creep over me an' I can't seem to shake it off. I'm startin' to feel bad about me somehow. I'm gettin' ashamed when I can't see a thing I done wrong. It's like feelin' disreputable, like there's somethin' in the air, some kind of tarnish comin' down on me. But I'm a good person, I believe that I am."

Suddenly the feeling was hurtling through her and her eyes stopped talking to the vacant air high above the lectern and flashed toward the empty pews, the corridor, the outside buildings, the crowded streets beyond.

"*As good as them others* —"

The words seemed to rocket about the room.

"Ain't I?" she whispered. "I need to find somebody to stick on my side."

A police siren started up on the street outside, quickly leaping up octaves in a whirling howl that eddied away into the distance. Abby-Jean's head tilted to one side, listening as the first accusative shriek became mournful then died out.

○

Abby-Jean could hear everything. How could she help it, with her chair right up against the wall (except for the six-inch dropping/leaping roach zone), and the speaker in the next room leaning against the wall and talking so loud? Even overhearing hadn't turned to listening for quite a while, as the second voice's responses dropped into the occasional silence — "Yaaas, *uh-huh, uh-huh,*" and "Praise the *Lord!*" — made the conversation sound like a Bible-study session. But there was something about the first voice — a reasoning and arguing tone that might carry on for five minutes or so before getting louder and hotter and then leaping off into a question (followed by the inrushing murmur of the second voice, anxious to please, "Thass right, praise God," "Blessed Gee-zus") — that made her stop to really listen to what she couldn't help having heard.

"—wish you'd just stop and think a minute about what I'm telling you, Mrs. Jackson, because when they come around to put the question to you — You ought to understand what it means. Look —"

When the voice became kind, it was harder to hear, dropping down gently, encouragingly. Affected by this empathy, the second voice blurted suddenly, "Y'aw a good gal, some boy gonna love y'aw for thet one day!"

"—Mrs. Jackson — Thanks. But what I'm trying to say to you, and this is important, is that the stock of low-rental housing units in the city is going down. Destroying buildings which presently provide housing for — A hundred? Are there a hundred women in here?

"Thass right, honey. Thass what y'aw said."

"Destroying buildings like this to make room for what? A hotel? Some development project, who knows what? And think, down the street there's another building gone, and across the street another, and two blocks up, another, and two blocks across, another. And every time I've said another, how many people —" She paused for breath. Her voice had gotten high, but when she went on, it was low and regular again. "Have to find somewhere else, don't you see? Maybe a lot of folks leap at some free rent or whatever in return for leaving, but where are they all going to go, think of that."

There was a moment's silence. Abby-Jean pictured old Mrs. Jackson leaning forward on her chair, her brown eyes so distant they seemed almost blue, making her look like she was remembering something from a very distant past, something drenched in mist and wonder. Each brown hand with its folds of wrinkles would be clamped onto the arms of her chair as she swayed forward gently, eager to return interest for interest, kindness for kindness.

"And think," the speaker took up again, "I'm still only talking about a small area downtown, and already you can see a trend that puts hundreds on the street, hundreds. Thousands of people, when you think of it going on all across the country, maybe millions in time to come. Some of those people are out there right now, sleeping in doorways, in the parks, flat out on the sidewalks —"

"Hallelujiah! Lord, it's a sin!"

"It's a *crime*. Why isn't there enough decent housing when folks are so in need? Who makes the policy decisions? What are their interests? Are they the same as ours? Any number of things in this world can be done, it's just a question of priorities, of who's deciding what the priorities are, of where they're sitting when they look out on the world."

The voice kept up a steady stream, its reasonableness rising from time to time to fever pitch, then restrained, disciplined into reasonableness again. It kept interrupting Abby-Jean as she was trying to think of something nice that might happen sometime, kept prodding at her through the wall as if expecting a *Praise God!* from over here. And every time she figured the woman had had enough, she'd draw in a big breath, say *Think* —, then ratta-tat-tat, she was off again.

Abby-Jean began to drift. She stared out her window to the window across the way where people kept passing up and down the stairs. Where was Louise? Margaret? Anybody? The heat was getting so bad nobody came home until as late as possible. Her luck to have missed them all going out, and be left here to suffocate, sitting drenched in the darkness waiting for the cool to fall. Across the way, a light went out, and the small yellow oblong cast through her window across her bed and onto the floor disappeared.

But what was that? She craned, half-rising on the bed to see more clearly.

"When you think of what could be done, Mrs. Jackson, that's when you know there's a crime going on. Are there things that need to be done? Building low cost housing, schools, roads, public recreation? Sure. Are there folks that can do it? Sure. Millions of people are aching for a job, eating out their hearts and wasting their lives because the capacities they have aren't being used. What about materiel. This is the richest nation in the world, and yet steel mills, lumber mills are closing down —"

What *was* that? What was that over there on the floor where the yellow oblong of light had been? Abby-Jean stood up, her feet swiftly, automatically, slipping into her thongs. It was another square of light, paler, not stretching so far into the room, its' source evidently not the building across the way. She approached, gazing out the window and up.

"Think. There are so many things that need to be done, so many people wanting to work, so much natural wealth in the country waiting to be used and developed. Being suppressed from use, even. What can it be that's stopping it, then?"

The moon! There was the moon, so high up in the sky that it was almost directly overhead! Naked, Abby-Jean drew near the window and gazed up at it. When the moon was highest in the sky, its light was strongest, outlining in silver all the dark shapes below, irradiating the silent sky with its pale eerie calm. And when the stars were out, when the sky was crowded, fiery with stars — in Beaufort anyway — Here there was just the moon —

"Think. All the basic ingredients for doing something are here — the needs, the people to do it, the materials to do it with. It's just a matter of getting it organized fluidly, you'd think. It's so simple surely, and yet they keep telling us it can't be done. What is it? What keeps holding it back?"

Abby-Jean stood full in the square, and the moonlight fell over her like silver rain — over her naked shoulders, her breasts, the taut protrusion of her stomach, her sturdy legs slightly convex from thigh to knee, slightly concave from knee to ankle. Down along her lower legs, the hair stood out starkly, sending rivulets of shadows shooshing down her legs like ocean waves after a departing sea. And across her arm as the gooseflesh came out: granulated ribbles of moon on sand. Turning halfway back, she caught her image in the mirror above the sink, the silver outline of upturned breasts, her square back arched into grace. Oh! Oh! Was there ever anything so ghostly beautiful? Oh!

"Things get done when they're in the interest of the rich. If they threaten their interest, the rich put a stop to them. That's all it is."

And he saw me, Abby-Jean was thinking. *And he said, you're beautiful. And he took my hand* — she lowered herself out of the moonlight square —

Lord it drove her crazy, that nagging voice! Even if it didn't really have a nagging tone, even if it was calm and reasonable and only saying things that seemed obvious and somehow startling, she was in no mood to hear. It was hard to have anything against rich people when she wouldn't mind being one herself. They had such beautiful things, she saw from the TV, that it made you want to get to know

120

them, to hang around with them. And even if that didn't happen, still she didn't want anybody thinking she was envious of their good luck, or greedy, or some kind of a poor sport.

"Think. Why do people live in a place like this? Because it's cheap? But it's not. Because it's so nice? Why."

The heat was bad enough, but to have a voice constantly trumpeting through her thoughts when she was trying to think of something nice, air conditioners or wind or — *Because they can't find anything else,* she wanted to holler.

"Because they can't find anything else."

"Praise God."

What business was it of hers, somebody blowing in from God knew where, trying to make them all feel ashamed, as if they didn't know how bad it was already? Suddenly Abby-Jean felt a warmth toward the decaying building that enemies within a family feel for each other when attacked from outside. This was her place, her life in here. What right did an outsider have to come and say it was no good?

"And whose interest is that in. Do you think the people who own this building, all the people who own buildings like these, want to see more low-cost housing ease the market? As long as it's tight, they can still squeeze rental blood from these stones until something better comes along. Every week, every month, year after year, people have to scramble to come up with money for rent, and there's no getting away from it ever — all just to pay for the pain of living here. When tenants have nowhere else to go, why should the owner bother with repairs? Why on earth let cheap government housing get built that would drive their rents down? Why build cheap housing themselves, when the real money is in building for the rich?"

Abby-Jean squirmed on the bed. The voice in the next room had gotten hot again. Somehow she felt as if she were being attacked. Who was there, after all, to endure all this but herself and Mrs. Jackson? She hated it when anyone pounded at her with something... And there was Mrs. Jackson nodding and rocking in her stationary hard-backed chair, saying "Thaas right, honey, y'aw a good sweet chile."

The voice laughed breathlessly. "I guess I get a little carried away."

"*Thaas right!*"

"Sorry. I try to watch it. But when you know what's going on —"

"Don't y'aw love to holler, honey? Ah know y'aw does. *Hallelujiah!*"

Abby-Jean grinned as Mrs. Jackson let out a whoop straight out of her belly. Lord, it sounded like it felt good, a great big heave of the voice, busting like a water balloon on the surrounding air. For a few minutes after, there was nothing but whoops coming from the next room, the visitor's whoops taking on more diaphragm as she practised under the instruction of a master. Abby-Jean listened hankeringly until at last the session dissolved in laughter.

"Ah-ah— Mrs. Jackson, I don't know."

"Go on, gal. Y'aw knows it all, aintch'aw been tellin' me?"

"Seriously, seriously —"

She would be wiping away tears of laughter, Abby-Jean thought. Maybe she wasn't so bad.

"To think that people have to live this way in the 20th century, Mrs. Jackson, when They're going to the moon."

"Nessie."

"What?"

"Y'aw call me Nessie."

"Short for Agnes?"

"Nestoria."

"Wow."

They talked about the name, the history of it, for a minute or two, then their voices lowered and Abby-Jean heard only the unmistakable click of snapshot on snapshot.

"But to get back to the point, Nestoria. You know, talk about crazy, sometimes I — Here I am sitting in your room, one moment saying it's terrible that people should be forced to live in a place like this, and the next minute arguing how we have to fight so you can go on living here. How we can prevent the owner of this building from selling out and getting it torn down?"

Abby-Jean craned toward the wall. Torn down? This building here? Somebody should have told her about that, you'd think?

"I go through these places and I think: This is what we're trying to save? These rat traps? Look at this building here anyway. It's hard to believe it can be saved. It ought to be torched, torn down, burned to the ground, and if the owner doesn't do it for the insurance, we should. It makes me feel — I don't know — crazy —"

"Aw now, y'aw don't want to feel bad. Here, here now, y'aw don't want —" Mrs. Jackson rushed in concernedly.

Abby-Jean put her ear flat against the wall. Now that she wanted to hear more, for a long while there was no sound from the next room.

"How can you be free when control of something as vital as your shelter is in the hands of somebody else, who's using your need to extort money. How free when you're scared all the time something's gong to happen so you can't pay the rent — like losing a job or getting kicked off some program. Or the owner raising the rent, raising it, raising it, until there's no way you can pay. You know what I mean?"

"It's a terrible thing."

"And even if you paid it year after year after year, one day he decides to go condo, and where are you then?"

"Y'aw straight in the hands of the Lord."

"You're straight in the hands of the landlord."

There was an abrupt frustrated silence.

"Mrs. Jackson —"

"Y'aw a good sweet —"

"We just can't let it happen. We have to fight for some control over it. We have to keep this building. Get it renovated. Build more —"

Abby-Jean sat up in her chair. All her struggling to get out of the women's residence when in truth she'd have to fight just to stay on? Even this little room, as if it were on rolling pins, silently, imperceptibly sliding out from under her. All the while the rolling pins turning, all the while herself thinking she was racing along them trying to get up to some better perch, when in fact she was racing, racing, just to keep from being thrown off and into the street. Surely they couldn't just throw a person out on the street, leave them sitting on the sidewalk where everybody could see what they'd done? Surely they couldn't consciously, knowingly, shove a person out who had nowhere to go? But if they found some other way to drive you out, that didn't make it look as if it was Them — She sank back into the chair. Even if she found a place, the loss of this phone would wipe out the job-hunting effort of weeks. It couldn't happen! She closed her eyes tightly, rigid with the conviction that it could. Her eyes began to smart. What was wrong with Them anyway? Couldn't they see how hurtful they were? Surely that had to be it. They didn't know?

"Anyway, you have to realize, if they come to make you some kind of an offer to leave —"

"Y'aw sech a nice gal, gonna he'p y'aw out best Ah kin."

"It's *not me*, Mrs. — But thanks. *Thanks.* I really appreciate your letting me talk to you. Some of the other women don't want to hear about it at all. They don't want to think about it because they don't think they can —"

"Folks got a lot on they minds."

"Yes..."

Mrs. Jackson's door shut, then Abby-Jean heard knocking on a door further down the hall. After a minute's pause, the knocking began again further down. On it went, as the visitor worked her way down the hall then across, back along the other side without a door being opened. Maybe she didn't know people stayed out as late as they could to avoid sweating like the walls here inside? Maybe she thought they were all closing their doors on her. Slipping on a shift, Abby-Jean went to her door, put one eye to the open crack. Across the hall, the visitor stood briefcase in hand, hands behind her back. She looked like she could be living in a place like this too. Her light green blouse was blotched with sweat. As she raised her head to shake her hair away from her face, Abby-Jean saw a streak of grey at her temples wave like a banner back through her short black hair. Mrs. Jackson's girl would be in her forties at least.

Before the woman could glance around and catch her eye, Abby-Jean closed the door. Maybe if the landlord saw he couldn't buy her out, he'd just throw her out on the spot? Even though she'd paid her rent and he couldn't do it, who was to say he wouldn't just the same, and let *her* worry about how it couldn't be done. Maybe she'd be asked to do something embarrassing or frightening? Maybe she and Mrs. Jackson would have to go over and give hell to somebody Big? Her eyes widened. Then They would tell her things — about the law or whatever — and who was she to know if they were true? And if they simply told her, too bad — what then? As the knocking in the hall drew nearer, she began to panic. It was wrong to stir everybody up when there was no chance. People weren't cowards; they weren't fools, either. On the other hand, if they were going to be thrown out anyway, why not get a little something —

There was no sound whatever in the hall. *Snake!* a droplet of sweat streaked down her back. Sweat, not a bug of some kind. She opened the door. Gone. Well, that let her off facing somebody Big. That was a relief.

She felt rotten.

"Hey, Mrs. Jackson? Mrs. Jackson?"

The door opened, and she gazed into the old woman's eyes, so distant that the brown seemed to be turning blue. Or was it cataracts?

"Hope I didn't get you up or nothin'." Abby-Jean stared at the sheaf of gestetnered papers spread out on the bed, interspersed with newspapers showing crowds carrying signs, then glanced at Mrs. Jackson as if she hadn't seen a thing. The old lady's distant eyes seemed to gaze past her — as if they had seen something delightful an aeon ago, and the impression of it still lingered. But it wasn't true. The old woman was fretting, embroiled about something.

"Looka this heah," Mrs. Jackson said, stooping over the papers, her hands moving among them, her ancient fingers inarticulate. She grasped a sheet, glanced at Abby-Jean worriedly, then put it down. Then as if duty bound, she picked it up again.

"Got all this stuff to read, see."

"This is what that lady gave you, huh."

"Y'aw see what it says?"

Abby-Jean glanced at the sheet, her eyes stumbling from "present policy considerations" to "overall effect." She nodded gravely.

"Y'aw wants to read it out?" Mrs. Jackson pressed more paper into her hands, nodding anxiously. "Save us two gittin' in each otheh-one's way. Y'aw do the readin' an' Ah jes' do the listenin' settin' back oveh heah."

Sitting on the bed, Abby-Jean began to read, her tongue stumbling over the difficult words. In the pauses that she took for breath, which were scattered throughout the lengthy sentences with complete disregard for periods, Mrs. Jackson put in "uh-huuuh, uh-huuuh" encouragingly from the corner. Reaching the bottom of the page at last, she stopped even though the sentence finished on one of the other pages spread out on the bed. "Uh-huuh," Mrs. Jackson murmured with finality. They glanced at each other shyly.

"What do it mean?"

"Well it's kind of hard to explain. 'Sides I was readin' it out an' that made it hard to think —"

They lapsed into silence.

"I phoned up a radio talk show once. Was I gonna get a college education, that's what I asked. The man said if I really wanted I would, but it was all up to me. I was thinkin' about it day an' night but I couldn't see no way."

"Y'aw kin make y'sef sick wif it."

"I had to stop thinkin' about it, that's all."

"But y'aw reads purty good, seems t' me."

"Yah, well."

They sighed.

"What you gonna do with these?"

"She were a good sweet gal."

"Next week she's gonna be back askin' you, maybe."

"Git one a' them comin' through once, twice a year," Mrs. Jackson reminisced, settling back in her chair. "They gives some good cause or t'otheh a good try, then they's gone."

Abby-Jean glanced at the papers on the bed. Somehow the urgency seemed to go out of them.

"You think they're really gonna throw us out of here?"

"Could be." Mrs. Jackson's horny wrinkled hands dropped into her lap, her head tilting back against the top rim of the chair.

"I'd like to fight to stop 'em from doin' it," Abby-Jean said. She rolled up the news sheet. She was going to take it with her.

"Shu y'aw would."

"'Course with any luck, I'll have a job an' be out of here any day," she added hopefully.

"Uh-huh, uh-huh. An' wif any luck," Mrs. Jackson's distant brown-blue eyes scanned the ceiling, "Ah be daid."

○

As the girls swept three abreast through the notions department, Yolande stouter than Abby-Jean and Abby-Jean the same amount larger than Lynn, for a moment they looked like three stages in a weight loss commercial. For a moment only, for every time a shopper came toward them, Lynn was forced to fall in behind. Rather than stick back there, she kept darting ahead, talking to the other two walking backwards, or grabbing Abby-Jean's arm and cracking them all like a whip off to one side to look at Norman Rockwellillustrated mugs or sift through a 99-cent panties bin. The trinkets set out for impulse buyers magnetized her, drawing her to candy K rations or tall cloth flowers in plastic beakers labeled "The Eternal Rose" or bubblegum the package inscription claimed LOOKS-LIKE-FRENCH-FRIES. Exclaiming "Cute, ain't it" or "Crappola!", she hummed as her hands scrabbled through the heaps of them, seizing then tiring, discarding, almost faster than the eye could see.

"Lookit this, huh? Bumper stickers with a l'il cracked heart for the stuff ya hate. Like: I hate my homework, I hate Liberals, Environmentalists, Rainy Days." She was reading down the rack. "That's a yuk, huh?"

"'I hate Preppies,'" Abby-Jean read. "What's that, Preppies?"

Nobody knew.

"I hate N.Y.," Yolande read.

"Aw hose me down," Lynn burst. "I gotta have that one. I hate New York! That's me. Fuck, I was born sayin' that. That's my — whatzit? — Motto. Yeah."

"Pipe *down*," Yolande complained.

They stared at her, then glanced about them to see who was looking. Yolande hadn't said so much since the three of them first met outside the residence and started griping about the roaches and the heat. The outburst surprised Abby-Jean, who for many blocks after their meeting had been leary of Lynn, feeling strange walking down the street with a girl who wore a WHITE MEN NEED JOBS TOO T-shirt, and had two-colored red and blonde hair. It made her crowd closer to the prissy Yolande even though Yolande's long-sleeved blouse with randomly somersaulting elephants was making her sweat profusely and exude an intolerable odor of violets. When after many blocks, they still hadn't drifted apart or tried to escape each other, they seemed to settle into being together. No matter how weird they seemed together on the face of things, they had a lot in common living in the same roach-ridden hole, enough to endure through an unbearably hot afternoon. When suddenly Yolande had darted into the climatized air of the department store, the other two had followed her in without a second thought.

"You sayin' I talk too much?" Lynn took up. "Fuck, I race like a train. It's 'cause I'm schizoid, see, sorta blipped out — Ka-joing! I'm crazy. Crazy! I never know what I'm gonna do."

Abby-Jean glanced down at her. Despite all that talk of craziness, she was even less afraid of Lynn than at first.

"Oh rats, here she comes anyway," Yolande complained.

"The floorwalker?" Lynn looked up apprehensively, then whispered "Shit."

"Lena Johnson, that's all. I saw her coming up the street and I thought I'd get away if I dodged in here." Yolande shrugged. "It's probably you she's after anyway."

"I never done a fuckin' thing."

"She wants to *meet* you, that's all."

"Oh yeah? Yeah?"

Lynn was staring eagerly at the huge black woman barreling down on them, an immense royal blue paper flower behind her ear, a small child reeling in tow. As she swept toward them, her eyes rolled from side to side until they seemed to flash, a broad smile fixed on her face that made a point of missing no one upon whom her sunshine might take.

"Come on, let's go," Yolande urged. "Let's not just stand here 'til she runs us down."

"Hey waitaminit. You said this spade chick wants to meet me, right? Fuck, now's her chance. Right? I mean, right?" Lynn was grinning recklessly, bashfully.

"She wants to meet both of you."

"Oh." Lynn's voice dropped.

"Yah?" Abby-Jean piped up.

"For heaven's sake, it's nothing personal," Yolande burst. "She's selling Rexall Nine Products, that's all."

"Geez, why'nt ya say it straight out. Christ Almighty," Lynn fumed.

"What's —" Abby-Jean broke off, tagged after them, glancing over her shoulder apologetically as Lena swept in.

They scattered through rows of head scarfs, nail polish and curlers just as the royal blue wave with its tiny tottering wavelet seemed about to crash upon them, before the words "Hiyall Yolandey, honey —" could spray all over them, and regrouped in the record department.

"You could've said hello," Abby-Jean accused. "What's wrong with hello? That was mean."

Yolande's plump under-chin seemed to tremble, the round soft swell of it giving her face the shape of a pear. She pursed her lips and said nothing. A wave of violets struck Abby-Jean again.

"Aw, them Rexall Nine people, they bug ya an' bug ya. Ya couldn't hold 'em off with a stick. There's nothin' to do but split," Lynn cut in. "They tell ya all this stuff about how ya can be millionaires too like they're gonna be. Zillionaires. Quadrupla-stupefyin'-multi-multi's."

"I think it's fifty thousand dollars," Yolande clarified. "Part time a year. If you work real hard." She sniffed.

"What's so wrong with that?" Abby-Jean demanded. It sounded good enough to her. She glanced around. Maybe Lena would catch up with them yet. She was willing to talk.

"She lives in a hole just like us," Yolande said.

"A hole just like us an' a zillionaire. That's a yuk."

"I never even thought of that until later. When I was in church two weeks ago, I saw her looking around at me with this great big smile, and I thought she was being friendly, that's all. Nobody else was paying any attention to me. Nobody else came up and said, 'Aren't you new?' I was dying for somebody to talk to, just for a little while, and she asked me back for some cake. I was thinking how maybe we could be friends. That's what I was thinking the whole time. We went back to this grubby little place with the kid lying sick on the bed, and us two crammed round this big store-bought chocolate cake, drinking diet coke. I wouldn't have taken the cake," Yolande fastidiously brushed invisible crumbs from the two heaves beneath the blouse that were her breasts, "But that was supposed to be what I'd come for. I couldn't say no, with her so friendly and all." Beneath the excessive modesty of her elephant-tossed blouse and full skirt, even Yolande's body seemed to take on the bottom-heavy roundness of an enormous pear. "When she started in about how Rexall Nine was making her rich, I never thought a thing, not even when she kept on and on. There we were eating the chocolate cake, the kid sick, and all the products out on the table in front of us. I thought she was just talking and showing me, like a friend. Even when she said I could sell Rexall Nine too, I just thought she was pointing out something good. It was making her so rich, she said. Didn't I want to be rich? Well sure, that's what I said."

"They suck up to ya, that's what they do."

"She asked me to a party after. She said to me, 'Don't worry, Yolandey honey, there's gonna be lotsa people like you.' A party. No matter how I was feeling from the cake and diet coke, I got excited. 'Cause I don't go to parties that much."

Abby-Jean nodded emphatically, wondering if there would be another? She was ready to give her eye teeth to go to a party. Parties weren't something you heard much of at the women's residence, while back in Beaufort, in her time —

"When she said the party was Tuesday night, I thought how lucky it was, coming on my night off at Friendly's, that's all. I never thought: how come not on Friday or Saturday?"

"I'm always partyin'," Lynn cut in. "Seven days of the week. I get so bored, that's how come I'm always partyin'. Christ I get bored. Then I party. Then I get more bored. I can't even do dope, ya know what I mean? It shuts me up, what the hell, fuck that. A lotta people want to be ghosts but not me. Not that I give a fuck."

"The party was in a hall. Some people showed up in cars. A lot of the men was dressed up in suits, nearly all of them was."

Lynn glanced at Yolande, then the muscles in her lips skewed tightly to one side. "Not that I give a fuck about a fuckin' thing. It can all blow to screamin' hell and it ain't nothin' but a yawn to me."

She strode off to the Rock section of the record department, leaving Abby-Jean and Yolande standing on the border between Country and Religious.

"I could've felt really awful," Yolande confided. "Coming to a party alone like that. But everybody was looking at everybody else and kind of smiling and a little breathless like me. And nobody was drunk, neither. Nobody was even bringing in alcohol. It didn't look to be that kind of a party so I felt real glad."

Abby-Jean nodded, her fingers ticking through a big stack of discount Country and Western albums. Even at the discount, she couldn't buy one — not that she had a record player anyway. She had nothing, she never could buy anything, it made her want to scream with all this here.

"I saw Lena at the entranceway. She was waiting for me there with two other ladies, I think one was a nurse 'cause she still had her white stockings on. We turned inside, and all the chairs was set out in rows instead of round the edges in a circle, so I saw right then there wasn't going to be dancin'. Wheeuw, that was a relief, I thought. We just filed into the row of chairs, me between Lena and the nurse. When all the rows filled up, this man came out to talk to us. It was like being in church. I thought he was prayin' by the sound of his voice, by the way he made us say after him what he just said, then louder 'cause he couldn't hear the sound of our voices. He says 'I believe I'm an eagle,' then we say I BELIEVE I'M AN EAGLE. 'I believe I can soar.' 'I BELIEVE I CAN SOAR.' When we didn't say it loud enough the first time, he made us say it again. There was folks just beltin' it out as if their lives depended on it. Everybody was hollerin' 'cause he kept egging us on, and everybody seemed kind of on-edge anyways, and ready to let go. And then, there were what looked like prizes on the dais behind him — a dishwasher and a beautiful car."

"Huh," Abby-Jean said, thinking how she would rather dance at a party any day.

"It was all about selling Rexall Nine, that's all."

"Fuck, you call that a party?"

Lynn bobbed in front of them brandishing a record from the Rock section titled *Virgin Killers*. The four band members on the record cover stared out at her like they drank blood. They looked like they were trying to look like girls who wanted to look like boys — gaunt faces, wild lipstick and jagged two-colored long-short hair.

"Lena never said that's what it would be. She said a party, that's all."

"Well, it's something to do."

"Shit," Lynn said. "Here she comes."

"Lena?" Yolande glanced about worriedly.

"The floorwalker. Her." Lynn's elbow pointed toward a sallow woman with heavy glasses who was staring at them from behind the Opera section.

"They don't have floorwalkers any more. They got those." Yolande pointed to the four-directional camera bearing down from the ceiling above.

"You wanna bet?"

Yolande and Abby-Jean stared at the floorwalker anxiously.

"Lemme just put this disc back on the shelf, there," Lynn trumpeted.

Hope nothin' got into my purse somehow, Abby-Jean thought.

Yolande picked up a Mormon Tabernacle Choir album. "I wonder if they got *Saved By Grace* on this."

The floorwalker's fingers flicked mechanically through double and triple albums of Italian operas, tipping the stack like a deck of cards. Head turned to one side, she seemed preoccupied, staring very hard into a space directly to her left. There was nothing in that space at all.

"I bet she was just going to church because there'd be more people to meet," Yolande muttered. "I bet she tries a different church every week to pick someone up. She probably wasn't a member at all. There was hardly no one black in that church but her."

"I don't see what she did that's so wrong," Abby-Jean said stubbornly, keeping her eye on the floorwalker. She dropped the Wailin' Bill Jennings album back in its slot as if it bored her to tears, and for several minutes as Yolande talked, she carried on a private little "See, I got nothin'" charade.

"At the party, the Rexall Nine man explained how it works. It isn't the selling you do yourself that gets you rich. It's getting other people hooked in and taking a piece off theirs. You get richest off of others working for you. You build your Empire on that, on how many you got. *That's* why she asked me. She only wanted to get me out there making money for her."

"Geez, can we get out of here?" Lynn butted in. "That old bat's givin' me the Holy Hey-Soos!"

"Here I thought she wanted to be my friend." Yolande fell in behind them down the aisle.

They passed out of the record department, on into radios, home computers and TVs. Two men lingering in the back doorway to a stockroom glanced up as they approached, then carried on with their conversation.

"Hey lookit this!" Lynn pointed to an immense video screen that transformed television into a home movie theatre. "Ain't that somethin'? A gi-normous 'lovin' TV!"

Abby-Jean stared at it a moment, then her glance wandered down to the string of portable TVs on two shelves, checking to see which had the truest color, then coming to rest, with a sudden pang of longing, on the small black and white set at the end of a row. One hundred dollars. Way out of reach, she thought in a sudden welling of despair.

"I gotta have one of these." Lynn stroked the video system. "Look here, the whole screen pops in and out of this cabinet. All you gotta do is —"

"*Don't touch it,*" Yolande cried, glancing fearfully toward the stockroom.

"Can't find the fuckin' — HEY!"

The two men in the stockroom doorway glanced in their direction questioningly.

"Hey could we get some service over here?"

"Oh come on," Yolande whispered. "Don't let's bother with it now. You can come back and see it some other time."

"Hey anybody workin' over there today? Hey, there's people out here, for fuck's sake."

"You better talk clean," Abby-Jean advised.

One of the salesmen turned his back, disappeared into the stockroom. The other kept talking to him with his back turned to the department floor. The three girls stared at him silently.

Lynn shrugged. "It's this thing here I really go for." Her fingers carressed a miniature TV/tapedeck unit. "You got every damn thing here an' it's a snap to lug it around." She touched it again with longing. "I'm gonna get one of these some day."

"Let's just go, that's all."

"This here is a better deal than that big gabonza over there," Lynn persisted. Suddenly her voice raised. "Fact, I'm gettin' one of these next week down at Radio Shack where they got some *service*."

As the salesman glanced over his shoulder, they filtered quickly back toward the main aisle.

"That fixed him."

Abby-Jean glanced back mournfully, doubting it, glad she hadn't said something like that now she saw how it looked when you did — as if you were the rude one. Preoccupied with the thought, she ran straight into Yolande, who had stopped abruptly in the aisle, seeing Lena sweeping toward them from the record department like a blue fire engine with all its lights flashing.

"You want to take the escalator to the second floor?" Abby-Jean suggested helpfully. "I think they got ladies clothes up there." She wasn't so sure she wanted to meet Lena any more. She didn't mind getting rich, but getting people to let you make money off them sounded like an unpleasant complication. What she really wanted was just to get a job and work, and leave getting rich to those who had the stomach for it.

"Fuck, I always feel weird in the dress department," Lynn muttered. "I always feel like somebody's lookin' to see if my nails are clean."

But Lynn's nails were bitten so far down they couldn't get dirty, Abby-Jean saw.

"I want to go," Yolande said petulantly, striking out in front.

The other two trooped along behind her. Looking back as they went up the escalator, Abby-Jean saw the floorwalker stare up after them, then redirect herself with a heave of the shopping bag she carried. Did that mean there was another one up on the second floor? Or were they free? Maybe if she sold Rexall Nine Products and got rich, she could buy the whole store and that would fix — she shrugged harriedly — everybody.

"I bet ya'd never believe I sold Lady Bright one time," Lynn said.

"Frankly —" Yolande said.

"Sure, hell, they'd let *anybody* sell — 'cause ya gotta buy the kit and that costs a buncha bucks right off. Every poor sucker lookin' for a job can grub together twenty-so bucks to try it. They make a pile on people just wantin' a job."

"I tried to get a job sellin' vacuum cleaners, but it wasn't no good," Abby-Jean said. "They wouldn't give me the job for sure 'less I brought in two sales first. How could I do that? What about your relatives, they said, but I ain't got none in town."

"Even if you sell to your relatives, it runs out after that," Yolande said.

So they all had tried it, Abby-Jean thought. Everybody tried selling, long enough to see it didn't work — unless maybe you were a certain type.

They spread out through the millinery department, placing hats on their heads, posing and grimacing.

"Fuck, people don't wear hats no more." Lynn tossed aside a pillbox-shaped hat.

Abby-Jean had on a small pert hat with a slight mesh veil. I don't know, where would I wear it, she was thinking. Not that she could buy it now, but still she could keep it in mind for someday. She glanced at herself again in the mirror and tore it from her head. It was a ridiculous thing. She'd even like to smack anybody she caught in a snotty little thing like that.

"I wish there was someone here I could ask about this." Yolande had on a bell-shaped hat with a business-like feather. "They never have anybody to help."

"Ya wanna buy it, I'll grab it an' head for the door. That'll bring somebody round."

"I just wanted to *ask*, that's all." Abruptly she replaced the hat on a styrofoam head. "Don't keep *at* me," she burst out. "I can't take people keeping *at* me."

"Me?" Lynn spun on her heel, asking the question to a small cluster of black velvet hats. "Me? Was I doin' that? No I never, I —"

"Oh shut up, dummy."

"Aw who gives a fuck," Lynn muttered, flushing.

"Oh let's go see the dresses," Abby-Jean said crossly. She was in no hurry to return to the scorching heat outside.

As if the same thought had occurred to the others, they crossed the aisle and fell upon the dress racks.

"Look at this!" Yolande exclaimed piteously, pulling out a striped dress.

"What about this!" Abby-Jean seized another. "Nope, this is more you than me, but still —"

The two of them went through the racks feverishly, tossing off remarks like "I love that there, the belt," "What d'you think, this color? Really?" and "No, you gotta be tall, tall an' thin —" as Lynn hovered about aimlessly.

"Did I tell ya I worked for Lady Bright?" she asked.

"You goin' to try those on?" Abby-Jean asked Yolande, who held out a dress in either hand.

"Did you see what they cost?" Yolande whispered.

"Who says we ain't gonna buy one? Who says?"

"I got money in my purse, but it's this week's money for food."

"Well they don't know that. 'Sides, people don't buy all the stuff they try. They never do. People try on twenty things an' never get one."

"But they could. They *could*."

"Look at this. I'm takin' in a blouse, here. A twenty-seven dollar blouse."

"I keep feeling that they know. That everybody's looking at me and thinking: she can't buy that, what's she trying it on for?"

The sweat glistened on Yolande's lips despite the air conditioning.

"It's a free country, ain't it?" Abby-Jean said fiercely. "Well I'm gonna try these."

She took up three more dresses and swept off to the fitting room, leaving Yolande and Lynn trailing behind.

A woman with bleached styled hair intercepted her in the doorway.

"How many?"

She took the dresses out of Abby-Jean's hands to count them, separating each dress from the others in case one should cling hidden to another.

"You can only take in three," she snapped, staring at Abby-Jean's eyes, then her neck, her shift, her bare legs, the glance dropping right down to her thongs.

"Here, you take in this." Abby-Jean handed Yolande the striped dress. "You liked it anyway."

Yolande glanced at the saleslady fearfully as she received a white tag saying ONE.

"I got nothin'," Lynn said sharply as the saleslady approached, then strolled in after them.

There was a loud click as the fitting room door shut.

"Wazzat? What the fuck?"

"She's locked it! She's locked the door!"

They stared at one another. A loud sneeze came from one of the fitting rooms further along.

"It ain't just us," Abby-Jean laughed breathlessly. "They do that to everybody. They got everybody locked in here."

"Makes you feel weird," Yolande said softly.

"Well fuck, *everybody's* a thief."

As Yolande and Abby-Jean got down to business in opposite boothes, Lynn leaned against the wooden partition.

"This one time when I was workin' for Lady Bright. I tell ya about that?"

She glanced at them over the changing room partitions which were only shoulder high. From the boothes came the muffled sound of undressing.

"They give ya a residential district where ya could walk to bloody death without nobody ever openin' the door. With the heat beatin' down and the cosmetics runnin' down yer face, fuck that, I said. Lemme try one of them boo-jie apartment blocks, they maybe got air-conditionin' in the halls, right? I mean, what the hell, I'm sellin' Lady Bright, I got a reason to be there. So I go to the door and ring one of the buzzers. When the lady answers, I throw her the line. This here's yer Lady Bright lady callin'. The door don't buzz open. Fuck that. I spread out two hands and rung all the fuckin' buzzers at the same time, like sendin' a screetch through the place. All it takes is one buzz, and I got it. I was in.

"Straight off two little old ladies come to check me out in the lobby 'cause they heard the door open. 'Who let you in,' they gotta know. F'Chrissake, I was in, wasn't I? What business was it of theirs? 'My friend Sandy up in 315,' I say, figuring there had to be a 315 up there. I was going to take the elevator, but they were on me like two sentries with their warnin' lights goin' off and on. So I took the steps, two at a time. It brung out the smell of Wild Country, the perfume from the sample case I was wearin', the way they told ya to do. Pugh! Ya coulda choked bloodhounds with the smell.

"I ring a doorbell on second. She's starin' at me through two inches of open door, and there's three chains goin' across. 'Lady Bright callin',' I says. She slams the door in my face, ka-thonk. Okay, I says, so I'll go on next door, I don't give a damn. I ring the bell. Somebody comes to the door but nothin' happens for maybe a minute. They're givin' me the onceover through the peephole an' it goes on forever. Shit, I wanted to put my finger up that eyehole, enough's enough. They got me feelin' like I'm some kinda germ. Then all at once the door swings open wide.

"'What're you doin' in here,' she says, this Princess-lookin' number with hair dyed honey-colored like it weren't dyed at all. Already she's mad as hell. 'Lady Bright,' I says. 'Who let you in? They don't — I *could scream* — Don't you know we don't allow pedlars in here?' I said I never saw no sign like that. 'People understand. People don't have to be told. If we had a doorman he'd —' 'Well geez, forgive me for breathin',' I said. That blows her away. 'I'm calling the Super,' she's screaming, 'I'm calling the police.' 'Yeah? Go ahead, fine, suits me,' I said, looking behind her into her bedroom where she's got this pink satin quilt-like thing on the bed, and there's a doll propped up on it, and filmy pink curtains goin' every whichway behind. A *doll.* Jesus Christ, I got over that at age three! Anyhow she's off to the phone, not shuttin' the door so I can see she's doin' it.

"Before she's even finished, I seen this guy in the hall. An old guy, big army type like my old man, and I'm headin' for the stairs before he breaks my ass like my old man done. The two old ladies got to be the ones that sent the janitor on up. So I beat it on up to the third floor. I was crackin' up, it was startin' to remind me of DONKEY-CONG. I'm standin' at this door knockin', and I can hear him comin' up the stairs, some kind of rattle in his breath. The door opens, 'Lady Bright callin', can I come in?' I says and she lets me. The door closes as he hits the top of the stairs, and there I am sittin' on a sectional starin' at this kid who's tellin' me ain't nobody come by from Lady Bright in years."

Lynn's narrow face was screwed up in a grin.

"Things are funny after, huh," she said.

Abby-Jean's face bobbed above the partition. "Nothin' looks good on me. Whyn't you go an' get me three more."

"Hey, I ain't no slave."

"I'd hafta get dressed, see."

It went on for about ten minutes after that, Lynn hauling in dresses for Abby-Jean in sets of threes, accompanied each time with another size of the striped dress for Yolande: 11, 13, 15.

"Can I try one of them smaller striped ones?" Abby-Jean asked, peering at Yolande over the partition while Lynn was gone.

Yolande was standing in her slip, staring at herself in the mirror. Her upper arms had the same long drooping pear shape as her body. Small flamey pustules were spattered along the backs of her arms and across her chest. Seeing Abby-Jean's face above the partition, she reached out quickly for her blouse, then let her hand fall back as if she hadn't tried to cover up.

"This on my skin just come up. I never had a thing like this before."

Maybe I'll just hold that size 11 striped dress up to my face in the mirror, Abby-Jean was thinking, instead of trying it on. Now she knew why Yolande put up with her long-sleeved elephant-tossed blouse in the heat.

"It's not what you think."

"What do I think?"

"You know what I mean." Yolande's head bent down. "It's not men."

Yolande was so pudgey-soft. Sort of trembly pudgey-soft, like the hemmorhoid-sufferer type on TV. In a white coat. Proper. Abby-Jean didn't think it was men.

"It has to be my room back at the residence. The room and the heat. 'Cause otherwise I feel okay." There were tears in her eyes.

"Well the heat won't last long, anyway, here's hopin'."

As Lynn returned, the saleswoman swept in behind her.

"Don't you think this is about enough?" she snapped.

The girls stared at her, cowed.

"Sometimes you gotta see a lot of things before you find the right one."

"Is that what you're doing," the saleswoman said.

"Yah," Abby-Jean said, instead of *No, cuttin' grass*.

She raised an eyebrow, then turned her back on them. The door clicked locked again.

"Hey, what's she in such a tizzy for?" Lynn burst out. "It ain't her fuckin' store, she don't own the place. She probably can't even afford to shop here. They pay her a stinkin' minimum wage and she's out bustin' her ass to protect some big dude's zillions. Izzat crazy or what?"

Somehow Great Auntie Tiffie from Davenport, now dead, turned out to be a millionaire with a Will, Abby-Jean was thinking, and then I buy the store and — no —

Grim-faced, Yolande got into the size 17 striped dress.

The department store catches on fire and there's only that saleslady and me, Abby-Jean was thinking, trapped on the second floor. Then, even after what that bitch done, I save her — no! —

"What do you think," Yolande repeated, louder.

"It looks okay." Maybe that was what Yolande looked like when something looked okay. "It looks good, really."

"I don't know. It's kinda tight still."

"Let's go, fuck," Lynn said, glancing over her shoulder. The saleswoman had come back.

"Well what about that one?" she demanded. "That's the third you've tried."

"I never thought the sizes would be so tiny, that's all."

"Okay, you girls run along now. Give me the dress." The saleswoman snapped several times with purple-lacquered fingernails.

The three girls glanced at each other.

"There's nothin' says you can't look. We got a right —"

"I'm not gonna shop here any more," Yolande quavered.

"Aw fuck her, fuck her," Lynn cut in. "Take the dress off, Yolande. It looks like shit."

At bay, Yolande's eyes darted from face to face, then she stared at the floor and stood very still. Like Dibsy, Abby-Jean thought, holding her breath when she got mad until she passed out. Turning blue slowly, terrifying them.

Slowly Yolande began unbuttoning the dress, unbuttoning the dress, then for an instant as it dropped to the floor, she stood before them with the inflamed crescent across her arms and breasts revealed. No one said a word as she stepped over the border of the dress to the sanctuary of her long-sleeved blouse.

"I'll take it," the saleswoman muttered, and took the dress away between two fingers.

"C'mon, let's go, huh," Abby-Jean murmured gently.

"It's the room," Yolande said.

They had to ring a buzzer inside the fitting room door to be let out.

"Hey, ya wanna frisk me?" Lynn dared. "Go ahead. Down both sides at once, arms and legs." Both her hands were braced against the wall, her body spread-eagled.

136

"C'mon, huh," Abby-Jean nudged.

Yolande had walked straight out without looking at anything, her head to one side and up. She had put gloves on, white nylon gloves that reminded Abby-Jean of Sunday and Church.

"All it takes is a l'il weenie match," Lynn tossed off as Abby-Jean pulled her away. "Ya got a match an' Zzzzzt—POUM—FAROUM! The whole place goes up, KaBLOUIE! It's no fuckin' loss to me."

The saleswoman glanced over her shoulder toward the fitting room, then stared back apprehensively at Lynn.

"Hey, ya see her?" Lynn bragged as they spun down the escalator after Yolande. "Starin' at me like to memorize my face 'case the whole place goes up some day. I shoulda said that at first, keep her on her toes. She'd take me more serious, she believed I'd do that. She'd know she couldn't do just any damn thing to me."

"Yah, she'd throw you out first thing."

As the escalator neared the main floor, they glimpsed Yolande halfway down the center aisle. She was standing in front of a small display table, her face screwed up in an immense pout, her eyes looking as if she were about to sneeze, staring at the small collection of things atop the table as if one of them had bitten her. Reaching in among them with her gloved hand, she gripped one of the small crystal half-moon shapes and raised it up above her head. She turned it upside down. Then, lowering her hand, she stood gazing at it.

"Whatcha got there?" Lynn demanded.

Yolande's palms closed, then opened again reluctantly as Lynn and Abby-Jean bent close. Trapped inside a crystal was a little white cottage covered in snow. Yolande raised the crystal high above her head, turned it upside down again, then brought it down cupped in her palms. As her fingers lifted off the cool smooth surface of the crystal, they saw a myriad of small white flakes pendant in the crystal sky, hovering there, floating lightly like diamond-chip fragments of cloud, then drifting down, gently down onto the cosy white building with its red-roof trim, down onto the white crescent of earth below.

"Geez, snow," Lynn whispered.

"You could watch it forever," Abby-Jean breathed. "I think it has a calmin' effect."

Yolande's gaze was fastened upon it, the soft burden of flesh that swelled her jaw suddenly dimpled, petulant.

"Going to buy it," she said hoarsely.

"Aw fuck. D'ya check out the price?"

Abby-Jean turned the half moon in her hand upside down. That much! A little thing like that, after all.

"There's no use to it," she advised. "After a while you'd get tired an' then —"

"It's for lookin' at. You've seen it now." Lynn placed the crystal back on the table just as the floorwalker, studiously not noticing them, lumbered by.

"Going to get something," Yolande hissed. "Don't care what it is."
The two girls stared at her. Yolande's face was ablaze.
"I'll *show* them," she breathed.

At the cash register, Yolande's shoulders straightened righteously as she doled out the ones, doled out the change, seriously depleting the week's money for food.

'*Believe I'm an eagle,* Abby-Jean thought, looking at her laboring back. *'Believe I can soar.*

"Cruddy little thing," Lynn muttered. "Real crappola."

Yolande came toward them with her little paper bag, her face red, timorous now, the paroxysm over and doubt setting in. None of them spoke as they swept toward the door and plunged back into the suffocating heat outside.

They straggled on down the street without a word.

"Anybody want a few packsa gum?" Lynn asked at last.

Nobody answered.

"It's free."

They shrugged.

She thrust her hands deep into her pockets and pulled out a fistful.

"The LOOKS-LIKE-FRENCH-FRIES fuckin' kind?"

○

"Trouble is, if you're not standin' here, you lose your place," Abby-Jean complained to Etta.

"How long have you been here?" Etta asked the woman in front of her.

"Long enough. If I don't get in soon, I'm gonna just go, I don't give a damn," the small woman croaked. Her thin hair, plastered to her face, looked like it had been slept on on every side. "If they got a line outside the Pearly Gates when I get there, I'm goin' straight down to Hell. I had it up to here in this life with standing in line." Her frail large-knuckled hand etched a line a foot above her head.

"God it's hot."

"You don't need to tell me."

"You hear anything in there?"

"Look, I saw her go in."

"Jesus Christ, look at all of you. If I'd know it'd be like this, I'd have stayed in bed." The woman in bright red slacks with a drycleaners press line grinned jovially as she lined up behind Abby-Jean.

"Nothing new for you, Bea," Etta snapped.

Trapped between them, Abby-Jean scuffed her thonged foot against the floor.

"I was up at the Sheraton yesterday," Bea said jovially. "The old gang likes to treat me. 'Sides, I sold them a couple of flash marker pens. I always pick up something to sell them. We spent the whole afternoon drinking champagne."

"You can pay me that dollar then."

"Soon as I get my check. And guess who we saw? Senator Patten of the Ways and Means."

"Figures, that you'd know somebody with ways and means," Etta said. Her clean-nailed fingers smoothed her black and white polyester dress which still, despite the heat, looked fresh.

"You're so hard to talk to, Etta," Bea complained. "Anyway, I went up and shook his hand."

Abby-Jean nodded. Bea was now talking to her.

"'Senator Patten,' I said. 'Do you remember Al Graham, the heart specialist up in Boston? Well I'm little Bea. Beatrice Graham.'"

Abby-Jean stared at her in confusion. Little Bea was fat as a breeding sow, over fifty, with fire truck orange hair.

"'Beatrice, is that right,' he said. 'Heaven's sake. Al Graham the heart specialist's daughter. Forgive me if I didn't recognize you after all these years.' 'Well you missed the best ones, Senator. I was a Ziegfield girl, did you know?' I gave him a little pinch on the arm. 'A Ziegfield girl, is that right now. Well, well, well, well.' He got a light in his eye too, the old goat. 'It's been quite a life, Senator,' I said."

"Huh," Abby-Jean said.

Ahead of them, the door opened and shut in front of the small woman who hated lines. They all moved a pace forward. A young black girl passed down the line in a dense cloud of perfume.

"You want to see this picture?" Bea offered.

Gingerly Abby-Jean took the snapshot showing a brick house that seemed too opulent to fit inside the photo frame. There was a silver Mercedes parked in an oval driveway out front. She stared at Bea blankly, then offered it to Etta.

"Seen it. A thousand times," Etta added as she glanced at her watch. "If there was somewheres else to go near here —"

"The family abode. The old stamping grounds." Bea's assertive face with its pointed nose protruding between the puckers of her cheeks seemed to rush forward to grip Abby-Jean in its enthusiasm.

"You lived here, huh?" Abby-Jean said lamely.

"Oh, years ago. Had to sell it in the end." Bea threw up her hands. "Well hell, it wasn't my kind of life."

Abby-Jean glanced at the snapshot again, hers since Etta wouldn't touch it and Bea was in no rush to put it back into her wallet again. The Mercedes looked brand new, the snap itself seemed new. Bea had gone back recently to take this picture of the house, years after it was no longer hers.

"I blew it all." Bea gave a great horsey laugh, nudging Abby-Jean. "You know what Ziegfield said to me?"

Abby-Jean shook her head. Who was Ziegfield? She wished the line would move.

"He said, 'Face it, Bea honey, you got a luscious bod —'" Bea broke off, looking like a thrown rider whose horse halted suddenly.

"This is ridiculous. Five more minutes," Etta said.

"Go on ahead then," the small woman who hated lines said. "I don't mind."

"Don't be silly. You were here."

They argued about it.

"'— but you handle it like an ox-cart.' That's what he said." Bea's mouth shut.

She didn't see the photograph extended in Abby-Jean's hand.

"Pfah, Ziegfield," Bea sniffed, then brightened and said, "Well, well, well, well." She seemed to see Abby-Jean again. "I crack them up, they never know what I'll be up to. I took 'em blue flash markers this time — they'd buy any damn thing — and we drank champagne for an hour or two. Senator what's-his-face was there."

Abby-Jean nodded. "I met the Mayor of Beaufort, Jody Burritt, at a barbeque one time." She reddened. What had made her say that?

"Well I had it all," Bea said, looking around. She took back the snapshot from Abby-Jean. "The right schools, the right people. Money —"

Or was it at a high school picnic, Abby-Jean was wondering.

"And now look what I've come to," Bea lamented. "Look where I am." Her face became piteous. "Here. Look at me."

Abby-Jean looked. "Yah, this is tirin'."

"I used to mix with celebrities, millionaires, and now look at me."

"You poor dear," the woman who hated lines burst. "You want to go ahead of me?"

"Here I am, down with the —" Bea stopped, but her hand had waved about her, taking them all in.

Well did you ever, Abby-Jean thought.

"You're not getting in front of me," Etta said. Her face had gone a little shiny with the heat. She took out a fresh piece of kleenex from her white plastic purse and dabbed at her face.

"Well I don't care," Bea sniffed. "Doesn't make a damn of difference to me. You people are so hard to get along with."

No one answered her.

"Well I've had about enough of this line," Bea said, talking to herself. "Let's see, what shall I do, who shall I call?" She gazed thoughtfully down the hall, her head tilted to one side like an enormous red-joweled rooster, then her eye blinked. "Well, well, I wonder what's in store for little Bea today," she murmured talkatively as she ambled back down the hall towards her room.

The three standing in line gazed after her.

"Off she goes drinking with her friends down at the Sheraton," Etta said. "And then what? Two or three days before her check comes, she's poking around in my room looking for bananas. 'Can't you give me something? I'm hungry, Etta.' She figures she doesn't have to look out, she can just come on over and poach off of me. Well, was I drinking champagne at the Sheraton? Not me. It's not fair."

"'Course it's not," the small woman croaked.

"What she gets is coming off my taxes as it is. You wouldn't believe how much they take off that dinky paycheck of mine. And here she comes along, 'Got any bananas,' she says."

"Geez, but if she's hungry —" Abby-Jean said.

"She never gets hungry enough to learn. There's always somebody giving her something."

"Well I can't help it," the small woman fumed. "What'm I gonna do with them apples, put them under the bed? You keep apples in your room, the smell gives you away."

Feeling bad-tempered, they nodded brusquely to the short-backed, broad-faced Spanish woman who waddled down the hall to join the line.

"Why don't she get a job? You can't tell me she don't know somebody who could give her one?" Etta carried on. "No. She's rather go bumming to the government."

"I heard of one who took what she got on Welfare and went on a cruise," the small woman chimed in.

"Yah, I saw that," Abby-Jean said. "It was in all the papers."

"Then Maybelle was tellin' me, out at the Safeways where she works, she seen a woman usin' food stamps, then loadin' two big bags of groceries into the back of a Cutlass Supreme."

"Yah, I heard a story like that too. Only it was Margaret tellin' me."

"Maybelle told it to Margaret."

"Margaret said she seen it herself."

"It makes me sick," Etta cut in. "Going on Welfare like it don't mean a damn. They got no pride at all. I'd rather die than touch a dime of it. I'd rather starve in my room."

"If nobody don' give me no job, it's nothin' on me. If they don' let me work, then don' call me no bum, that's all," the Spanish woman's pebbly voice broke in. "If there's no jobs, there's no jobs, si? It got nothin' to do with me. You Inglish got to be better than everybody," she added slyly. "That's how come the Welfare's so hard for you."

"Well I don't know. I always got a job. I always came up with something. I don't see why other people —"

"Aiee," the Spanish woman muttered softly, then was silent.

Almost as an echo, they heard a distinct *Meow* coming from one of the rooms down the hall. The sound had been produced by a human voice.

"Hah there, look, she's come out at last." The small woman who hated lines stepped back a pace so that the long-haired faded beauty who once complained to Abby-Jean about the mouse could pass by. She moved swiftly down the line, not looking at anyone, trying to avoid eyes. "*Now* she's in a hurry. Pah, the smoke in there. Go ahead, Etta, I got nowheres to go."

Etta stepped into the dank steamy smoke, disgust breaking through her concentration as she closed the door. The three women stared at their feet.

"The other toilets still clogged up?"

"Yah."

Meow.

"Well I sure don't like the idea of that Welfare," the small woman took up again, looking directly at the Spanish woman as if daring her to argue. Then she shrugged. "They won't give it to me anyhow."

"How come?" Abby-Jean asked. "You haven't got anything. 'Least —" She stopped, embarrassed.

"I do!" the small woman protested. "I do too." A sprig of her plastered down hair came loose, coiled upward. "I got $4,000."

"You tell the world like that, you won't got it long," the Spanish woman warned.

The small woman sighed. "You take a piece of money like that, $4,000. I don't know what to think about it. It took me all my workin' life to save it up and that makes it a lot, but when I think what to do with it, I can see how it's nothing. I wisht it was gone sometimes rather than to have to watch it dwindle away — like I was one of them African mothers on TV with her starvin' kid — watchin' it go down an' down, an' I wisht it was over an' done with an' gone. Then I think of just blowin' it some ridiculous way to put an end to the misery, but I haven't got the heart. I think of what I suffered to get it. Then I move to a place like this to try an' save it. To prolong it some." Another curl pried loose from her neck, pinged up. She had to clear her throat to go on talking, not talking to them but to the money. "I wisht it was gone so's I could fall onto the Welfare and get it over with. What'm I gonna do to save myself with a little bit like that? And still, long s' I got it, I got it, you know what I mean. I'm still somebody who got $3,000 to dip into at a pinch." She stared defiantly at the Spanish woman, then shrugged bleakly. "Long as I got it, they won't give me a thing."

"Why you got to tell them you got it anyhow?" The Spanish woman was genuinely irritated.

"Why? Because it was the truth!" The small woman stared at them, blinking. "They asked me things and I told them. What about bank accounts, that's what they said. 'We want to know what you're worth,' they said. And I —" Her gaze wavered away from the Spanish woman's face, "Couldn't say 'Nothin'."

The Spanish woman snorted, then glanced about her up and down the hall. She began to mutter to herself in Spanish.

"Maybe you could just take it out of the bank and tell 'em that it's gone," Abby-Jean suggested.

"Where'd I put it then? In my closet? Under the bed?"

Down the hall, they heard another *Meow*, then a door opened. A woman with dark brows and wild hair shot them an alarmed glance, murmured "*Sorry! Sorry!*", then slammed the door again in her own face. They stared at the door a second, preoccupied.

"You got a relative could put it in their name?" the Spanish woman suggested.

"Don't you see? They'd still know it was gone. They'd want to know how," the small woman said helplessly. "It's not nothing, $2,000, after all. You can't just get rid of it overnight."

"It's gonna be gone soon anyway. You oughta buy somethin' nice 'fore it's too late," the Spanish woman advised. "You oughta get somethin' out of it at least."

"Yah, 'fore they got you whittled down to a stump," Abby-Jean said.

"I buy a big colored Tee Vee and then I go on Welfare, an' they'll be writing me up in all the papers, next thing you know. GOES ON WELFARE, BUYS TV."

"You're doin' it the other way round," the Spanish woman pointed out.

"It's not honest. 'Least they wouldn't see that it was."

Abby-Jean frowned. The honesty of it hadn't occurred to her. You had to look at it a certain kind of way for the thought of that to come to mind, and she had only been thinking of the small hoarse woman with crushed dank hair and carrot-chip freckles on her pale, pale hands.

The Spanish woman closed her eyes, raised her brows, and for a moment she seemed immobilized like a heavy statue, all ponderous squarish globes, from her brazziere-buttressed breasts piled upon the blocks of her thighs to the fist that lodged obdurately against the bulge of her hip. Sweat gleamed in the dark-furzed channel above her upper lip. A pungent odor like earth cellars radiated from her, became almost palpable in the heat of the hallway, contrasting sharply with the thin acrid odor of the small woman on Abby-Jean's other side.

"I'm honest too," the Spanish woman muttered, an edge to her voice. "I'm honest like me." Her chin thrust out.

The small woman's returning stare was diverted momentarily toward the door behind which the meowing woman had disappeared, as a brief rapping sound came from behind the door, followed by a pause as if for listening, then two more raps, louder still.

"You're honest like Them," the Spanish woman said.

"I am not!" the small woman burst, sensing an accusation in it somewhere.

There were two more raps on the door, louder yet, then after another pause, two raps that cracked out like pistol shots. A volley of knocks followed, frantic in their urgency.

"Oh for Pete's sake," the small woman croaked. "Come on in."

The door opened and the meowing woman burst into the hallway, nodding at them several times, quick jerks forward of her head that were like bows. Muttering, she took her place in line behind the Spanish woman.

"She was knockin' to get *into* the hall," Abby-Jean whispered. "To get *into* it."

"Fruitcake," the small woman shrugged impatiently, her face craning anxiously toward the Spanish woman who ignored her.

"She was knockin' to get *out of* her room," Abby-Jean kept up. "This hall don't belong to nobody. You don't knock to get into somewhere public. That's like knockin' to get into the world."

"I got standards, that's all," the small woman shot out.

"*Their* standards you got," the Spanish woman returned phlegmatically. "Let them bury you down in this doghouse 'til you're bled dry, you think it's right."

"It gives me the willies," Abby-Jean muttered. "Honest to God."

The door to the washroom opened and Etta burst out, her entire face glistening. Her black and white dress clung to her body in patches, revealing slip straps, fasteners, through the drenched polyester. Though her frizzy white hair had gone damp, the neatness of the severe summer clip held. She expelled her breath into the hall, then walked past them without a word, nostrils dilated, eyes unblinking.

"Okay, it's you now," Abby-Jean prodded.

"You go ahead. Go on, I say, go ahead." The small woman who hated lines motioned her past with an impatient wave. Her gaze was rivetted on the Spanish woman.

Abby-Jean stepped forward, pushed the washroom door open with a forefinger. Entering was like an immersion. A thousand odors streaked dirty fingers across her face, making her gasp then hold her breath. Why didn't they do anything about it? God knew everybody had told Vandernikke in the office downstairs. He had gone into the inner office and barricaded himself inside. Off and on, you could hear water running in there. The women were trying to get out of the residence harder than ever. Maybe, driving them out? That's what the owners were up to?

As the door shut her in, she could still hear them going at it hammer and tong outside, the small woman's voice plaintive and demanding, the Spanish woman's answers perfunctory, the monotone of the self-evident.

"I'm gonna pull my own weight as long as God gives me breath. The Lord's with them what helps themselves. I believe in that."

"Si, but who you helping, tell me that? Who says you gotta help do yourself in? They gonna wait til you got nothing, then let you die."

Meow!

"Honest to God."

○

There was no doubt the long forecast Killer Heat from Texas had arrived. For days the white and swollen sun set the tumescent air abroil, the short nights' cool coming as an asthmatic gasp before dawn. Throughout the midnight hours bricks, pavement and sidewalks radiated back the incandescence of a long day's scorching, pumping stored heat into the fluid odor-choked air, leaving the city simmering by night as by day it had boiled. In the residences, in the rooming houses and flophouses, in the cheap apartment clusters that sucked in and compacted people with the dense absorption of black holes in space, children, women and men sweltered and staggered and drew long suffocated breaths that left them dizzy by daylight. Feverishly they scanned the tabloids to track the heat wave's course. The corn had withered in Idaho while the death toll mounted in Louisiana. Smalltown Texas streets were as quiet as if under military siege. Already some public buildings had opened to accept refugees.

Though it was long after midnight, Abby-Jean was pounding on Louise's door with both fists.

Down the hallway, the yellow bulb shed its malarial glare like a toxic bubble afloat on a poisonous pool. A week ago midnight as she left the humid relief of the tri-walled shower, an enormous three-inch flying roach struck the bulb overhead then rebounded zzzzblatt into her hair. The last straw, a roach Master Race attacking from above. Her scream sent spirals through the air. She shrank back, but not a door had opened, not one. And the roach onslaught from above was only the battered frenzy of a strayed June-bug trapped like herself in this fetid Northern hole. Her chagrin gave way to dread. A scream like that, and nobody even looked out into the hall, the women lying breathless, stupefied behind their doors. That or dispersed like disintegrating ghostly fragments in the murky stew outside, seeking refuge in bars, in franchises, in 24 hour drugstores, in churches, God knew where in the streets until the small hours dropped into cool.

For several nights, Abby-Jean had banged on Louise's door, afraid to walk the streets alone, knocking until her knuckles throbbed, her heart pounding, despairing in the silence. Maybe Louise had moved on at last? Maybe she had gone off with some man? Off with some man just for the air-conditioning? Or giving in to what it was to be lonely "that way" again, giving in as both heats coincided. Louise, with her dark lipstick, short iron grey hair, and her head craning up as if she hoped to see over the tops of trees, of buildings, beyond the horizon itself. Louise, whose belly would be heavy, whose breasts would droop, whose legs were still like a girl's. Somewhere in that body, changing, unchanging: Louise. She felt the presence of a dreadful intimate mystery, too immense for questioning.

"Hey Louise!" Her voice dropped to a whisper.

The door opened. Louise's face glistened like a peeled egg in the darkened room. "Okay," she muttered, "Okay."

Abby-Jean went in, moved some clothes from the bed to sit down.

"If I leave it open, it's just the same," Louise explained as she closed the door.

They sat in the darkness, not speaking, sweating.

"Glad you're back," Abby-Jean said at last, instead of "Where you been?"

Louise nodded.

"I been knockin' about three days," Abby-Jean probed.

"I was away." Louise looked out the window.

"Yah. Yah, well." Abby-Jean looked out the window too.

Louise's eyes softened, became wistful. "It was marvellous."

"Yah? Where —"

"Charles had to get back to Williamsburg."

A police car passed on the street below, not too fast yet with its blue lights whirling and the siren mesmeric, sinking into the humid darkness like a launched ocean liner subsiding into the sea. Striations of blue passed from one wall to the next, cutting across their face and hands.

"His family's there," Louise said.

They said nothing for a while.

"I thought we could go out, walk around, you know —" Abby-Jean began.

There was a muffled thud against the wall behind her.

"It's after midnight. There's nowhere to go."

"We could just maybe sit out on a bench or something?"

Something struck the wall behind her in another place. The sound was dull, heavy, as if some large padded object had struck it then rebounded again.

"People know you're out wandering the street 'cause of the heat. If we only take our keys, nobody's gonna try to rob us."

Louise flicked on the television, and again they were bathed in a blue-black glow. On the screen, the Saint was playing cards in a casino in Las Vegas, the sweat coming right out on his forehead. The camera cut to his hand, showing a ten to king run in hearts, plus a spoiler, the seven of spades. Blondes with immense exposed breasts leaned toward him on either side. Jaw tightening, he discarded the seven and held out for a flush. The ace of hearts came up. So he won. The four gangsters shook their heads and glowered at each other. Plainly *this* was a man to be respected.

Maybe she can smell me, Abby-Jean was thinking.

"If I could sleep —" Louise said.

"Nobody sleeps. Nobody sleeps in this heat. You gotta face it an' do somethin'."

"Lot more people drinking, I think."

146

"Yah. I hear 'em staggerin' through the halls."

"Stupid. You get to sleep but you wake up early. It brings your body heat up."

Abby-Jean slapped her knees and jumped to her feet to prod Louise on. Behind her, there was another thunk against the wall, followed swiftly by two more and two more, as if something soft and heavy were pelting down along one wall. They heard a cry and glanced at each other.

"Someone's *killin'* someone. Oh Geez."

They listened intently.

"Geez, you aren't opening the door, Louise. Wait a sec or two —"

Louise stepped out into the hall. Abby-Jean heard the grate of the key as Louise locked her door behind her out of habit.

"Hey! Hey!"

The door opened promptly. "Sorry," Louise whispered.

They stood listening, heads tilted, breath low, outside the door next to Louise's. On the street outside, high heels took two steps, then paused. Abby-Jean could hear the scrape of the heel against pavement, yet beyond the door in front of her, the sounds were blurred, as if cargo had come loose in the hold of a boat, and with each ocean swell it blundered from side to side, indecipherable in the murky charged depths.

They pressed together, eyes on the door. There was a short panting cry, then another thud.

"Hello?" Louise called.

Geez, *hello*, Abby-Jean thought, trembling.

Louise's forefinger touched the door. They heard another bump as the opening door let a yellowish irradiation into the room. A blanched nightgown, an ankle, a bare arm passed like a projectile in front of them, slamming against the wall in full flight like a lamp-crazed moth. The body struck the wall face full on. The nightgown shuddered as the invisible flesh rebounded. Despite their presence in the doorway, the floundering continued back and forth. With each impact of the body against a wall, the strange muffled thump came again.

"Here," Louise cried. "Here — don't —"

The shadowy figure crashed against her blindly as if she were a wall. Louise's arms encircled the strangely inert ricocheting form and together their bodies hurtled onto the bed. The constant *huh-huh-huh* shrill of breath that Abby-Jean only now heard gave way to a shriek. She fumbled for the light.

"Yolande!"

"Lie across her legs —"

"Geez — Yolande —"

"*Lie!*"

She lay. Yolande's legs bucked beneath her, raising her into the air, feet askew. Louise lay across her chest, pinning down her arms. A low gurling sound issued from Yolande's mouth as if she were being smothered. They got off and she lay there rigid, still choking.

"Yolande —"

There was a loud crack of flesh on flesh, then Yolande burst into sobs. Louise shifted, cradling the face she had struck in her lap, smoothing brown hair back from a battered pear-shaped face. Abby-Jean reddened. She could hear what Yolande was saying now: *hate-hate-hate—*

Yolande heaved, struggling to rise.

"I'll hit you again," Louise hissed, pushing her back.

"*Hate-hate-hate—*"

"So help me God —" Louise's hand raised.

"Don't *look* at me," Yolande shrieked, then sank back.

Abby-Jean raised herself, sat on the side of the bed by Yolande's feet, then looked. From her toes, her thighs, her pear-shaped arms to her forehead, red pustules swarmed over Yolande's body so completely it was as if she were being devoured. Her plump mottled arms were raised, covering her face.

I lay on that, Abby-Jean thought.

Louise was stroking Yolande's hair, mesmerically stroking Yolande's hair.

Still nothin' bare of me touched her, Abby-Jean thought.

"It's not that bad, Yolande," Louise said, her hand leaving Yolande's hair, grazing lightly over her tortured cheek and upper arm, stroking them.

"I lost my job. Nobody wants me serving food looking like this. They're scared something's gonna come off me and into their meal. Looks like I got some disease. Looks like I been —"

"What," Louise said smoothly, her glance leaving Yolande to rest on the poster on the wall above her that showed a man in a business suit, his vivacious blonde wife and two immaculate children with their expensive new home in the background. Taken from below, the photo placed their heads against a blue-blazoned sky, making them seem to stare into the future like champions. I AM THE WAY AND THE LIFE, the caption read. It was the TV evangelist Oracle Hobard and his singing wife, Joan. A flag flew on their flagpole and there was an eagle with talons descending over their front door.

"—Up to something bad," Yolande whispered.

"Geez, Yolande, will you come off that? It's the room, huh, you said," Abby-Jean murmured, wanting to stand up, resisting it. She glanced at the bureau where a snapshot was wedged into the mirror. Resting cool and serene atop the burn-poked surface sat the small snow-covered house trapped in crystal. The room looked like the others. But who knew what was thriving here that couldn't be seen.

"I bet you get out of this room, that crap on your skin'll go down," she advised.

Yolande's chest began to heave again. "See — see —"

148

"Maybe there was somebody here before who had somethin', hey Louise?" She stood up. She was good and ready to go now. Perhaps whatever it was would cling to her clothing. Maybe already it was filtering outward through the walls, on to Louise's room, then up to her own.

"Maybe Lysol," Louise said.

"If it's just the room, it means you got nothin' yourself, if you know what I mean."

"Did you to to a clinic or see a doctor about it? You can go to Emergency, it's free —"

"Oh they don't know. They told me it was psycho-somethin', that's all."

"It's the room, like I say. All you gotta do is move."

"See — See — How can I get out of here when I've lost my job? I can't get better 'til I get out of here, and I can't get out of here 'til I get another job." Yolande was panting. "And how can I get another job, see, when I look infested like this?"

They stared at her.

"I'll never get out!" Yolande shrieked.

The walls seemed to seep towards them. Abby-Jean shuddered. Trapped in this room with that invisible thing invading you, crawling all over your skin —

Like a fired larvae, Yolande's enflamed body convulsed. She tore loose from Louise and reeled into the wall in full tilt. Numbed, they watched as she staggered from the impact, then hurtled blindly against it again.

"*Huh! Huh!*"

"Oh Jesus God Yolande —"

They pinned her down on the bed again. Her face was swollen and black.

"I hate me," she shuddered, her voice low, obsessed. "Hate me." Her head wrenched from side to side.

"*Never* say that," Louise trembled.

Yolande lay beside them, rigid, her hands fists to keep her fingers from scratching her skin.

"Everybody hates me. I don't know what it is."

"Not us, we don't hate you, right Louise?"

"Not you, not you. *Out there.*"

"Oh," Abby-Jean said softly. She gripped Yolande's toes.

"It ain't even this thing on my skin," Yolande cried. "I don't know why it is, I feel it everywhere, that's all. When I go outside — there are knives in their eyes an' I shrink right down to a pea. I wouldn't ask for a thing and have their eyes at me but I got to live, that's all. I breathe, I take up space, I got needs. I got to have things — what can I do about that? There I am. I don't just go up in smoke 'cause nobody wants me. I'd feel like I wasn't there at all, if it wasn't for always needing something or getting in the way. Always asking for something, always saying *please, please.* I hate to hear it, the sound of my voice, *please, please.* Please can you let me have a job. Please can I live in this place you got. Please can you let me walk around or look around or hang around or just sit down here. When I hear that voice goin' *please-please-please,* I'd like to tear my whole body in two." She lay back, shivering. "No wonder they hate me. Oh God."

Abby-Jean turned away. Despite herself, she was hating Yolande.

"Nobody hates you," she heard Louise say. "Look, it's just one of those days —"

Abby-Jean stared at her, frowning. Suddenly she was furious.

"Yah, well I'll tell you what it is, Yolande. It ain't just one of those days, right, if it goes on all the time. They hate you cause you got nothin'."

They sat brooding on it, sweat trickling down their backs.

"They hate you 'cause they're scared your nothin's gonna rub off on them. They know you gotta come askin' for somethin' an' they're prepared in advance. They hate you 'cause they don't want to share nothin' or get put out to give you a chance. They hate you 'cause that makes their conscience feel bad an' they don't want to face up to that. They got to believe you're bad an' deserve to have nothin'. If you got nothin', they want to see you suffer an' get served right for bein' one of them types. They don't want nothin' good to happen to you. It's almost like they was takin' revenge."

"But I never did a thing to them," Yolande cried.

"I don't have nothing," Louise interjected flatly. "I have traveled, and more."

"Go on, Louise. You know everybody's always kickin' down. Whenever they feel bad about how things are for them, they got to start kickin' an' blamin' the ones below. But how can we be the cause of it all when we ain't the ones running the show? It wasn't me that set things up like this-here. I been doin' the best that I can."

"That's right, so've I," Yolande burst. Her eyes unscrewed, opened wide. It seemed to put a light where darkness had been.

"Well then," Abby-Jean said.

"I hate them," Yolande whispered.

"I don't hate anyone," Louise said. "Anybody's life can be marvelous, it's all up to them." Her face was glistening with sweat as if layered with cold cream.

Abby-Jean stared at her. How *could* she go on?

"I don't want to hate anybody," Yolande cried. "I want to be happy, that's all."

"Yah, well who doesn't." Abby-Jean sighed. "Anybody want to go outside?"

She glanced at Louise levelly. Louise's head was tilted up, her face tight, pained. She grimaced. She wasn't going to take a word of it back.

150

"There'll be no trouble for sure, now we're three." She butted Yolande with her elbow.

Louise glanced avidly at the space on the wall where a window might have been.

As one, they sprang toward the door.

"'Sides," Yolande cried. "Anybody bothers us, we can always say I got the Plague."

○

"Shit, it's dark. You bring the lights?"

"Got to go back to the fuckin' car. Jesus Christ."

"Hustle your butt. Two minutes in this fuckin' dive —"

"How's my makeup?" (A woman's voice.) "I think I feel something running down my —"

"We don't have to shoot you, Carole. All you have to do is ask the questions and fork over the fan. There's no need to stick your sweet bod' in it at all."

"You can kiss my ass, Sol, all right? Just kiss my ass." She pronounced it A.S., letting a Southern accent pop out.

"How many fans you got?" (Pause) "How many?"

A muffled response.

"Okay, okay, that might do it. First come, first served."

"Maybe there's nobody here —"

"I happen to know the place is full up. I do have some professional talents, sweetheart."

"Yeah, I saw you talking in the Office. Big deal."

"Christ, can you breathe this air? It's like being trapped inside a fart!"

A spurt of laughter.

"Miller! For fuck's sake —" (Whispered amid giggles)

"Well damn it, it is."

"C'mon, let's get serious, here. Let the Lady lead us. Up we go."

"Onward Christian soldiers."

Abby-Jean and Mrs. Jackson peered over the second floor railing, overlooking Elizabeth, Margaret and Louise who hovered near the landing on the floor below, all of them alerted by the sound of male voices and excessive banging on the stairs. Mounting toward them came two jean-clad boys carrying floodlights and a TV camera, and leading them, a very young woman dressed all in white. The noise, profanity and delay in their progress upward stemmed from the fact that each one was carrying at least three electric fans.

"I swear I'm going to fucking drop this, I — *Hi there!*"

From above, Abby-Jean saw the young woman reach the first floor landing and suddenly glimpse the three women there who had been silently watching her. She hesitated a moment, her face gleaming smiles and uncertainty, then she put down a fan and stretched out her hand. As she was still some distance from the women, who had backed away from the landing as she approached it, she had to walk several paces with her hand outstretched before reaching them.

How haggard Elizabeth, Margaret and Louise looked, Abby-Jean thought suddenly. How worn and drained.

"I'm Carole Preskie? Oh this is terrif — That's Sol? That's Miller — Ernie — How are you. Hi? Hi —" She was standing in front of Elizabeth with her hand stretched out. "Well how are you. Hi, hi —"

"Good," Elizabeth grunted, then stood gawking as her own outstretched hand, shaken once with a firm yet limp motion, was immediately relinquished again as Carole pressed on toward Louise, all the while glancing over her shoulder to rally the boys carrying the equipment onward. In the instant that her face was turned, Margaret quietly shrank back into her room and closed the door. Carole's hand slipped into Louise's, then lingered there a moment longer than in Elizabeth's, as if coming to rest, having picked out the leader.

"It's hot in here, very hot, don't you think? It must be terrible if you didn't have any form of air-conditioning, like a fan. That's why we, or rather they, the women of Bethesda, what's it again Ernie? the Bethesda Second Wednesday Action Group, B-SWAG, thought that a good project would be to rake up some fans for some under-advantaged people who needed fans in this heat, and then they called up the Station to ask if maybe we knew some, and then —"

"—the rest is History," the bespectacled boy carrying the camera finished ascerbically.

From the second floor, Abby-Jean saw Carole Preskie's grimace, invisible to Louise, as turning, her lips formed the syllable *shhh* at him, her face showing complicity and chagrin.

Can't be much older than me, Abby-Jean thought, and here she's got two guys and equipment in tow. Yet somehow the young woman in white seemed much younger than herself, shiny and effervescent as a bubble.

"Weren't there three of you?" Carole Preskie asked, turning again to Louise. "I thought I saw three."

"Two," Louise said. It was the first word she had spoken.

"I wouldn't want anybody to miss — of course we'll knock on doors but still a fan, after all — see, look! — just because they didn't know that we —"

"You made enough noise to raise the dead, if you ask me," Elizabeth said laconically, then added, "But whoever does?"

152

"Oh." For an instant Carole Preskie stood perfectly still. Then she gave an ingratiating little shrug as if to say: well I mean so very well, don't you see.

"You mean to say you're giving away these fans to us," Louise said.

"That's it," Carole Preskie murmured, visibly relieved.

"What about them?" Louise's head, tilting up, indicated the two boys behind her who, having unburdened themselves, were standing with fingers lightly on their hips, looking down.

"Well, it's a story, don't you see. Because of the heat. People want to know how everyone's doing. They want to know if you're okay."

Behind her, the boy who had been carrying the TV camera coughed.

"I already have a better fan than that," Louise sniffed, pointing to the fan the young woman still held at a careful distance from her radiant white slacks. "You can give it to somebody else. I don't need it."

"I'll take it," Elizabeth said, stretching out her strong brown arm again. "I could use one of them."

The young woman handed it to her, glancing quickly over her shoulder as if to alert the boys.

"I'll take another for my friend Margaret, next door here. She could use it too. She's in there listenin' behind the door." A devilish grin passed over Elizabeth's face as she imagined Margaret smarting behind the door at being given away like that. Before Carole Preskie could stop her, she had been relieved of a second fan. She turned quickly to the boys behind her, signaling with two abrupt jerks of her hand for them to lower their equipment again. Clasping her booty to her chest, Elizabeth looked like she had reaped a bonanza of fans.

"They're gonna be out of fans before they get up here," Abby-Jean whispered to Mrs. Jackson. She leaned over the railing covetously.

"They gonna take your picture, you go down there."

"You think?" Poised at the stairwell, Abby-Jean held back to consider this price for the fan.

"Wouldn't thet be nice," Mrs. Jackson said benevolently. "Seen y'sef on Tee Vee."

"You goin' down?"

"Cain't do much mo'n creep to muh chair."

As she turned back to her room, Abby-Jean stared at the back of Mrs. Jackson's pale shapeless dress where the varying rings of dried sweat stains were. The dress had been worn a long time, starting to turn the dun color of dirty sheets, the marks of interminable sitting, of heat, ingraining themselves in the cloth.

It wasn't until she reached the landing half a floor above the TV crew that Abby-Jean remembered she wasn't wearing any shoes. Abruptly she squatted, ready to scramble upwards if the camera pointed her way. Already from Elizabeth's room, she could hear the sing of the fan.

She's givin' an' maybe I'm takin' an' we both the same age, she thought. A heat intensified in her face.

The TV crew was left alone in the hallway. The boy carrying the TV camera lit a cigarette, flipped the match on the hall runner. Carole Preskie was standing with her ear to Margaret's door. She knocked again but it remained tightly closed, even though Margaret's radio blared the President's half piteous, half righteous voice into the hallway. Carole Preskie knocked at the next three doors to no avail.

"Hey, try yelling *Fire!*. That would get them out."

"Smart ass."

The fourth door opened, but before the finish of Carole Preskie's laborious explanation it had closed again. She was left standing outside it waving her hand to beat back the suffocation she had unleashed, the woman's frightened refusal in some unknown language ringing in her ears.

"See, Carole? Some days you just can't give it away," the bespectacled boy with the camera said, trying to sound hard-boiled.

"Christ, we're only trying to help. If there were some publicity maybe — I don't know —" She stopped, not bothering to think it through, taking one of his fans and leaving it outside the door.

"Can I say something here?" the boy with the lights demanded.

"Shoot."

"The next door that opens, Carole just hands them the fan and we shoot it quick. Presto. Fini."

"But she didn't want —"

"Plenty of people get shot that don't want it, and you're giving them the fan, for fuck's sake," Sol cut in. "Where's your professionalism now?"

Quietly Abby-Jean sat down on the stair, watching as they seemed to creep on down the hall past Louise's room. After a few moments of total silence, the floodlights suddenly came on, illuminating the hall with an eerie white light. Carole Preskie grasped a fan in one hand, prepared to knock with the other, glancing over her shoulder to be sure they were ready. The door next to Louise's was so transformed by the blaze of light that every chip, every flake of paint, even the grain of the wood stood out in stark clarity. She knocked, waited, then the door opened. A girl stood transfixed, agape, utterly exposed in the pitiless gleam, the red swarm on her face, her shoulders, concentrating into a red sludge that poured down the cleft left visible by her nightgown between her breasts. Yolande. Opening the door to an explosion of light. Silence, then an incredulous wail. The slamming of the door a thunderclap through the hall.

"*Jesus.*" (Whispered.)

"Well how was I to know?"

"Don't touch the walls."

"Christ, you suppose a doctor knows about that? Maybe it's some rare communicable thingamajig."

"This was a dumb idea in the first place. Who knows but you plug in half a dozen electric fans in this dump and you blow the wiring sky high. I say we split. We wash our hands. We call it a day. Presto, fini."

"We'd look like such asses coming back with nothing."

"Oh Christ."

"What if we said there was nobody here. Or that we couldn't find the sort of place —"

"You're kidding! You've really got to be kidding. Who in God's name is going to believe that?"

"Oh Christ. Oh Hell."

They lapsed into a disconsolate silence, seemed to Abby-Jean sitting mute on the stairs, to shrink a little. The young woman lit a cigarette and, turning her back on the others, paced to the end of the hall. Tap-tap, tap-tap, flecks of her ash sputtered out all along the runner like beads of sweat from the agitated fiery point. Her face was flushed, her lower lip thrust out in a savage pout. It was all going wrong for her. She looked ready to kick the wall. They were about five feet apart. Still Abby-Jean said nothing, didn't move.

Glimpsing her suddenly, Carole Preskie's eyes dilated. Motionless as a fixture on a wall, a gargoyle but without the grimace, more sober— Sullen? Suspicious? She went over the adjectives permissible in a story of this kind. How long had that barefoot girl been there, their little scene below dropping into her eyes like stones silently dropping into a well. She felt a twinge of embarrassment at her new white slack suit, wilting now and soaking up foul smells in the heat. Sitting there envying her, no doubt. Hating her? The question came to mind almost automatically, and it steeled her. Well let her, then, too damn bad. She didn't have to answer to anyone.

Abby-Jean's face was twitching. It was all she could do to hold back laughter. Why good Lord, that little girl her age was wearing a tie!

"Hot, huh," she said, looking down to hide her hilarity.

"Sol, will you come here a sec? I've found someone." Carole Preskie brushed back her hair with the hand holding a cigarette. "Just a sec, okay?" she said to Abby-Jean smoothly and winked.

Behind her in the hall, the boys had gotten rid of their fans outside doors where there had been no response. Sitting there in a row, the fans looked like so many rejected babies outside a hall of church doors.

"Too young, for Chrissake, too young," Sol said tiredly, approaching them, then adding "Hi there," for Abby-Jean. "We got to get somebody who looks more —"

Old? Abby-Jean wondered.

Carole Preskie nodded. She smiled at Abby-Jean brilliantly, perfunctorily, the kind of smile career women reserve for their housewife friends' children out on display.

"Is there anybody else here?" she asked.

"Mrs. Jackson, she's here."

"Well show us where, for Chrissakes. Sorry, this heat. I mean just — show us where."

Abby-Jean's eyes dropped. A mistake. Maybe Mrs. Jackson didn't want to see them. Because she couldn't think how to tell them that, she stayed motionless, looking down. A feeling was setting in slowly: she didn't want to show them anything. She began to feel shock at their presence, the way touching ice takes time to register a chill.

"They're shy," Carole Preskie said.

"Look, look, I'm sick of this. Two more minutes of this air and I barf. C'mon hey, will you?" Sol took the steps two at a time, swaying slightly with the weight of the camera.

"Hi, how ya doin', there," Ernie grinned back as he passed her, trying to be friendly.

Abby-Jean followed them on up. The broad beam of light going into Mrs. Jackson's doorway reminded her of pictures in a Sunday school book showing a small child gazing awed before just such an opened, light-brimming door. AND LO, THE KINGDOM OF HEAVEN IS AT HAND, the caption read beneath. She stood outside the doorway behind Ernie, who was smiling and nodding as inside, Carole Preskie introduced him to Mrs. Jackson. But he had had the lights on her even before that.

"Ain't thet nice," Mrs. Jackson was saying, blinking into the lights, rocking softly in her rigid chair. They had set a fan up on the bureau which was blowing directly onto her face.

Carole Preskie was looking around the room. In the blinding light, the dim shadows on the wall around Mrs. Jackson's bed, the oily residue of a body's perpetual contact over months or years seemed blanched away. As if with the eyes of a camera, her gaze swept over the bureau on which there were three small barrettes, a shoe horn and a large family Bible. She nodded at the Bible, glancing at Sol. He nodded.

"Is this your Bible, Mrs. J?" Her voice sounded like she was talking to a very small child.

"Thaas right."

"It must be a comfort to you."

"Oh Lawd, sweet Jeezus —" Mrs. Jackson's large wrinkled hand dabbed a freckled knuckle to one eye. "Y'aw don't know what muh Jeezus mean to me."

"I suppose when times were hard —"

156

"Winter time, see. Ah be lyin' heah wif nuffin' but this Book a-coverin' me. An' Ah wuz wa'm, Lawd. Ah jes' be lyin', an' it put a heat up through muh ches'."

"Why don't you show us, Mrs. J?"

The question was really addressed to Sol. He shrugged, nodded. Mrs. Jackson heaved herself from chair to bed, one arm propped on each to make it across. Then she lay flat on the bed, her eyes staring at the ceiling, her legs still hanging off the side of the bed, one hand tugging inobtrusively at her dress to be sure it was down.

"See, Ah were —" Mrs. Jackson began, her eyes staring at the ceiling, her brow furrowed with thought, anxious to tell them exactly how since they seemed so interested to know.

"Wait a sec. The Bible."

Carole Preskie reached for it, grasping the heavy volume at either end of the spine. As she raised it, the leather covers, worn soft, buckled, and the thin-leafed pages went slap-slapping down, releasing a shower of keepsakes that had lain hidden between its pages: a pressed flower, an ancient sienna photograph of an Afro-American in uniform, a four-leaf clover, numerous small torn pieces of paper from a magazine which must have been marking out special passages, falling now to the floor like the shedding petals of a magnolia blossom. Carole Preskie knelt, stuck them back between the pages here and there.

"Ah were like this on the bed," Mrs. Jackson was saying, opening her arms to receive the Book. Unprepared for the sudden weight of it as it passed from Carole Preskie's arms to her own, she let it slide down an inch through her fingers, a soft *hunhh* escaping her lips as it struck and lodged against her chest. She opened the pages in the middle, and straddled it against her.

"Ah were like this when Ah were cold," she explained to Carole Preskie, turning her head still flat on the bed. At the foot of the bed, raised so that it peered down on her from above, the camera began whirring. "Then when Ah got wa'm, y'aw see —" She didn't notice it, intent on her explanation to Carole Preskie who was kneeling by the head of the bed, nodding at her, eyeing the camera swiftly from time to time. "—Ah'd pick it up an' read agin."

"Maybe you'd like to read something for us," Sol suggested, attracting her glance toward him, toward the camera.

For the first time, Mrs. Jackson peered at the camera, her face grave. The light whirring sound carried on a few seconds, then stopped. She squinted into the eye of it, then licked her finger, turned a page, her fingers quivering against the rim. Sol moved from the foot to the side of the bed, recapturing her face, which had been obliterated from view by the raising of the Book.

The old woman glanced over the side at him, then turned back to the Bible, her face wet, her fingers fumbling through the pages.

"Righto, Mrs. J," Carole Preskie prodded, staying out of range of the camera though, after much wiping of her face in the heat, she looked less out of place. As if to compensate for appearance, an intense alluring scent exuded from her that challenged the other odors in the room.

Breathing in the perfume deeply, Abby-Jean closed her eyes. Opening them, she looked away. It was hard to look at the young woman in white now that she envied her. One stubby-fingered hand clutched the shoulder of her other arm. She felt hurt for herself.

Mrs. Jackson kept fumbling through the pages, a wettened finger crushing slowly forward and back, the bottoms of the frail pages tearing slightly with the unaccustomated haste.

"It doesn't matter what you read, read anything, just go ahead."

The old woman was muttering to herself. Between the thumb and finger of her left hand, she held one of the many small scraps of paper that had fallen out and been indiscriminately replaced. All the passages specially marked out over the years had receded again into the dense unyielding text.

"Okay listen here, Mrs. Jackson. We're starting shooting — NOW —"

The old lady's head jerked toward the book. "And Joabim, the fourth son of the Canaanite, Hebemoth, rose and looked upon him and saith, Who is this Gawd thet we should be a-feared of him? But the Lawd saith —" She glanced into the eye of the thing, fixed on her now, and cleared her throat, the better for the pagan world outside to hear. "And the Canaanites rejoiced against the Lawd Gawd but it were a sign that he who slew —" Her distant almost blue eyes returned its prying stare with solemnity, giving equal reverence to all the words she believed were God's. "And when the Lawd looked on the heathen with they heedless ways —"

"That's enough. Let's wrap it up. Jesus, I —"

"But the Lawd, not wantin' to release unto them the sons of Ishmael, spake unto them with —"

"Hey Mrs. J, you got your new fan, hey? How about that?"

The old lady glanced up, bewildered, her finger marking the spot where she had left off. She had intentionally chosen a short chapter, but it wasn't finished yet. She skipped down a few verses.

"Elohim, first chile of the comin' generation, when he had reached the age of —"

"Oh God —"

They were off.

Standing at the railing staring down on their flight, Abby-Jean saw the last fan, tucked beneath the arm of the woman who once had been beautiful, disappear two doors down from the door it had been resting in front of. A trod-upon cigarette remained in its place, as if in exchange.

"If you say anything about the expression on their faces when we give them these fans, I'll bust your sweet —"

"I don't see how they can stand — I think it's horrible that they have to —"

"Can I say something here?" (Breathlessly) "I think we just did a piece up there on what it's like to be *cold?*"

Silence. The commotion of feet on the stair came to a halt.

"Oh Christ. Oh Hell."

"Well I tell you what we'll do. We'll work it out *in the car.*"

The thunder of feet resumed as they raced down the stairs toward the air-conditioned car.

"Well, that's it," Abby-Jean said, stepping back into the room.

Mrs. Jackson's finger was still pointing at the place she had left off. "They gone?"

"Guess so."

Abby-Jean put her fingers in front of the fan, wiggling them, turning them over, grasping at the relief offered by the hot current of wind.

"The Beatitudes. That's what Ah were lookin' for," the old woman lamented.

"Anyway you got a fan," Abby-Jean said shortly, her whole body in front of it now. "Wish I had one," she added plaintively.

"Y'aw take mine."

"Geez, I couldn't," she murmured, suddenly mortified. They were both running with sweat. Mrs. Jackson's face had a green tinge to it, like slime on damp earth.

"Take it. It don't matter to me."

"But a *fan!*" Tears came to her eyes.

"Ah got muh Book. That's what matter to me."

"I'll bring it back in an hour," Abby-Jean vowed. She couldn't bring herself to refuse it altogether.

The old woman's brow was still furrowed. She was agitated with thoughts of the people that for a brief time had rocketed about her room. The shock of them lingered like the heady exquisite perfume.

"We aw gonna die," the old woman said, touching the Book, rocking in the rigid chair. "We aw come to thet, no matter who we be. Thet be the same for everybody."

"Yah well," Abby-Jean cried out angrily. "What about the years an' years an' years 'til then?"

☻

The sky was nearly white. Only the intermittent strokes of lightning, so swift, so diffuse they seemed like momentary dilations of the eye, showed it wasn't. As if scorched into incandescence from above, the thin sheen of cloud gave off a glare that penetrated the recesses between buildings where in sunlight, shadow might have been. From brick, glass and pavement the irradiation rebounded, shooting the humid groggy air with filmy ripples of heat. On an unseen horizon, the sky was deepening into grey, veined with lightning, the thunderclaps merging into one another until they became a continuous single reverberation threatening rain.

As if in feverish activity before the storm, cars entered the traffic circle from all directions then spun out again, limousines wheeling from a south of monuments and marble to glide toward the embassies in the north west, careening family-laden cars spinning off east beyond the Riot Corridor toward relentless rows of narrow houses that culminated at last in apartment barracks beyond, dotting the city limits like buttresses on some sprawling fortress. The irregular whorl of their passage beat like fanned flames upon the air, obliterating from instant to instant the drone of air-conditioning that merged with the thunder beyond, setting a rushing swooshing sound through the dusty glistered trees.

Human voices broke through in singular isolation, in clarity, like so many single notes creating at last a concatenation of their own. Crowded thigh on thigh on all the benches that formed a disjointed ring within the traffic circle's tiny park, the women from the surrounding buildings sat, leaned against, struggled to find solitude among, argued with, baited, consoled and ignored one another. As if spilled over from an original allotment, some crouched, some sat, some lay stretched out as if collapsed upon the parched reedy grass beneath trees whose shade had vanished. From time to time, grunts or a cry of triumph broke out from one of the several tight knots of bending, kneeling men intent beyond pleasure on games of chance they willed into games of skill. At the water fountain, the biggest boy of a gang of small children tried to fend off all comers by forcing jets of lukewarm droplets from an aperture that barely released water at all. The children shrieked, their laughter peeling as they raced against him more to capture than avoid it, mouths agape, flesh tingling for the touch of spray. Black children, Spanish children, Vietnamese. Black and white women, old men. Anticipating the storm, waiting for it, wet-faced, heat-drenched.

At one end of the circle, several reedy high-pitched voices burst into song, matched by an irregular clapping of hands that sounded like the smattering of huge droplets across a sidewlk. Legs askew, four skinny black women crowded on a bench were beating out:

Look who's callin' out, JESUS!
Oh Lawd it's me
Look who's callin' out, JESUS!
Oh Lawd it's me

but the song petered out as people started looking at them. Petulantly, their bodies kept up angular motions that followed where

160

the song might have been, had they carried on aloud, then like an irrepressible stream, it surfaced again. Other voices joined in, adding to the reverberations in the air.

A few benches down, what had begun as an argument became a monologue. An immense old woman, leaning forward elbows on thighs, her breasts two burdens slung between, reached into her purse hefty as a mailman's sack, and drew out a pamphlet from between her out-turned knees. The posture drew her dress up above her knees, exposing tan elastic support bandages on legs over which veins coursed like choked streams. She wheezed slightly with the effort, the newsprint pages trembling between red freckled fingers of what had once been a mighty hand.

"And vot of the flock?" she boomed, waving a booklet whose title proclaimed *The Kingdom is Coming.*

Her companion, a neat woman whose smaller purse perched upon legs studiously pressed together, gazed timorous encouragement down upon the women who encircled them whether they wished to or not, sitting or stretched out, lethargic, spent with heat.

"You are Catholic, you are Protestant, vot?" the huge woman demanded, glancing about her, her great hand braced against her knee. One of her eyes, red with an affliction, was watering constantly, forcing a tear to drop down her cheek from time to time. "Sunday you get songs, a sermon, everythink, then they pass round the dish. Take the money. Okay. *Good-bye.* See you next veek, ve do it all again. The next six days, it doesn't matter vot's vit you. Maybe you sick, you dyink, you got problems in the family, in the job. No job. Okay who cares, seventh day sing the song, take the money, *good-bye.* For six days and six days and six days," she was pounding on her knee, "Vot of the flock? Who comes to see you, to talk vit you? Who cares?"

The murmur of the women was lost in the whishing of cars, the exclamations of the gamblers, the gospel rhythms beaten out against the reverberations of thunder.

"Now we got big stars on TV. Billie Graham, Jimmy Swagger'. Vot hoppen? They comink down from the sky to a place, thousands people come. Thousands people step up and say, I gonna follow God from now on. Next day vot hoppen? Gone! Back into the sky, you never see them again. Thousands people come out with their hearts in their hands. Thousands people ready turn to goot like maybe never gonna happen to them again. Vhy they leave them to be good and all alone after that? They not used to it so much yet. All they say: I write you a letter, my secretary write you a letter out of some place, California, send you a picture, a book. Big noise, big TV, vot of the flock? Nothink." Her hair, orange-grey, seemed to fly out in kinky tendrils as if blown by the wind.

But there was no wind yet. The women's faces bore a concentration that was their bodies' mute resistance to the heat. It encompassed them, this heat that hovered at the threshold of endurance, turning every touch of glass, of metal, of pavement, cement, brick and flesh into an abrasion, a blistering scorching torture to the skin. It beat upon them, enclosed them, invaded their lungs and wrung their clothing limp with sweat. Bodies slowed, became silent within as in the dark shade of the soul, exhaustion bred fear. Older men and women listened to their hearts with panting breath. Relief was a thing that money could buy, and those who had none sought refuge in the parks from the cauldrons of their rooms.

Look who's singin' out, JESUS!
Oh Lawd it's me
Look who's cryin' out, JESUS!
Oh Lawd it's me

Louise's hair was sticking to her face. She raised her head and raked it back with her fingers. Her eyebrows and lashes, limned in sweat, took on a chiselled look.

"I know the type, believe me. You run into them all the time. Everywhere. All she wanted to do was talk to me about her religious experience. 'Look,' I said, 'I phoned about your ad for an air-conditoined room. I don't want to hear —'"

Abby-Jean nodded. She too had returned to looking for another place to live, struggling with the other women at the residence for a turn at the phone, everyone now trying desperately to get out. She had answered an ad reading "Cooperative household of four seeks non-smoking fifth in tune with her/himself and open to the universe" that had been tacked to the notice board in a small vegetarian restaurant where once, amid strange long-haired types, she had eaten a small cautious meal. Her meeting with the four had been a failure. She didn't know why. They would ask her a question: "What foods do you eat?" and when she answered "Hamburgers 'n that," their glances met and connected around the room. "What turns you on? I mean, do you see yourself as involved in a spiritual sort of — like, in terms of relating to the cosmos, do you —?" "My folks was Baptist but I'm still sorta up for grabs. That what you mean?" Again the glances. Then they told her she could go and they would phone her if — It was worse than applying for a job. And now, over on the far side of the traffic circle, two of them were seated on an Indian bedspread, the man reading a book, the woman with a little flute, not the pair that she had thought was a couple at all.

"They never seem to think you might have had a religious experience yourself," Louise was saying. "That you might have experienced something — *marvellous* — and don't need to hear about it from anybody else." Her face was intense, inward.

162

Look who's shoutin' out, JESUS!
Oh Lawd —

It was as if a great sighing, a great moaning were mounting heavenward from all the scorched and squalid rooms, the teeming buildings that jammed and crammed the densely trafficked streets. Entombed in all the whistling heat-licked corridors and cubby holes, women struggling and agonizing and brewing God's image from their own life's sap. Their troubles and sorrows, their thwarted love releasing a lament that beat upon the skies.

To the left of the singers, a tall raw-boned black woman was nodding her head in time to their music, slow heavy nods that caused her body to rock mesmerically. In the pauses between verses, her loud voice intoned:

"Yehass, the Blessed Jeezus, He were pore like me."

The women strung out along the benches nodded and murmured among themselves, not looking at her, staring out instead over the dirty grass that clung for life amidst the dirt, over the roofs of swift oblivious cars, over the Congressional dome incongruous and irrelevant on their horizon.

"He were pore, He didn't have no nickel to His name. He weren't no rich man drivin' no Cadillac. He were pore like me." The woman's face was strengthened, justified.

Abby-Jean frowned. She didn't want to be poor, though. Maybe for a little while, but not for always —

"He were rejected and despised like me. He were brought low."

Abby-Jean's heart panted within her. She didn't want that! She didn't want that!

"He were trodden underneath. He were tortured and betrayed. He were laughed at and reviled. He were swindled and ignored and cheated on jes' like me."

The murmuring among the women was like a constant shooshing heave of deepwater tides, an ecstasy of misery and affirmation.

"Yeh, you tell me, sisteh," a voice pierced through. "You tell me how He BLECK like you." The wiry old black woman's fist was waving, her face unblemished with scorn.

The women's response was like a crashing on the rocks that ebbed away into turbulent silence. But from a different quarter, the tumult of argument began anew and spread. The mighty orange and grey-haired woman drew a handkerchief from the sack between her knees and wiped her dripping eye. To no avail. It brimmed and flowed again. She swung her head, firm, her voice laden with the burden of reasoning.

"Vot ve got in today's vorlt, I tell you, but corruptions? Nobody tell the trut', everywhere lie, kill, steal. Little childrens bring into the vorlt, nobody care nothink but making money, getting successes. Ve got in countries peoples killink peoples, who knows who, does it matter, vot?

163

Ve got vars all kinds, ve got famines, millions people die. Ve got poisons in the airs, in the foods. Ve got everybody's cheatink and make bribe, ve got you sleep mit my wife and I sleep mit the corner boy, ve take pictures of the kiddies, no clothes, put 'em in a plastic cover book and sell next door."

She took a mighty breath.

"Nobody think of God, nobody think of the little chilt, the old voman. They say is Christian country, this. Vot Christian, the neighbor sleepink on the street? Vot Christian, makink heroes big killers, big crooks? In the government puttink them, in the university, lots of talk and get rich quick. Everybody to the people tellink nothink, anythink — is no goot. Is pagans, these peoples, believe in nothink." She shook her head slowly, grimly, and her running eye loosed a drop. "Vot you think all these troubles means? Not for nothink these bad things hoppen. Signs, is these things. The Lort Got not goink take it no more. You think Got don't care nothink when peoples is bad? You think Got goink let it go on forever?"

A flurry of speculation raced among them.

"This here heat wave is a sign of God, that's what I think. Whenever you seen a heat wave like this? Never, that's what they say on TV. They never seen a heat wave like this here. It's scorching the earth right down to the bone. Out there in the South West, you hear they're dyin' —"

"We had a death in our own buildin' yesterday, old Mrs. Gench, it was. She started quick to stink. It don't take but a day, then we all knew she was gone —"

"—and 'course you get to wonderin', anybody would, how come the weather's gone queer like this, when it never done before. An' I'll go as far as this, that's all, that it's a Sign."

The murmuring among them grew.

"A sign of what, I'd like to know," Louise interjected skeptically, head tilted upward. But the women, grasping for an understanding, seized on it.

"God's punishing us, it must be."

Their sweat-blanched faces turned toward each other, toward the white lightning-shot sky.

"A punishment, that's what it is. Like he done to them Children of Israel."

"When you think of some things America done." The woman had dark features, black eyes, an untraceable accent. "God punishing America." Her eyes flared.

There was an instant commotion among them, first of protest, then of debate. A story circulated among them that made Abby-Jean's eyes open wide.

"Anything America done, the Communists done worse," a square-jawed woman retaliated.

"Is America getting the heat wave, no?"

"It's *us* getting it," Abby-Jean said aloud though nobody heard. God's punishment was falling hardest on people who had never had much say in what the country did at all. That's how it seemed to her.

"Is time of big troubles," the voice of the Prophetess with the weeping eyes boomed. "Is time of volcano and earthquake. Is time of the godless on eart'. Is evil peoples got the vorlt in their hands. Everywhere you see them, evil peoples, don't care nothink for nobody at all."

The thunder crashed above them. For a moment it seemed as if the surrounding buildings had quaked in response to some enormous suction in the sky.

"Our President ain't evil. How could God let somebody evil be President?" The square-jawed woman's face was bellicose, frightened. "I believe in him. The President. If the President of the United States ain't good, who is?"

"Jesus knows who the good ones is," a small woman piped up. Through the soft furze of red hair, her scalp was visible. On her lap sat the scarf-hat that had either caused or covered the thinning of her hair, removed at last due to the heat. "Maybe they ain't much in this world but Jesus knows 'em and recognizes how they been. It's Jesus, bringin' Justice when He come."

The women scrutinized her face, wondering if she thought she was one, if they were one themselves in that case. Their faces became irritable, obdurate, pensive, alarmed. As the wild unclaimed children shrieked and raced among them, their glances labored backwards along the length of their days, and their flesh, distorted by time, bad food, labour, disease and abuse seemed to remain behind like incipient wreckage on their bones.

"There's gonna be weepin' and wailin' and gnashin' of teeth, no doubt about it," the small woman carried on, her impassioned eyes sweeping the horizons. "There's gonna be fires and floods and terrible devastations all over this world. The mighty is gonna be brought low and consumed in a pit of fire. They're gonna call out for an escape and there's gonna be none. 'Cause it's the Last Days. They're gonna be thrown in torment forever and ever. All the things they thought they got away with gonna catch up with them then, and only the good will survive."

"How are the good going to survive with the earth on fire?" Louise cut in. "Tell me that."

"They're disappeared!" the small woman reasoned ecstatically. "Before it happens, Jesus is gonna come back and take 'em off someplace with him. One day they'll be here and the next, poof! Gone! Vanished! They ain't nowhere to be found. Then the ones left behind'll know Jesus come to get 'em out of here at last." She half rose from the bench in her excitement, as if hoping at any moment to be evacuated into the stratosphere: poof!

165

The wind began rushing in the trees, sending styrofoam cups and wax paper sheets tipling across the beaten grass. Thunder encompassed them, tossed them in its reverberation, and cries of the forthcoming floods and fires seemed to belabor the air.

"When you think of the atomic bomb, like, it makes you think," Abby-Jean yelled to Louise. Imagining herself sitting here on a park bench suddenly consumed in a whorl of fire that stretched over all the globe, it seemed as reasonable to think of it as God's doing promised in Revelations as to think of it as something done by mere human beings, a crime so enormous that it was completely beyond grasp.

Over the tops of buildings, the black rumbling clouds swept in, driving the brilliant white light away. The women's bodies bent into the wind, their faces turning to the side, the front, eyes closed, shielded against bursts of wind-driven grit by a hand licked by blowing hair. The first heavy drops raced toward them *splat! splat! splat!* across the dust. The four black singers, silenced now, huddled in a cluster beneath a tree until a lightning crack sent them skittering fearfully away from it, back toward the unprotected benches. The Prophetess with the weeping eye had given way at last to her companion, who was searching out arcane numerical proofs of the Paradise to come, losing and finding them as the wind tore the flapping pages of the Book from her hands. A howl went up from the knot of gamblers, the men standing now, arms folded or bodies gesturing emphatically, rhythmically into the wind, glancing round at the slowly eddying mass of women as if refusing to be first to be driven away. Only the water fountain had been deserted. The women and men seemed thrown together, hurtled about, caught in a whoosh of wind and noise, clinging to the open space of agitated grass and swirling grit.

"You want to go back?" Louise yelled.

"Not yet. Wait just a little. Feel the cool."

Their arms spread wide, letting the wind buffet through their garments as if they were clothes hung out to freshen on a line. The drops fell more softly, in greater concentration.

"Don't that feel good?"

"Them drops hit my head, I hear 'em sizzle, I swear."

"Seven! Seven!"

With a cataclysmic crack of thunder, the deluge broke. The men and women scattered toward the trees, huddled there, still holding out. The smell of wet hair, clothes, bodies — animal scents — seemed clean and leathery in the rain.

"I don't want to go back," Abby-Jean yelled hoarsely, feeling the water coursing down her back. Cool! It was cool!

Louise's hair was plastered to her face. It made her eyes and mouth look enormous. "What do you want to do? Just stand here in the rain?"

"Sure. Why not? It's only water." The water streamed over her face, making it hard to keep her eyes open.

"Get hit by lightning?" Louise's hand was jerking at her dress. She was inexlicably angry.

"I'd rather die. I'd rather die than go back in there."

For a dazzling instant she could see nothing but white, then the earth seemed to jerk beneath her as the thunder smashed through the air.

It was the kind of storm that left broken tree branches on the Beltway, thickened the dead underbrush in the ravines and littered Embassy lawns. Left gasping by the deluge, alone, in pairs and in swarms, the men and women scattered and fled for cover.

The sound of the residence door closing, *whoomff*, was like the thickly shielded door of an oven closing as the heat rushed out. For a moment, they couldn't see each other in the darkness, standing there with the water dripping off their bodies. Abby-Jean heard the flicking of Louise's hand as she brushed water from her clothes, heard the droplets splat against the dirt-sodden runner on the floor. The heat seemed to fasten onto their rain-purged bodies like a parasite, sticking on them, covering them, drawn by and adhering to the water on their skin.

"I hate it," Abby-Jean cried. She heard her voice, disembodied — almost a shriek —

Louise's hand hesitated, then continued pummelling the water from her clothes in the darkness.

"I hate it! I hate it! That door closin' on me every time like it's never gonna open again. I'm never gonna get out of here. My life! — What's gonna happen to me — Oh God —" She was trembling, her breath hurtling out of control, careening, full of silent whistling screams. Her head was ringing. Something had given way inside her and in the torrent it unleashed, she was going under, drowning. Terrified! Everything strange. Louise's ghostly eyes. Oh Lord, was she here, where was she? This dark landing. A streak of yellow crossed her inner eye. The top of her head tingled, seemed to shoot away, shrieking, toward a vanishing point like a punctured balloon. Her hand reached out, reached out —

Louise was gripping her, shouting.

An irradiation of prickles exploding like stars all over her skin.

"Cut it out! Stop it! So help me God —" Louise's voice harsh, threatening, her hot breath burning, her grip wrenching her arm.

The pain brought her back to her body. They stood together trembling, Louise gripping her arm.

"You watch that," Louise hissed.

"I never — I never —" It had come on her so quickly.

"You want to end up raving on the street? You want to get put away?"

"Oh God I just —" The shower of stars came again.

"I *know* what it is. Just stop it. You stop it right now. You start letting that happen and you're through."

"It's okay. Okay," Abby-Jean choked.

"This is real. *Real.* This life is real."

"Okay."

They stood panting in the darkness.

"It's like I was a radio signal goin' off the end of the dial."

"I know."

"You think I'm goin' crazy?" Abby-Jean cried.

"When it happens to me, I bite my fingers. The pain brings me back."

Abby-Jean stared at her, able to see her face clearly at last, streaked with rain. Or was it sweat? Or was it tears?

"Oh Louise, are we gonna get out of here? Are we ever gonna get out?"

As if it were an echo, her repetition of the question seemed to send it rebounding up the narrow stairway, ricocheting from floor to floor until it seemed the question was torn from a thousand throats.

In the silence that swept back no response, Louise dropped the words, "I'm gong up now." Calmly, purposefully, she climbed the stairs.

Abby-Jean stood there. She waited for something to happen. Nothing happened. She climbed the stairs.

Hot. It seemed hotter than before, hotter than ever before. Groping along the hall, she turned into her room with the relief of abandoning herself to private torment, then she gasped. It was intolerable — surely — she couldn't breathe! She couldn't breathe! The air was a tight hot presence smothering against her, searing her eyes, ramming up her nostrils, down her throat, everywhere a suffocation as if some alien had swallowed her and was squeezing her to death. She groped about, arms outspread, wide-eyed yet blinded.

The radio in Mrs. Jackson's room was still on, blaring as it had since early evening the day before, locked on to a Bible station that preached twenty-four hours non-stop. Through the wall it raged at her, *"There were Canaanites to the east and west, Amorites, Hittites, Pherezites and Jebusites in the mountain regions and Hevites at the foot of Hermon in the lamd of Maspha. They came out with all their troops — all their troops, amen! — an army numerous as the sands on the seashore — that's what it says, oh Lord save us —"*

Tears were running down her face. She stuck her hand by the window jammed open by her knife, waved it about. Maybe if she prayed? She wanted to pray. Heaving about the room in the darkness, she touched the side of her bed with her fingers, then grazed the top of the rough shag pyle. She wanted to pray but the thought of kneeling on her bare wet knees on the roach-infiltrated rug sent her reeling about the room.

On the bed! Kneeling on the bed. She could pray from up there.

168

"Do not fear them, the Lord said to Joshua. This is important. Do not fear, the Lord said. And why? For tomorrow, tomorrow, I will stretch them slain before Israel. Slain..."

"God?" She choked.

"God kept his Almighty Word. Right here in Joshua 11, it says it right here. It says the Lord delivered, yes! The Lord delivered them into the power of the Israelites, who defeated them and pursued them to Greater Sidon, to Mesrephoth-maim, and eastward to the valley of Maspha —"

She couldn't hear, couldn't think, couldn't breathe. She tottered on the bed.

"Oh help me, God, get me out —"

A terrible thunder and rumbling just above her head. A clatter, a rattle, then a mighty crash, as the window once propped open by her knife slammed shut, driving the knife deep into the heart of the frame. She toppled onto her side.

"Joshua did to them as the Lord had commanded. Remember this was what the Lord commanded. The Lord commanded this —"

She was up, prying at the window, her nails scraping and breaking against the wood. The window was sealed forever. She stared at it panting, then her hand gripped her chest in terror. Buried alive in this room! Sealed in forever! Like a sign, a damnation. She reeled back nauseated, felt a thousand inner stars explode.

No!

She staggered off the bed. Breathing against the glass, she saw a thin crack shooting up crookedly from the bottom of the sill. She pressed against it and it deepened, pressed again and the window seemed to bulge out slightly, the crack shooting up, farther up. With a cry, she struck it with her fist, and a shard of glass hurtled out through the night and shattered on the pavement below. She struck again. Again! The night air was filled with the splinter and shriek of fragmenting glass. Her ears rang. It was as if forty windows eye to eye across the alleys and recesses had shattered outwards, as if uprising, rebellion, ecstatic destruction were released in all the other rooms until the skies exploded in a silver holocaust of bursting glass.

She leaned out the window, euphoric. Her hand was bleeding, her head was clear. A sweet buffet of rain-cleansed air dropped its dew upon her cheek and wafted into her room.

Never such satisfaction.

○

The luminous twilight hours just before dawn, the water a silver winding pathway through the reeds. Waterfleas dipping soundlessly over the boat's wake toward the shadowy labyrinth of coarse pole-like stems. Everywhere the gentle, regular rustle of water against vegetation, a rising and falling, the water breathing among the rushes. A creaking noise as Bud shifts his weight, leaving the oars still at last, turning toward her, his face damp from the rising mist. "Here," he says, reaching for her fishing rod next to his own, the red one. "Here," he says, the mist rising about them, her hand trailing in the limpid water. The land beyond the coiling of the canal invisible, the lush dank green-brown marsh hushed in mists skimming like fallen clouds along its bristled surface. The borders of the sky becoming vague, disappearing, the reeds disappearing, nothing but Bud's voice, "Here," his face preoccupied, purposeful, the mist rising between them, his hand stretched toward her with the green rod. Hers, the green rod. Her hand reaching out — A mystery rising between them — Bud's glance — "Here!"

Abby-Jean was suddenly, lucidly awake. Still *here*, her heart cried out.

There was a commotion of some sort in the hall. She listened, her body suddenly tense. Strangers, excited, somewhere down the hall. So alone and yet never alone in here. Always the abrasion of other lives at any hour. They were running, Lord at four in the morning they were running down the —

"Fire!"

Did they say that? Did they say fire? She shot up in the bed, listened again, heard Mrs. Jackson's radio as it droned relentlessly *"And it came to pass that night that an Angel of the Lord came and slew in the camp of the Assyrians a hundred and eighty-five thousand —"* No, she was just thinking that surely, because deep within she was always thinking that here, the same way unexpected late night firecrackers always gave rise to fear of Russian bombs exploding overhead. If there was a fire, surely they'd call it out again, they wouldn't just —

Nothing. A small jet of wind struck her through the gutted window. She glanced at the paint-crinkled ridges on the outer frame, thinking how if she left the blind down during the day, the maid in her infrequent rounds would never notice. For several moments she stared at it, then shrugged. She didn't care who saw. She had no regrets, she'd smash it again. Sooner the next time.

There was no sound.

It wouldn't hurt to take a little — She was up, thonged, out in the hall. Dark. It smelled foul. Her senses quickened. Smoke, wasn't that — She breathed again, electrified. With the second breath, the acrid fumes seemed to cut her throat, enveloping her suddenly as if flaring at the gusty opening of a door, augmented threefold from one breath to the next. She took a tottering step forward. Yell fire? Had she actually seen the flame? She stole along the hallway, crept down the stairs into a thickening haze.

The smell of smoke was pervasive all along the corridor of the second floor, mounting, mounting, and still the eerie silence down the semi-blackened halls remained unbroken. Her own voice strangely caught in her throat, herself terrified of the shriek of it upon her ears that would make this real. Nice, a thought struck her confusedly, this scent of burning wood — like home —

Still no one in the halls. No doubt now — Why couldn't she —

A door opened slowly, and Elizabeth's head craned out. Their glances locked in a long vacuous stare.

"Fire," they whispered, then as one they yelled "FIRE!"

Abby-Jean stared blankly at Elizabeth's neck, the way the cord had swollen there. Elizabeth's gaze was fixed somewhere distant beyond her head. Had nobody heard? What time was it? How many behind the doors? Why still nobody?

Water was streaming down her face. Impossible! Tears? She felt a hiccough of laughter along her throat, forced it ack, forced back the thought, *excitin', this is.*

"Don't breathe! Keep yellin'!" Elizabeth cried hoarsely. "You go that way, I'll go this." Lurching away, her fist slammed at the next door down the hall. "Which way's it comin' from?" she called back to Abby-Jean.

"That way." Abby-Jean's finger stabbed toward the direction in which Elizabeth was running. Or was it coming up the stairwell from the first floor? Coming from behind her, then? Why was it so hard to tell? So foolish if all this was only — people would be so mad — Reluctantly, almost apologetically, she began pounding on the doors.

The phone. Somebody should phone the fire department.

"Hey, you got change?" she cried to a figure speeding toward her from the end of the hall. A man. Pulling a lime green net shirt over his head as he ran.

"Are you nuts?" His eyes rolled toward her as he passed, his face angry.

"It's for the phone —"

Crashing down the flight of stairs, two, three at a time, he was gone.

Maybe the fire would whoosh up sudden, Abby-Jean thought, panicking, then remembered how they always said the smoke would get you first. Or poisons in the air, depending on what was burning. Maybe you didn't even have to see the flames to — Die? Die? The laughter hurtled through her body, erupted aloud. Maybe she should forget everything and just run out right now?

"Fire!"

Women in the halls. It was as if a dam had burst. They were half-dressed, their hair awry, clutchng plastic bags, paper bags of belongings, lugging suitcases, one dragging a stand-up shopping cart lined with a blanket from which a grease-oozing frying pan protruded. Seeing her, not seeing her as they buffeted past, knocking into her as she struggled against the tide back toward her room to grab some things of her own. Macabre, the silence that sucked them along despite the buffeting, the banging, the sound of breaths and complaints as their belongings struck each other's and lodged. Macabre, the dark hurtling effort that groped and collided silently, anxious and sweat-ridden, blundering back and forth after things dropped, lost, forgotten in mid-tide.

"Why're you goin' that way? Why?" A woman clutched her arm fearfully. "Is there somethin' blocked down there? They're goin' slower —" She scanned Abby-Jean's face for any signs of special knowledge.

"Goin' up to my room. Let go." She pulled loose.

Another woman stared at her, stricken. "I left my best brown sweater back there —"

"For Chrissake," the woman behind her pushed. "You don't need to worry about no sweater right now."

"It was warm. I never had a sweater so good as —"

The woman turned in behind Abby-Jean, abandoning her suitcase on the stair. In her struggle to get past it, the woman behind her knocked it and gently it slid down several stairs, coming to rest again like a boulder in a stream. She stared after it helplessly then continued upwards, choosing the brown sweater over all she had in there.

"Y'ever think there was so many people in here?" Abby-Jean panted, looking back over two flights of craning, struggling bodies. Faces she had never seen before crowded past her on the stair. "Just look at everybody!"

"I'm gonna lose everything," a large black girl cried, a suitcase in either hand. "All my Lionel Ritchie records and a radio back there." Tears were streaming down her face.

"My God, I just grabbed this coffeemaker here. I left the snaps of the folks in the bottom drawer."

Two streams eddied against each other, one toward the door below, a second struggling back up the stairs.

"Somebody phoned the Fire Department? You think they know?"

"I'm gettin' out, that's all I care."

"Them women takin' their sweet time down there. They ain't thinkin' none about us back here on the stair."

"I didn't have any change or I would've —" Abby-Jean said.

"You dial O, that's all," Yolande burst, passing on the downward stream. She had a scarf wrapped about her head and neck, and was wearing two dresses, each of which covered up spaces that the other would have left bare.

"What if all this is just a joke?" somebody suggested hopefully.

"What if it were a trick, dig, to get us out of our rooms and then —"

"Soon's I get out, I'm gonna park right outside that door. Somebody comes out with my toaster, I'll bust her ass."

"I knew somethin' like this was gonna —"

"Who says it has? Who says it has? You seen any fire? Who —"

172

"Jes' smell, for Chriss—"

"At four o'clock in the morning, they don't pull no fire drills, girl."

"How fast it goes up depends if someone set it, I heard."

"How fast's fast?"

Someone began to cough. Immediately two or three others began to cough.

"Make up your mind, for God's sake." This to a woman who had been pushing up the stairs carrying a heaping armful of clothes. Turning now, she was trying to get back in the down line and holding up both lines. They caught the cloying musty odor of unwashed clothes.

"Why'nt you leave that stuff behind. Do it good."

"Quit pushin' me. It ain't my fault. I think they got some problem down at the door."

"How fast's fast? For God's sake —"

The lights flickered. A low moan rose among the women on the stairs.

"You hear that?" Silence. "I tell you I hear it."

"Can't breathe."

"It's the fire eats up the air."

"What air. This smoke —"

"To think of them finding me dead in here with —" Bea's face, her jowels glistening. "God! Not here! I don't want it to end like —" She was carrying nothing at all, using her free arms to squeeze and elbow forward.

"I'm gonna pee!"

As Abby-Jean reached the top of the stairs, the crush of women seemed to ease. She stared down over the straining that clogged the stairs below, its progress blocked by abandoned belongings and the few women who still struggled to salvage something they had maybe grabbed at random, chosen thoughtlessly in the blind urge to save, to cling to something, anything, not to lose it all.

"What I got up here anyway?" Abby-Jean breathed aloud.

She stood a moment, mesmerized by the line below. Directly below her, freed too from the crush of women that was now confined to the stairs, Elizabeth was still pounding on a door.

"Margaret! *Margaret!*"

"What's wrong?" Abby-Jean craned over the railing.

"She's gone and locked the goddam door. She's dead to the world in there."

Abby-Jean stared at her, uncomprehending.

"Things was building up to one of her toots. I knew they was."

Margaret? Abby-Jean thought, almost grinning. Toots?

She straightened up, glanced down the two dusky corridors of the third floor, one partly hidden by partition walls. Were there still others in here? Had anybody checked to see? There were sounds rising up from the women on the stairs. Cries. Maybe now they could see the flames.

Oh God, I'm still standin' here, she thought.

"*Amen!*" (A sound of clapping) "*Amen Lord!*" (Amen, amen, amen.) "*Aie-mayan, swee' preshus Jeezus.*"

That many people still — Mrs. Jackson's radio.

There's no time to go make sure nobody's here, Abby-Jean was reasoning as she ran toward the far hall behind the partitions, crying "FIRE!" and banging on doors. Can go out here anyway, she thought, seeing the red exit light above a door, heaving against it, then slamming up short. It wouldn't open. She felt feverishly along the rim, unable to see why it wouldn't.

Turning, she saw a crack of light beneath a door frame, and within that crack, a shadow that moved. Someone standing listening at the door.

"Good Lord, fire, don't you know?" She banged on the door.

The shadow moved as if feet had shifted but there was no other response, no sound of a voice, no opening of the door.

"Fire! Fire!" Abby-Jean was pounding on the door. Abruptly she stopped. Her fists were throbbing. With every blow, the door had rattled, but it held. She stared at the crack beneath the door. Whoever was in there was listening, standing pressed right up against the door.

"Who is it," a voice quavered. Very old. Frightened.

"Me. Abby-Jean. You don't know me, what's it matter? FIRE!"

A silence, unbearably long. Abby-Jean began to cough.

"How do I know," the voice trembled. "Maybe you're tricking me."

Abby-Jean's cheek pressed against the door. "There's a fire, honest." Her voice was gentle, urgent. "I swear to God."

"Maybe you just want me to open the door and then — " The voice broke off, choked by its own fears.

"Good Lord, you do what you want. I'm goin'!"

Abby-Jean made off down the hall. Still the door didn't open. She stared back at it, wet-faced. A pig-headed old woman, ruining her life by guilt forever if she didn't go back, maybe costing it if she did. Her face contorted, sharp needles of feeling shooting through it. No consideration! No thought for others who wanted to live, who craved to live, who still had a whole life with God knew what might have been possible — A pang for that life — She surged back toward the door, feverish with indignation.

"*Look —*" It was almost physically painful to soften her voice. "Don't you smell no smoke?"

Silence. What was that below? It sounded like wind through fissures, clothes beating on a line.

"*You listening to me?*" She struck the door with all her force.

"I got nothing! Don't hurt me! Oh God!"

A secretary, she might have been, or self-supporting, anyway. She might have married and had children. To be cut off like this before

174

things got good — Abby-Jean was leaning against the door, crying bitterly.

It moved against her fingertips. She felt the faintest frailest push from the other side passing to her like a tremor through the wood. She stepped back. The door opened 60 degrees before lodging against a dresser with a huge oval mirror. A haggard fear-filled face craned past her down the hall.

"I smelt it," the old woman whispered to herself.

Behind her in the room, there was barely space to stand. The passage between bed and bureau was taken up by the dresser, with a coffee table up-ended upon it.

Their eyes met.

"I had some furniture from before," the old woman apologized. "Some special things."

Abby-Jean snorted impatiently. They didn't look so special to her, the wood chipped, piled there uselessly atop each other, taking up what little space there was for standing. There was no room for a past in there.

"Don't you think I could take —"

Abby-Jean propelled her, frail and wispy as a tumbleweed, toward the stairs. Pausing a moment where the amens got louder, she glanced over the railing for Elizabeth before checking Mrs. Jackson's room. Still there, the thickening haze between them dimming Elizabeth's figure, making it strange, like a blotch striking out. Hard to hear her fists striking the door with the babble of smoke-disembodied voices below and the praying behind.

The hall lights died. An instant of shattering blackness struck her eyes.

"Elizabeth!" Abby-Jean screamed.

"*Margaret!*" from below.

Through the dense smoke, the far walls danced with new light. From below, a cry from the women rose like a burst of frenzied applause, then peeled again, terrifying. She could see their light-flickered forms anguished and tumultuous on the narrow stairs.

The old woman stood panting at the head of the stairs, her face panic-stricken at the smoke billowing up. As the continuous stream of women surged toward escape below, the forced open door ventilated and fueled riot in the flames somewhere above.

"Go on," Abby-Jean urged her. "You go quick, you'll be alright."

The old woman took a tottering step, her body trembling violently. Her fingers reached out for the railing. Strangely large, knotted with arthritis, they could barely cling to it.

"I'll be right behind in just a sec," Abby-Jean tried to reassure her, her hand softly pushing against the back of the woman's head, her fingers touching hair crinkly and dry as Spanish moss. So frail — as if, touched by flame, she would go up in a sizzle and a puff of smoke, her whole body no more substantial than a tangle of hair, extinguishable in a second.

"No!" The old woman recoiled suddenly, her eyes ablaze with accusation, as if she were being pushed to her death.

"It's the only way! There's no other!"

"No!"

Lord, was there no end to her? Abby-Jean burst into a fit of coughing that left her face streaming with tears.

The old woman stared at her, fear illuminating her face at the sight of the tears. Her gaze jerked away. She took a trembling step down the stairs.

Released, Abby-Jean shot toward Mrs. Jackson's door.

"You still in there?" she cried.

She heard a voice, very low, and pushed against the door. It opened. Pitch-dark. One of the windowless rooms. With the suffocation of air mingled a curious sweetness. She heard the voice whisper again and stepped inside. The door tipped shut behind her, snuffing out all light. Quietly, lucidly, almost poignantly the thought struck her: she was going to die.

She stood rapt, all her perception probing the blackness, forgetful of her lost future now, glancing hesitantly toward Death. Her soul leapt mightily, a white bird above blackwater rapids flailing then diving backwards into an infinite night sky. The air rushed in her ears as all the person that she was dropped behind in little pieces, releasing a purest current that was not she, not not she, at once yearning, serene —

No! Not quietly — so much pain first — She reeled with horror and her hand reached out —

Cold, its' surface granulated like fine stucco, a rigid protruding object. Her fingers pressed once uncomprehendingly against its granite immobility then fluttered lightly back along the irregular abrasive surface to its uppermost extremity. She shrieked and sprang away, choking in the suddenly recognized sickly sweet stench of death. The stalagmite projection was a human foot. She had grasped the toes.

"Mrs. Jackson?" Her voice was low, horrified now of a response beyond the incoherent murmuring of prayers behind her that came from the radio.

To touch again — she had to. Her fingers reached out, skimmed the cool sweaty pipe that was a leg. She touched further up, and then recoiled. Completely naked, her breast a stony rock. No more than the rest of them could Mrs. Jackson endure this black heat furnace in the immolation of her clothes.

Dead now. Cold now. Leave her here to burn? Maybe a better thing, if souls could watch — who knew? No eyes of strangers on her ancient heat-choked nakedness. But how long like this? How long?

She touched again, not afraid of the body now. Mrs. Jackson, this was. A thwarted useless tenderness flew out from her, an outrage that batted blindly against the converging walls. Out of here. She turned. Away from Death, this incomprehensible vestigial chill amid a blaze of heat, out of this black inferno that crazed before the relief of death. Her own living body spasmed again with horror, blundered in the darkness groping for the door. Life! life! life! oh god she —

— collided with another body in the pitch-dark room and screamed.

"It's me. Me. *Lorinda Beddoes!*" a trembling voice clarified urgently.

Who?

Abby-Jean reached out, touched hair like Spanish moss.

"I couldn't. You left me. I —"

They were touching each other's faces, fingers inadvertently in eyes, nostrils, mouths. Wet, the old woman's cheeks. Tears? Sweat. What did she look like again, this life she was clutching at, encircled tight within her arms as if to save both their lives at once.

"There's no more goin' down. We're gonna die."

Abby-Jean stroked the withered face. There was a singing, a rushing in her ears.

"No," she said. "It's okay. I'm here."

"Hail Mary, Mother of Grace —"

"Don't breathe. Stop that."

"Hail Mary —"

The words were choked off in a fit of coughing that rocketed the old woman like a series of inner explosions.

"— out a window. Mine's broke already. Somebody's gonna come, down below." Abby-Jean butted and bumped the old woman around the half-open door into the hall.

Heat seared across them like an iron. Naked flame beat against the walls below, sending sparks and flamey gassy fissures up the stairs.

"No!"

Lorinda Beddoes had slithered around in her grasp, was struggling to plunge back into the pitch-dark room. They strained chest to chest. A sudden whiff of urine cloyed the air.

"Let me back —"

"No!

"Get outta my — I'll kill you —"

"No!"

"Whyyyiiiee —"

Abby-Jean had grasped her below the buttocks, heaved her over one shoulder, nearly flinging her for the old woman had no weight. Her room, just feet away. As she ran toward it, Lorinda Beddoes body bumped against her back, forcing a series of grunts out of her that needed only breath to turn to shrieks.

A heart attack, anything, a spark in her hair. Fearfully Abby-Jean clutched the old woman's thighs, her hands moiling in the urine-soaked dress. Inextricable from hers now, this stranger's life whose face constantly fled her memory. See — jerking, wavering before her eyes, a rip in the hem of the slip Lorinda Beddoes wore beneath her dress despite the heat. Tangerine. A tangerine slip. The old lady. A heart beating against her back. She gasped, heaved them both inside her room, flung the door shut.

"See there. The window. Get up on the bed."

She was shoving her towel along the crack beneath the door. Who knew but that given a fire, now there would be a mighty current between her window and the door. Lorinda Beddoes was tottering on the bed, clutching the window sill, craning into the alley below.

"Yell!"

"I can't —"

"So help me God, *you old bitch* —"

"*Help!* Somebody see me! I'm up here —"

Abby-Jean's glance clambered blindly over her belongings with sudden avarice, looking for something to save. For a moment in the silence within the room, it seemed unintelligible that destruction could be climbing toward them. She grabbed her suitcase, her typewriter, a small bundle of clothes, wedged the shampoo beneath her chin, then glanced up. Lorinda Beddoes was watching her quietly, her face lit from the light in the alley below. Abby-Jean's grip loosened, and the hoard dropped to the floor. Crazy, surely, to have thought of that now. And yet she hadn't been able to help it, sweeping everything on her desk top into her purse, thinking: just this one thing.

"There's no one," Lorinda Beddoes said in a clear voice. "No one hears us."

She was staring at Abby-Jean as if seeing her for the first time, her head turned to one side, scanning her face closely, almost wistfully, all her concentration there and nowhere else. Abby-Jean's eyes lowered before the naked earnestness of the regard. In that second when her gaze was down and Lorinda Beddoes scanned her face, something passed between them flesh to flesh, skin to skin. A boundary melted. They were starting to flow into one another.

"Sure they'll hear."

In one motion she leapt upon the bed and hurled her purse to the street below. It sailed down, down, then struck the pavement with a shudder. Her wallet bounced out. Say goodbye to that, she thought fleetingly.

"I grew up in Portland, Maine," Lorinda Beddoes was saying.

"Help! Hey up here! Help!"

Incomprehensible, mysterious, rayed with beauty, the half-lit silent stairwell in the building beyond, its serene half-shadowed vacancy so short a chasm away, there where the dull torpid welter of life seemed now to flow in grandeur through empty halls. Like pebbles, her cries, dropped in that torrential silence. Paradise just beyond and in the vacuous light-smeared alley below...

"Look there! See that ledge? If you can just lower yourself to that ledge then creep along —" Her voice broke euphorically.

Lorinda Beddoes craned outside, her glance dropping six feet to the narrow ledge below.

"No," she said softly. "I couldn't."

Abby-Jean glanced at the arthritic knotted fingers which couldn't even cling to the railing of the stair. Her heart sank.

"Sure you could," she lied.

"You go."

"Yah, an' leave you here?" She was shaking her head, trembling. "Somebody's gonna come. They got ladders."

The old woman was stroking her hair, her withered thorny fingers rough against her cheek. A creased forehead, dewlap cups of flesh puckering a thin abstemious mouth, Lorinda Beddoes coming toward her in light through the disguise that had converged her features towards the common mask of age. A young girl, a woman flowing toward her in those eyes. The naked yearning dissolving in an agony of tenderness.

"Don't think you can —" Abby-Jean cried. "I'm not gonna —"

"I don't think I was pretty ever," Lorinda Beddoes whispered, touching Abby-Jean's face with her thorny hands as if she was reaching toward her from far away. "But Buck loved me."

Pure. The old woman becoming incandescent before her, a terrible impersonal clarity making a tunnel of her eyes.

"It's all right to go," Lorinda Beddoes said, absolving her.

"Any minute they could —" Abby-Jean was shaking. Terror to the point of nausea. Impressions coiling at her, coming loose like reels of film, skittering, rattling away. She clung to the sill.

A mighty hiss behind them, and all at once the door was a river of upward-flowing smoke, outlined in a brilliant blue.

"No!"

Lorinda Beddoes was struggling with her, pushing her out the window. For an instant they tottered, straining against one another with recognitionless eyes, then Abby-Jean collapsed forward. Lorinda Beddoes' plump weightless body was hurtling toward the door, her wraithlike hair sprung out as if in ecstasy. She pulled at it, unleashed an explosion of yellow flame that sent her reeling backward then sucked her somersaulting, torched, into the conflagration. She crackled like a leaf, then was gone.

The sight a whiplash across Abby-Jean's eyes —

She was clambering over the sill, hanging, then she dropped.

❂

The night air was filled with flashing crisscrossing beams of light that swept the crowds and dissolved in the brilliance of naked flame. Coils of hose slithered across the bright wet pavement beneath a rebounding spray. Piercing through the thunder of the flames, sharp explosions traced the bursting of window panes, the glass shattering again on the sidewalk below. Black smoke mounted in flamey fissures into the sky.

The women were gathered in silent clusters gazing up, some in sleeveless night clothes, some barely clad, some with coats and dresses slung over arms, over backs, with radios, small TVs, suitcases, paper and garbage bags at their feet. Among them, around them, through their ranks, young boys and late night couples craned and jockeyed for a better view, only to be swept sideways and back by police and firemen redefining their battlefield, back against the stoic groups of victims who stared at the flames or blankly elsewhere, but rarely moved.

"I lost all my clothes in there. I got nothin' to wear."

"You can thank sweet Dottie it weren't your life."

"They's two women died in there."

"We all got out."

"It was twelve died, I heard."

At once there was a rash of names of persons seen and not seen. A silence followed, then the spattering of voices gusting over them like so many heavy random droplets began again.

"You think a toaster burns? I had a toaster in there."

"That shit I had? I said to the fire, go on bitch, you jes' *take* it. I got so miserable sick of lookin' at that crap, I like to throw in mysef what the fire don't take firs'."

"This here fire set me back ten years," a small woman snapped.

"I got nothing," a thin woman in a white cotton nightie was weeping. "I got nothing now."

"Take this coat. Go on. You can't stand around out here like this."

"Anybody seen Abby-Jean?"

"I didn't even try to take a thing — and I had a good five minutes, I think. Damn. You lose your head."

"There ain't nothin' worth my life."

"What started it? What're they sayin' over there?"

"It coulda been a thousand things. A thousand."

"Somebody started it, I bet."

"Who?"

"I know what I know."

Speculation flashed through the clusters of women, giving rise to new possibilities, anger and argument as the light danced on their faces. Several feet away a TV camera left the fire and probed their faces for emotion, then returned to the blaze again. As a helmeted man approached to herd them back with outspread arms, the women moved slowly, resisting, as if hungering after the flames.

180

"It was the wirin', I think. Everybody got something electric. They don't take into account all of that."

"Smokers, that's what it was. Lyin' in their goddam beds with their goddam cigarettes. They could've sit up in the chair, but no, they got to lie on their backs."

"The thing is, you never know who's in there. You never know how crazy some of 'em is. They could be just like kids playin' with matches and never understandin' a thing. I try an' help 'em out, the ones I see, but you can't be after 'em all the time. They don't like you helpin' too much."

"What's it matter now what it was."

"We could've been killed!"

"That don't matter to them," said the woman who knew what she knew, her arms folded across her chest, her nostrils flaring. "They wanted us out, that's what. This space where we is, it's valuable now. Right downtown space, that's what it is. Free and clear."

"I figure it were done intentionally by somebody who got mad."

"Mad how?"

"Mad cause they got throwed out. Mad cause they got bugs. Mad cause of the heat. How do I know? It coulda been a thousand things."

The small woman who had been set back ten years glowered. "Yeah well I get mad myself but I never done a thing like that."

"That's right."

"Even if I might've wanted to, I never did."

"That's right."

"And there were times when I felt like it all right, that dump."

A low chuckle, more like an emphatic release of breath, passed among the women within hearing distance, and was followed by hoots and catcalls.

"There was days I could've took a axe to it."

"Yeah I remember feelin' like that."

The women strained toward the building again with brilliant eyes, some seeking amid the flames the cubicles where their lives had been, some staring off into different distances, their glances vacuous, bitter, dumb. From the gutted interior came a series of rendings and crashes. An array of sparks gleamed momentarily like tinsel above the flames.

"Well I'm out of there, anyway," someone muttered laconically.

"That's what I say."

"It were home! It were a roof! Good God, where now—?"

From somewhere deep in the crowd, a voice sand out "*Burn, baby, burn!*" and the cry was repeated across the crowd like a stone skipping over water.

"Anybody seen Abby-Jean?"

"Over there."

She was standing quietly by an ambulance, the back doors of which were open waiting. There was no one inside. The driver was sitting on the opposite fender, smoking and listening to an after-midnight radio talk show on sexual trauma. Facing away from the fire, Abby-Jean's glance was fixed on empty space.

Several feet beyond, an uncoiled hose slithered across the pavement toward the blaze. It caught and held her gaze for several moments. When her eyes shifted at last, her face contorted suddenly, becoming for an instant raw and anguished before lapsing into vacuity again. Without signification, the sight of Louise running toward her, jumping the hoses in her flat black shoes, water splashing up her bare legs, her mouth opening soundlessly, closing, opening wide again. Louise's arms around her. Louise. Louise's face. Louise's cheeks.

"What are you doing over here?" Louise shaking her. "Are you okay?"

"Sure."

"You're okay!" Louise was hugging her again. "When I didn't see you, my God I almost wondered —"

"I'm okay."

Louise scrutinized her, then tossed her iron gray hair back and glanced behind her at the dying fire in one motion. Her hand was trembling on Abby-Jean's arm.

Abby-Jean's glance turned toward her slowly. "You get your things out okay?"

Louise's skin, pale and wet, seemed to shine, the contour of her cheek like a half-illumined moon. "Oh I lost everything but my purse," she said, tossing her hair back again. "Anyway it's time for a change." An agitated hand raked her hair back yet another time. "I'm not getting much work here, you know."

Abby-Jean was staring again at the hose slithering past.

"It's an ill wind that blows nobody good," Louise shrilled, turning toward the blackened dripping frame.

"I saw two people. One was dead an' I saw the other one die."

Louise turned away, saying nothing.

"Mrs. Jackson, she was the one that was dead already. Remember her?"

Louise shook her head.

"Sure, she was in the room next to me. You remember her."

"There's a lot of people," Louise said harshly. "I've seen a lot of people come and go."

"She was black but she had these eyes nearly looked blue? And Lorinda Beddoes. What about her?"

"No."

Tears spilled over Abby-Jean's cheeks. "Well I remember 'em, an' I'm waiting for 'em here."

"Maybe they didn't suffer —"

"Are you kidding? Mrs. Jackson, I think maybe she smothered in there. An' Lorinda Beddoes went up like a torch."

Louise's head raised. "Well, they're free of it now."

"Free of what? Free of bein' alive?" Abby-Jean cried.

Pungent with the scent of water on burnt wood, the night air swept down on the lingering clusters of women spread out across the blockaded streets, cooling as the fire shrank and sizzled into ash, leaving dank blackened brick and flame-eaten timber behind. Several blocks away, the trees in the rotary circle shimmered at an intermittent passage of wind. Down the quiet side streets, moving leaves obliterated then revealed a row of streetlight moons.

"Hey it ain't so bad out here. Don't that air feel good? I swear I feel it right up my back."

"Better than in there."

"Better here than in there even before the goddam fire."

They laughed almost exhuberantly, remembering again with the dying of the flames, that other heat.

"You know, I was thinkin' of doin' this. I was thinkin' of movin' out onto the street.'"

"Yeah, it's okay now with everybody here, but how it'd be by yourself. Think of that —"

As the passing spectators dispersed and drifted away, as the TV camera quit shooting but didn't leave, the blockaded street seemed quieter, almost relaxed. Stirred by a febrile excitement, the women were moving about freely, talking to other women they didn't know, exchanging stories and wisecracks about the clothing they'd snatched or been caught in, examining and comparing the things under arms, between feet, in suitcases and bags of all sizes. Some sat on the steps of neighboring buildings; others were squatting, sitting on clothes, on bundles out on the pavement. As the tumult of conversation slowly sputtered out, their scattered encampment was swallowed in a pall of silent conjectureless waiting.

Suddenly by the ambulance, a brilliant artificial light glared through the softening darkness, cutting a channel across the rubbled pavement to blind two stretcher-bearers picking their way without urgency toward the open ambulance doors. Their burden was wrapped in a coarse grey blanket that completely covered an indecipherable shape.

Abby-Jean started forward.

Louise's hand gripped her arm. "You won't know who it is. You won't even know what color they are."

For an instant they froze in the floodlight's eerie gleam, felt more than saw the TV eye upon them.

"Get away," Abby-Jean cried harshly.

It lingered momentarily on her face then flicked mechanically away.

"They want to look but they don't care," she cried.

Stumbling toward them through the floodlit channel, a tall half-naked woman, her body blackened in the places where her night dress had been scorched away, her short hair standing out in singed tufts.

"*Elizabeth!*"

Elizabeth staggered forward, struggling to evade the light, distinguishing their faces at last, her large eyes incredulous, scintillated with pain. Her hand jerked toward the stretcher left on the ground waiting to be loaded into the ambulance.

"*Margaret!*" she howled.

"Get back," a cop shouted as he swept in between them. "Everybody get back, get back. Here, you. You too. Get back, get back."

They retreated backwards across the pavement, herded by two uniformed men toward the tired gathering of waiting women.

"Okay everybody... Come on, let's go, let's go. We're opening up this road again. You can't sit here, we're letting the traffic through."

Slowly the women rose, picked up their belongings, receded in a wave from the pavement back toward the far sidewalk. Beyond the gutted building, the sky was incandescent in the east.

"Is that all?" one asked another. "What next?"

"I don't know."

"Where're you goin', then. You don't even know," she accused.

"Well we can't just sit here forever. We got to go someplace, ain't we? We got to go get us another goddam room."

❍

"Looks like you're finally gonna make it out of Washington," Abby-Jean grinned, her eyes full of tears.

Louise was fumbling with the green cardboard suitcase, lifting it easily because it was empty, picked up at a second hand store to protect her from appearing destitute. She placed it beside a row of suitcases waiting to be loaded onto the bus, then studiously looked away, disowning it as the driver lifted it, glanced about questioningly, then shrugged and tossed it into the bin. She raked her hair back, then glanced at Abby-Jean.

"Oh it takes a while, but I always do what I say I'm going to do."

Disembarking passengers from Baltimore pressed toward them in a horde from the stall beyond, driving a wedge between two waiting lines of boarders, the passageway momentarily transformed into a seesaw of coming and going. For an instant in the crush, they were swept apart, Louise's face craning, bobbing away. They struggled towards each other again.

"It's hard to believe," Abby-Jean said.

"What?"

184

"Oh, that maybe we're never gonna see each other again. Maybe never in the whole of our lives." She turned away blinking, the water in her eyes blurring the shapes of people in the bus station waiting room beyond, turning the rows and lines of them into spasmodic languorous blots. "I miss you already, Louise." As she turned to face Louise, the tears spilled over.

"Here."

Louise was handing her a kleenex. A snort of laughter convulsed Abby-Jean at the sight of it, and broke loose in more tears. Kleenex. She had thought to pick up kleenex, too.

"We can keep in touch though, can't we? We can write?"

"Neither of us have an address to write to. That's a fine start."

"What about your sister in North Carolina?"

Louise's face seemed to clench. "I'd never let her know where I am."

"Well there's Beaufort. You can always reach me through there. You send it in care of Mrs. Dottie Brown. Mums works at the Post Office so I'm gonna get it for sure eventually."

"In care of Mrs. Brown, Beaufort," Louise repeated.

"She'll send it on to me — wherever I am — an' then —"

Louise was smiling at her with quiet distant eyes. She wasn't going to do it, Abby-Jean realized with a pang. Her eyes searched Louise' face, less pale now without her intense lipstick. She was going to get on the bus and disappear forever, plunging on into her future without looking back.

"Don't you like me, Louise?" she whispered.

"You'll meet a lot of people in your life. You'll forget about me."

"I'm never gonna!" She was crying bitter tears.

"I won't blame you." Louise' face was wet. "People can't keep up. You'll see. You move and then you move again. It doesn't take more than two or three moves, and then you're gone forever."

"It's not like that in Beaufort."

"Well you're not there." Her voice was gentle as she suggested, "You could still go back. It's easier for girls to go home."

"Yah well," Abby-Jean muttered, her face tightening. How to tell Louise that it was already too late for that? That she was wounded, the city hurting her more the longer she stayed. Changing her, until it was only the craving to even the score, to reclaim what had been stolen and torn away that kept her hanging in. The need to go out whole, the way she'd come in. To get a lick of her own back. She was hungering for that.

"So," Louise breathed softly, understanding. Her eyes probed Abby-Jean's face, searching the future there, revealing nothing of what they saw.

"Williamsburg," Abby-Jean countered, trying to get a feel of the town by the sound of its name. "I guess it's small. That oughta make things better, don't you think?"

185

"I don't know." Louise flinched. Rallying, head raised, she added, "Of course, I hear it's a marvelous place."

Abby-Jean's gaze dropped. Already carrying on about marvelous again. For a fleeting instant she had a vision of Louise alone beneath an enomous tent, trying to raise it by herself, the dark voluminous canvas weighing down on all sides. How long marvelous in a downtown room? Lord, how long could she go on like that, her will against all reality, before the outside rammed its way in?

"So we are off on our separate ways," Louise said.

The passengers had started to bump along past them onto the bus. Louise's arms were around her, clutching her.

"I hope your life is —" Louise's mouth pursed, the tears running down on either side of her nose.

"Oh Louise — I love you, Louise —"

They clung to each other, tears in each other's hair.

"Beaufort — always —"

"I will — I will —"

And then the bus was sliding backwards out of the stall. Abby-Jean paced down the row of windows, squinting at profiles through the shaded glass. Nowhere at the window, no sight of Louise. She felt a twinge of horror, like seeing someone sink beneath the water, not seeing them rise. Louise already swept away. As the bus turned the corner, she stared after it wistfully, almost forgetting to wave, then waving in strokes broad enough to be seen for miles. Louise was in there somewhere looking back at her, even if her head was turned away.

"Well," she said, then cleared her throat and wiped her eyes.

Alone. On the street.

Terror swept in.

She turned toward the bus station waiting room where people were squeezed into and sprawled over rows of single-seat chairs that prevented lying down. New, all that, since the first time she was here. Her eyes scanned the waiting room, going directly to the phones. A good sign that, remembering where they were. She paused, reflecting on the sudden happy thought that losing her suitcase and typewriter to the fire meant that she didn't have those heavy weights to lug around while looking for a place.

On her way to the telephone she paused to squint through the door at the city beyond.

And get a lick in for Lorinda Beddoes, she thought, for Nestoria Jackson, for Elizabeth and Margaret and Louise if ever some sweet day —

But what she needed now was quarters. For the phone.

○

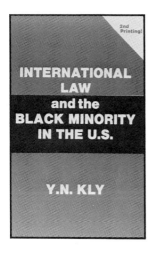